THE HEPPENHEIMER FAMILY HOLOCAUST SAGA

WHAT REMAINS IS HOPE

Based on a True Story

BONNIE SUCHMAN

Black Rose Writing | Texas

ISBN: 978-1-68513-655-0
LIBRARY OF CONGRESS CONTROL NUMBER: 2025935676
PUBLISHED BY BLACK ROSE WRITING
www.blackrosewriting.com

Printed in the United States of America
Suggested Retail Price (SRP) $23.95

What Remains is Hope is printed in Baskerville

*As a planet-friendly publisher, Black Rose Writing does its best to eliminate unnecessary waste to reduce paper usage and energy costs, while never compromising the reading experience. As a result, the final word count vs. page count may not meet common expectations.

The Lazarus Heppenheimer Family

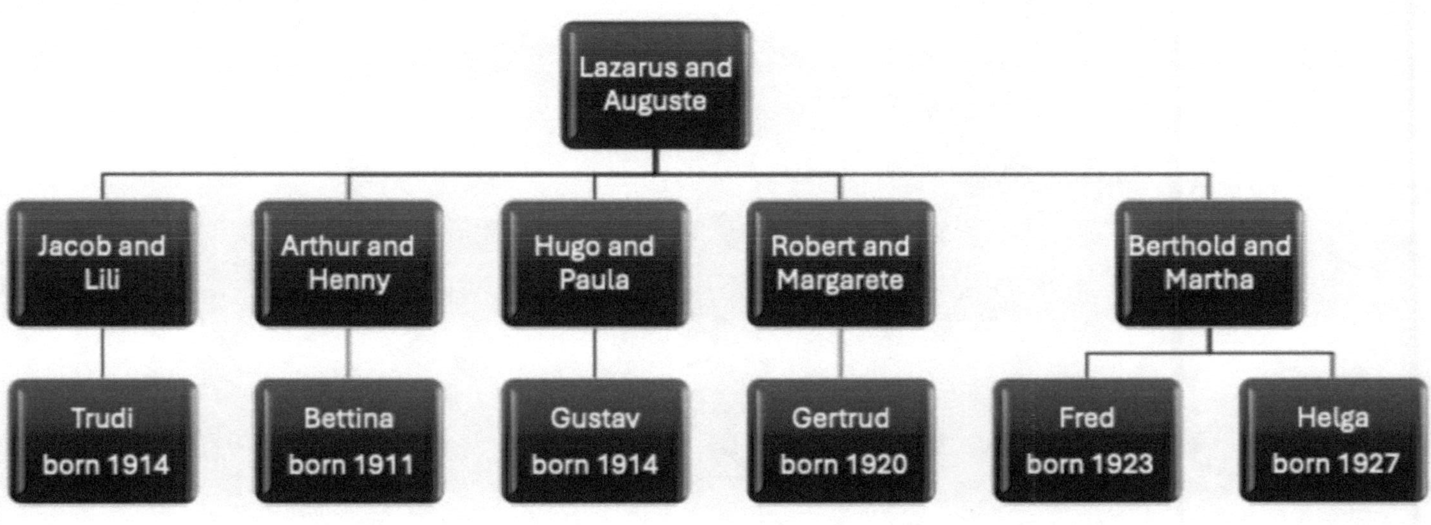

WHAT REMAINS
IS
HOPE

"Remember that hope is not a gift given from God to us; hope is a gift, an offering, that only we human beings can give to one another."
–Elie Wiesel, Commencement Address at Wagner College, May 18, 2012

"Hope is the pillar that holds up the world.
Hope is the dream of a waking man."
–Pliny the Elder

PROLOGUE

Frankfurt
June 1996

A taxicab pulled up to the hotel's front door, and the old woman walked outside. The driver got out of the car, presumably to help her. She waved him back into the car. "Thank you, but I can get into the taxi without any help. I just need you to take me to the Hauptwache." It felt strange to speak with him in German, but she didn't want the driver to think she was a tourist, to overcharge her. But the truth was her German felt rusty, and everything around her was unfamiliar.

As the taxi navigated the narrow streets, she tried to get her bearings. She had not been in Frankfurt since the end of the war. The buildings she now saw were mostly modern and functional. Nothing seemed to remain from the Frankfurt of her youth. The Allied bombings during the war had seen to that.

The taxi soon reached the Hauptwache. The driver stopped the car and got out to help her. This time, she let him. She paid the fare, including a generous tip, and walked into the plaza. Looking around, the only building she recognized was the small building in the center, where she would be having lunch with her cousins - Café Hauptwache. While planning her trip, she had read an article about how the government had preserved the café while they were digging for the subway, since it was one of the few buildings in the inner city not destroyed during the war. She remembered the café from her childhood and thought this would be a good place to meet her cousins for lunch. Standing in the plaza now, she realized she had made the right decision.

She had no memory of ever going to Café Hauptwache with her cousins. They frequented a different café since Café Hauptwache was too fancy for them. Instead, she went to Café Hauptwache with her mother after a morning of shopping on the Zeil, the main shopping street in Frankfurt. There had been plazas on either end, sandwiching the Zeil. She and her mother would start at the Konstablerwache Square on the east side of the Zeil and walk west until they reached the Hauptwache. If it was a warm day, they would eat outside. But on cooler days, they would go inside and enjoy the warmth and coziness of the café.

She looked at her watch. She still had an hour before lunch. She had intended to arrive early for lunch but had not expected to be this early. She decided to walk along the Zeil to pass the time. As she was leaving the plaza, she noticed a giant shopping mall, perhaps ten stories tall. Certainly not anything like the stores she remembered. In fact, she had the same feeling she had in the taxi — nothing was familiar.

Sitting down on a bench, she caught sight of the building to her right. It was a nondescript structure, with shops on the first level. But something was so familiar about the location. She stared at the building. And then she remembered. This was where Kaufhaus Wronkers had been. She could almost see it now. It had been the largest department store in Frankfurt and her favorite place to shop for clothes, with multiple floors of ready-to-wear clothing and a shop for tailor-made items. The Wronkers were well-regarded philanthropists in the Jewish community, and her mother always spoke with Frau Wronker when she was in the store. That special store was just one among many driven out of business by the Nazis. The building was destroyed during the war, and the Wronkers were murdered in Auschwitz.

She stood up from the bench and continued her walk, searching for something else that was recognizable, but even the names of the streets were unfamiliar. She remembered one street that was near the Zeil – Allerheiligenstrasse – but she couldn't find it. That was the street where Café Goldschmidt had been. The café she and her cousins always frequented. The café was four stories and had multiple rooms, including a gaming hall and a ladies' salon. The cousins preferred one of the smaller rooms on the first floor that served the café's famous cheesecake. They would sit for hours, talking and drinking coffee, until one of the waiters would finally ask them to leave. The café was often referred to as "Café Jonteff," which meant holiday in Yiddish, since Jews could come on the Sabbath and pay for their food later in the week. But Café Goldschmidt had closed during the 1930s and its owner perished in one of the camps. As she continued down the Zeil, she tried to remember the site of her favorite dressmaker and the local cinema. Newer buildings had replaced them. She felt like one of those old buildings, out of place in this new Frankfurt.

Glancing at her watch, she saw it was time to walk back to the café. She felt surprisingly good at the moment, notwithstanding a bit of jet lag. Friends often told her she acted like a much younger woman, and she did feel that now. She also kept her sense of humor, smiling as she recalled how she invited her cousins to lunch. She sent them letters in code – the cousins' code. The code that allowed them to evade the censors. The code that helped them keep track of each other during the war. The code that sometimes kept them alive. She hadn't used the code since the war ended, but it came right back to her as she was crafting the letters.

She retraced her steps back to the café. She was still a little early but walked in anyway. She was ready to sit down. A number of tables were empty, including a few near the windows.

A waiter came up and asked, "Meine Dame, how can I help you?"

She replied in German, "I would like a table for four for lunch by the window." She was feeling a little more comfortable using her German. The waiter smiled at her and grabbed four menus.

As she sat down and looked at the menus, she realized her error, but said nothing to the waiter. *I'm sure it's just jet lag*, she said to herself. Or she was feeling anxiety about the day's upcoming event. She had a knot in the pit of her stomach. Or, perhaps, being back in Frankfurt has triggered old habits, when there were four of them. Because now there were just the three.

She felt the hole the few times the three had been together since the end of the war, without the fourth cousin. The cousin who had perished in the Holocaust.

The old woman had come to Frankfurt this time, as had her cousins, to attend the opening of the Holocaust Memorial, which would include blocks on a wall memorializing all the victims of the Holocaust from Frankfurt, including that lost cousin. That was one of the reasons they were meeting in Frankfurt. But the other, and more important, reason was that they had made a promise to their cousin that they needed to fulfill, together, and in Frankfurt.

PART I
BEFORE THE WAR

CHAPTER 1

Frankfurt
April 1930

It was a lovely spring morning with just a bit of a chill in the air, but Gertrud was hot, and her mother's sweaty hand was just making her hotter. As they were leaving their apartment, her mother had insisted that Gertrud wear her winter coat, woolen stockings, a winter hat, and warm gloves. Gertrud had taken off the gloves, but that really didn't help. She knew better than to unbutton her coat. *Like always, I will just have to suffer*, she said to herself, grimacing.

Gertrud looked around at the small crowd gathered at the cemetery. She knew the family members, but the others – mostly old women –were unfamiliar to her. Only the old women were crying. Gertrud herself was far from heartbroken. Even though she lived in the same city as her grandmother, she didn't see her often. And when she did, she found her grandmother to be cold and distant.

Gertrud often heard her mother complain about her former mother-in-law, and she recently asked why. Her mother first paused, then said, "Your grandmother was never nice to me. I don't know why. Maybe it's because I'm not Jewish and never converted, like her other daughter-in-law. Or may it's just because she is not nice." She never remembered her mother being so candid, but then her mother changed the subject, making it clear she was finished discussing the matter. Gertrud knew better than to ask her anything else about her grandmother.

Gertrud felt a little guilty that she was actually feeling happy at the moment. Her grandmother's death brought her father back to Frankfurt for the funeral. Her father had come home the day before and spent the entire evening with Gertrud. She loved her father and was always so happy to see him. He tried to come back to Frankfurt once a month for a visit, but it had been nearly three months since she had last seen him. They wrote to each other often, but writing was just not the same.

But Gertrud was especially happy because her father had told her he was moving back to Frankfurt. Three years earlier, her parents had sat her down and told her they were getting a divorce, and Gertrud had been devastated. She didn't even know what a divorce was. Her mother explained they would no longer be living together. She was didn't understand what her mother was saying, but then her father told her he was leaving Frankfurt and moving to Strasbourg in France to work for his brother Jacob, and Gertrud started to cry. Her father hugged her hard, but was gone the next day.

Before that moment, her father had never been away from her, and then suddenly was living in another city, in another country. *I was such a baby then*, Gertrud thought to herself. She was only seven years old at the time, and she cried for days after her father left. They did not have a telephone, so Gertrud's mother would occasionally take her to her grandmother's apartment, and they would call her father from there. But her grandmother would usually remind her the call was "long distance" and would stand by the telephone, so she never really felt free to speak with her father. But no more of that. Her father would be moving home for good.

Gertrud saw the rabbi cut small pieces of cloth from each of the jackets of her father and his three brothers. They said some prayers in Hebrew that were not familiar to Gertrud, then her father and uncles each took turns shoveling dirt into her grandmother's grave. Almost as soon as it began, the ceremony was over, and everyone started to leave. Once they were beyond the gates of the cemetery, her mother waved to Bettina, who came right over. Bettina was wearing a simple black dress, a black cloche hat, and low-heeled black pumps.

Gertrud's mother gave her niece a hug and said, "Bettina, could you take Gertrud to your grandmother's apartment? I need to go to work."

Bettina nodded and said, "Sure, Tante Margarete."

Margarete looked at her ex-husband and said, "It looks like your Onkel Robert is having a serious discussion with his brothers."

Bettina smiled and sighed. "Whenever they're together, they always look like they are having a serious discussion. They could be talking about the weather, and they would all look that way."

Margarete laughed and hurried away without giving her daughter a chance to say goodbye. But Gertrud didn't care. She loved her cousin. And while Bettina was nine years older than Gertrud, the two had spent a lot of time together, particularly when her parents were still married. Before the divorce, Gertrud's father had worked for Bettina's father Arthur in the scrap metal business. Bettina was often enlisted to babysit Gertrud when the adults went out, which Gertrud always looked forward to. When she was really young, Bettina would read her stories, and, as Gertrud got older, Bettina would tell her stories about friends and family. Gertrud loved hearing those tales.

"Gertrud, aren't you hot in that coat and hat? I'm getting hot just looking at you."

Happy to hear those words, Gertrud immediately unbuttoned her coat and took off her hat. "You know my mother. She's always worried I might get sick, which would mean she would have to take off from work. I was so hot I could hardly breathe. This is so much better!"

"Okay. One problem solved. Now let's go find Trudi and Gustav and the four of us can walk back to the apartment together."

Trudi was Onkel Jacob's daughter and Gustav was Onkel Hugo's son. She never met Onkel Hugo – he had been killed in the Great War – and she had spent less time with Gustav than with Bettina, but she still adored Gustav. Trudi had moved to Strasbourg when Gertrud was four years old, and while Trudi often visited Frankfurt, Gertrud didn't know Trudi as well as she knew her other two cousins. Both Trudi and Gustav were sixteen years old and liked to spend time together and with Bettina, but the three always encouraged Gertrud to join them. Gertrud loved being with her teenage cousins. She certainly wasn't going to spend any time with Onkel Berthold's two children, who were younger than she. And Gertrud, Bettina, Gustav and Trudi shared one more bond – until Gustav's half-brother Alfred was born the previous year, all four cousins were only children, and that seemed to connect them to each other.

"Trudi, Gustav, over here," Bettina called out to her cousins. They both waved and immediately came over to Bettina and Gertrud. Trudi had arrived just before the service had started and had not had a chance to say hello to her cousins. Trudi was wearing a matching black dress, coat, hat and shoes, and her bobbed auburn-colored hair was a little longer than the last time Gertrud saw her. Gertrud thought she looked like she had just stepped out of a fashion magazine. Trudi gave Bettina a big hug, then Trudi hugged her younger cousin. After Gustav gave Bettina a hug, he lifted up Gertrud. "Hello, spätz!" Gertrud would only let Gustav call her a little sparrow, and she loved it. She held his hand as they started walking back to their grandmother's apartment.

"I can't believe we arrived so late. We almost missed the funeral. I don't know why we had to drive here. We could have taken the train like Onkel Robert did yesterday. But Papa just loves driving that car. Or riding in that car, since Georges does all the driving."

Bettina started to laugh. "Admit it, Trudi. Your father enjoys showing off that fancy car."

"That is so true! I think he likes that car more than me and Mama."

Bettina grabbed Trudi's arm, and they began to walk arm-in-arm. Gertrud was always a little jealous when the two were together. Bettina and Trudi would always include her and Gustav in their conversation initially, but at some point, the two would go off and have private time with each other. But Gertrud understood – unlike her and Bettina, Bettina and Trudi really were raised like sisters when they were little.

Gertrud's Onkel Jacob had been living in Strasbourg before the Great War, but was forced to leave the Alsace area in 1919 after Germany lost the war and lost Alsace to the French. Gertrud's uncles Arthur and Berthold had started the scrap metal company *A&B Heppenheimer* – "A" for Arthur and "B" for Berthold – and Jacob joined his brothers in business as a partner. Gertrud's father Robert worked for his brothers but was never made a partner. The wives of Jacob and Arthur – Lili and Henny – worked in the business, as well, and Bettina and Trudi became very close. Something happened among the brothers that was never explained to Gertrud, and Onkel Berthold left to start his own scrap metal business in 1921. Jacob remained in Frankfurt until 1924, when France allowed Germans to return to Strasbourg. Bettina was thirteen years old and Trudi was ten years old when the girls were separated. Six years later, the separation seemed to have had no effect on their relationship.

Gustav turned to his cousin and asked, "Trudi, what plans does your father have for you when you graduate from high school?"

"What plans does any Heppenheimer have for his daughter? Working in the scrap metal business, of course. Until she gets married. I really do hate that business. It feels dirty in the office, even though there's never any actual scrap in the office. But I don't know what else I can do. I am not interested in attending university, and I don't think my parents would want me to go, anyway."

"You mean you don't want to run off to Nuremburg like our second Cousin Alice?"

"What? To open an arts and crafts studio? I'm not that daring, Gustav."

Bettina looked back at Gustav. "I don't want to hear any complaints from you when you graduate from high school next month, since you actually get to do something you like!"

"I do like the work, and it's certainly better than being in the scrap metal business. Although wouldn't it be nice if I had a choice."

Bettina smiled at Gustav. "You mean like being a starving artist? Well, I certainly didn't have a choice. Still, it's been three years since I graduated, and I've loved every moment at *A&B Heppenheimer*!" Bettina winked at Gertrud, and the three cousins started to laugh. Gertrud didn't really understand what was funny, but she decided to laugh along with her cousins. She always wanted to feel a part of this group.

They entered their grandmother's apartment building and climbed the stairs to the second floor. The door to the apartment was open, and the small apartment was already filled with people and food. Gertrud was still holding Gustav's hand, but she could sense the private time with her cousins was over. Bettina and Trudi were already in a corner of the living room, speaking to each other in hushed tones. Then Gustav dropped Gertrud's hand and walked over to his mother, who immediately handed over his baby brother to Gustav. Gertrud was now on her own.

Gertrud walked towards her father, who was sitting with his three brothers. They had the same serious faces from the cemetery. She wasn't usually interested in listening in on grown-up talk, but she was curious about what they were discussing, since it might have something to do with her father's decision to move back to Frankfurt.

Her Onkel Jacob seemed to be dominating the conversation. That was not a surprise to Gertrud. He was the oldest, but also the most successful of the brothers. At least, that's what her mother told her. Gertrud placed herself behind her father, but remained quiet.

"Robert, I will not continue to pay for this apartment. I was fine paying for it while Mama was alive, but now that she's gone, I no longer want that burden. You'll just have to find another place to live."

"Jacob, my living here is only going to be temporary. I can contribute some to the rent until I find a place to live."

"Well, I would have expected some contribution. I'm assuming Arthur will be paying you something to come work for him."

Arthur grunted loudly. "Jacob, you know things have been slow for me. The depression has affected all our businesses. Well, maybe not yours, but both Berthold and I have lost business. We need to be careful with our finances. Of course, I'm happy to have Robert come work for me. My health has not been great, and Henny has begun doing some of the trading. Robert will be a real help to her and Bettina. But I can't pay him what I would have paid him before the depression."

"Arthur, all of us have been affected by the depression, even me. Robert, I can pay the rent on the apartment for the rest of this year, but you will need to find something by January."

"Jacob, I'm sure I can find a place to live by January."

Gertrud looked at her Onkel Berthold. He was saying nothing to his brothers and was now even looking away. Gertrud knew there had been a problem among the brothers when Jacob was living in Frankfurt, but didn't know the details, and no one discussed it. At least, not in front of her. Berthold got up abruptly and walked over to his wife and two young children. Her father rose from his chair and turned around. He seemed surprised to see Gertrud.

"Liebling, I didn't know you were here. Why don't we get something to eat."

"Papa, are you going to be living in Oma's apartment? And working for Onkel Arthur?"

"Yes, I told you I was going to be moving back to Frankfurt." He seemed a little annoyed with Gertrud, and she didn't understand why.

"Papa, all you told me last night was that you were moving back to Frankfurt. But you didn't tell me where you would be living and what you would be doing." She could tell her father was still annoyed, so she added, "But I'm happy you'll be staying at Oma's apartment and working for Onkel Arthur. I like him. Plus, I'll get to see more of Bettina." Gertrud could see that the last words did the trick. Her father smiled at her and took her hand.

"I like Onkel Arthur too. Now let's get something to eat. I'm famished."

The table was loaded with food and Gertrud wondered how they'd be able to finish it all. Neighbors and friends had brought over platters of meat, fish, and vegetables. The fancy Sabbath tablecloth covered the table. She had not been to Sabbath dinner since her father moved to Strasbourg in 1927, but she remembered the tablecloth. Her mother was raising Gertrud as a Lutheran, but she remembered the Sabbath dinners, some fondly, and even remembered some of the prayers.

Gertrud and her father found a place to sit on one of the couches. They were old and worn, and Gertrud struggled to find a place that wasn't lumpy. Gustav sat down next to her father.

"Hello, Onkel Robert. I hope you found a comfortable place on the couch."

Robert laughed. "Hello, Gustav. This couch is so old, I'm surprised it hasn't collapsed. If I remember correctly, my father bought this couch, used. Since he died in 1903, you can assume it's over thirty years old."

"And it feels it. So, I understand you're moving back to Frankfurt and working for Onkel Arthur. Welcome back. I guess you got tired of working for Onkel Jacob?"

Gertrud looked up at her father. She wondered what he would say. Her father's smile seemed forced when he said, "No, nothing like that. I just really missed my daughter and the rest of the family." Gertrud assumed she would never really learn the truth.

"Well, I'm sure Gertrud is happy to have her father home. And we're also happy to have you back."

"So, Gustav, I understand you're going to work for your stepfather and become a tailor."

"That's right. They've been pretty busy, even with the depression, and Papa is eager for me to start. But he also knows I'm interested in learning about the new fashions, and he's trying to find me an apprenticeship. I have to say between being a tailor and being a scrap metal dealer, tailor wins."

"Your father, of blessed memory, would probably still be in the scrap metal business had he survived the war, and like the rest of the Heppenheimer men, you would not have had a choice. But it seems to me you will actually like being a tailor. You certainly dress like someone who likes clothes."

Gustav blushed. "I don't dress nearly as well as Trudi!" They both laughed. But then Gustav stopped laughing and looked at his uncle and said, "If he had lived, I wonder who my father would be in business with."

Robert smiled, shook his head, and said, "I really don't know." Gertrud knew about some of the upheaval in the business lives of her father and uncles. Gertrud assumed had her uncle survived the war, he would probably have been part of the drama.

Gertrud yawned and suddenly felt exhausted. She turned to her father. "Papa, how long are we staying?"

"Not much longer, Liebling. I need to speak with Onkel Jacob again. Why don't you stay here, and I'll be right back." Her father stood up and walked towards her uncles.

Gertrud knew it could be at least an hour before they finally left. Her father was never very good at time, and she sensed her father had some important things to discuss with her uncle. She looked around the living room. Bettina and Trudi were still in the corner, whispering to one another. Gustav had left the couch and was holding his brother Alfred and talking with people Gertrud didn't recognize. She was bored and really wanted to leave.

Gertrud's eyelids began to droop, but a bounce jolted her awake. Someone had sat down next to her. She turned and saw an old woman she didn't recognize.

The woman immediately asked, "Who are you?"

"I'm Gertrud, Robert Heppenheimer's daughter."

"Oh, the shiksa."

Gertrud didn't respond. She knew what the word meant. Her father explained it was how the Jewish community referred to a woman who wasn't Jewish. But Gertrud knew it also wasn't meant as a compliment, and this woman sneered when she said it. But she was old, and Gertrud had been raised to respect her elders, so she said nothing.

"And where is your mother?"

"She had to go to work after the funeral."

"What, she couldn't come? I know your parents are divorced, but how could she not come?"

Gertrud said nothing, then saw her father standing before her. She was so relieved to see him.

"Frau Stein, it's so nice to see you again. Thank you so much for coming to the funeral. My mother really valued your friendship and would have appreciated that you came."

"Robert, it's nice that you came in for your mother's funeral. She often spoke to me about how she missed you. Your mother was the salt of the earth. Did you see I brought my noodle kugel? That was her favorite. She was always trying to get the recipe." She cleared her throat. "I have been having a pleasant chat with your daughter."

"Frau Stein, thank you for the kugel. I am afraid that I need to take Gertrud home. But it was lovely to see you again."

Gertrud immediately got up from the couch and took her father's arm. "Papa, thank you so much for rescuing me. That woman was not very nice to me. She called me a shiksa. Then she criticized Mama for not being here."

"Liebling, don't pay any attention to that woman. Even your grandmother didn't like her. As soon as I saw her sit down on the couch, I knew it was time to leave. Your Onkel Jacob will be in Frankfurt for two more days, and I can speak with him another time. Let's get your coat and leave."

•   •   •

Gertrud spent the rest of the afternoon with her father. They first went to Gertrud's apartment, and she took a much-needed nap. After she awoke, they walked to the zoo and her father bought her an ice cream. She thought it was a rather strange day, having attended her grandmother's funeral in the morning, then having a fun day with her father at the zoo. But she didn't care. She never felt very close to grandmother.

As they neared her apartment, her father turned to her and said, "Gertrud, your mother told me she is getting married again. Do you like the man she is marrying?"

"Karl is a little old. But he's nice to Mama, and he buys me treats. I know he wants me to like him. She told me not to talk to him about you or my cousins. She says it's better that Karl doesn't know."

Robert put his arm around his daughter. "Yes, she did tell me that. She thinks it's better that Karl doesn't know that she was married to me. And that I not come to your apartment to get you after she marries."

Gertrud started to breathe fast. She worried things weren't turning out how she'd hoped. "Papa, now that you're back in Frankfurt, I want to see you all the time. How am I going to see you if you don't come to the apartment? I don't care what Karl thinks. Mama wants me to call him Papa. Did she tell you that?"

"She told me. But don't worry about what you call Karl. If your mama wants you to call him Papa, that would be okay. We both know I will always be your papa. Don't worry about my seeing you. We'll figure out a way for us to see each other all the time. But it's important that we do what your mama asks."

Gertrud grunted. "I really don't understand, but if you think it's important, then I won't say anything to Karl. Mama says that, once she's married, we need to move. I'll need to go to a new school, and I won't be able to see my old school friends, which is okay, since I really don't like them. But I still don't understand why she cares who knows about you."

"Gertrud, sometimes I forget that you are only a child. But your mama is probably right. There is a lot of anti-Semitism in Frankfurt, and it has only become worse because of the depression. Many people are out of work, and some blame the depression on the Jews. You and I both know that's wrong, but we can't stop people from believing what they believe. Your mama thinks if the new neighbors don't know that I'm Jewish, they'll be nicer to you. And I guess she might be worried about Karl knowing."

"But, Papa, I'm not Jewish. Why should it matter that you're Jewish?"

"Liebling, unfortunately, for some people, it matters. You'll be living with your mama and Karl once they're married, so you will need to do what they say to fit in. But it won't matter for us. We'll still spend a lot of time together. Your mama will take you to where I'm living, or we can meet someplace. It will be fine. It might even be fun, like a little game."

"Papa, that sounds crazy. I don't like that you can't visit me at my place, and I don't like that I have to hide you."

"I wish this were a different world and people were different. But your mama is just trying to keep you safe. Now that I'll be living in Frankfurt, she's worried people will find out about me. But when things get better and people go back to work, I'm sure your mama will think differently about this."

Gertrud looked at her father and thought he might not fully agree with her mother. But her mother had always been the boss, even when her parents were still married. Whatever her mother said was the law. And now her mother had decided they would deny her family, and he had agreed. And Gertrud could never defy her mother.

Gertrud never really felt a connection to her father's Jewish background, but she felt a little sad that she now needed to deny it. Perhaps she was simply feeling badly about the denial of her father. She knew her mother would have been just as happy to have her father remain in Strasbourg. So, Gertrud decided it was up to her to make sure her mother continued to allow her to see her father.

As they walked toward her apartment, Gertrud was lost in thought and not really paying attention to the woman coming up to her and her father. Gertrud nearly bumped into the woman.

"Herr Heppenheimer, I thought that was you. I haven't seen you for ages. And don't tell me this is little Gertrud! You have gotten so tall. You're almost taller than your father! But, of course, who can forget that face! You look just the same as you did when you were little. The same blue eyes and blond hair, just like a real German girl."

Her father seemed startled by the appearance of this woman. He offered her a fake smile, then said, "Frau Müller. It is nice to see you again. I hope you are doing well."

"As well as can be expected. My rheumatism is always giving me trouble, but I'm not one to complain. I hope you are well. Where are you living these days?"

"I actually moved to Strasbourg, although Margarete and Gertrud still live in Frankfurt. I am here visiting." Gertrud noticed her father said nothing about moving back to Frankfurt.

Frau Müller seemed to almost sneer at her father when she said, "That's so nice that you stay in touch with your daughter. It's so important for fathers to be close to their children. My late husband was very close to our children. Since your wife, I mean your ex-wife, moved out of the building after the divorce, I no longer see her. We were such good friends, and now not a word. I really miss our chats over coffee."

"Frau Müller, I know Margarete is very busy with her job. I'll tell her I saw you. But we are already late for an appointment, so we must be on our way. But it was nice to see you. Goodbye, Frau Müller." Her father grabbed Gertrud's hand and nearly dragged her across the street.

Gertrud could hear the old woman yell, "Make sure you tell Margarete that I would like to see her. And Gertrud, it was lovely to see how you have grown! You can't even see the Jew in you!"

As soon as they were out of earshot of the woman, Gertrud asked her father, "Why were you in such a hurry to get away from Frau Müller? I didn't even have time to say hello. I remember her. She was always nice to me when we lived in the old apartment. She always gave me candies."

"She may have been nice to you, but she was horrible to me. She scowled at me every time she saw me. I told your mother that I thought she was an anti-Semite, and you heard what she just said about you. You should avoid that dreadful woman, especially since your mother doesn't want anyone knowing about me. She could make trouble for you" Her father then smiled at Gertrud, but she could see it was strained. Still, she took her father's hand, returned his smile, and they walked to her apartment.

•　　•　　•

The following evening, the family gathered at Onkel Arthur's apartment for dinner. Gertrud's father told her this was to be the last dinner for the brothers before Jacob left Frankfurt for Strasbourg. Gertrud didn't know Jacob well – he left Frankfurt when she was four years old, and when he visited Frankfurt, he always seemed too busy to talk to her. Plus, her mother always talked about how rich he was, so she was a little intimidated by him. But she always like Trudi, and especially loved to see the different outfits Trudi would wear, hoping one day to dress just like her older cousin. And now that she was ten years old and feeling a bit more mature, she wanted to spend even more time with Trudi. She secretly hoped that Trudi would take her shopping for dresses, if her mother allowed.

Her father knocked on her uncle's door once, but then just walked in. Gertrud had been in her Onkel Arthur's apartment many times, but always knocked and waited for him to open the door. But her father never waited, and her uncle never seemed to mind. Gertrud knew her father was closest to Onkel Arthur, and maybe this was why he always felt comfortable just walking into the apartment. While Onkel Arthur's apartment was much larger than Gertrud's, she always felt at ease there. The living room had two comfortable couches, and the flowered wallpaper was always inviting to her. Onkel Arthur's wife Henny was warm and kind and always encouraged Gertrud to sit anywhere she wanted. Gertrud had been in other apartments where children were never allowed in the living room. That was not Tante Henny's way.

Gertrud and her father were the last to arrive. As they entered the apartment, Gertrud saw Onkel Berthold, his wife, and their two children, Onkel Jacob and his wife Lili, and Gustav and his mother Paula and stepfather David. She assumed Gustav's baby brother was home with a babysitter. She could hear Henny, Bettina, and Trudi in the kitchen. Gertrud knew no one was expecting her mother to come, so no one asked where she was.

Henny came out from the kitchen, noticed Robert and Gertrud, and said, "Good, everyone is here. Dinner is ready, so why don't we set up the tables. Arthur, take the folding table into the living room, and take the chairs from the other rooms." Once the tables and chairs were arranged, her aunt Henny took out two tablecloths, and then all the women began to set the tables.

Fifteen of them had gathered for dinner, and the family arranged themselves around the tables. Gertrud sat between her father and Bettina. The last thing she wanted was to be forced to engage with her younger cousins. Henny brought out a platter filled with roasted chicken and brisket. She served spätzle, asparagus, a large salad, and a bowl of green beans. The family passed the various platters around, then Arthur brought out several bottles of wine, which were also passed around the table.

No one said anything while the food was being passed, but as soon as the last platter was put down in the middle of the table, Onkel Berthold said, "So Robert now gets to stay in Mama's apartment and doesn't have to pay a thing?" Gertrud was surprised by the comment. She looked around and noticed that her cousins were surprised, but not their parents. She felt like she'd just stumbled into the middle of an argument. Perhaps this was just a continuation of their conversation at the funeral.

Jacob tried to play peacemaker. "Berthold, we already discussed this yesterday. It's time to move on."

"I'm not ready to move on. I don't understand why Robert just gets to move into Mama's apartment."

"Berthold, why do you care where Robert lives? Besides, I'm the one who has been paying the rent on Mama's apartment. And I'm paying the rent on the apartment until the end of the year. It really isn't any of your concern."

Gertrud could see that Berthold was only getting angrier. "Jacob, I was paying my share of the rent until the stock market crash wrecked the economy and my business. Arthur is also struggling and had to stop paying his share. Frankly, I don't know how you've been able to weather this storm."

"How my company is doing is none of your business. I said nothing to you when you told me you couldn't help pay Mama's rent and you shouldn't say anything to me about Robert living in Mama's apartment."

"It's not just that he's living in the apartment. That furniture is all of ours. The china and the silver are all of ours. We should be able to get our share and not have to wait until next year."

Gertrud heard her father loudly exhale. He clearly had had enough of his brothers talking about him as if he wasn't there. "Berthold, if you want the furniture so badly, take it. In fact, you can take it all. I have asked nothing from you in the past, and I won't ask anything of you now. Just take it."

"Robert, I don't want to take it now. I just want to be fair. And fair is that we all get our fair share of what's in the apartment. I can go to the apartment in the next few days and make an inventory of what's there, and we can then decide what each of us will get. I think that seems fair. What do the rest of you think?"

It was quiet until Robert said, "Berthold, do what you want. I'm starting work with Arthur tomorrow. You have a key to Mama's place. Just go when I'm at work."

"I'll do that. Really, I am just trying to be fair to everyone."

Gertrud couldn't understand why Berthold cared so much about what was in the apartment. She glanced at her father, and he seemed upset about the exchange with his brother. She took his hand, and he looked at her and smiled. He then turned to Jacob and asked, "When are you and the family leaving tomorrow?"

"I want to be out the door by nine a.m. Do you hear that, Lili and Trudi? We really need to get back to Strasbourg tomorrow."

No further arguments arose for the rest of the dinner. Gertrud did notice that her father spoke with everyone except Berthold, and Berthold only spoke with Gustav's stepfather, David. It was probably better that way, so the brothers avoided any more fighting. Henny served a strudel for dessert, then Gertrud and her father said goodnight to everyone and goodbye to Jacob and his family.

On the way back to her mother's apartment, Gertrud asked why Berthold was so upset about her father living in her grandmother's place.

"I really don't know. Maybe he wants to make sure he gets some of Oma's silver." Then he quickly changed the subject. "Did you have a nice time this evening with your cousins?"

"I didn't really get a chance to speak with any of them. It's hard to speak when we're all at the dinner table. But I do wish I could spend more time with Trudi. She doesn't come to Frankfurt enough."

"Well, maybe someday you could visit her in Strasbourg."

"I would like that."

•   •   •

Gertrud arranged to see her father the following Friday and to stay at his apartment for the weekend. Her father told her to meet him at *A&B Heppenheimer* after school, and he would leave early. When Gertrud arrived at the business, only Bettina was in the office. But that was fine with Gertrud, since she hadn't seen her cousin since the family dinner.

"Hi, Gertrud. Your father had to deliver some scrap to a client. He should be back in about an hour. He told me to tell you that you could walk over to the apartment if you didn't want to wait."

"I'm fine waiting, if it's okay with you."

"It's fine with me. It's a little slow, and I was going to get a cup of coffee. You want some water?"

"Water would be nice. Thanks."

When Bettina returned with their drinks, Gertrud asked her what she had been wanting to ask since that dinner. "Bettina, why was Onkel Berthold so angry at my father at dinner?"

"Did you ask your father?"

"I did, but he really didn't answer my question."

"Well, you're ten years old, old enough to know some things about the family. The Heppenheimer brothers never tell their children anything and rarely fight in front of us. I was actually surprised to see Berthold so angry in front of all of us last week. They must have been really fighting at the funeral."

"I did see them together a lot, both at the cemetery and then in the apartment, but I only heard small pieces of the conversation. And nothing about why Onkel Berthold was angry."

"I'll tell you what I know, but I'm pretty sure it's not the whole story, and I may have some of it wrong. But I've heard my mother and father discuss things between themselves over the years. I'm guessing they don't want us to know, but I think we all have the right to know what's going on."

"Well, I would be happy to know something."

"You asked me why Berthold was so angry at your father. I actually think Berthold is furious with all his brothers. You know Berthold and Hugo were in business together before the war and that my father and Berthold were in business together after the war – they started *A&B Heppenheimer*. They were both partners, but had Robert work for the business. I always thought it was strange they never made your father a partner. When Jacob was forced to move back to Frankfurt after the war, he was made a partner and the four of them worked together. I have the sense that things were fine when it was just my father, your father, and Berthold. But when Jacob joined them, I heard Berthold thought Jacob was trying to control the business. The two of them began to fight. My father tried to stay out of the mess, as did your father. Finally, Berthold announced he was leaving the partnership and asked to be bought out. My father tried to convince him to stay, but I have the sense that Jacob was happy to see him leave. That was around 1921, so I was around 10 years old."

"My age now."

"That's right, but I don't think I was as mature as you. Anyway, after Berthold left the business, I rarely saw him. I do remember that he married just before Onkel Jacob left Frankfurt, so that must have been 1924. We all went to the wedding. I remember Oma complaining that Berthold was her second son to marry a non-Jew, even though Tante Martha had converted just before the wedding. And, of course, I remember the fight. At the wedding."

"I don't remember a fight. Of course, I was four years old."

"Well, the rest of us certainly remember it, and it was quite unexpected. I believe Berthold's wedding was the first time Jacob and Berthold had seen each other since Berthold left the company. My mother was hoping the wedding might help heal the rift between the two. She thought it was a good sign that Berthold had invited Jacob to the wedding. I don't remember how the fight started – all I really remember was Berthold yelling that Jacob had ruined *A&B Heppenheimer* and was now leaving a wrecked company behind in his move back to Strasburg. He said, 'It's just like the first time you left Frankfurt.' Then Jacob stormed out of the wedding."

"Do you know what he meant by 'It's just like the first time?'"

"I never found out. I do know that he left Frankfurt for the first time in 1910, so I assumed that's what Berthold was referring to. I asked my mother after the wedding, but she told me she didn't know. I didn't believe her then, but I knew not to ask her again, nor to ask my father."

"If Berthold is so angry with Jacob, why does he take it out on my father?"

"I really don't know. Maybe he's too afraid to directly confront Jacob. Or maybe he doesn't like that Jacob has always helped your father. My mother thinks Berthold has struggled as a scrap metal dealer since he left *A&B*, and she thinks the depression has been especially hard on him. But he doesn't have to be so mean to your father."

"I agree. Thanks for telling me." She shivered, not understanding why her family had to disagree so much. "Is it okay if we change the subject?"

"Of course. It is a bit hard, isn't it?"

Gertrud nodded. "Yes, it is." She waited a moment and said, "It was so great to see Trudi. She has really changed since I saw her last year."

"You're right. She has really grown into a beauty, don't you think? And the outfits she wears! She could be a fashion model. I wish I had the figure to dress like that. Or the money."

"Bettina, I don't know what you're talking about! If you dressed like Trudi, you would look just as great as she does."

Bettina blushed. "Well, I don't know about that. But could you imagine me sitting in this office and wearing clothes like Trudi? Still, it really was fun being with her, even though it was for a sad reason."

"Wouldn't it be great if just the cousins could go away together? Maybe to Bad Kissingen. It's in the mountains and is supposed to be beautiful. Mama and Papa went there on their honeymoon."

"I wish we could. But money is a problem now, and I'm always needed in the office. Maybe when things get better. But it is a nice dream to have. Just the cousins!"

"Yes! Once things get better, the cousins can go. But not Berthold's bratty kids."

"Gertrud, that's not nice!" She waited a few seconds, then laughed. "Well, they are pretty bratty. Okay, just the four of us!"

•　　•　　•

Gertrud was sound asleep when she heard noise in the dining room. Her father had promised he would buy her treats for breakfast, and she assumed he had just returned from the bakery. Her mother had warned her not to eat too many sweets, that she might get fat or ruin her complexion, but she didn't care.

She was too excited to stay in bed. Gertrud left her bedroom and walked into the dining room. She saw her father looking over a stack of papers. In fact, the table was covered with papers.

"Good morning, Papa."

"Good morning, Liebling. I hope I didn't wake you up. It's still early. I haven't even gone to the bakery."

She had no idea what time it was, but she didn't want to make her father feel bad about waking her. "No, Papa, I just got up early. But what are all these papers?"

"I'm helping prepare booklets about the importance of protecting the workers." He motioned for his daughter to come closer. "Liebling, this is really important. Do you want me to tell you why?"

Gertrud was really hungry, but she could tell her father really wanted to discuss what he was doing, so she nodded.

Robert began, "Gertrud, after the Great War, the German people had the opportunity to create a government that serves all the people. That's the Weimar Republic. Have you learned about the Weimar Republic in school?"

"Of course, Papa."

Robert smiled proudly at his daughter. "You really are so smart. Well, then you know the chancellor had been a Social Democrat, and I am a Social Democrat. Unfortunately, the coalition the Party formed to run the government collapsed last month, and President Von Hindenburg used emergency powers to appoint a very conservative politician named Heinrich Brüning as Chancellor. We worry that Herr Brüning will try to undo all the important work the Weimar Republic has done for workers. So, the pamphlets are designed to educate the German people about what's going on. Like I am educating you."

"Papa, do you think the German people will listen to the Social Democrats?"

"They must. What we did for the German workers is too important to lose. Plus, many people are worried about some of these right-wing groups gaining power."

"My teacher at school told us about the Nazi Party. He said the Party is trying to make Germany a stronger country."

Robert raised his voice and said, "Gertrud, don't listen to your teacher. The Nazi Party is trying to take away all the workers' rights. The only Party that cares about the worker is the Social Democratic Party. I promised your mother I wouldn't discuss politics with you, but this is something you should know about and care about."

Gertrud answered quietly, "Okay, Papa."

Robert looked at Gertrud, took a breath, and said, "But enough of politics. I was hoping to have finished assembling these pamphlets before you were up, but you look a little hungry, so I'll finish them later and we can walk over to the bakery to pick out our breakfast."

"Oh, Papa, I would love that! Maybe we could eat our breakfast at the zoo?"

"Yes, let's do that. And Gertrud, let's not tell your mother about these pamphlets. It'll be our little secret."

"Of course, Papa. I understand."

"Gertrud, you really are wise beyond your years."

Gertrud smiled at her father, gave him a kiss on the cheek, and went into her bedroom to change. *Secrets,* she said to herself. *Always secrets.* Her mother told her not to tell anyone about her father. There was a time just after her parents divorced that her mother told people she was a widow and told Gertrud not to tell them the truth. And her father was always talking about politics but told her not to tell her mother. Secrets and lies. Secrets and lies. She loved her parents, but sometimes found them a bit exhausting. She hated keeping their secrets and telling their lies.

CHAPTER 2

Strasbourg
January 1932

Gertrud and Bettina knocked on their cousin's bedroom door. Not hearing a response, the two opened the door and jumped into Trudi's bed. The large bed was roomy enough for all three. Trudi gradually opened her eyes and growled at both her cousins. "Why did you wake me up? I was enjoying my last night of sleep before my big day! I was having this great dream about climbing up a snowy mountain in my wedding dress!"

Gertrud snuggled against her cousin Trudi. "We thought you might be lonely, so we decided to keep you company."

"Plus, we are too excited to sleep. You're getting married!" Bettina exclaimed.

Trudi smiled. "Well, Bettina, from what you told us last night, you might not be far behind me."

Bettina blushed. "I've just seen a few movies with him. But remember, both of you, don't say a word about him to the family."

"My lips are sealed! Same goes for you, Gertrud."

"Don't worry about me, cousin. I'm used to keeping secrets. Besides, I really don't think it's a big deal. After all, I'm not Jewish."

"Well, Gertrud, technically, you're half-Jewish. Hans, on the other hand, is 100 percent Catholic."

Gertrud grunted. "But who cares, anyway. If you love him, that's all that matters."

"Spoken just like a twelve-year-old! And I don't love him. We've just gone out a few times. Although we talk all the time, and he's easy to talk to."

"How long have you known him?" Trudi asked.

"My parents hired him about six months ago. Just after Papa had his first heart incident. The doctor said he could no longer do any heavy lifting and couldn't visit the customers alone. Hans had never worked for a scrap metal dealer, but he's a hard worker, and my parents both like him. But they don't know that we've been spending time together outside of work. No need for them to know if nothing comes of it."

Trudi took her cousin's hand. "Bettina, I'm really sorry your parents couldn't come to my wedding, but I completely understand your mother needing to stay behind to care for your father."

"Both regret not being able to come. They've always considered you a second daughter. But Papa's heart troubles have them worried, and a train ride here would have been too much for him."

"My father also felt badly about not being able to come, but he felt he needed to help Tante Henny as well." Both Bettina and Trudi knew that their Onkel Robert could only afford to send his daughter to Strasbourg, but neither said a word. "Plus, it's fun to have just the cousins here to see you married and Gustav was so much fun on the train!"

"Speaking of Gustav, let's wake him up. I get to do what I want today. After all, I am the bride. And, besides, I'm starving!" The three giggled, got out of bed, and raced down the hall to wake up their cousin.

Gertrud was the first to reach the door. She knocked once and opened the door, not waiting for an answer.

Gustav was already sitting up in bed. "Good morning, spätz. What took you so long? I could hear your cackling."

Gertrud made a face at her cousin.

Trudi said, "Gustav, as the bride, I order you to get out of bed and join us downstairs for breakfast. We're starving. I told Marie we would likely be getting up early and that all of us would want her wonderful crepes. Unless, of course, I'm the only one who likes Marie's crepes."

Gertrud raced out of the room, yelling, "I'm getting the first crepes!" The others laughed, but immediately joined her. No one ever said no to the family's cook's crepes!

•　　•　　•

The four cousins were in the spacious dining room, eating Marie's crepes. The table had twelve chairs, but leaves could be added to accommodate twenty. Trudi loved sitting in the dining room but was worried that the ornate furniture and the Henri Matisse painting on one of the walls would remind her cousins of how well her father, their Onkel Jacob, was doing in the scrap metal business and how their families were struggling. The depression was hurting most businesses, but she knew that Onkel Arthur's illness was also affecting *A&B Heppenheimer*. Tante Henny was essentially running the business with Onkel Robert and Bettina, and Trudi knew from her father that none of them were an effective replacement for Onkel Arthur.

But leave it to Gertrud to lighten the mood. "This room is so fancy! Do I have to worry about damaging anything when I spill something? Because you know I will spill something at some point."

Trudi smiled at her cousin. She was surprised at how grown-up Gertrud was looking, although moments like this reminded Trudi that Gertrud was still a child. Happily, they had become closer in the last year. Gertrud was a small child when Trudi moved back to Strasbourg, and they hadn't spent enough time together to create the kind of bond she had with Bettina. But the week she spent with Gertrud last year when she and her mother came to Frankfurt to buy a wedding dress brought them closer. Gertrud was spending the week with her father during a school break (having told her new stepfather that she was visiting a cousin in Mannheim), and Gertrud accompanied Trudi and her mother to virtually every shopping destination. Trudi and Gertrud had even found time to go out on their own. Now giggling at her cousin, she said, "Gertrud, you can spill anything you want. After all, it is my wedding day."

"We can eat when we want, where we want, and can spill what we want. So, what can't we do on your wedding day?"

"Well, Gustav, you can't be late for the ceremony!"

Almost in unison, the girls said, "Like you always are!" They all laughed, then told stories for the next hour, until Jacob and Lili joined them for breakfast.

"Good morning, children. I see everyone is still in their pajamas. This house is pretty big, but I could hear the four of you talking and laughing for the past hour. Trudi, it's a good thing your mother is a heavy sleeper - and was wearing earplugs."

Her mother laughed, and said, "Trudi, darling, the hairdresser is coming at noon to do your hair. And then we need to be at the synagogue at four p.m. to get ready. Remember, everyone, especially Gustav, the service starts promptly at six just as the sun is setting."

"Mama, we know, we know. Everyone will be on time. Why do you think we started breakfast so early? But we have a few hours until the hairdresser comes, and the cousins need some more time alone."

"You four had time alone last night. Don't you three want to spend time with your favorite aunt and uncle?"

Bettina rose from her chair and gave her aunt a huge hug. "Tante Lili, I think Trudi will be a little busy tonight and tomorrow. Our train doesn't leave until tomorrow night, so we'll have plenty of time to spend with you and Onkel Jacob."

"I will hold you to that promise! Okay, you four, go have fun."

The four quickly left the dining room and moved into the parlor, closing the door behind them. Trudi switched on the large radio.

After it warmed up, classical music filled the room, and Trudi twisted the dial until she found jazz.

Gustav nodded and said, "Much better. And this song is one of my favorites. Trudi, how about you and I cut the rug, as they say in the American movies, and dance the foxtrot? I just learned a few new steps."

Trudi smiled and said, "I thought you would never ask!" Gustav took her hand and the two began to glide their feet to the music. After a minute, Gustav turned to Bettina and said, "Your turn," and the two began to dance, Gustav leading his cousin in the new steps.

Not wanting to feel left out, Gertrud took Trudi's hand and said, "I've watched enough. Let's you and I try these new steps." The four continued to dance until the song was over. Then the four collapsed in laughter. Gertrud stretched herself out on the large divan, and the other three moved chairs together around her.

"I see the queen has chosen the best spot and is taking up the entire space."

"Thank you, Gustav, for recognizing my royal position. I am the queen of this divan, and no one else may sit here but me."

"Don't worry, spätz. No one will bother you."

"Gustav, stop calling me spätz. I'm no longer a child."

"Sorry. Old habits. It's sometimes hard to grow you up in my head. When you said goodbye to Onkel Robert yesterday, I noticed you are actually taller than your father. But, of course, your father is short, just like all the Heppenheimer men!"

"But not you, Gustav," Bettina said. "You clearly got your height from your mother's side of the family. And with those eyes of yours, the women must be throwing themselves at you!"

"Yes, all the old women coming into the dress shop just throwing themselves at me. Besides, I'm only eighteen years old. Trudi can get married at eighteen, but I have lots of time. Of course, we could also talk about your prospects, Bettina. Hans is his name, right?"

Bettina blushed. "Enough of all this marriage talk. Trudi's getting married today and only Trudi. So, let's change the subject. Trudi, I heard your father say that Berthold is not coming to the wedding. Do you know why?"

"I know my parents sent him an invitation to the wedding, and I believe they heard nothing back. I don't believe my father has spoken to Onkel Berthold since Oma's funeral. Bettina, has your father spoken with Onkel Berthold recently?"

"I know there was some communication involving the sale of Oma's things after Onkel Robert moved out of the apartment. But I haven't seen his family since the funeral."

"I haven't seen them since the funeral either, but I can't say that I'm unhappy about that. His children were always brats. But I do remember how angry Onkel Berthold was about Papa living in the apartment. It seemed pretty unfair to me that he was being so selfish about that apartment, particularly because Papa had just moved back to Frankfurt and had no money. Maybe it had to do with Berthold saying something to Onkel Jacob about being forced to leave Frankfurt. Trudi, do you know what he was talking about?"

Trudi looked at Bettina and then at Gustav. She took a deep breath and said to her young cousin, "Gertrud, I guess you're old enough to hear the truth. You're always talking about how your parents force you to tell lies and hold secrets. Well, I also had to hold a secret in our family. I recently told both Bettina and Gustav, but no one knows in Strasbourg, and you must not talk about this to anyone. Even your mother. Promise?"

Gertrud sat up on the divan and looked excitedly at her cousin. "Ooh, someone else's secret! But seriously, Trudi, I won't tell anyone, including Mama. I promise."

"There are actually two secrets, one related to the other. Bettina and Gustav learned the first from their parents, but I told them the second. You know that Opa Lazarus died a long time ago. What you don't know is that he committed suicide. Like his brothers, he was in the scrap metal business. But unlike his brothers, he was never very good at the business. His brothers Henry and Joseph had started *Gebrüder Heppenheimer* even before Opa moved to Frankfurt, but never invited him to join their business. And when Opa's business began to fail, they didn't help him out. At the end of December 1903, he walked onto the thin ice on the Main River and drowned."

"Oh, my goodness! I had no idea. All Papa said was that Opa died. He never said how and I never thought to ask."

Trudi shrugged. "Well, why would you ask? Plus, in our family, we never ask. My father was twenty-three years old and suddenly became the man of the house. He had been working with Opa, but had never been in charge. Bettina, your father had also been working with Opa, and he and Papa started to run the business. The younger three brothers were still in school, although Onkel Hugo soon joined them. I believe the three of them struggled in those first few years. Opa's brothers Henry and Joseph were never much help to Opa, or at least that's what I was told. I guess we will never really know. All I know is that, at some point, Papa started to do some trading with *Gebrüder Heppenheimer*. Great Onkel Henry had already moved with his family to America, but Great Onkel Joseph was running *Gebrüder Heppenheimer*, and maybe he wanted to help his nephews. But something went terribly wrong. In 1907, Papa was arrested and charged with selling stolen metals to his cousin Adolph at *Gebrüder Heppenheimer*. Adolph was Henry's son and had remained in Frankfurt. I don't know how the stolen metals were discovered, but I do know Adolph claimed Papa sold him the metals and that Adolph didn't know they were stolen. Papa wanted to make sure no one else got into trouble, so he said that neither of his brothers knew anything about the sale."

Bettina spoke up. "Trudi, remember I told you that, based on things I've heard, my father and Onkel Hugo knew about the stolen metals and that Adolph also probably knew. The brothers were probably desperate at the time to make money, and perhaps Adolph was taking advantage of his cousins. But as wealthy as

Adolph was, he wasn't going to prison. And Onkel Jacob, as the head of the family, was not going to allow his brothers to go to prison, either."

Gertrud sat up, wide-eyed. "Onkel Jacob went to prison?"

"He did, Gertrud, for a year. When he was released, he moved to Strasbourg to start over. He told no one here that he had been in prison. In fact, instead of Jacob, he started using the first name Jacques in business. And Papa started doing well. When Papa went to prison, Onkel Arthur and Onkel Hugo closed the business and started their own separate businesses. When Onkel Berthold graduated the eighth grade, he went into business with Hugo. Gertrud, your father worked for Onkel Arthur, although not as a partner. After the war and Hugo's death, Arthur and Berthold went into business together as *A&B Heppenheimer,* but had a falling out after my father moved back to Frankfurt and the three were in business together. Things have been bad between the brothers ever since. Gertrud, when Onkel Berthold made that comment about my father being forced to move to Strasbourg, he was referring to my father having gone to prison."

Gustav grunted. "I know almost nothing about their businesses since I don't really remember my father and my mother doesn't really like to talk about my father, but maybe I'll ask her one day."

Trudi smiled at that last comment. "Or maybe not. Since no one in our family likes to talk about anything. But it is still my special day, and I want to talk about my wedding and how happy I am that we four are together! Although, Gustav, you will need to leave the three of us alone soon so we can look beautiful for tonight!"

"You three are already beautiful, but I'm happy to leave you. I promised Onkel Jacob I would talk with him about my apprenticeship."

"Oh, right! With all this wedding nonsense, I forgot to ask you about the apprenticeship. How do you like Würzburg? And how do you like making ladies' dresses?"

Gustav glared at his giggling cousins. "I'm sorry, but I like both men's and women's fashion. A lot of the newer fashion is in women's wear and my parent's shop is only for men, so this is a good apprenticeship for me. My boss is very skilled and is interested in the newer fashion designs, so I'm learning a lot."

Bettina shushed her cousins and said, "Gustav, I'm sorry we were teasing you. Perhaps at least one of us is a little jealous that you're doing something you like. I'm stuck trying to help my parents keep the business from sinking, and if I'm being honest, I actually hate the scrap metal business! But I have no choice."

"That's really one of the great things about marrying Joseph, other than that I love him. I will no longer have to go to that office. But, Gustav, do you plan on staying in Würzburg after your apprenticeship is over?"

"I'm not sure. While I really like my boss, someday I would like to open my own place, a place that specializes in fashionable clothing for men and women. I'm not sure where. Maybe in Frankfurt. Maybe even Berlin. But right now, Würzburg is okay. The only concern I have is that it is a bit anti-Semitic, at least that has been my experience. But you know I'm not at all political. I'm just staying focused on my job, which I really like."

"And I refuse to discuss politics on my wedding day. Besides, we're all too young to be political."

Gertrud sat up and said, "If we can't discuss politics, let's discuss religion."

The other three cousins groaned in unison.

"No, I'm serious. Do you know this is the first time I'll step into a synagogue since Gustav's bar mitzvah and I barely remember that day."

Gustav smiled and said, "It wasn't a big event. I said a few prayers and then we ate a lot."

"I'm not nervous. I'm just wondering what I should expect. Do I need to do or say anything? I once went to a Catholic church with

Karl and Mama, and people were going to the front of the church at some point, being fed crackers."

Trudi laughed and said, "I think they call them wafers, and you don't need to do anything. Just sit there and watch me cry. We'll say a few prayers, then Joseph will step on a glass. It will go very quickly. And then we'll eat."

"When I went to the Catholic church, it felt like I was in another world. Mama sometimes makes me go to Lutheran church, but we just sit and listen to the sermon. Or Mama listens. I usually think about other things."

Bettina said, "We used to go to the synagogue for Rosh Hashanah and Yom Kippur, but stopped a few years ago. Trudi, you've joked that the only reason Tante Lili insists you go on the high holidays is so she has an excuse to buy you and herself new outfits. Gustav, you may be the only one who still goes to services other than for the high holidays."

"Not very often, now that I'm living in Würzburg. I only really went because it made my stepfather happy. He never insisted that my mama go – she also only goes for the high holidays – but he has always enjoyed going with me. I would go almost every Saturday when I was younger. After my bar mitzvah, he stopped insisting that I go and left it up to me, but I liked seeing him greet his friends and showing me off, so I still went while I was living in Frankfurt. I've never felt like a stepson to him, and that was particularly the case when I accompanied him to Saturday morning services. He has started taking Alfred, but I still go with the two of them when I visit Frankfurt."

Trudi looked at the clock and said, "Gustav, you need to leave so we can get on with our beauty treatments!"

After Gustav left, Trudi said, "Gustav has really become a handsome man. Sandy brown hair and blue eyes. That smile! And I have to say that he is certainly looking even more fashionable these days. I loved that double-breasted suit he was wearing yesterday and he never seems to be without a scarf. Bettina, does he ever talk to you about dating? I'm assuming the girls are all over him. How else would he know those dance steps?"

"He never talks to me about girls. But you know Gustav. He loves to talk, but never about himself. I wouldn't be surprised if, someday, he just shows up with some girl and announces that he's married! But don't worry, Gertrud. You'll always be Gustav's special girl."

Bettina winked at Trudi, and they started tickling Gertrud until they all collapsed on the floor, laughing.

•   •   •

It was nearly midnight. The house was quiet when Trudi and her new husband came home from the wedding. *My husband*, Trudi said to herself with a smile. She thought her wedding was perfect. Well, nearly perfect. Joseph looked so handsome in his top hat and tails. She loved her white silk dress and long veil and she was happy she was able to convince her mother to allow her to wear a dress that fell just below the knee. Her father spared no expense in decorating the synagogue with flowers, which was a particular challenge given the time of year. The flowers made the sanctuary, already beautiful with its large stained-glass windows and ornate architecture, even more impressive. The Reform service still had enough religion to satisfy her mother and was done in French and German to satisfy both of her parents. The lovely dinner after the service, in one of the adjacent halls, was wonderful. The only thing that Trudi regretted was that the dinner was small – her father allowed just fifty people – mostly family – to attend the dinner.

When he first told her that the wedding needed to be smaller than she had wanted, Trudi had strongly objected. "But Papa, I have so many friends and so does Joseph. I'm your only child. I really want this to be my special day."

"Trudi, just getting married is special. Every day I'm married to your mother is special."

"Yes, I know being married to Joseph will be wonderful. Still, I was hoping for a really special wedding."

"Trudi, believe me, there is nothing I would ever want to deny you. You have always made me proud. I seldom speak about my business, but because we are in the middle of the depression, we need to be careful. We're doing okay now, but we need to be cautious about how we spend money. More importantly, we don't want to be showy in front of the business community, particularly because we're Jewish. But I promise you will have a lovely wedding."

Trudi tried to hide her disappointment, but she knew her father could see it, anyway. Still, she said, "Papa, I do understand, and I know the wedding will be wonderful, even if it is a little small."

And it was wonderful. They could not invite all their friends, but the most important ones were there and much of their family was there too. Most importantly, her three cousins from Frankfurt were there.

Joseph took Trudi's hand and led her to her bedroom. When she opened the door, rose petals covered the floor and an opened bottle of champagne awaited them. She had a lot to drink at the wedding dinner, but clearly, she was not done drinking. Joseph led her to the table and poured the champagne into two flutes. They lifted their glasses and toasted to their new life. Trudi thought to herself, *I can't imagine my life will be anything but perfect!*

CHAPTER 3

Frankfurt
September 1933

Bettina woke early and began making breakfast for her parents and husband. Husband, she sighed to herself. She was a newlywed, but didn't really feel much like a newlywed. She and Hans had married four months ago, but she felt like she had gone from unmarried woman to part of an old married couple. Hans was living in her parents' apartment and Bettina, who had been cooking for both of her parents, was now also cooking for Hans.

Bettina never expected a wedding as lavish as Trudi's wedding. Even though her cousin had said she was forced to scale down the event, it didn't feel scaled down to Bettina. But there was no question that Bettina's wedding was scaled down. Bettina, Hans, and her parents went to city hall around noon on a Thursday. Bettina wore her best dress, a blue and white flutter-sleeved dress with a matching cloche hat. She had set her hair the night before, so that her shoulder-length light brown hair had a subtle wave. Onkel Robert and Gertrud, who left school early, were the only family present at the ceremony. A few of Bettina's friends also joined them, and then the group went to a restaurant to toast the new couple. Bettina and Hans went home to change and went to the office. No time for a honeymoon. Nor could they afford one.

Her father was the first to come to the breakfast table. He was not sleeping well, and Bettina could tell that he was happy to have an excuse to leave the bedroom.

"Good morning, Papa. How are you feeling this morning?"

"Good morning, Liebling. I can't complain. If the coffee is made, I would like a cup."

"Just half a cup, Papa. Remember what the doctor said about drinking less coffee."

"What do doctors know? But half a cup would be fine. And some fried eggs would go well with the coffee, don't you think?"

"I agree, Papa. Why don't you sit down, and I'll get your breakfast."

"Has Hans taken care of the Fleischmann order?"

"Papa don't worry about the order. Hans is working with Onkel Robert to make sure everything is taken care of."

"You know how difficult Herr Fleischmann can be. Plus, with all the pressures now on the business, I want to make sure our most loyal customers don't worry about doing business with a Jewish company."

"Papa, remember the doctor told you not to worry about the business. We have everything under control. The only thing you need to do is rest."

Her father smiled at her and drank his coffee. But Bettina was worried. And there was reason to worry. Her mother had obtained a scrap metal trading license the previous year when the doctor had first told her father to cut back on work, but her mother didn't have the skills her father had in identifying the different alloys. Hans was learning the business, or at least claimed he was learning, and Onkel Robert never could learn the different alloys, or perhaps really didn't care. Bettina had to finally admit to herself that her uncle might not be suited to work in the scrap metal industry. But they weren't about to let him go, not in the middle of a depression and not in the middle of what seemed to be a war on Jews.

Bettina looked up and saw her mother and Hans coming to the table. She served her father his fried eggs and toast. She cracked six eggs into a bowl and poured them into the pan to make eggs for the three of them. "Mama, Hans, sit down. The eggs will be ready in a minute. I'll get you your coffee."

Before either could thank Bettina, her father immediately asked Hans, "Are you seeing Herr Fleischmann this morning?"

"Papa, Hans has barely sat down, and you're already bothering him with work?"

"Bettina, that's fine. Yes, Papa, I am seeing Herr Fleischmann as soon as I finish breakfast. I'm picking up Robert on the way. Herr Fleischmann told me he needed some brass and copper. I should have enough supply to take care of the order."

"Hans, remember Herr Fleischmann is one of our oldest and most loyal customers. These days, companies are using any excuse to stop using Jewish scrap metal dealers. We don't want to give our customers an excuse to leave us."

"Relax, Papa. I have everything under control."

Her father knew he had no other choice than to trust his son-in-law. But Bettina knew better. It would soon be clear to their clients that her mother and Hans were not a satisfactory substitution for her father. Perhaps, in different times, the company could have managed the loss of her father at the helm of the company. But these were not normal times.

When Adolph Hitler was named Chancellor in the beginning of the year following the Nazi Party gains in the election, her father told Bettina not to worry, that the Jews would still be protected because Von Hindenburg was still president and promised to protect the Jews. But that promise didn't protect the company from the one-day boycott against Jewish businesses in April of this year. Her father stopped coming into the office after the boycott, and Bettina noticed a steady decrease in their business. Bettina couldn't tell if it was because of the Nazi Party's anti-Semitic rhetoric or because their customers didn't trust the business without her father.

Bettina had spoken to her mother and Hans about the loss of business. Hans' response was to tell her that business would pick up, particularly because he was now the face of the company, and he was not Jewish. Despite his reassurances, Bettina worried his over-confidence in his abilities might actually cause a loss in what business they still had. But the reality was that he was now the face of the company, and her father was not coming back. She needed to have faith in Hans.

Hans was already finished with breakfast by the time Bettina sat down to eat.

"Bettina, I need to go. Will you be okay getting to the office without the car?"

"Yes, Hans, I was already planning on taking the tram to the office this morning. And Mama will go in with me. I'll see you in the office after your meeting."

"Okay. See you then." Hans gave his wife a quick kiss and left the apartment. Bettina finished her breakfast quickly and began to wash the dishes. She could see her mother ministering to her father. Bettina tried, as much as she could, to lighten her mother's load. She now did most of the shopping and cooking. They could no longer afford a maid, and so Bettina also did most of the cleaning. Her mother did what she could when she wasn't taking care of her father. And while her mother was the only one in the office with a license to trade, she was working fewer and fewer hours.

After she finished the dishes, Bettina quickly made a chicken salad for her father for lunch. She then signaled to her mother that it was time to leave. They each grabbed their purses, coats, and hats, said their goodbyes, and left the apartment. On the street, Bettina could tell it was going to be a hot day, but the temperature at the moment was cool.

"Mama, it's a beautiful morning. Why don't we walk to the office. It will only take an extra fifteen minutes, and we have nothing pressing now."

"Bettina, that would be perfect. I would like to talk with you, anyway."

As they began to walk, Bettina asked, "What did you want to talk about?"

"Bettina, I know you do the books for the company, but even I know what's going on. And so does your father. We're both worried about the long-term viability of the company."

"Mama, you know I don't really follow politics, but Papa says that President Von Hindenburg has promised to protect the Jews from the Nazi Party. I have to believe that we'll be fine."

"I do worry about all this horrible anti-Semitism, but that's not the problem. I worry we can't run the business without your father. Your Onkel Robert has never really been good at the business, and I'm not sure Hans can do what your father did, regardless of what he says. Maybe he would be better suited for another line of work. You know, we could always sell the business."

"Hans has been working hard at learning the different alloys and believes he'll be successful in the business. He thinks the depression is the problem and that the business will soon recover. Please give him a chance."

"Well, we don't really have to do anything now. Let's see how things are in the next few months."

As they continued their walk, Bettina noticed all the posters on the walls and lampposts promoting the Nazi agenda, but also demonizing Jews. Cartoons showed Jews grabbing money or Jews stepping on the backs of workers. She tried to ignore the posters, but they were seemingly everywhere. She hoped her father was right, that President Von Hindenburg would protect Germany's Jews. Bettina rarely worry about politics, but she wondered whether she should start.

CHAPTER 4

Frankfurt
June 1934

Gustav waved to his mother and brother as he bounded down the stairs of the train. He was relieved to be home. He had expected to miss his family and his friends when he left for his apprenticeship in 1931, but he was excited to be living in a new city, to be experiencing new adventures. But the last year had been really hard, and he was happy to be home.

Unlike Frankfurt, which had a sizeable Jewish population, Würzburg's Jewish population was small. When his stepfather found the apprenticeship at a Jewish-owned firm, Gustav's mother worried about the Bavarian city's history of anti-Semitism. But Gustav was so excited about the opportunity that he ignored his mother's concerns. And while that worked for the first two years of the internship, everything seemed to change after the Nazi Party came to power in 1933. After the April 1933 one-day boycott against Jewish businesses, anti-Semitism increased. In the early spring of 1934, a car equipped with loudspeakers began driving down the streets, calling for Germans to boycott Jewish stores. Several times, Gustav found leaflets left outside his shop, calling for a boycott.

Gustav's apprenticeship had been scheduled to end in May, and his boss asked him to sit in the back office at the end of a particularly busy day in April. Even with all the calls for boycotting, they had never been busier. Gustav sat down in a side chair and his boss said, "Gustav, as I've told you before, you have been a wonderful apprentice. You are skilled in even the most difficult stitches, but more importantly, you are interested in women's fashion and have helped me to design dresses for our customers. You are really talented, and I predict great things for you. Unfortunately, that won't happen with me. But not because I don't want you as an employee. It's because I'm selling the business and going into business with my brother in Berlin."

"The brother who has the dress shop?"

"That's the one. He is very busy and said he could use the help. But my wife is also tired of all the anti-Semitism in this city. Our son has been knocked down several times by bullies. Berlin will just be safer for us, away from Bavaria."

"Don't you worry about the Nazis in Berlin?"

"I worry about the Nazis everywhere. But I think there will be safety in numbers. On top of that, the fashion capital of Germany is Berlin and the fashion world in Berlin had always been controlled by Jews. I know they've had problems since the Nazis took control, but there is still plenty of work. I'm sorry that I can't hire you permanently, but with your skills, you should be able to find work in Würzburg."

"That's nice of you to say, Herr Gruenbaum. But if you're leaving, there really is no reason for me to stay here. I'm also a little worried by all the recent anti-Semitic actions. I think I might just go back to Frankfurt."

"That's a good decision. Like Berlin, Frankfurt is a city with a large Jewish population and even recently had a Jewish mayor. Of course, that was before the Nazis forced him out. But I think you will be safer there. I would imagine your mother will worry less if you were living in Frankfurt." Gustav nodded his head and smiled.

They spent the month of May packing up the store and getting it ready for the new owner. Gustav left the same day his boss and family left Würzburg. And now he was back in Frankfurt, with his mother and brother running towards him. He was home again.

•   •   •

"It's cousin's night! Gustav, you can't go home! We just got here!"

"Gertrud, we got here three hours ago! I'm exhausted and so is Bettina. We're old people with jobs and responsibilities!"

"You do sound like old people! Just one more coffee and one more song."

Bettina and Gustav looked at each other and laughed. Then they nodded their heads. Gustav was thinking that neither of them could ever say no to their little cousin. Who was not so little anymore. At fourteen years-old, she was already taller than Bettina. Her hair was still blonde, and her blue eyes lit up when she smiled. Gustav had teased her earlier in the evening, "You look like a poster for the perfect Aryan girl!"

Café Goldschmidt had recently added a jazz trio on Friday nights, and the three were enjoying the music – along with being together. Gustav had been home for about a week, and Gertrud had been pestering him for several days to go out for "cousin's night." Gustav had convinced Bettina to join them for Friday night at the café. And he told her to leave Hans home. "Gertrud insists – only the cousins." Gustav found Hans to be a bit of a bore, and he often tired of Hans trying to prove himself to Gustav, so he was just as happy to leave Hans out of the evening's activities. He never understood why Bettina had married Hans but said nothing to his cousin.

"Gustav, you haven't really told us anything about your life in Würzburg. I know you worked and worked and worked. But what else did you do? Any girls?"

"I've been home several times since I first went to Würzburg and told you all about my life every time I visited. My life didn't really change from the last time we had this conversation, Gertrud. But I want to make a toast to Trudi and her new baby girl!"

"We already toasted baby Laure. Stop changing the subject. You say the same thing each time you've come home, but you never really tell me anything. Who were your friends, what did you do, who did you date?" Gertrud put an emphasis on the last part of the question.

"You don't know any of my friends there, so telling you their names won't make a difference. My friends and I went to the cinema, went to the cabaret, went to dinner at restaurants. But, understand Gertrud, I mostly worked. Just because I moved to another city didn't mean it was all fun and games!"

"I know that, Gustav! But did you go to the cinema with anyone special?"

Gustav looked over to Bettina as if to say, "Please rescue me!"

"Gertrud, not everyone is as obsessed with dating as you seem to be. And correct me if I'm wrong, but I have not heard about any special someone in your life!"

"I'm only fourteen. Besides, both my mother and my father tell me I'm too young to date. But, if I were old enough, there's this really cute boy in my school who I've been having lunch with."

Taking advantage of the distraction, Gustav said, "Tell me more, cousin!" And Gertrud spent the rest of their evening at the café talking about boys.

• • •

Early the next morning, Gustav walked to his stepfather's shop, eager to be the first to arrive. He often smiled as he passed the sign: *David Seidel and Wife: Men's Tailor.* His stepfather used the more German-sounding name rather than the Polish surname Zeydel, but didn't include his mother's name. His mother was just as good a tailor as his stepfather and she contributed most of the money to start the business, using the rents she received from a building she had purchased just after the Great War. His mother was a strong-willed person, and Gustav didn't like that her name on the shop sign was just "wife." But he understood this was the old way of doing things.

The shop on Taubenstrasse was just a five-minute walk from his parent's apartment on Bronnerstrasse. Considered the inner-city, they were near the two main Jewish sections of the city: the East End (to the east) and the Westend (to the northwest). Gustav always liked this part of town since it was convenient to restaurants, the theater and the cinema. It was also an easy walk to the Main River, where he liked to stroll on a warm summer evening. Often, he would bring his sketchbook and draw.

Gustav had never intended to stay in Würzburg forever. Herr Gruenbaum had taught him a lot, and he would have been happy to have worked for him a few more years. But he never enjoyed living in Würzburg. The newer fashions from Berlin seemed to have skipped over that provincial town and Gustav had been harassed by street bullies a few times and had actually been chased one evening after leaving the cabaret with a friend. They were able to hop on a tram just as the hoodlums were almost upon them. After that incident, Gustav decided to be more careful, and that was especially the case after the Nazi Party came to power the previous year. By the time he finally left Würzburg, Gustav was mostly keeping to his room after work.

While Gustav felt safer in Frankfurt, he was not kidding himself about a return to normalcy. Frankfurt had changed in the three years he was living in Würzburg, and he saw first hand the effects of Nazi control on his hometown. There were no trucks with loudspeakers like in Würzburg, but anti-Jewish posters were everywhere. Gustav hated to see the posters on his way to work and the artist part of him also hated the garish designs. Friends of his were leaving Germany; a few had been lucky enough to find a sponsor in the U.S. and receive the coveted visa, but most were satisfied to emigrate to Palestine. He sometimes wondered if he should also think about leaving, but for the moment, he was happy to be back in Frankfurt.

Gustav looked at his watch. Eight a.m. They had customers coming after 9:30 a.m., but before that, the morning was clear. Enough time to prepare for the day and even have a leisurely cup of coffee. His stepfather would be coming in around nine, his mother a little later, after she had dropped off his brother at school. He was just about to get his coffee when he heard a knock at the door. He went to the door and saw that it was his Onkel Robert.

"Onkel Robert, is everything okay?"

"Yes, yes, I didn't mean to startle you. I thought I would stop here on my way to work to ask a favor. Maybe I should have called first."

"That's quite all right. Come on in. Can I get you a cup of coffee?"

"Coffee would be very nice. With a little milk and sugar. Thanks."

Gustav walked to the back and poured them both coffee. He joined his uncle at a small table at the front of the store.

"Gustav, this is not a big favor. Just a little bit of your time this evening. I received a call last night from the Party. They're having an emergency meeting this evening. I told them I would be there, but after I hung up, I remembered that I promised Margarete I would meet Gertrud after a school program. Margarete doesn't want her walking home alone. Personally, I think she's afraid Gertrud might walk home with a boy. Anyway, I can't make it in time for the end of her program. Could you do it?"

"What time is the program over?"

"Six p.m."

"That would be fine. Just give me the address of the school."

"Well, you won't be meeting her at the school. Margarete had arranged for me to meet Gertrud at a nearby café. Margarete still worries about people finding out about me and doesn't want me to be seen with Gertrud. Let me write down the name of the café."

"But when I take her home, won't people see her walking with me?"

"Oh, you won't be taking her home. Margarete will meet you at the café at seven. She just can't get out of work in time."

"Onkel Robert, this all seems like such a lot of work. I still don't understand why Margarete has made such a big deal about hiding Gertrud's lineage. And I can't believe that you've gone along with it."

"Gustav, we need to keep the peace. She hasn't prevented me from spending time with my daughter, so I live with it."

Gustav thought his uncle was a little too interested in keeping the peace with his ex-wife. He really didn't understand why this needed to be hidden, and he thought both parents were putting a little too much pressure on Gertrud to keep the secret. But it wasn't his place to butt in.

"Onkel Robert, are you still involved with the Social Democratic Party?"

"No, no, the Nazi Party banned the Social Democratic Party last year and a number of its leaders were jailed. The rest are now living in Prague. When the Party was in control of the Weimar government in 1928, that was a very exciting time for all of us. But then the Party made concessions to the conservative groups to stay in power, which failed anyway, and the government collapsed in 1930. President Von Hindenburg appointed a new cabinet without going through the Reichstag and the Social Democrats said nothing. So, some of us left the Party and formed the Socialist Workers Party. The Social Democrats still supported Von Hindenburg in the 1932 elections, thinking it was a way to prevent Hitler from taking power. But look how effective that approach was! Hitler and his thugs now control everything, and Von Hindenburg is just a puppet. The Socialist Workers Party is one of the few parties left that will fight against the Nazis."

"Onkel Robert, given what happened to the Social Democrats, do you think it's a good idea to stay involved with the Socialist Workers Party?"

"Gustav, I can't sit back and do nothing. The Jews are suffering, the workers are suffering. We must make the rest of the world see how dangerous Hitler is! But you don't need to worry. Our leadership met in March in Dresden and agreed that we needed to go underground but also establish foreign bases of operation. The Nazis banned our paper last year, but there are still things we can do here. And if I ever need to leave Germany, then I will leave."

Gustav always liked his uncle. But he was a little surprised at his uncle's forceful position against the Nazis. He was generally mild-mannered and rarely challenged anyone. That was particularly the case with his ex-wife, who generally controlled Robert's relationship with his daughter. But Robert was committed to the Party, and didn't seem to appreciate how dangerous his involvement was.

"Onkel Robert, you understand these are dangerous times for anyone challenging the Nazi Party. Particularly for Jews challenging the Nazi Party. Please be careful."

"Gustav, don't worry. I'm always careful. But I have to do something." Robert remained silent, staring at the wall and drinking his coffee. He didn't seem to be in much of a hurry to leave the shop.

"Onkel Robert, don't you need to get to work?"

"Oh, don't worry about me. Things are a little slow at work. I think we're still feeling the effects of the anti-Jewish boycotts." Robert then continued to slowly drink his coffee.

Gustav had lots of things to do that morning, but didn't have the heart to ask his uncle to leave. So, he remained seated and said, "Onkel Robert, for as long I've known you, you have always been involved in political parties. Why?"

Robert took a slow sip of his coffee and said, "Gustav, believe it or not, no one in the family has ever asked me that question. My brothers always thought it was a folly of mine and my ex-wife always thought it would get me into trouble. But no one asked why I do this, why I attend rallies and put together pamphlets. My answer to you is that I have always believed we could all live a better life, and no one person should be denied that better life. If we don't work to make that happen, it will never happen."

Gustav smiled at his uncle and said, "Onkel Robert, it sounds like you have hope." His uncle gave his nephew a quizzical look, and so Gustav continued, "I was recently at services with my stepfather, and the rabbi was speaking about hope. As you can imagine, many in the congregation are worried about what the Nazis are doing to the Jews. The rabbi said we must not sink into despair but must remain hopeful. He spoke about how Jews were once slaves in Egypt but remained hopeful and were ultimately freed. He also said there's no word in the Hebrew language for 'hopeless.' The Jewish response to trouble has always been *tikva*, the Hebrew word for hope, and that must continue."

Robert nodded his head and said, "That's good the rabbi has encouraged the congregation to have hope that things will get better. But things can't get better just by hoping they will. I'm actually doing something."

Gustav nodded and said, "I'm glad you are." Gustav stood up and took their empty coffee cups to the back of the store. He really needed to begin his work, and the last thing he wanted was a political discussion with his uncle first thing in the morning. When he returned to the front of the store, his uncle rose from his seat, shook his nephew's hand, and said, "Gustav, please don't mind my ramblings. But I do need to get to the office. Thanks again for the favor."

After his uncle left, Gustav thought again about what his uncle had said, about not just having hope, but also doing something. He knew he had dreams about what he wanted to do with his life. Open a dressmaking store selling fashionable clothing, eventually marrying and having a family. He understood it was not just a dream, but also a hope. And a hope because of the current climate, where Jews were finding it harder and harder to be in Germany. While his uncle wasn't religious, Gustav was struck by the fact that his uncle was actually engaging in the important Jewish tradition of *tikun olam* - healing a broken world. Joining a political party was not anything Gustav ever wanted to do, but he was wondering whether he would need to do something more than just hope.

CHAPTER 5

Frankfurt
September 1935

Gertrud's singing lesson went longer than she had wanted, and she was already running late to meet her father. Her teacher was frustrated with her progress and had even suggested that Gertrud might consider stopping the lessons. It had been her mother's idea to take the lessons in the first place, thinking that her only daughter could grow up to be an opera singer. But Gertrud didn't enjoy the lessons, and not just because of her teacher's criticisms. She felt distracted and she was worried, mostly about her father. She understood it was getting harder to be a Jew in Germany. He never spoke with her about that, but she knew. He had stopped talking with Gertrud about his political activities, but she suspected he was still involved with the Socialist Workers Party, and she worried that he might be arrested one day. She decided she would say something to him at the café.

As she approached the café, she saw her mother sitting at an outdoor table. Her father had always insisted that they meet indoors and in the back (just in case someone she knew walked by), so why was her mother there and sitting outside?

"Mama, why are you here? I know I'm a little late, but you aren't supposed to be here for another hour. Is Papa inside?"

"Gertrud, let's go inside."

Gertrud looked at her mother and saw fear in her eyes. She had never seen that look before, and it rattled her. She followed her mother to the back of the café, sat down, and asked, "Mama, what's wrong?"

"I need to talk to you about two things. First, I need to tell you something about your Papa. I don't know why, but he was always involved in political organizations. He always talked about helping the workers, but I never saw the point of any of his involvements. He should have thought about just one worker, himself. And I didn't know that he was involved with the Socialist Workers Party, which has been banned by the government. I hope he never spoke to you about this."

Gertrud lied. "No, he didn't."

"Well, that's good. Anyway, he came to see me at work today and told me he had to leave Frankfurt right away, that the police were looking for him."

"The police? Oh, no. Where is Papa now?"

"Your Papa left. He packed his bags and took a train to Prague. He told me there are Party members living in Prague and they'll find him a place to live and maybe a job. I can't believe how irresponsible he has been. That is just like him, worrying about the workers and not himself or his family! I told him to stop this nonsense when we were married, and I warned him not to start again when he moved back to Frankfurt from Strasbourg. He didn't listen to me when we were married, and he clearly didn't listen to me when he came back. He's paying dearly for such recklessness by being forced to leave Germany."

"Slow down, Mama. Papa has already left? He is in Prague?"

"Gertrud, pay attention. That's what I've been telling you. Your father had to leave Frankfurt and is on his way to Prague. He should be there soon. He promised he would send a telegram once he arrives in Prague. Of course using a different surname, in case Karl sees the telegram. Or the Gestapo."

"I can't believe this. He didn't even say goodbye."

"Believe me, Gertrud, he had no time to say goodbye. He couldn't go to your school – you know why. And he couldn't wait until this evening, since he might have been arrested. He did the right thing for once and left when he did."

Gertrud was devastated - and heartbroken. But she knew that her mother would not want to see any tears for her father. She took a deep breath and told herself she would cry later. Then she remembered. "Mama, what's the other thing you wanted to talk with me about?"

"Oh, yes, the other thing. You've probably not been paying attention to the morning papers – why would you? The Nazi Party has been meeting in Nuremberg, like they do every year, but this year they issued new laws relating to Jews. They're now defining half-Jews as those with two Jewish grandparents, and you have two Jewish grandparents."

Gertrud had been picking at a fingernail, like she usually did when someone was discussing politics, but as soon as she heard that last part of what her mother had said to her, she looked directly at her mother. "I don't understand. What does that mean?"

"Your father's parents were both Jewish. According to the Nuremberg Laws, you are half-Jewish."

"But I still don't know what that means!"

"According to the newspapers, it means that, for the most part, you will be treated by the government as a Jew."

"But I'm not a Jew. I'm Lutheran. I've been baptized. Can't you just explain to the authorities that I'm not Jewish?"

"Unfortunately, it doesn't work that way. That's now the law. And we now have another problem. Before I enrolled you in your new school, I needed to provide them with a birth certificate. Remember I told you that you would be using my maiden name as your surname in your new school, so that no one would know about your father? In order to enroll you in that school under the name 'Auelmann,' I needed to change your birth certificate and your baptismal record."

"You changed my records?"

"I had to."

Gertrud shook her head several times to try to clear the noise. Finally, she said, "So, let me understand what you're saying. I am Jewish, my records are fake, and we have committed crimes by using them."

"Well, actually, I think only I have committed a crime. Although, they might also charge you with committing a crime. But it doesn't matter, since no one will know. As far as anyone knows, I gave birth to you out of wedlock, I don't know who the father is, and your surname has always been Auelmann."

"Wait! So, I'm also a bastard?"

"I thought you knew this last part. Why else would I tell you to use my surname when you started the new school? What have you been telling everyone?"

"I told them that my father died."

"Well, you need to stop that. If anyone asks me, I'll just say I told you your father died so you wouldn't know you were born out of wedlock. That's what I told Karl when we first met. Although, fortunately, he's never seemed to be that interested."

"Oh, all these lies! Mama, I can't sit here anymore. I need to take a walk by myself. I will just meet you at home."

Her mother took Gertrud's hand and said, "Gertrud, the lies were meant to keep you safe. Now remember not to say anything to anyone about what we just spoke about. Especially not Karl."

Gertrud grunted loudly. She got up quickly from the table, took her satchel, and left the café. She was walking quickly, and, before she knew it, she had reached the Main River. It was still light out and she decided to sit down on one of the benches.

Lies, all lies, she said to herself. *All they've done my whole life is to force me to tell one lie after another, to keep one secret after another. And now those lies are finally catching up with us.* Gertrud thought, *I was raised Lutheran and never felt Jewish. Maybe it was because my father never tried to teach me anything about Judaism, or my mother wanted to make sure I was not Jewish. They both made me hide my lineage and lie about his being Jewish. And now she tells me those lies could get us into trouble. Real trouble.* She needed to talk with someone, and not her mother. None of her friends knew about her father. There was only one person who she wanted to see at that moment, and she went right over.

By the time Gertrud reached the second-floor apartment, she was out of breath. She knocked twice and waited for the door to open. Her aunt opened the door, wiping her hands on her apron. Henny looked at Gertrud, then down the stairs, expecting to see her mother. Seeing no one else, Henny grew alarmed.

"Gertrud, are you all right? It's after eight! What are you doing here without your mother?"

When Gertrud didn't answer, Henny took her niece's arm and gently pulled her into the apartment.

"Gertrud, talk to me. Are you okay? Did something happen to you?"

"Tante Henny, I am so sorry to bother you. I'm okay, but I just needed to talk to Bettina. Is she here?"

Her aunt nodded, patted Gertrud's arm, and quickly left the room. In a few seconds, she returned with Bettina, with Hans trailing behind the women. As soon as Gertrud saw her cousin, she started to cry. Bettina gave her cousin a hug, then walked her into the back bedroom. She closed the door and told Gertrud to sit in one of the chairs.

"Gertrud, take your time. When you're ready, you can tell me why you're here." Bettina sat in the chair next to her cousin and took her hand. After about a minute, Gertrud took a deep breath, then told her cousin everything her mother had said.

Bettina squeezed her cousin's hand and said, "That's quite a lot to hear all at once. Gertrud, you must feel like your life has been turned upside down."

"That is exactly how I feel. I don't think my mother was really thinking about how all of this would affect me. I just couldn't talk to her anymore, but I needed to talk to someone, and I knew that someone was you. I can't believe any of this! My father is gone, my mother is a criminal, and the world thinks I'm a bastard."

"Gertrud, I'm so sorry you must go through this. You're upset right now, and you have a right to be. But we'll figure out all of this and make sure that nothing happens to you."

"Bettina, all my life I've had to hide things, to avoid telling people things. Secrets and lies, that's my family! And now I need to make sure no one knows about the secrets and lies since my mother could go to jail, or maybe even me! And what was my father thinking when he kept going to those Party meetings? He stopped talking about it, but I knew he was still going."

"As long as I've known your father, he was always political. But I agree with you he should have been more careful. With everything we know now, he did put you at risk by staying involved with the Party. But you know your father. He really was committed to the worker."

"Well, I wish he was a little more committed to me, since who knows when I will see him again. But I'm sure my mother is relieved he's gone. It makes it less likely that anyone will find out that I have a Jewish father and that he is still alive!"

Gertrud was no longer crying, and the color had returned to her face. She knew seeing her cousin would make her feel better. Bettina was like a rock, always there for her and always knowing what to say to make Gertrud feel better.

"Bettina, would it be okay if I spent the night here? I could sleep on the couch in the living room. I just can't see my mother right now."

"Of course you can stay here, but there will be no sleeping on the couch. You can stay in my bed with me and Hans can sleep on the couch! Just like when we were younger."

For the first time that evening, Gertrud smiled. Then she realized she was starving.

"Bettina, do you think your mother has anything for me to eat?"

"I'm sure Mama is already preparing a plate for you. But first, you need to call your mother to tell her you'll be sleeping here tonight."

CHAPTER 6

Frankfurt
November 1936

Trudi had arrived in Frankfurt with her husband Joseph and her parents the night before. Tante Henny's apartment was too small for the four of them, so they were staying in an older hotel in the inner city. It had been hard to find a Jewish-owned hotel that was still in business, and no other hotels would accept Jews. Not up to the standards of her parents, but it was near her aunt's apartment. Trudi had been back to Frankfurt a few times since the Nazi Party came to power, and things were worse with each visit.

As they drove to her uncle's apartment that morning, she saw the same sign in many of the store windows: "No Jews allowed." She remembered being told, as a child, that certain hotels and restaurants in Germany did not allow Jews. But those were rare. Now, it seemed the opposite was the case in Frankfurt. She struggled to imagine that, just a little more than a decade earlier, this city had been so welcoming to her father after he was forced to leave Strasbourg after the Great War. What a difference from Strasbourg now! She had always loved visiting Frankfurt. Now she couldn't wait to leave. And this visit was made harder by the fact that she had to leave her new baby home. She knew it wouldn't have been appropriate to take her daughter Laure and baby Ruth to Frankfurt on this sad occasion.

Their car pulled up to the apartment building and Georges got out to open her door. Trudi thought it was silly to have Georges drive them to Frankfurt, but her father only trusted Georges with his beloved car. And her father was worried about them, as Jews, taking a train through Germany. After the four were out of the car, they walked up the stairs to the first-floor apartment and knocked on the door.

Bettina answered the door, and Trudi pushed past her family to give her cousin a hug. She then looked around and saw the mirrors covered. "Bettina, I am so sorry for your loss. How are you doing?"

"I'm okay. It was not a surprise – he had been sick for several years. Joseph, Tante Lili, Onkel Jacob, thank you so much for coming on such short notice. Mama will be so happy to see you."

Bettina hugged her aunt and uncle, and Jacob and Lili went to find Henny. Joseph stayed with his wife.

"Bettina, is there anything we can do?"

"No, Trudi, there really isn't anything to be done. Because of the new rules imposed since the Nuremberg Laws, we can't bury my father until after dark. We won't have the ten men we need for a minyan, but what can we do? We just have to stay here until the sun goes down, and then we will go to the cemetery."

Trudi noticed her cousin's tone was flat, like she was reading off a script. Not like the Bettina she knew, who always managed a smile, even in the most challenging of situations. The last few months had been very hard on Bettina and her mother since Onkel Arthur was essentially bedridden. Trudi and Bettina had been writing often, so Trudi was aware of the heavy responsibility placed on Bettina's shoulders. And she wasn't sure how much Hans was helping.

"Bettina, who else is coming to the funeral?"

"Tante Paula, Onkel David, and Gustav will meet us at the cemetery. They're leaving Alfred home with a neighbor. I know my mother spoke with Onkel Berthold, but he was worried about the Gestapo seeing him at a funeral. He said he should be receiving his

US visas soon and doesn't want to give the Gestapo a reason to delay their emigration."

"What is he talking about? Why would the Gestapo care? His own brother and he can't even manage to attend his funeral?"

"Trudi, I really don't care. Papa had not spoken with Berthold in a while and I don't think he would be disappointed, or even surprised, that Berthold would not attend his funeral."

"I'm assuming Tante Margarete isn't coming."

"I called her, and she expressed her condolences, but told me she had another engagement. But that she would tell Gertrud. Then she hung up. As much as she can, she tries to pretend that none of us exists." Bettina then exhaled, probably louder than she intended.

"Bettina, when was the last time you were out of the apartment?"

"Not since yesterday. I know what you're going to suggest, and the answer is yes. Let me get my coat and hat."

Trudi turned to her husband. "Joseph, stay and see if there is anything they need help with." Joseph nodded his head in agreement. Trudi grabbed her coat and hat, and the two cousins walked down the stairs and out of the building."

"Bettina, I didn't see Hans in the apartment."

"He went to the office. We were expecting a scrap delivery, and Hans was worried we would never see the scrap if he delayed the delivery. A number of our customers have stopped doing business with us. I don't know how much longer we can keep the business going, but I can't possibly deal with this today." Bettina's voice cracked a little with the last statement.

"Bettina, I will always remember how kind your father was to us when we had to move to Frankfurt after the Great War. He was a wonderful man, and he will be missed."

Tears ran down Bettina's cheeks. Trudi took Bettina's hand, and the two walked together in silence for a few minutes. Then

Bettina stopped, looked at her cousin, and said, "I need to hear something happy. Tell me about your beautiful daughters."

Trudi was happy to provide Bettina with a distraction. "The girls are wonderful. Laure is like a little mother, constantly bossing around her sister, and Ruth is as stoic as ever. I don't think she has ever cried, even when she was born. But they do get into their share of trouble. Last week, when Marie was about to bake a chocolate cake, she noticed that the chocolate was missing. She went to the girls' room, asked what had happened to the chocolate, and Laure denied knowing anything. But the chocolate stains on their dresses gave them away, and Laure finally admitted taking the chocolate and sharing it with her sister. We had a different cake that night, but no dessert for the girls!"

Bettina laughed, took her cousin's arm and said, "I could imagine you and me doing the same thing when we were young. And I am sure those stained dresses were stylish and matching." They both laughed, but Trudi could hear the pain in the laugh.

•　　•　　•

While the funeral could not take place until after the sun set, the family was hoping they could begin a little early, so they arrived at the cemetery at 6:30 pm. Gustav and his parents were already there. Trudi could see Gestapo officers at the cemetery gates monitoring all funerals. Henny and Bettina walked up to one of the guards and told him they were there for the Heppenheimer funeral. The officer looked at a piece of paper and said, "You'll need to wait until seven p.m. And family only. Several family members came earlier to dig the grave."

Bettina quickly answered, "Yes." The regulations provided that only family members could dig Jewish graves, but Henny was able to hire two Jewish men who posed as family members to dig the grave. They would return later to finish covering the grave.

At exactly seven, the family walked over to the gravesite. The casket was already in the hole. Jacob had volunteered to lead the prayers. Just before Jacob began, Trudi saw someone walking quickly towards them. It was Gertrud! *How wonderful that she came,* Trudi thought, *and how wonderful for Bettina.* Gertrud walked right up to Bettina and hugged her tight., then embraced Henny and Trudi. Jacob soon began.

The service was short – Jacob said a few heart-felt words about his brother Arthur, and then they said the Mourner's Kaddish. Trudi could hear Tante Henny crying while they said the prayer for the dead. After they finished the prayer, the few family members in attendance each took a handful of dirt to throw into the hole. Then the service was over. Henny invited everyone back to her apartment for a late dinner.

Gustav walked up to Bettina, gave her a hug, and said, "Bettina, your father was like a second father to me when I was little and before my mother married my stepfather. He continued to be a source of comfort and wisdom. I will remember him always." He grew quiet for a moment, then continued, "I don't know whether this will help, but I learned in Hebrew School the Kaddish is also a prayer for better days, a prayer that expresses hope for the future."

Bettina sighed and asked, "And where will I find that hope?" Gustav didn't respond, but gave his cousin another hug. Trudi also hugged Bettina.

Bettina approached her mother and said, "Mama, Gertrud needs to go home. Her mother doesn't know she came to Papa's funeral. Gustav, Trudi and I will walk her home and will meet everyone else back at the apartment." Henny knew better than to try to separate the four cousins. Hans and Joseph also knew they needed to let their wives have time with their cousins.

After they passed the Gestapo officers at the gate, Trudi asked, "Does the Gestapo monitor everything that Jews do?"

Gustav was the first to speak. "It certainly feels that way. It's bad enough that we're limited in where we can eat, movies we can see, theaters we can attend, but they're harassing us more and more. Believe it or not, my parents have started talking about leaving Germany."

Bettina looked directly at her cousin and said, "This is the first time I'm hearing this. Have you been speaking with Onkel Berthold?"

"No. It's been a while since I've seen Berthold and only heard about him trying to emigrate from you. But my mother is worried about the business. Since the Nuremburg Laws were enacted last year, our business has shrunk. We're finding it harder to get supplies, and the Finance Office has started harassing my parents about made-up taxes. My mother believes that the Nazis will continue to take from us until there's no more to give. You three know me. I was never political. But I agree with my mother. Things will only get worse for us."

Trudi looked at Bettina and could tell she was startled by what Gustav was saying. Trudi was thinking that she was fortunate her father had left Frankfurt when he did. But while he was now a French citizen, he had also expressed his own concerns, and she decided to share those with her cousins. "Gustav, my father told me he is also worried about Hitler affecting us in Strasbourg. Because Alsace was part of Germany before the Great War, there are still a lot of Germans living in Strasbourg and some of those Germans are supportive of Germany and the Nazi Party. The government has even started discussing plans for the evacuation of the city, in case Germany invaded France."

Bettina was now white as a ghost and Trudi realized that what she'd said had made her cousin feel worse. "Bettina, I didn't mean to imply that things are going to be bad for all of us. I actually feel quite safe in Strasbourg. Plus, your marriage to Hans should protect you, don't you think?"

"Trudi, I really don't know. It certainly hasn't helped with the business, although I don't know if the reduction in business has to do with the fact that the business is Jewish-owned or that Hans is just not very good as a scrap metal dealer. Maybe it's both. I doubt we can keep the business running for much longer. Some of our competitors have offered to buy the business, at a great discount, of course, but Mama wouldn't talk with them while Papa was still alive. That may change now."

Gertrud, who had been unusually quiet, finally spoke up. "You're all talking about leaving! You can't leave! It can't be all that bad. Plus, you can't leave me. Who would I have left? My mother?"

"Don't worry, spätz. No one is leaving you, at least not for a long while." Gustav put his arm around his young cousin.

Trudi smiled at Gertrud. "I have an idea. Bettina, if you think it would be appropriate, we could stop at Café Goldschmidt for a quick coffee. Gertrud, since your mother doesn't know where you are, arriving home even a little later shouldn't matter. The punishment will be the same."

"Don't worry about me. I've already come up with a lie to tell my mother. But unfortunately, we can't go to Café Goldschmidt. Like other Jews, the owner was forced to sell the café a few months ago. The new owner makes the worst coffee, and he's rude to everyone. But there is another place nearby, although it won't be quite the same."

Trudi thought to herself, *Another place lost to the Nazis.* But she wanted to spend more time with her cousins and said, "Okay, Gertrud. Let's try this new place."

The four cousins walked arm-in-arm to the café. As they got closer, Gertrud stopped walking and turned to her cousins, very agitated, and said, "But what happens if things get bad for the three of you? Gustav and Bettina, what if you're both forced to move, and I won't be able to see you? And what happens if I can't communicate with you? You know my mother doesn't want me seeing any of you. She even told me not to attend the funeral, but how could I not? She still worries people will find out I'm half-Jewish. Trudi, my mother doesn't even want you to write to me. She's worried Karl will ask who you are, which is absurd, since Karl barely notices I'm alive." Gertrud was quiet for a second, and then her face lit up. "I know! We need a special code, so we can communicate with each other and never have to worry about anyone interfering. Especially my mother!"

Gustav laughed. "You've seen too many Thin Man movies."

But Gertrud was not laughing. "I'm serious. We need to come up with a system."

Gustav was still laughing. "Then you could write it in invisible ink that disappears in a week."

Gertrud responded loudly, "I am not kidding!"

Gustav stopped laughing and Bettina hugged her cousin and said, "Gertrud, I think that's a great idea. We should agree on this system now while we're all together."

Gertrud nodded and said, "We'll come up with the code, and then we'll practice. Actually, it won't really be practice when you send letters to me, Trudi, since we'll need to fool my mother. She's so sneaky that, if we can fool her, we'll know we've succeeded." She smiled to herself, proud of her suggestion, and the four resumed their walk to the café.

After their coffees, the cousins walked to within a block of Gertrud's apartment and then said their goodbyes. They knew better than to say goodbye in front of the prying eyes of Gertrud's neighbors. Then the three walked back to Bettina's place.

They remained silent for the first minute of the walk until Trudi broke the silence. "Did you notice Gertrud said nothing about her father? Do you know if they're in touch with one another?"

Bettina said, "She doesn't really like to talk about him. She stills sometimes comes to the scrap metal office after school to work and I pay her a little. Not much, since there really isn't much for her to do. She stocks some of our shelves, but I think she mostly comes just to talk. Mostly about boys. But occasionally about Onkel

Robert. I know he's sharing an apartment with a friend from the Party who also needed to leave Frankfurt. He was able to get a job in a hotel selling papers. It doesn't pay much, just enough for food and rent. Gertrud writes constantly and hopes to visit next year. When he first wrote to her, Margarete told Karl that the letter was from her uncle, but he didn't seem to care. Onkel Robert is using a different surname, just in case the Gestapo is monitoring their mail."

"Poor Gertrud," Gustav said. "Tante Margarete has locked them into the lie, and being found out now would get them both into trouble. It was unfair for Tante Margarete to force Gertrud to carry that burden. But who knows? Maybe it will make her stronger - and safer - in the long run."

Trudi turned to Gustav and said, "I understand why you're thinking about leaving Frankfurt, but maybe your family could move across the border to France instead of going all the way to America?"

"I'd be happy to move to France, but my mother is worried that France might not be safe in the next few years. She wants to leave the continent. They haven't made the decision yet, at least in terms of applying for a visa. Once you apply, the Nazis move all your assets into a blocked account, and the Gestapo puts the family under surveillance. My parents aren't quite ready for that. But we may be soon. Bettina, do you think Tante Henny will also want to emigrate?"

"Between the business and my father, I haven't spoken to my mother about leaving. But I have spoken with Hans, and he's opposed to us ever leaving Germany. Instead, if you can believe it, he's thinking about us moving to Munich."

Gustav was visibly shocked. "Munich? The birthplace of the Nazi movement? Everyone knows that being a Jew in Munich was hard even before 1933."

"Gustav, I agree. But Hans has family in Munich, and they could set him up in a business there. And Hans believes his family would be able to protect me and Mama, even if things get worse for German Jews."

Trudi looked at her cousin with concern. "Bettina, do you really think Hans can protect you and Tante Henny?"

Bettina hesitated, then said, "I have to believe it. He's my husband."

The cousins soon reached the apartment building and walked up the stairs to the first-floor apartment. Bettina used her key to open the door.

The family was in the living room, sitting on chairs with plates on their laps.

Henny came to the door. "Bettina, where have you been? It's after nine p.m.! We couldn't wait anymore and started to eat."

"I'm sorry Mama. We were talking and lost track of time."

Her mother smiled. "When the four of you are together, you always lose track of time. But there is food in the kitchen. Get something to eat and join us in the living room."

Trudi could see her father sitting in the largest chair. He was speaking, and everyone seemed to be listening to his every word. She knew he enjoyed his role as patriarch of the family, which was made easier since he was the most financially successful of the brothers. Of course, it helped that he could still do business in Strasbourg, while the German Jews were being strangled economically.

After she filled her plate, Trudi found an empty chair and sat down. Her father was still talking.

"I thought I was prepared for the changes to Frankfurt, but I guess I wasn't expecting to see Nazi posters everywhere."

"Onkel Jacob, they took the posters down just before the Olympic games this summer, hoping to fool the world, I guess. But after the world left, the posters went back up, serving as a constant reminder that we are not wanted."

"Gustav, it really must be hard to see them every day. In Strasbourg, we've seen an increase in anti-Semitic activity, but nothing like this."

Henny nodded sadly and said, "Jacob, seeing all the posters is hard for all of us. But worse are the things that you cannot see. The boycotts have been hard on our business, as has the loss of customers to 'Aryan' businesses. Now we're battling the Finance Office with phony taxes and neighbors who used to talk to us now look through us as if we don't exist."

Gustav's mother Paula said, "It's not much better in the tailoring business. We used to have non-Jewish customers, but they're gone. Only our Jewish customers have remained, but there's less business. Some of our customers have emigrated, while others don't have money for new clothes. David and I are actually talking about leaving Germany if things don't get better."

"I hope you all know that you always have a place with me and Lili. You just need to give us a call first, so Lili can make sure we have enough food." They all laughed, but Trudi could tell that part of the laughter was from anxiety. She was anxious for her Frankfurt family, particularly her cousins. She would be leaving Frankfurt the following day and could put the anti-Semitic propaganda behind her. But Bettina and Gustav were not so lucky. She was relieved that Gustav and his family were thinking about leaving. But Bettina moving to Munich? Gustav was right, that would be crazy. Gustav had once told Trudi that he didn't believe Hans was taking the rise in anti-Semitism seriously enough. And now, hearing that he might force a move to Munich, Trudi had to agree. Bettina was always the sensible one of the cousins. So why was she willing to let Hans make this decision for all of them? A decision that could put Bettina's life in danger?

CHAPTER 7

Frankfurt

September 1937

Bettina was sitting at the dining room table, carefully wrapping Bohemian crystal wine glasses. The radio was on, playing a Richard Wagner opera. Bettina's mother had purchased these glasses on a trip to Paris early in her marriage, and Bettina knew how precious they were. They were hardly ever used these days – not much to celebrate – but Henny still liked to display them in the hutch. Bettina was sure these glasses would be among the first items unpacked by her mother once they moved into the new place.

Gustav called out from the kitchen, "Bettina, are you ready to start packing the china? If you are, I can bring in the bowls."

"I'm almost finished with the wine glasses. I needed to take my time with these glasses. I think they're more precious to my mother than I am."

Gertrud peeked out from the kitchen. "Well, they may be more precious than you, but probably not more precious than the baby you're carrying."

"I have to agree with you there. So, I guess I come in third place. But that's okay. I'll always come ahead of the everyday china in Gustav's hands. My mother hates the pattern, a gift from her mother."

Gustav placed some dishes in front of Bettina, who grunted and said, "Gustav, you don't have to treat me like an invalid. I can get up from the table to get them myself. I'm actually feeling better. The mornings seem to be the worst. I had hoped the morning sickness would end after the fourth month, but no such luck!"

Gustav winked at his cousin, and said, "I'm glad you're feeling better, but before your mother left this morning, she made me promise that I would have you sit while you're wrapping the dishes and under no circumstances was I to allow you to carry anything. Those were her orders, and I'm obligated to follow them. Your mother will know if I let her down, so Bettina, for my sake, please stay in that chair."

"Well, fine, but only if you get me a cup of coffee. And I'm lonely, so Gertrud, you need to come sit with me."

"And what would Tante Henny say if she knew I was sitting while she was out?"

"Who would tell her?"

"You heard Gustav. Your mother would just know!"

"Then we'll tell her you did it to prevent me from getting up and carrying dishes."

"I like that excuse. Okay, Gustav, bring us both cups of coffee."

"If you're planning on sitting with Bettina, I think it is only fair that you get the coffee. Besides, my hands are full of dishes."

"Fine, I'll get the coffee and while I'm there, I'll bring us back a few cookies. Don't worry, Gustav, I'll bring coffee and cookies for you as well."

"That's the best idea you've had all morning. I've certainly worked up an appetite. Time for our coffee and cookie break." By the time Gertrud returned with the coffee and cookies, Gustav had moved the dishes to a separate table and the wrapped wine glasses to the box on the floor.

As the Wagner opera ended, the radio began playing a recent Hitler speech. Gustav immediately stood up and said, "I refuse to listen to this nonsense. All we hear on the radio now are Nazi speeches and Nazi-approved music. Let's see if I can find something better." Gustav turned the dial and stopped when he heard swing music. "Well, this is a nice surprise. I don't know how this radio station received permission to play some swing music, but I'm not complaining. Gertrud, let's show this old married lady how to dance to swing."

"Gustav, you'll need to show me. I like swing music, but I don't know any of the dances."

"Okay, this is called the Lindy Hop. I'll start out slow." Gustav began the dance, and Gertrud picked it up quickly, so he quickened the pace. When the song was over, the station started to play a Nazi speech, and Gustav found a station playing Mozart.

"I guess that's all the swing we'll hear today. But Gustav, where did you learn that dance?"

"Gertrud, did you like it? A friend taught it to me. The Nazis have banned jazz on the radio, which they call "Negro music," but you can still hear swing now and then. Like we just heard. But Gertrud, your mother better not catch you dancing to that music!"

Bettina smiled and said, "Gustav, you really are a man of mystery. You know about swing music and swing dancing. How? You never tell us anything!"

Gustav shrugged his shoulders, added milk to his coffee and asked his cousin, "Bettina, when are the movers coming?"

"Okay, Gustav, mystery man, I guess we're changing the subject. They're coming in three days. Mama and Hans are supposed to finish the paperwork this morning on the sale of the business and will be back after lunch to help us with the packing."

"I can't believe you're leaving Frankfurt and moving so far away!"

"Gertrud, Munich is not that far away. Just five hours by train. It is certainly not as far as Prague, and you went to Prague to see your father this past summer. Plus, we'll get to perfect the cousins' code. I certainly could use the practice."

"Bettina, stop complaining about the code. It's not that hard — just use Goethe's poem *Prometheus* like I showed you. And as far as visiting you, I know I can visit, although I will have to come up with an excuse for Karl. It's just that I can't visit whenever I want. I still don't understand why you need to leave Frankfurt. Especially since you're pregnant. Who will babysit the baby? You don't know anyone there."

"Gertrud, you know my mother had to sell the business, and Hans' uncle offered to bring him into the family business. Hans doesn't really have good job prospects here, so it makes sense for us to move there."

"But of all places, Munich?" Gustave said. "Bettina, they really hate Jews in Munich. Worse than Würzburg. Jews are leaving Munich. I'm sure you and Tante Henny are the only Jews actually moving to Munich."

Bettina was doing her best to control her face, but her cousins knew her too well. She finally gave up and released a loud sigh. "Gustav, do you think I don't know all about the problems Jews have had in Munich? I know Hitler formed the Nazi Party in Munich in the early 1920s and was arrested in Munich after a failed attempt at revolution in 1923. Munich has been a nightmare for Jews ever since. Do you really think I want to move there? And to take my mother there? But Hans' uncle owns a munitions factory and has arranged for him to be a manager at the factory. He'll be making good money."

Gustav shook his head. "How can he take his Jewish wife to that horrible city? I really don't understand why he can't find a job here."

"Trust me, Hans has tried. He just can't find anything. And certainly nothing that pays what his uncle will pay him." Bettina was tempted to tell her cousins the other reason why her husband was so desperate to take his uncle's job. Hans didn't want to be drafted into the army. Hitler had reinstated the draft in 1935, and Hans was worried that he would be drafted, particularly if Germany actually went to war. Hans' uncle assured Hans that he would be exempt from military service if he were employed in the munitions factory. Bettina knew her husband was not especially interested in working in the factory, but he was much less interested in being drafted.

"What about your mother? How is she going to fare in Munich?" There was now anxiety in Gustav's voice, and his face was getting redder. Bettina needed to calm her cousin.

"Gustav, Hans' uncle is an important person in the Munich business community. He will keep me and my mother safe."

"No Jew will be safe in Germany, even with important relatives. Bettina, you and your mother really should focus instead on leaving Germany."

"Gustav, I can't leave. I need to stay with my husband. Besides, I'm pregnant. I can't go anywhere until the baby is born. And you know my mother. She won't leave me, even if I told her to leave. I know I'm being a little selfish, but I will really need her once the baby is born."

Gustav looked at Bettina with a sad smile. "I understand, cousin. I know you need to be with Hans. You know I never used to think about politics, but I don't seem to have a choice now. And I worry about you and Tante Henny. I just wish things were different for all of us."

Bettina nodded her head and said, "So do I. But we must have hope." With that last statement, Gustav quickly stood up from the table, grabbed a pencil, and walked to one of the boxes. He quickly drew a picture of a butterfly.

When he was done, Gertrud gasped and said, "Wow, that's beautiful. How can you draw something so beautiful so quickly? But why a butterfly?"

Gustav said, "You both know that I was never much of a scholar. But I did love learning about Greek mythology, and I particularly loved the myth of Pandora and her box. I'm sure I've told you this myth, but I'll tell you again to explain the butterfly. Pandora had been given as a wife to another god and her dowry included a box that she was told never to open. But she was curious and opened it anyway. Just like you would do, Gertrud." He winked at his cousin, who smacked his arm, and he continued, "When she did, all the world's evils leapt out of the box and attacked her and her husband with hate. She quickly closed the box, but then heard a scratching noise in the box. When she opened the box a second time, a lovely blue butterfly flew out of the box that soothed her and her husband's pain, and they were happy again. This butterfly was hope. So, while there is pain and suffering in the world, there is also hope. And that is why I drew it on the box, your own Pandora's box. To give you hope, Bettina."

Bettina hugged her cousin and wiped a tear from her cheek. "Who knew you were so poetic, Gustav? And what would your rabbi say about you quoting Greek mythology?"

Gustav laughed and said, "He would be surprised that I was actually paying attention to any subject in school. But, for your information, Judaism is actually a hopeful religion and believes that people can make the world better by working together. Bettina, remember I told you at your father's funeral that the Mourner's Kaddish is a prayer for better days. So, on some level, the lessons of the myth are also Jewish lessons."

Bettina laughed and exclaimed, "Wasn't it you who picked Goethe's poem, another Greek myth, for the cousins' code? Gustav, the scholar! You are wasting your time at the sewing machine!" But she grew quiet for a moment, then said, "Gustav, I agree, it would be nice to think about a better world, so thanks for the butterfly and the reminder of hope. I will treasure both." Bettina traced the outline of the butterfly, then shook her head and said, "All this talk of evil is making me sad, so let's talk about something else. Gustav, have you told Gertrud about your little distraction?"

Gertrud looked up at her cousin with anticipation. "A little distraction? This sounds like something I would like to hear about."

"It's not really that important. I've started to spend some time with the daughter of our fabric supplier. We've known each other for years, but when I came back to Frankfurt, we started to work together on orders and got to know each other better. Over the last few weeks, we've started to see each other outside of work, taking long walks together."

Gertrud was clearly happy for her cousin. "Oh Gustav, finally! We have been talking all this time about how handsome you are and how you need to find a girl. This sounds so exciting!"

"I didn't say I found a girl. I just said I have been spending some time with someone. Bettina is making too much of it."

"I am not making too much of it. Her name is Gretel, and when Gustav talks about her, his face lights up. What girl wouldn't swoon over your fashionable scarves, Gustav! I particularly like the one you are wearing today! I think our cousin may be in love, Gertrud."

"I am not in love. I'm just spending some time with her."

"Spending time is fine, but you have to be careful."

Gertrud was clearly surprised by the comment. "Careful? Bettina, what do you mean?"

"Gertrud, you didn't know that your cousin is a criminal, just like you. Gretel is not Jewish and Gustav is violating the Nuremberg Laws by spending time with Gretel."

"I am not violating the laws. I'm just walking and talking to her. The laws don't prohibit walking and talking."

"Well, Gustav, just make sure you keep it to walking and talking. If you do anything else and you're caught, they can arrest you and send you to a concentration camp. They just need to suspect you of something to arrest you. You need to be careful."

Gertrud was clearly excited about this new relationship, which agitated Bettina even more. "Gertrud, calm down! Don't you see that your cousin is putting his life in danger?"

"Sorry, but I'm a hopeless romantic. I'm so happy that Gustav has found someone to spend time with. Plus, on a selfish level, I like that Gustav has to keep a secret. I've had to keep this secret about my past, and sometimes it can be exhausting. I like it that someone else has to keep a secret about their Jewish background. And trust me, the longer you keep the secret, the better you get at it."

Munich

September 1937

The last of the furniture had finally been delivered, and Bettina began to take things out of the boxes. The three of them had stayed with Hans' uncle and aunt, a childless couple, for the past few days, but the arrival of the beds meant they could finally move into the apartment on the ground floor. The small apartment building was owned by Hans' uncle, who lived in the first-floor apartment, one floor up from the street level. The ground-floor apartment had two bedrooms. Henny had told Bettina that she would be happy to sleep in the second bedroom with the baby. But Bettina told her mother the baby would stay in Bettina's bedroom, or maybe in the living room. Henny just smiled and said, "Well, we shall see."

The apartment was much smaller than their Frankfurt apartment and also seemed a bit dark and dated. Bettina was thinking it could be the small windows or the faded flowered wallpaper, but it also could be her mood. She was feeling sad about the move away from Frankfurt, and away from her cousins. It didn't help that she was also anxious about moving to Munich. It was hard enough to be a Jew in Frankfurt and now they had moved to Munich, a more dangerous place for Jews.

When Hans had first told her about the possibility of a job in his uncle's munitions factory, Bettina said nothing, hoping the job prospect would simply vanish. But when the uncle called with the news that he had secured Hans a managerial position at the factory and Hans told Bettina they would move to Munich, Bettina simply smiled and gave her husband a kiss. Bettina knew she was strong when it came to business decisions. She made sure customers paid their bills on time and she convinced her mother to sell when it was time to sell the business. But she abandoned her independent, decisive temperament by not even challenging the move.

Hans had told Bettina not to worry, that his family would protect her. But Hans had said a lot of things in their marriage that turned out not to be the case. He had said he would be able to take care of the scrap metal business while her father was sick. And that he would be able to maintain the business after her father died. Neither were true. The business failed and had to be sold. Hans said it was because everyone had associated the business with its Jewish founder, but she wasn't so sure. But that no longer mattered. They were now living in Munich, and she had to trust that Hans would be able to make a living. And that he would be able to protect her, her mother, and their baby. She was placing her hopes in him.

Bettina opened a box containing dishes, the box with Gustav's butterfly drawn on the outside of the box. She took out the dishes and put the box on the floor; she would cut out the butterfly later and save it. They had to sell the fancy china and the silverware. They needed the money, not the fancy dinnerware. Bettina didn't know anyone in Munich, and she wasn't expecting to entertain. She knew once her neighbors found out she and her mother were Jewish, they would likely avoid the family. She unwrapped the eight plates and eight matching bowls and put them in the cabinet. She then unwrapped the coffee cups and matching saucers and placed them in the adjacent cabinet. Bettina thought to herself that the cabinets were a little old but would be adequate for their needs. But she was very happy the apartment had recently been wired for electricity, and the kitchen had a new electric refrigerator. Her father had replaced the old coal-fired stove in their old apartment with an electric stove in the beginning of the 1930s. This new apartment had an older gas stove, but at least it wasn't a coal stove!

It didn't take long for her to finish unpacking the kitchen. She next went into her bedroom to unpack their clothes. She could hear her mother in the other bedroom, humming a familiar tune. It was the Strauss wedding song, a particular favorite of her mother's. Bettina put down the box and went into her mother's bedroom. Bettina joined in the singing, and then the two began to dance around the bedroom. They soon sat down on the bed, laughing.

"Bettina, you need to be careful in your condition. This is particularly the case when dancing a Strauss waltz."

"Mama, it's not like either of us is a prima ballerina and I would bet that neither of us would win a singing contest."

Henny laughed. "Agreed. What time is it? Remember, we have to be downtown by two p.m. If you've finished unpacking the kitchen, we could go to the store after our meeting."

"Everything in the kitchen has been put away. It's almost noon. But I don't understand why I need to go with you downtown for a meeting. We just moved to Munich, and we still have a lot to do here. You could reschedule the meeting, and we could just go shopping together for dinner."

"Bettina, I already explained to you that this meeting is important to me. I didn't really complain when you announced we needed to move to Munich. Even when all my friends told me the move was crazy, I kept my mouth shut. But I told you that if I were to move here, I would need to make connections with the Jewish community and I would need to do that right away. This will just make me feel better about having to leave Frankfurt and move to this place. Plus, it will do us both good to get out of this apartment."

Bettina grimaced to herself. Her mother had done nothing but complain when Bettina told her they would be moving to Munich. Bettina had presented it to her mother as a decision that both she and her husband had made, but it really was a decision that Hans had made. But she didn't see the point of sharing this information with her mother.

Henny had made an appointment with someone in the Munich Jewish Community office. The office was in the main synagogue, which her mother thought was fortuitous, since she had also wanted to visit the Reform synagogue. Bettina thought this was odd, given that her mother hadn't attended any services since her father got sick. But her mother was actually excited about this meeting, and this was the first time her mother had been excited about anything having to do with Munich, so Bettina was supportive of the meeting. She just wanted it to happen on a different day.

The two had a quick lunch and left the apartment just after one. Henny told her daughter that she had been told that the tram would take about thirty minutes and would let them off just in front of the synagogue, but she wanted to leave a little early, just in case they encountered any delays. The tram came relatively quickly, and Bettina found two seats towards the rear of the car. They sat down, and Bettina ignored the stares from the other passengers. *Maybe they think we're Jewish*, she thought to herself, but she wasn't wearing anything that would make it obvious. *Or maybe they just know we're outsiders*, she thought. Either way, the staring was making her uncomfortable, so she decided to distract herself by talking about dinner.

"Mama, do you have anything in mind for dinner? When Hans left this morning, he thought he would need to stay at the office until at least six, so he should be home by 6:30. Maybe we could just make a chicken stew. That should cook relatively quickly."

Her mother didn't respond. Bettina glanced at her mother, who was staring out the window. "Mama, did you hear what I just asked you?"

"I'm sorry Bettina. I guess I was just miles away. What did you ask?"

"I was just asking about dinner, but we can decide later."

"That's fine, Liebling." Her mother continued to look out the window, and Bettina knew something was troubling her. But with everyone staring at them, she thought it would be best to wait until they were off the tram. Before she knew it, the tram had reached Lenbachplatz, and the two left the tram. They still had thirty minutes until their meeting, so they walked over to a nearby bench. The plaza was quite spacious, with a large fountain near the center. They could see the synagogue, which was on the other side of the plaza.

"Mama, this is quite a plaza and that is quite a synagogue. How lucky the Munich Jews were to be able to build their synagogue right on the plaza."

"Yes, it is a beautiful place for a synagogue," her mother said with little enthusiasm. Her mood was such a contrast with her earlier enthusiasm about the meeting. While she intended to ask her mother what was wrong once they reached the plaza, she had second thoughts. Perhaps it would be better to ask her after the meeting.

"Mama, you still have a little time before the meeting, but I think it would be okay for you to arrive a little early. You don't know where the office is, and the synagogue looks pretty large. Are you okay if we just walk over now? I'll help you find the office, and then I'll sit in the plaza and wait for your meeting to finish."

Her mother said nothing but stood up and began to walk towards the synagogue. As they drew near, Bettina could see how grand the structure was. The façade was dark red brick, and two towers stood on either side of the building. Bettina and her mother opened the large door to the main foyer. Inside were large stained-glass windows, with light streaming from multiple directions. They walked down the hall and could see the large doors to their right that led into the sanctuary. They still had some time, and Bettina walked over to the doors, with her mother trailing behind. She opened the door and was impressed at once with the grandeur of the sanctuary. Pews lined both sides of the aisle, leading to a large and impressive bimah at the end. There was an upstairs gallery for women. Looking up, Bettina could see stained-glass windows to her left and right.

Noticing that her mother was looking up at the windows, Bettina said, "Mama, this really is a beautiful sanctuary, although a little ornate for my tastes. I actually prefer the more modern design of Frankfurt's Westend synagogue. But I do love the windows." Bettina looked over at her mother, who seemed not to have been listening to her daughter. So, Bettina said, "Mama, let's try to find the Community office. It's nearly two p.m." Her mother nodded, and the two left the sanctuary and walked down the hall. On the door at the end of the hall was a sign for the Jewish Community Office. Bettina opened the door and walked up to the woman sitting at a large desk.

"Good afternoon. I am Bettina Schnitzler, and this is my mother, Henny Heppenheimer. She has an appointment with Dr. Neumeyer."

"Yes, Frau Heppenheimer. Dr. Neumeyer is expecting you. Frau Schnitzler, would you like to join your mother?"

Before Bettina could respond, her mother said, "Yes, she would." Bettina glared at her mother but said nothing.

"I am Frau Levy. Why don't the two of you follow me." As Frau Levy walked the two to Dr. Neuermeyer's office, Bettina looked over at her mother. She wanted to signal her displeasure, but her mother kept her eyes forward. Bettina wanted to leave immediately, but that would have embarrassed her mother.

Frau Levy knocked on the door and opened it without waiting for a response. "Dr. Neumeyer, this is Frau Heppenheimer and her daughter Frau Schnitzler."

A small balding man with a mustache walked over to the two women. He had kind eyes, which put Bettina somewhat at ease. "Frau Heppenheimer, Frau Schnitzler, I am Alfred Neumeyer. It is a pleasure to meet both of you. Please, have a seat." Bettina saw two chairs in front of the desk. She took one and her mother took the other.

"Frau Heppenheimer, Frau Schnitzler, I understand from Frau Levy that you have recently moved here from Frankfurt. Lovely city, Frankfurt. I have been there several times, although not recently."

"Yes, our city really is a lovely city. Herr Dr. Neumeyer, thank you so much for meeting with me and my daughter. I am grateful for you taking the time out of your busy schedule to meet with us.

Of course, I would be happy to meet with one of your subordinates if you're too busy to see us."

"Frau Heppenheimer, I did, at one time, have a larger staff. But unfortunately, the office is now just me, Frau Levy, and some volunteers. We still have the same amount of work, we just work longer hours. But I'm sure that's not why you're here. So, first, tell me about your decision to move here. To be honest, I'm a little curious, since the only Jews moving into Munich these days are from the rural towns in Bavaria. They're generally moving here because they believe it will be easier to make arrangements to emigrate. Actually, I can't remember the last time I met any Jews moving here from a large city like Frankfurt."

Henny looked first at Bettina, then said to Dr. Neumeyer, "We moved to Munich because my son-in-law, Hans Schnitzler, who is not Jewish, decided we should move to Munich. Hans had worked for my husband's scrap metal company, which is how he met my daughter. My husband, of blessed memory, passed away last year but couldn't work for several years before that, and I was running the company. Because it was a Jewish company, I was essentially forced to sell the business. Hans has an uncle who owns a munitions factory and offered him a job. Hans took the job, and that's why we're here. Two Jewish women moving to Munich, when every other Jew is trying to leave."

Bettina immediately said, "Mama, you know Hans could not find another job in Frankfurt, certainly not one that would pay enough for us to live."

"All I know is that you announced Hans had this new job in Munich and that we were moving here. To Munich, of all places!"

"Frau Heppenheimer, it sounds like you did not want to move here."

"Dr. Neumeyer, would any Jew want to move to Munich? It's hard enough to be a Jew in Frankfurt."

"Frau Heppenheimer, I understand your concerns about Munich. But could you not stay in Frankfurt?"

"Bettina is my only child, and she is newly pregnant. I couldn't leave her. So here I am."

"Mazel tov, Frau Schnitzler. I understand the need to be with an only child and a new grandchild. But tell me, Frau Heppenheimer, how can I help you?"

"Dr. Neumeyer, this is my first time in Munich. Before we moved here, I read about the problems Jews were having living in Munich. But I would like to hear from the Munich Community Office what those challenges are and what you think we as Jews have to look forward to."

So Bettina finally understood the purpose of this meeting. Her mother had been unsuccessful in convincing her not to move, so she decided to enlist the help of the head of the Munich Jewish Community. She was pretty sure Dr. Neumeyer had not known the actual purpose of the meeting when he had agreed to it, but she was reasonably certain he understood now. And Bettina could tell it was making him uncomfortable.

"Frau Heppenheimer, perhaps I could tell you what this office does and some of the limitations we have right now. I wish I had a crystal ball to know what will happen to German Jews, but we'll just have to make do with what we have. It may be helpful to give you a little background on the Jewish Community Office. I actually helped establish the office in 1920, just after the Great War, and have been its president ever since. At the time it was established, I was a judge, and the office was run by a large staff. They were responsible for the welfare of the Jewish community in all of Bavaria. We even had our own newspaper. After the Nazi Party took over the government, I was removed from my position as a judge and came to work at the office full-time. Since then, we have seen the government support diminish. And while the community has had to take on more of the costs of support, there is less money. We've actually had to rely on support from American organization likes the Joint Distribution Committee. We are unable to adequately support institutions like hospitals and orphanages. The government forced us to discontinue our newspaper last month. I don't think I need to tell you, Frau Heppenheimer, that we have more needy with fewer resources for them, but we are doing the best we can."

Bettina was relieved. Dr. Neumeyer was not going to tell Bettina that she and her mother should immediately move back to Frankfurt. Not only would it make no difference, since he must have realized they had no choice but to remain in Munich, but it could also get him into trouble with the Gestapo. Still, they were here, and Bettina decided to take advantage of the moment. "Dr. Neumeyer, we know the situation is somewhat dire for many German Jews. I am fortunate, as is my mother, that my husband is not Jewish and now has a well-paying job. Since we don't need the financial assistance of the office, is there some way my mother could help? Before she was forced to sell our business, she worked with me to maintain the company's books. She's very good with numbers."

"Frau Schnitzler, I am so glad you asked me that. Frau Heppenheimer, we could always use more help here. After our meeting, I will ask Frau Levy to speak with you about ways you could assist Munich's Jewish Community. Our beloved Rabbi Baerwald's wife is quite active with the Munich Jewish Women's League. They recently started a home economics training program for young women hoping to emigrate. I am sure they would benefit from your experience and expertise, Frau Heppenheimer."

Bettina looked at her mother out of the corner of her eye and could see that she was frustrated. She clearly had hoped that Dr. Neumeyer would scare Bettina into moving back to Frankfurt. But that had not happened. Bettina understood Munich was a hard place to be a Jew, but so was Frankfurt. The only truly safe place for a Jew would be out of Germany. But she had Hans to protect her and her mother. And her baby. Still, she thought it was good they had the meeting with Dr. Neumeyer because it did provide her mother the opportunity to make new friends and have something to do. Her mother had worked hard all her married life, and it would be good for her to have a job, even as a volunteer.

Sensing that the meeting was nearing an end, Dr. Neumeyer looked seriously at both women and said, "The one piece of advice I can give both of you is to exercise caution when in public places. It is better for you if you just try to stay invisible. That also applies to you, Frau Schnitzler. Even with a non-Jewish spouse, even in a privileged marriage, you need to be careful."

After the meeting was over, her mother spoke with Frau Levy. Bettina told her mother she wanted to walk around the building and that she would meet her in the plaza. As she walked down the hall, there was a faint but familiar smell. It reminded her of the Main Synagogue in Frankfurt. She wondered if all synagogues had the same smell. It was likely that there had been a recent event that had served some Jewish food. She liked the smell, and it brought back good memories. But it also made her a little sad. She hadn't attended services in years, even when her parents continued to go for the high holidays, but she still felt some connection to being Jewish. But that connection would not extend to her child. After she found out she was pregnant, she agreed with Hans to raise the child as a Catholic. Hans was Catholic and had said that was the only way he could protect her and the baby. Bettina had not told her mother and thought it best to wait until after the baby was born. Still, she worried. Under the Nuremburg Laws, the baby would still be half-Jewish. And a baptism wouldn't change that.

CHAPTER 8

Frankfurt
April 1938

Paula brought out the tea from the kitchen and sat down with her family at the dining table. Given everything that had happened in the last few years, Gustav knew his parents thought Alfred was mature enough to be part of the discussion. Perhaps in another time and place, the nine-year-old would be outside playing with friends. But the Nazi actions of the past few years had matured Alfred. He would now play a role in the family's decision.

Gustav's stepfather David began. "We have talked about the need to leave Germany and emigrate to America. Once we start the process, everything will change for us. The Gestapo will begin to monitor our every move, and they will arrest us if there is just the hint of some wrongdoing. All our money will be placed into a blocked account, and we will need permission to spend any of that money. Not that we have a whole lot of money left. We thought we had more time to decide, but that changed this week with all the new edicts. I believe that now is the time to begin the process of emigration."

Alfred barely let his father finish his last statement when he said, "Yes, I hate it here. Let's leave. The sooner the better."

Gustav smiled and said, "I agree with Alfred. What do we need to do to prepare?"

Paula said, "Papa and I went to the Jewish Community office yesterday to speak with them about all the things we need to do to get started. The most important thing we need to do, before we alert the Nazis of our intention to emigrate, is to find a sponsor in America. The Americans require that an American citizen agree to be financially responsible for all of us. Gustav, your father's Onkel Henry has a son-in-law, Adolph Keller, who has sponsored numerous Heppenheimers. I'm going to write to him to see if he would, at least, sponsor you. And, of course, I'll ask him if he would sponsor the rest of us, or if he knows anyone who would. Once we find a sponsor, we'll put our names on the waiting list for a US visa and seek permission from the German government to leave. The three of us adults – that includes you, Gustav – will need to obtain a tax clearance certificate from the Finance Office saying that we owe no taxes. But hopefully, that won't be too difficult."

Gustav asked, "How will we move all our things? We have a house full of furniture. I'm assuming we won't be leaving our things behind."

"We'll sell some things and ship the rest to America. The Community Center explained to us we'll need to pay a tax on everything we purchased after 1933, including shoes and socks, and we won't be able to take any jewelry or art. Not that we have any art, and most of your mother's jewelry has already been sold. But we don't need to worry about that now. There is one thing, however, that Mama and I wanted to discuss with you, Gustav."

Gustav was worried about what they were going to say, that they would tell him to stop seeing Gretel, but he waited for his mother to speak.

"Gustav, you know how much we like Gretel. She has become like a member of the family. But you will need to be careful. What you do with Gretel puts you at risk, but it also puts the rest of us at risk. I know you are always careful, and we would never think to ask you to stop seeing her. We just want you to be extra careful."

Gustav was relieved. He nodded his head and said, "Yes, of course. I have been careful. But now, I will be even more so."

Alfred stood up and announced, "A toast! I always see people making toasts in movies and have always wanted to make one. And now we have an excuse. Every year, we say 'next year in Jerusalem' at the end of the Passover Seder. So here is my toast: next year in New York."

The other three stood, smiling, and they all clinked their tea glasses.

Munich
June 1938

Bettina left the apartment with the baby, happy to be away from Hans' aunt. Hans' uncle had mostly ignored Bettina and her mother, but when Gregor was born in February, Tante Helga became a constant fixture in her apartment. Any time the baby cried (which was often), there would be a knock at the door, and Tante Helga was there with food in hand or a new baby rattle. She had lots of advice for Bettina, who smiled but then ignored the advice. Tante Helga often volunteered to watch the baby, and sometimes, in a moment of weakness, Bettina agreed.

Her mother was out most mornings and often missed the visits from Tante Helga. That worked well since neither seemed to like the other. Bettina was happy that her mother's offer to volunteer her time to the Munich Jewish Community was readily accepted, since it kept her busy. Henny had even started attending Saturday morning services at the synagogue. Bettina didn't give voice to her own fears that her mother's involvement with the Jewish Community might put them both at risk.

Before she left that morning, Henny asked her daughter if she wanted to join her for lunch. Bettina was just about to say, "A lunch with the two of us would be wonderful," when her mother said, "And bring my golden boy, Gregi. I told everyone in the office I would have him come by so they could see how big he is."

When Gregor was born, Bettina explained to her mother that Hans did not believe in circumcision, that he thought it was a barbaric custom. Her mother said nothing, but Bettina knew her mother disapproved. Recently, Henny had been asking her daughter to stop by her office with the baby. Maybe her mother hadn't given up on Gregor being Jewish. But Bettina was so tired of being in the apartment that she said to her mother, "Yes, and I will bring Gregor."

"Wonderful. Come by at noon, and we can have lunch in the plaza. I already made a few sandwiches, which I will take with me." Then her mother was gone.

As Bettina walked to the tram stop later that morning, she was smiling to herself, thinking, *My mother had already made sandwiches when she asked us to join her for lunch. I guess she assumed I would be tired of spending the day avoiding Tante Helga, and she was right.* But it was a lovely day, and she was happy to have something to do with the baby.

As they approached the plaza, Bettina could see a small crowd gathered in front of the synagogue. As she walked towards it, she saw her mother and waved. Her mother immediately walked over to Bettina and hugged her daughter. Bettina could hear her mother crying. After a minute, her mother pulled away from her daughter and said, "They're going to tear down the synagogue. He said it is an 'eyesore.' We have just today to remove everything of value from the building."

"Who said it is an eyesore?"

"Who do you think? Hitler. He doesn't like that the synagogue is near the German Artisan's House, which he apparently loves, and so he said that it must go."

"Mama, this makes no sense."

"Bettina, what makes sense these days? All we know is that we have the day to remove everything – the Torahs, the prayer books, the candlesticks, anything of value. Except, of course, the organ, which we just purchased. Some church is coming today to take it away and paying us almost nothing for it. We were just told, and we need to get organized. I am so sorry, Bettina, but we have to postpone our lunch."

"Mama, don't worry about the lunch. Is there anything I can do? I know I have the baby, but maybe I can help in some way."

Henny took her daughter's hand and said, "Liebling, there is just one thing I would like you to do. We are having a final service later today, and I would like you and Gregi to attend. I haven't asked you to attend any synagogue services, but this is important to me. It will be before sundown, so it will give you enough time to get home and not be missed by your husband."

Bettina knew this was important to her mother and said, "Of course I will come."

"Thank you. There is chaos now, so you should probably leave. But be back here at five p.m."

Bettina returned to the synagogue at 4:30 p.m., carrying one of her mother's nicer dresses. She knew her mother would want to wear something that was more appropriate for a service, and her mother gave her a hug when Bettina handed her the dress. By 5:00, a crowd of people had gathered in the plaza. Bettina assumed everyone was Jewish but wondered if there were any Gestapo present. She knew Hans would be angry at her for attending the service – particularly with his baptized son – but she knew she needed to do this for her mother.

An old man started a prayer, and everyone stopped talking. Her mother turned to Bettina and said, "That is the retired cantor, Emanuel Kirschner, who was asked to come back to lead the final service. This is a sad moment for all of us." The cantor began the prayers, which were not familiar to Bettina. Then she looked up and saw several men carrying out the Torah scrolls. People began to cry, including Henny. Once all the scrolls were outside, they were placed in a large van and driven away. The cantor soon stopped singing, and Bettina heard everyone say in unison, "Amen."

Henny turned to her daughter and said, "I still need to do some things in the office. You should not wait up for me." Her mother then turned and walked quickly into the synagogue.

•   •   •

Several weeks later, the paper announced "German Art Day" to celebrate the greatness of German art. Bettina was not much of an art critic – leave that for Gustav – but even she knew that this great German art was anything but great. But what was most significant to her was that the day also marked the day the synagogue would be completely demolished. Her mother had said nothing to her, and she wasn't sure if her mother had returned to the demolition site, but she needed to see it for herself. Bettina asked Tante Helga to watch Gregor, and she took the tram to the plaza after lunch.

Bettina wasn't sure why she needed to go to the plaza. Maybe she really didn't believe the Nazis would actually demolish a synagogue. She had read that the Jews in Nuremberg had been asked to voluntarily demolish their synagogue, but, so far, nothing had happened. *I guess they decided not to ask the Munich Jews,* she thought to herself as the tram approached the plaza. As she left the tram, she gasped. It was gone. Totally gone. Not a single wall, not a single window, nothing was left of the magnificent synagogue. And it was magnificent. Perhaps not to her more modern taste, but it had represented the success of this Jewish community. She looked around and found a bench to sit down. She found herself crying, and then she became aware that someone was standing in front of her. At first, she thought it was her mother, but quickly realized the woman only looked like her mother – she was her mother's age and wearing something her mother would wear. She was about to say hello to the woman, to apologize for crying in public. But before Bettina could say a word, the woman spat at the ground and said, "No one wants your kind here, Jew." Then the woman walked away. Bettina, stunned, dried her tears and left the square.

Frankfurt
October 1938

Gustav was focused on his work and didn't hear the knocking until Gertrud practically broke the window. He smiled, put down the pants he was mending, yelled to his mother and stepfather that he would be back a little later, and went outside. Gertrud gave him a hug, and the two left for their weekly coffee date.

"Okay, Gertrud, where are we going today?"

"There is this little café that I discovered in the Northend. No one cares who goes in or out. It's a perfect place to just sit and catch up."

"You are just a wealth of information when it comes to these out-of-the way cafes. This place sounds as perfect as all the other ones."

Gustav was very careful these days about only frequenting places that allowed Jews, which were essentially only Jewish-owned establishments. He knew Gertrud was just as concerned about getting caught with Gustav, so he wasn't worried about the places she had chosen. He assumed they would soon run out of places to go since more and more of the cafes were being forced to close.

But Gustav was also being careful, because he and his family were now being monitored by the Gestapo. As soon as they notified the authorities they were applying to emigrate to America, their money was moved to a blocked bank account and their movements were being scrutinized. So, he was being especially careful these days. Both with Gertrud and with Gretel. He didn't tell either that he was concerned about the Gestapo watching him, but he took extra precautions. When either said something about the circuitous routes they were taking, he would tell them he enjoyed exploring the different streets in the city.

"So, who goes first today? I vote for you, Gertrud. Tell me everything that has happened this week!"

"That's not fair. I wanted to hear about your love life. Okay, I'll tell you my news, but then I want to hear everything about you and Gretel. With this new route of yours, I'll have more time to tell you about this new boy in my life. But once we get to the café, I want to hear all about Gretel."

As Gertrud was telling him every little detail about her recent date with this new boy, Gustav was thinking how much he liked this weekly routine and how much he would miss it once they emigrated. Adolph Keller, his father's Onkel Henry's son-in-law, had agreed to sponsor the entire family. But his stepfather was having some tax issues with the German Finance Office, and this was affecting Gustav's ability to obtain his own tax clearance certificate since he worked in his stepfather's business. He was hoping the tax issues would be resolved soon, and they could obtain their passports, since it had become almost impossible to make a living as a tailor. The government had recently put restrictions on the amount of fabric and supplies they could purchase, and each month brought fewer and fewer customers to the shop.

By the time they reached the café, Gertrud had finished telling Gustav all about her date. They sat down at a table away from the windows – Gustav wanted to be sure no one could see them – and they each ordered a coffee.

"Okay, Gustav. Enough stalling. Tell me how Gretel is."

"Gretel is fine. We actually went to the cinema last night. The movie was dreadful – it was some silly Hollywood romance and with lots of Nazi propaganda before the movie even started. But it was still nice to see a movie. It's one of the few activities Jews can still do. And Gretel and I are very careful when we go – no holding hands and no kissing, so you don't have to worry."

"I don't worry about you, Gustav. You have always been careful. Even with me. You think I don't know that you worry about the Gestapo and that we always take crazy routes to avoid being followed? Do you really think I believe you're interested in the back streets of Frankfurt? You always hated dark alleys when we were younger. In another life, you could have been a spy. I just feel badly that you must hide your love. This is a crazy time."

"And I hate that you and I have to hide our relationship. We're family, and yet we can't let anyone know, or you and your mother could be in trouble with the Gestapo. Maybe it would be safer for you if we stopped our weekly café visits."

"Gustav, don't say that! It's the only thing keeping me sane. I hate working at the bakery. It's even worse that I must work alongside my mother. She's always watching me, worried that I'll say something that will get us into trouble."

"And she doesn't suspect that your weekly art class is a visit with your Jewish cousin?"

"She doesn't seem to suspect. You know, I'm not a bad spy, either! Maybe you and I could team up. We could even be detectives, catching cheating husbands." They both laughed, then returned to discussing another boy Gertrud was interested in.

•   •   •

Gustav was losing feeling in his left arm, but he didn't want to disturb Gretel. He always loved listening to her snore. She denied she snored, but he knew better. It wasn't particularly loud, but occasionally, she would snort, which always made him laugh. He sometimes wondered if he would ever be able to sleep through the night with her snoring. He assumed he would get used to it once they were able to spend the night together, after they were married. He looked over at the clock. It was nearly 10:00. He needed to get up before Gretel's parents came home. They had gone to the opera and then to dinner at friends. That usually involved some after-dinner drinking, which usually meant they would be home late. Gustav had never met anyone who drank like Gretel's parents. His family never really drank, and neither did his friends. Gustav pulled his arm out from under her head, careful not to wake Gretel.

He got up from the bed, walked over to the chair, and sat down. Looking over at Gretel, he knew he had to sketch her. It might have been the light streaming in through the window or the way her golden curls rested across her face. But at that moment, she looked perfect to him. He found a pencil on her dresser and a piece of scrap paper and began to sketch. After a few minutes, Gretel began to stir. Gustav stopped sketching.

"Hello, sleeping beauty. Did you have a nice nap?"

"I did. What time is it?"

"It's a little after ten. I need to get dressed and out of the apartment before you parents get home."

"Don't worry about them. They're out with the Strausses. Once my father and Herr Strauss start drinking, there's no stopping them. Why don't you come back to bed for another snuggle."

"You know I would like nothing more than another snuggle. But it's late, and I want to avoid seeing your parents on the way out. Plus, a Jew walking the streets at ten p.m. is different than a Jew walking the streets at midnight. We still need to be careful. After all, you and I are breaking the law. In fact, I never even jaywalked before I met you. My cousins always teased me that I was such a rule follower. And now I could go to prison for years. You're a terrible influence on me, bringing me into a life of crime."

"Yes, your shiksa girlfriend corrupting you. How can I ever forgive myself?"

Gustav looked over at Gretel. She really was beautiful. It was all he could do not to return to her. But he really needed to go, to keep them both safe. "There's nothing I would like to do more than to stay with you tonight and every night. But we both know I need to leave. But remember, we're having dinner tomorrow night at my friend Leo's apartment. I'm cooking, so maybe you'll want to eat something before you get there."

"Remind me – have you ever cooked in your life?" She giggled, then said, "But don't worry. I'll bring plenty of dessert."

Gustav gave her the sketch and a quick kiss. He knew a longer kiss would cause him staying longer and he really needed to leave.

"When did you do this? While I was sleeping? It's beautiful."

"You are beautiful."

"Gustav, you are so talented. Just a pencil and a scrap of paper and you did this."

Gustav said nothing in response, but simply smiled at Gretel.

As he left the building, he looked left and right. Seeing no one in the street, he began to walk home, but still added a few additional streets to the walk, just in case. As he approached his apartment, he could see a car parked in front of the building. Two men were sitting in the front seat. Gestapo! Another Jewish family lived in the building. They could be monitoring their activities, but he didn't want to take a chance. Gustav carefully walked to the back of the building, picked up a pebble, and threw it at his bedroom window. Alfred quickly opened the window.

Alfred whispered, "Are they still outside the building?"

"They are. Throw down the rope ladder."

Alfred threw down the ladder and Gustav climbed up to the first-floor window.

"Thanks, pal."

"I saw the Gestapo park outside the building earlier this evening, so I assumed you would be coming through the window at some point this evening. So, I waited up until you came."

"You are the best brother. Are Mama and Papa asleep?"

"Papa went to sleep about thirty minutes ago. He said he has an early morning shipment coming in. You know Mama is waiting up for you. I'm going to bed."

Gustav ruffled his brother's hair and turned out the light. As he walked down the hall, he could see his mother sitting in a chair in the living room, reading the newspaper.

"Anything good in the news, Mama?"

"Is there ever anything good in the news these days?"

Whenever he talked with his mother, he was always struck by how thick her Polish accent was. She had moved to Frankfurt from Poland as a young woman just before the start of the Great War, hoping to become a seamstress. She had learned German quickly and met Gustav's father. They married and Gustav was born just before his father volunteered for the army. Gustav had no real memory of his father, who was killed in the Great War when Gustav was three years old. But as hard as his mother tried, she could never get rid of the accent. Gustav knew she had always been a little embarrassed by the accent, since she felt German Jews thought less of her. And she knew that the accent was even more of a problem now, since it branded her as a foreign Jew.

"Sorry I'm home so late. I saw the Gestapo out in front, so I came through the back window."

"I don't think they're here for us. I think they're monitoring the Langs. Frau Lang told me yesterday they just received their tax clearance certificate, so the Gestapo are probably spying on them." Gustav was always surprised that his mother never said anything about his climbing in the back window or where he was coming from. He knew she was aware of where he had been, but she seemed to trust that he was being careful. She also knew he would have had a hard time just staying home and waiting for the tax clearance certificates and not seeing Gretel.

"Mama, there's something I want to talk with you about."

Paula looked at her son and could tell this was important. "Should I wake up Papa?"

"No, I actually want to talk with you first. You know that Gretel and I have been spending a lot of time together. She knows that we're trying to leave Germany. She also doesn't like it here. I think she has been waiting for me to ask her to leave with me. I'm ready to do that. I'm making dinner for her at Leo's apartment tomorrow night – he has the night shift at his factory – and I'm going to ask her to marry me and to join us in America once we can finally emigrate. I know we can't marry in Germany, but I would like her to know I'm committed to her and want to make a life with her in America. I guess I'm asking for your blessing and maybe my father's blessing as well. I don't remember him, but I would like to think he would not disapprove of my marrying a non-Jew."

"Gustav, you know I think the world of Gretel. I know your father, of blessed memory, would have thought it more important that you find a woman who is good for you than that she's Jewish. Your stepfather has accepted that Gretel is in your life, but it probably would be better if I told him. I would give you the engagement ring your father gave me, but the Nazis already made us turn in all our valuables."

"I don't have a ring to give Gretel, but I will give her my promise that I will buy the most beautiful ring I can find once we are both safely in America."

"What do you think her parents will think about Gretel leaving Germany?"

"I really like her parents, and I know they like me. But I don't know. I think we will probably keep our engagement a secret, at least for now, assuming Gretel accepts my proposal."

"That is probably best. I know and trust the Webers, but there's no point creating drama in another family."

•   •   •

When Gustav's mother heard he was actually planning on cooking dinner for Gretel, she came over to Leo's apartment with her son and made the stew he was planning to make. When she first told him that she would be helping him cook, she joked, "You do want her to say yes to your proposal, don't you?" Gustav tried to tell his mother that he could cook a simple stew, but he was secretly relieved when she dismissed his protestations. She also made extra stew for her, David, and Alfred, so she wouldn't have to cook twice.

As she was leaving the apartment, she said to her son, "Now all you have to do is heat up the stew and make sure that the flame is low so the stew doesn't burn. And, Gustav, good luck this evening. She would be a lucky girl to have you as a husband." Paula gave her son a kiss on each cheek and left the apartment.

Gustav returned to the kitchen to stir the stew. He was breathing a little heavily and was surprised to find himself nervous. He and Gretel were in love, and he knew he wanted to spend the rest of his life with her. She had even strongly hinted that she would go with him to America. So why was he nervous? Certainly, she would say yes and they would have a wonderful life in America. But what if she said no? Or what if she said yes, but the Nazis refused to issue the tax clearance certificates? He had friends who had been waiting years for the certificates. He shook his head and said aloud, "Stop worrying!" Just as he said it, he heard a knock at the door. He put down the spoon and went to answer the door.

There she was, as beautiful as ever. He could hear his voice catch when he said, "Gretel, please come in."

Gretel giggled. "My, you're so formal this evening. Well Gustav, I would be honored to enter the establishment of your good friend Leopold. Lovely weather we're having, don't you think? I personally love just a little chill in the air."

"Okay, okay. I did sound a little stiff. Come in."

"Mmm, something smells good. It smells like a stew." Gretel walked into the kitchen and looked into the pot. "Thank your mother."

"How did you know?" But why ask? Gretel knew everything about him. They knew everything about each other. But he really couldn't wait any longer – he was just too nervous.

"Gretel, could we sit down for a second? I was hoping to speak with you during dinner, but I'm just too nervous to wait." Gretel gave him a quizzical look, but nodded and sat down. Gustav sat next to her and took her hand.

"Gretel, you know my family has applied to emigrate to America. We're waiting to receive our tax clearance certificates so we can receive our passports. We already have a sponsor in America. As soon as we're able, we're leaving. But leaving would be dreadful if it meant losing you. Gretel, we can't marry here, but would you agree to join us in America after we emigrate and marry me there?"

"Gustav, I would marry you anywhere! My life is with you." Gustav's eyes began to tear up and tears began to fall down Gretel's cheeks. They both stood up at the same time and kissed. They completely forgot about the stew until Gustav noticed a burning smell.

Leo didn't have a telephone in his apartment, so Gustav and Gretel decided to walk over to his apartment to tell his family the good news after dinner. They walked in separate directions to the apartment, and Gustav made sure the Gestapo was not sitting out front before he climbed the stairs to the first-floor apartment. Gustav opened the door to see that Gretel had beaten him there. He had added a few extra streets to his route. so he wasn't surprised. He was expecting merriment but instead saw long faces on his family and on Gretel.

"Gretel, did you tell them the good news?"

His mother walked up to him. "Gustav, we have news, and it is not so good. An hour ago, the Gestapo came to our door and handed us a notice. Our residency permits have been revoked and we must leave for Poland."

Gustav was feeling a little dizzy, not quite understanding what he was hearing. "What residency permits? What do you mean we have to leave for Poland?"

"Not you. Just me, Papa, and Alfred. Because your father was a German citizen, you are a German citizen. But your Papa and I never became German citizens. There was no way we could. But we have residency permits, have always had residency permits. Now the German government has revoked those permits. Papa needs to board a train tomorrow. Alfred and I have three days before we need to board the train."

"This is crazy. You've lived here for years. Alfred was born here. Why are they making you leave?"

His stepfather answered. "This is a fight between Germany and Poland, and we are stuck in the middle. In March, Poland revoked our citizenship. I really didn't worry about it, especially since we had other things to deal with. But now Germany is trying to force Poland to take us. Poland also doesn't want us, but we don't have a choice. We will need to leave. Gustav, you will be in charge of the shop. We don't have much work, but you will need to keep it open. Hopefully, we will be able to return soon."

Paula looked over at her son with tears in her eyes. "Liebling, I had hoped that we would be able to celebrate your good news. And Gretel told us it was good news. Hopefully, we will be able to celebrate soon." Then his mother broke down crying.

Gustav could not remember the last time he saw her cry. He was frozen, unable to move. But he saw Gretel immediately go to his mother and hold her until she stopped crying. *I will love this woman forever*, he said to himself.

Gretel left soon after, and David asked Gustav to join him in the dining room.

"Gustav, I need to talk to you about our finances, just in case I don't come back. As you know, we formally requested our tax clearance certificate last month. I know you filed for yours at the same time. I've been trying to sell the building your mother and I own on Kolstergasse. As you know, the city has been interested in buying the building and has discouraged others from trying to buy it. They offered us only RM 6,500, even though the building was assessed at nearly RM 15,000 in April. But I really don't have a choice, so I will accept their offer in the morning before I leave. They will then deposit the money in my blocked account. You should check to make sure the money has been deposited. I don't trust those vultures. And you should try to get permission from the

Finance Office to use the money to purchase your steamship ticket for America in case we don't return."

"Papa, I will take care of everything. Don't worry. You should just try to get back as soon as possible. Take care of Mama and Alfred."

"You know I will. As much as I can. And Mazel tov on your engagement. Gretel is a lovely girl." Gustav nodded and smiled. Then David got up from the table to pack.

Gustav's stepfather left the next day, and his mother and brother left two days later. Gustav's first night alone was lonely – not even the radio was a distraction. Only German classical, German opera, or German folk songs were playing. He and Gretel agreed not to meet at his place. The risk of being caught there was far too great. He woke the next day and went to the shop. Things were quiet there. No one came, likely because the Jewish Community already heard about the forced deportations to the Polish border. Gustav closed early and went home. He wasn't very hungry and went to sleep early.

Early in the morning, he was awakened by the front door closing. He raced out of bed and grabbed an umbrella, thinking a burglar had broken into the apartment. When he opened his bedroom door, he was stunned to see his family. He ran to them and hugged them tight.

"I can't believe you're here. How are you here? It's only been two days since Mama and Alfred left."

His stepfather spoke first. "I don't understand it myself. On the day I left, the train took us to the Polish border and left us there. The Polish government refused to admit us, so we just remained at the border, sleeping on the ground. By the time your mother arrived, there were thousands of Jews, tired and cold and hungry. I don't really understand how it happened, but late yesterday, they announced that all people from Frankfurt were to line up in front of a train. We then boarded the train and left. We didn't know where we were going – no one would tell us – but then we started to see familiar sights. When we arrived at the train station, we were told to go home and that we would be receiving a notice in the next few days."

Paula said, "I don't care about the next few days. Right now, I'm going to draw myself a bath and I don't want to be disturbed. I'm assuming you gentlemen can get yourselves breakfast."

"Mama, don't worry about Papa and Alfred. You take your bath and I'll make everyone breakfast."

Gustav started to hum to himself as he checked the refrigerator. He was so happy to have his family home. But then he stopped humming. What did his stepfather mean about this upcoming notice? He felt a chill run down his spine. He thought to himself, *This can't be good. We need to get out of Germany as soon as possible. All Jews need to get out of Germany as soon as possible.*

Munich
November 1938

Bettina was pushing Gregor in the pram, enjoying the quiet. Gregor was nearly eight months old, but he still wasn't sleeping through the night, and often cried during the day. The doctor said he would outgrow the colic, but Bettina worried she might have to wait until he was a teenager before she got a goodnight's sleep or even a restful afternoon nap. The only thing that seemed to settle him was a walk in the pram, and Bettina often found herself taking long walks with the baby. Today was a bit chilly, but he had been especially fussy this morning, and she was grateful when he fell asleep as soon as they started their walk.

Her apartment was about six kilometers from the old town, but even on her street, people were celebrating the anniversary of the November 1923 Beer Hall Putsch, when Hitler had tried, but failed, to topple the Weimar government. *Why celebrate a failure?* she thought to herself. Still, Hitler was in Munich to mark the event, with a noon march to the Feiderrenhalle and a dinner at the Old Town Hall. The celebration was an annual event and Bettina always tried to stay close to home on the day. But this year seemed different to Bettina. More people were on the streets than in past years, and the chants against Jews were particularly virulent.

For Bettina, things seemed to have changed within the last two months, really since the signing of the Munich Agreement at the end of September. They had all come to Munich – Italy, France, and England – and had agreed to give Germany the Sudetenland, in western Czechoslovakia, to avoid war. She had worried how this would affect her Onkel Robert since Prague was near the Sudetenland. She also remembered the grand celebrations after the signing of the agreement, and she could feel that continued excitement today. While the newspapers claimed war had been avoided, she worried Germany was actually closer to war. And things had become much worse for Germany's Jewish population. So, she decided to stay close to home today and just walk around the block a few times.

By the time she neared her building, Gregor started to stir, and she knew he was probably hungry. Maybe today he would eat, then settle down for an afternoon nap. She could certainly use a nap herself. She opened the door to her building and climbed the two steps to her apartment. As she opened the door, she could hear the upstairs door open as well.

"Bettina, is that you?"

"Yes, Tante Helga. Gregi and I are just returning from our walk."

Tante Helga started to walk down the stairs. "I wanted to make sure everything was all right. I was hoping little Gregi wasn't bothered by all the noise." She didn't wait for Bettina to respond, but reached into the pram and took Gregor out. Bettina sighed to herself and opened the door to her apartment.

"Surprisingly, Gregi didn't seem to be bothered at all by the noise. He started to fuss a little as we walked home, but I think that was because he's hungry. If you watch him for a bit, I'll make his lunch."

"I would be happy to watch the little angel."

Bettina went into the kitchen to make the oatmeal that Gregor seemed to love. She lit the old gas stove, thinking how much she loved her electric stove in Frankfurt. She could hear Tante Helga singing to Gregor and thought it wasn't so bad to have someone who could watch her child, someone who cared for him as much as Tante Helga.

•　•　•　•

Bettina was in the middle of making dinner when her mother came home. Bettina looked at the clock. Four p.m. Her mother rarely came home this late.

Bettina called from the kitchen, "Good afternoon, Mama. They kept you working late today." When her mother didn't respond, Bettina wiped her hands on her apron and walked into the living room. Her mother was sitting in one of the chairs, looking out the window.

"Mama, is everything okay?"

"It was a long day. I think I'm just tired. Where's the baby?"

"Believe it or not, Gregi is actually asleep. Tante Helga kept him awake longer than I had wanted today, but he went to sleep after she left and has been sleeping two hours. A nice gift for me." Henny said nothing in response, so Bettina knew that something was wrong.

"Mama, let's take advantage of the quiet and have some tea." Her mother nodded and Bettina put the kettle on the stove.

After they sat down, Bettina asked about her day.

"Oh, you really don't want to hear about my day."

"I spent the afternoon with Gregi and Tante Helga. I would love to hear some actual adult conversation."

Henny smiled weakly and said, "We have a lot of applications for welfare benefits, so I spent much of the day helping to process those applications. It's hard to work in the cramped space, but we're making do. More Jewish families need assistance. People continue to lose their businesses and their jobs, and it remains a real challenge to leave Germany. Sometimes, it feels like we're swimming upstream."

"Mama, I know how hard it is for you, but you're doing very important work."

"Maybe, but sometimes I wonder what the point is. Every day, the German government is making it harder and harder for Jews to live in Germany. At some point, I'm afraid we'll no longer be able to help."

"I can't imagine how some of those families survive. I'm just grateful that Hans has a good job and can protect us."

"Yes, but for how long?" With that last comment, Henny looked directly at Bettina for a moment before continuing. "Bettina, I worry about what will happen to you and the baby. I know you are protected now, but what about tomorrow? Or next year? Can we really trust the Nazis to keep their word about privileged marriages?"

"Mama, I have to believe that Hans and his family can protect me and protect you."

"I hope so. Maybe I would feel differently if we lived someplace other than Munich. Maybe it's today's celebration about the failed Putsch. Or maybe I'm remembering what Hitler did to our beautiful synagogue because he didn't like that it was so close to his favorite art museum." Bettina could see a tear falling down her mother's cheek and she moved closer to give her mother a hug.

Following the destruction of Munich's main synagogue, the Community Center was forced to move into an abandoned cigar factory on Lundwurmstrasse, which also housed a replacement synagogue. Bettina knew the demolition further fed into her mother's fears about Bettina's privileged marriage, and Bettina worked hard to allay those fears. Perhaps the Putsch celebration was simply re-opening the wound. Bettina decided to try to distract her mother.

"Mama, would you like to help me finish up dinner? I could use your help."

"I would be happy to. Let me just change my clothes and I'll meet you in the kitchen." At that moment, Gregor began to cry. "I have a better idea. Let me see what is bothering my grandson." Bettina smiled to herself, happy that her son decided at that moment to cry.

• • •

The next morning, Bettina woke at 5:30 a.m. by her reliable alarm clock – Gregor. She tried not to disturb Hans, who hated to wake before seven. She grabbed her bathrobe and quietly walked into the living room. She smiled to herself, wondering why she was tiptoeing when the baby was wailing loud enough to wake the neighborhood. Thankfully, Hans and her mother were used to the crying and slept right through it. She lifted Hans from the crib and brought him over to the changing table. She changed his diaper, which seemed to stop his wailing. Now he was simply whimpering. Because the noise had lessened, she could hear yelling outside. With Gregor on her hip, she walked over to the window and saw men carrying clubs and lit torches, yelling something that seemed to include the word "Jew." She also could see flames in the distance. Something was wrong.

Bettina knocked on her mother's bedroom door and went in before her mother could respond. Her mother's eyes were open, and Bettina assumed her mother had been awakened by Gregor.

"Bettina, no need to be quiet. I've actually been up for several hours. I could hear yelling outside the building. I guess Hitler's thugs are having a bit too much fun."

"Mama, I think it may be more than that. I'm going to leave Gregi with you and wake up Hans." Bettina put the baby down and walked into her bedroom. Hans was still asleep and grunted when Bettina began to shake him.

"Why are you waking me so early? It isn't even light out. Is there something wrong with the baby?"

"Gregi is fine. But I think something's going on outside. There is a lot of yelling, and I can see fires and smoke in the distance."

"You woke me for that? You know yesterday was the Putsch anniversary. I'm sure they're still celebrating. Some of those old Party members love an excuse to drink." Then Hans turned over, ready to go back to sleep.

"Hans, this is different. There are young men outside carrying clubs and torches and yelling things that include the word 'Jew.' I think something bad may be happening in the streets."

Hans grunted again, but this time, he got out of bed.

"I'm sure there's nothing to worry about, but just to show you nothing's wrong, I'll go outside. Then I'll go back to sleep, okay? I have a very busy day today and could use another hour of sleep."

"Thank you, Hans. And please be careful."

Hans quickly dressed and went out the front door. When he returned after thirty minutes, Bettina ran to the door. "Hans, you were gone so long. I started to worry. What's going on outside?"

"I'm not really sure. I saw Nazi brownshirts and Hitler Youth walking with torches, but I saw nothing damaged in our neighborhood. I could see smoke northeast of us, so it may be the damage was limited to the Jewish quarter. I'll go to work now and try to find out more information. You and your mother need to stay home. Do not take Gregi out under any circumstances. Okay?"

"Yes, I'll stay home. But please come home as soon as you can."

It didn't take long for Hans to return. Bettina assumed it was because he knew how worried she was. Both Bettina and Henny were sitting at the dining room table, and he joined them.

"Onkel Otto called some of his friends and found out what this was. It was a nation-wide attack on all Jewish businesses and all Jewish synagogues. The fires we're seeing in the distance were the last of the synagogues in Munich on fire, and some of the Jewish businesses and homes were also damaged. Mama, I believe your offices may have been damaged. Nothing happened in our neighborhood, which is a relief. Things are now calmer in the Jewish neighborhoods, so I think it's over. Nothing either of you need to worry about, but you should stay home for the rest of the day, just in case."

"Hans, thank you for coming home so quickly. I know you need to return to work, but I feel better knowing that it's over." Bettina worried about her mother, whose workload would only increase because of the action, and she hoped that her mother's offices were not too badly damaged. Then she thought about her cousin Gustav.

"Hans, you said this was a nation-wide action. Does that mean Frankfurt, as well?"

"It does mean Frankfurt, and no Bettina, you may not telephone your cousin Gustav. It's too expensive, and the Gestapo could find out that you called him, which could be a problem for all of us. If there's something to report, he'll send you a letter, like he always does."

Bettina nodded. She knew he was right, but she still worried. With everything that had already happened to Gustav and his family, it wouldn't be fair for them to have their business destroyed. Maybe it wasn't as bad in Frankfurt.

Frankfurt
November 1938
Gustav carefully navigated the streets to the shop. It was normally a five-minute walk, but broken glass was everywhere and Gustav needed to be careful. To complicate matters, Nazi brownshirts were still in the streets, looking to inflict more damage. Everywhere Gustav looked, there were broken windows and defaced storefronts. They lived in the East End of Frankfurt – often called the Jewish section – and the hoodlums knew where to focus their attention. Gustav had been awakened in the early morning hours by the sounds of yelling and glass breaking. Parting the curtain carefully in his apartment, Gustav could see the Nazi

brownshirts carrying torches, randomly breaking windows. The family decided it was safer to remain inside and away from the windows and wait until the violence ended. By eleven a.m., things were quieter, and his stepfather announced he was leaving, walking out the front door without waiting for a response. His mother yelled to Gustav to get dressed and follow his papa, which he did.

As he reached the shop, Gustav could see his stepfather picking up trash in front of the building. The windows were all broken and large swastikas were painted across the front door. Someone had entered the store through the broken windows, since Gustav could see that most of the few remaining bolts of fabric were gone. Gustav went up to his stepfather and said, "Papa, there's not much we can do right now, and it's still not safe for Jews. Let's go home."

His stepfather stopped picking up trash but didn't move. "We can go home, but I need to see one place first. I need to see the synagogue."

"Okay, but let's hurry."

To reach their synagogue on Friedberger Anlage, they walked along the Zeil – the main shopping street in Frankfurt – and Gustav was shocked at the level of destruction. Windows were smashed, and swastikas were painted on the walls. Looters were running out of the stores through broken doors and windows. Gustav wanted to run home, but he knew it was important for his stepfather to see the synagogue. His stepfather had moved to Frankfurt from Poland after the Great War, part of an influx of Polish Jews looking for a better life. The Polish Jews settled in the East End and were welcomed to the Orthodox synagogue established years earlier by Rabbi Samson Raphael Hirsch in opposition to the movement of many German Jews to a more liberal religious practice. His stepfather was not particularly observant, but found a community with the members of the synagogue, mostly Polish Jews. He tried to go as often as possible to services, and Gustav had his bar mitzvah there. The synagogue was the largest in Frankfurt, and Gustav, as a child, would marvel at the numerous cloakroom attendants who would take the men's hats and exchange them for the silk top hats worn for the Saturday morning service.

Gustav could smell something burning as they neared the synagogue. Once they turned the corner onto Friedberger Anlage, he saw the synagogue in flames. They walked as close as they could, but a large crowd had already gathered and included youths with large clubs. Every window had been broken. Worse, the Torahs and prayer books were in a pile in the street, and they watched in horror as a Nazi youth set them on fire. Gustav knew it wasn't safe to remain there long, and nudged his stepfather to leave.

His stepfather ignored Gustav, and said softly, almost to himself, "Baruch Dayan Ha'emet." The blessing one recited in the face of a terrible loss, usually a death, but a blessing that also expressed faith that God had an ultimate purpose for this terrible loss. Gustav could not bring himself to repeat the blessing. He just couldn't imagine there was any purpose for the destruction of this beautiful synagogue. Instead, he put his arm around his stepfather's shoulders and guided him away from the synagogue. As they walked away, they saw firemen spraying water on the neighboring buildings to prevent the fire from spreading but ignoring the burning synagogue. His stepfather turned to Gustav and said, "I will always remember this day, November 10th."

• • •

Two days later, there was a knock at the door. Gustav answered the door, always worried it could be the Gestapo. Instead, it was his mother's good friend from down the street.

"Good day, Frau Klein."

"Good day, Gustav. Are your parents at home?" They were both coming out of the bedroom as she said. "Good, you're both here. I need to be quick since I told Felix I would come to you and then go right home. We have been told they are arresting Jewish men in the streets. Anyone younger than sixty years old. I'm not sure whether they're also going to Jewish homes, although Felix is sixty-two and should be safe. But who knows? I just wanted to make sure you knew and stayed inside."

David said nothing, but Paula spoke to her friend. "Ilsa, thank you for coming and letting us know. We will be sure to stay inside. Hopefully, nothing serious is going on. But you need to get home. I'm sure Felix is worried." Paula hugged her friend and closed the door.

Paula turned to her husband and son. "You both heard. You need to stay inside, particularly you, Gustav. I don't know what it means that they are arresting Jewish men, but there's no point in taking a chance."

Gustav walked over to the window. He couldn't see anything and wondered if Frau Klein was exaggerating the actions being taken. Maybe the Gestapo was simply harassing Jews who were wearing yarmulkas, and no arrests were being made. But he knew better than to challenge his mother. And he was happy to stay home, anyway. For the past two days, he and his brother had been helping his stepfather clean up the store. Almost anything of value had been taken by looters, and they mostly swept up the glass and tried to clean the Nazi graffiti off the door. Gustav decided to get a cup of coffee and read the newspaper.

Just after he sat down there was another knock at the door. He thought he would let his mother talk to another one of her friends about this latest drama. But when a second louder knock followed, he put down his coffee cup and went to the door. His mother was already there, and as she opened the door, he could see two Gestapo officers standing at the entrance. The taller of the two asked, "Is this the home of David Zeydel and Gustav Heppenheimer?"

His mother just stared at the two officers, so Gustav answered for her. "Yes, I am Gustav Heppenheimer, and behind me is my stepfather, David Zeydel."

"Herr Zeydel and Herr Heppenheimer, we have orders to arrest you both and take you to the local police station."

Gustav's stepfather stepped around his wife and asked, "Why are you arresting us?"

"No questions. Just get your hats and coats and come with us."

"I don't understand. Why are you arresting me and my stepson?"

"I said move, now!"

Gustav and his stepfather took their hats and coats and followed the officers down the stairs. When the officers reached the bottom of the stairs, one of them turned around and said, "We will either put you in the car and take you to the station, or you will give us 800 Reichsmarks."

David looked at Gustav, then responded in as neutral a tone as possible, "That's a lot of money. I can't give it to you right now. I would need to go to the bank, and the bank has already closed."

"We will be back tomorrow morning. Have the money or we will arrest you both." With that last statement, the two left the building.

Gustav and his stepfather walked back up the stairs, and when they opened the door, Paula ran and hugged them both and asked, "What just happened? Why are you still here?"

"We need to give them RM 800 tomorrow or they will arrest us."

Paula took her husband's hand, and they both sat down. "The Gestapo must know we have money, that the sale of our building was just recently approved. RM 6,500 – half of what it was worth. And now they want a chunk of that. But we have no choice, do we David?"

David kissed her hand and said, "No, schatzi, we have no choice. We need to do whatever they tell us to do so we can get out of this rotten country before it's too late."

PART II
THE WAR

CHAPTER 9

Frankfurt
August – September 1939

Gertrud raced out of the apartment. She had promised Gustav she would meet him at the zoo at noon, and it was a quarter to twelve. She ran to the tram stop and leapt onto the steps as the doors were about to close. Gustav had picked an out-of-the way section of the zoo, and she didn't want to keep him waiting. It had been a month since she had seen her cousin, and she had a lot to share with him.

When the tram reached the zoo, she leapt off the stairs and walked quickly to their arranged meeting spot. As always, she didn't want to draw attention to herself, but she also didn't want to be late. It was a warm Sunday and lots of families were visiting the zoo. A perfect place to blend in, Gustav had said to her in the note he left at the bakery, written in the cousins' code. Gertrud reached the monkey cage and saw Gustav, surprised that he was actually on time. *And as handsome as ever*, she said to herself. She waved to him, he walked over, and they hugged.

"Gertrud, each time I see you, you get prettier and prettier."

"And I was thinking that you've never looked more handsome. Particularly with that new scarf!"

"Who can love us more than us?"

"No one!" They laughed, and Gustav steered his cousin to an empty bench.

"It has been so long since we've seen each other. I just had to see you, which is why I wrote you the note. Your mother didn't see it, did she?"

"She actually did see it, but I told her it was from Franz and that it was personal. Franz is the man I've been seeing. So, she didn't bother me about the note."

"A man? Tell me about this man."

"He's a little older than I am. He's tall, handsome, and very nice to me. He is a corporal in the army and his unit is based in Frankfurt, so we see each other a lot."

"And does this army man know your little secret?"

"You mean that I'm an extremely caring person?"

"No, I mean your other little secret."

Gertrud looked around, answering quietly, "No, he does not."

Gustav also lowered his voice. "And what would happen if he found out?"

"I really don't know. But I promised Mama I wouldn't tell anyone. She even made me promise not to tell Franz."

"And what would happen if Franz found out by accident? Is he someone you could trust with your life?"

"There's no reason why he would find out. But it's not like we're getting married, anyway. Now, you didn't ask me here to just talk about my life. What's going on with you? You look a little nervous."

Gustav took a breath and said, "I have two things to tell you. First, I received a letter from your father." He handed Gertrud the letter. "Of course, I read it. Given everything that's going on in Prague, he's doing well. Much of it was censored, but you can see from what they didn't censor that he still has a place to live, and he has been able to sell his magazines, although he's no longer welcome to sell them in the hotel."

Gertrud put the letter in her purse. "I'll read it later. I must say I think this system is working well. I send letters to my papa, and you receive them from him. I'm so glad we came up with this approach after my mother told me it was too dangerous to receive letters from him after Kristallnacht, even with the different surname. Did she really think I would stop communicating with my papa? Of course, we never talk about my father now, so she wouldn't know. Now, Gustav, what is the other thing you needed to tell me?"

"You know all about the challenges we've been having to obtain our tax clearance certificates, particularly since my parents came back from the Polish border. First, they struggled to sell that building. They thought the sale was done just before their forced deportation. But when they returned, my stepfather asked the city where the money was, and they told him they thought he wasn't coming back. Then they said they needed court approval for the sale, since the contract price was below the assessed value. They finally approved the sale, but the Jewish Levy that was assessed on all Jewish property after Kristallnacht took most of what had been given us by the city for the property. And let's not forget the extortion money we had to pay the Gestapo to avoid getting arrested after Kristallnacht, although that did keep us out of the Buchenwald concentration camp."

Gertrud noticed her cousin's voice lower when he mentioned Kristallnacht. She took his hand. "Gustav, I remember that horrible day last November. When I heard from my stepfather that Jewish businesses had been destroyed and synagogues set on fire, I walked to your shop the next day. I saw you and your mother sweeping up broken glass and your brother and stepfather trying to wipe the swastikas off the door. I wanted to help, but you put up your hand up to stop me. First, you were forced to clean up the mess caused by those hoodlums, then you had to give the government the money you received from the insurance company for the damage, then you were assessed the Jewish levy and finally you had to shut down the business. I was so angry."

"I was too. Then my parents started receiving letters from the city's chief of police directing that they leave the city because they are Polish citizens, which we couldn't do without the tax clearance certificates. Well, we finally received the certificates a week ago."

Gertrud's eyes widened and started to tear. "Does that mean you're all leaving for America? Is that why we're meeting, for you to say goodbye?"

"Not quite. Not America, anyway. England."

"England? Why England?"

"Even with the tax clearance certificates, we would still be waiting a while for our numbers to come up on the waiting list for US visas. But after Kristallnacht, England eased their immigration restrictions for Jewish refugees. My stepfather has some relatives there and has been in touch with them. We're all getting our passports next week and then our visas. My stepfather is leaving at the end of this month to set things up for us, and the three of us are planning to emigrate to England in the middle of next month. It's not America, but it's better than staying here."

"And what about Gretel?"

"Gretel will join us as soon as she can."

"And do Gretel's parents know about your plan?"

"Not yet. There's a lot we need to do between now and the day we leave, but I wanted to let you know. And don't worry, I'll see you a few more times before I leave, and we can write often once we are in England. In the cousins' code, of course. Who knew I'd still be reading Goethe poetry?" He gave his cousin a wink.

"Oh, Gustav, I will miss you terribly. But I'm so happy for you, to be able to live your life without fear and to marry the love of your life." As she said the last part, she wondered if she would ever be free of worrying about being discovered, whether she would ever be free from fear.

Gustav took an audible breath and smiled. "I must admit, I'm pretty excited about being able to marry Gretel and being able to hold hands and kiss in public without worrying that either of us will be arrested. But we're not leaving today, so no more long faces.

Let's walk around the zoo, starting with the monkey cages. I know how much you love to make faces at the monkeys."

"Gustav, I am not five years old! But, as long as we're so close to the monkeys, let's walk over and see what those rascals are up to."

As they approached the monkeys, Gertrud began to feel a profound sadness at the upcoming loss of her last cousin. First Bettina, and now Gustav. She hadn't seen Trudi for more than a year. She had friends, and maybe even a boyfriend, but she had no one like her cousins. They knew all her secrets, and she knew all theirs. What would she do without her last cousin in Frankfurt?

•   •   •

Two weeks later, Gertrud woke early and went into the kitchen to make her breakfast. She had been dreaming about Gustav, and in her dream, Gustav was being arrested by the Gestapo. She woke with a start and gave up trying to go back to sleep. She assumed she would sleep better once she knew her cousin was safe in England. Gustav had told her last week that his stepfather had made it safely to England and that Gustav and his mother and brother were making their final preparations to join him. Just a week and they would all be together! But she still worried.

No one was in the kitchen. Gertrud knew her mother was still asleep and assumed her stepfather was out buying the morning paper since he always woke early. Gertrud was putting her oatmeal into a bowl when she heard the front door open. She walked into the dining room with her breakfast and waved to her stepfather.

"Good morning, Gertrud. Is your mother awake?"

"I haven't heard anything from her room, so I'm assuming no. I have the early shift at the bakery, which is why I'm up early."

"Well, I guess she can wait for the news, but I'll share it with you. England and France have just declared war on Germany. Big headlines in the paper. Remember I told you two days ago that

Germany had invaded Poland? England and France had promised to protect Poland, so I guess they're living up to their promises. We are at war, but you shouldn't worry. We signed a non-aggression agreement with the Soviet Union, so I imagine this war won't last very long."

Gertrud tried never to discuss politics with her stepfather. He supported the Nazi government, which he said would make Germany strong again and would recapture the territory and important resources Germany had lost after the Great War. He ranted regularly about how the Jews had forced Germany to sign the Treaty of Versailles and that the treaty was to blame for Germany's inability to recover from the war. Gertrud needed to ask him a question now, but she needed to be careful how she phrased it.

"What does it mean that England has declared war on Germany?"

"Both England and France. At this point, we'll likely be fighting over Poland. But we might be fighting over other lands, as well. But I see why you're asking. You shouldn't be too worried about Franz. I'm sure this will be a short war, over before we know it. And, of course, Germany will win and win back what is rightfully ours."

Gertrud thought to herself, *Good, he thinks I'm worried about Franz, so I can ask my question.* "I guess when you're at war with a country, you can't visit that country?"

"Silly, why would you want to visit England or France? Maybe you and Franz were thinking about a romantic trip to Paris. But no, you'll have to wait until the conflict is over. All the borders between our countries are now closed." He shook his head and muttered to himself, "Visiting Paris. Silly girl."

Oh no, Gertrud thought to herself. *Will Gustav and his family still be able to emigrate to England?* She needed to see Gustav right away. She would need to take the risk of getting caught.

Gertrud stood up from the table quickly and said, "I need to go to work."

"But you hardly touched your oatmeal."

"I'm actually not very hungry. Say goodbye to Mama for me." She put her bowl in the kitchen sink, picked up her purse and hat, and quickly left the apartment.

She raced to the tram stop. The tram was actually still at the stop, and the driver was kind enough to wait for her to board. She easily found a seat – it was still early – and took the tram to a stop close to her cousin's apartment. Since they were forced to close the business after Kristallnacht, she knew they would all be home. She practically ran to their building and was out of breath as she climbed the stairs to the apartment. She knocked softly, so as not to alarm them, and tried to smile when Paula answered the door.

"Gertrud, this is a surprise! Are you okay?"

Gertrud didn't respond and didn't wait for her aunt to invite her in. She hurried inside and closed the door. She didn't want any nosy neighbors listening to their conversation. She looked up and saw Gustav and Alfred sitting at the dining room table with the newspaper opened and other papers spread about the table. She could tell from their faces they knew what had happened.

"As soon as I heard, I came right over. Is it true, are the borders really closed?"

Gertrud hadn't realized she had started to cry until her aunt hugged her. Then she couldn't stop crying. She was really worried about her cousin. Actually, she was worried about all three of her cousins. They were all Jewish and the Nazis were at war with the Jews. And if they knew about her background, they would be at war with her as well. Suddenly, everything seemed very real. It was one thing when it was simply one edict after another applied to Jews. But war? After a minute, she was able to gain control of her emotions and joined Gustav at the dining room table. He was staring at some documents.

"What are those, Gustav?" But she already knew the answer.

Gustav looked up at her blankly and said, "These are the tax clearance certificates. And these are our passports. And these are our visas. A lot of good any of them will do us now! We can't go to England now. We're stuck here."

Gertrud pleaded, "What about America? You're still on the waiting list, right?"

Gustav's voice grew louder as he answered, "It will be a couple of years before we're called. What are we going to do? The Frankfurt police want my mother and brother to leave Frankfurt because they're not German citizens. We have no money coming in since the Nazis forced us to close the shop after Kristallnacht. We have little money left in the blocked account since they've taken almost all of it. We want to leave, but we can't get out!"

Gertrud had never seen her cousin so upset - and angry. The two could always say the right thing to each other, but she didn't know what to say now. So, she decided to let him rant. "They hate us; they want us gone! We've been working so hard to leave! Germany couldn't wait just one week to invade Poland! We were so close, so close!"

Alfred then spoke up, his voice breaking. "And what is Papa going to do? Is he going to wait for the boat to arrive? We won't be on the boat. Mama, we have to call Papa."

"Alfred, Liebling, I am going to the telegraph office when they open to see if I will be allowed to send a telegraph to your father. He must be so worried about us. He wanted all four of us to go together, but I told him to get himself settled and we would join him in a few weeks. I thought, what could possibly happen in a few weeks? Boys, I am so sorry I didn't listen to your papa."

Gertrud could see Gustav quickly recover from his anger to rescue his mother. "Mama, no one is to blame. Your idea of having Papa go first was a good one. No one could have expected a few weeks would matter so much. It was just bad luck."

Gertrud looked at her watch. It was eight a.m. Her shift started at 8:30, and her mother would hear if she was late. And that would raise questions. She needed to leave, but she felt bad about leaving this family now.

"I am so sorry this happened. I need to get to work now – Gustav, you know my mother will ask questions if I'm late – but I would like to come over after work. I will be more careful this time."

Her aunt answered before Gustav had a chance. "Gertrud, you know how much we love seeing you. But war now means we need to be even more careful. Wait a couple of days. Gustav will get in touch with you."

Gertrud knew her aunt was right, that it would only be harder for Gertrud and Gustav to see each other without raising questions. She simply nodded, hugged Gustav, Paula, and Alfred, and quickly left the building.

As she walked to the tram station, she thought about the fact that Jews were even more at risk in Germany and that things would likely get worse for them. Even though her mother had warned her not to say anything to Franz about her father and about herself, Gertrud had not been convinced she should say nothing, particularly if they decided to marry. But everything that had happened this morning convinced her she needed to stay quiet. Franz was a good man, but he was in the army. She could not run the risk that Franz might say something. Even if they did decide to marry, she knew she could never tell Franz she was half-Jewish and that she had been hiding that fact for years.

Strasbourg
September 1939

Trudi was serving her daughters an early breakfast when she heard a glass break in the living room. She turned to her daughters and said, "*Grand-mère* is not going to be happy about that." Both girls giggled but remained focused on their breakfasts. Marie the cook had made her famous crepes, and no amount of noise was going to distract the girls from this treat. This was to be the last breakfast at the house for who knew how long, and Trudi thought it would make the move easier for her girls if they had crepes. Trudi heard the front door open and close and went to greet her husband, who had gone out for the paper. He was taking off his hat and coat as she entered the foyer.

Joseph handed his wife the paper and said, "Take a look at the headline. France and England have declared war on Germany."

Trudi took a deep breath. "So, it's really happening. I guess the government was right in ordering us to evacuate Strasbourg today."

"Everyone could see we would be going to war with Germany. It was like watching a collision in slow motion."

"Except you and Papa saw it even earlier. It was so smart of you to arrange for a house for us to live in until we can return and to begin packing earlier than everyone else." The French government had developed an evacuation plan months earlier for all the cities and villages along the French/German border, but Joseph had convinced his father-in-law that evacuation was an inevitability given everything Germany was saying and doing. When they received the notice on August 30th to evacuate on September 3rd, the family was ready.

Trudi heard something else fall in the living room. She turned to her husband and said, "You should join the girls in the dining room for some crepes. I'll go into the living room and see if there's a problem with the packers."

As Trudi entered the dining room, she saw her mother speaking with one of the packers they'd hired. She didn't seem happy.

"Mama, I heard some noises. Is everything all right?"

"They need to be a little more careful with our things, and I told them so. They broke a vase from my mother. I understand they need to move quickly, but I don't want them breaking everything we own."

"Mama, they're doing a good job. It's inevitable that something will break, and you never liked that vase, anyway."

"I suppose you're right about both things. I guess I'm a bit nervous about getting everything done in time. The moving van will be here shortly, and your father is still not back from closing up his office. He knows we need to leave Strasburg before noon, since he hoped to get to Villeurbanne before dark."

"Mama, I'm sure he'll be here soon. You shouldn't worry – we're nearly done packing."

Trudi looked around the large living room and could see they were nearly ready for the movers. But yesterday had been a very long day. Their cook Marie distracted the girls by baking cookies for the trip, while she and her mother identified for the packers what would go with them and what would remain in Strasbourg. Joseph had convinced his in-laws that nothing of value would be safe once they left, so they worked to identify all the things they truly cherished. Jacob loved collecting things and seemed to cherish everything, and Trudi felt like she was spending most of yesterday saying "No" to her father.

Trudi heard her father walking through the front door. He came into the living room and looked around. "I'm assuming we're nearly finished."

Lili gave her husband a kiss and said, "Yes, and with little help from you."

Jacob winked at his wife and said, "I actually was helping by staying out of your way. But something smells delicious, and I'm assuming Marie made crepes. Lili and Trudi, put down what you're doing and join me for our last breakfast in the house."

The three joined the rest of the family in the dining room. Joseph waved to his father-in-law and asked, "Did you see the crowd at the train station? Thousands of people were already waiting for the train. It's hard to imagine how the entire population of Strasbourg – 200,000 people – will be able to leave the city in a single day. And where will they go?" Trudi was wondering the same the thing. Like them, everyone in Strasbourg had received the notice on August 30th that they would need to evacuate the city. She was just grateful they had the resources to make this journey easier.

As they were finishing their crepes, there was a knock at the door. Lili stood up and said, "The movers are here. I need to make sure the packers are done. Trudi, could you help me?"

Trudi knew her breakfast was over. She stood up to join her mother.

For the next three hours, the house was mostly in chaos. The packers were still finishing their work while the movers were moving the designated furniture. Jacob had decided to take one of the buffets and the credenza, as well as Lili's family's Persian rugs. They couldn't take the massive dining room table, but decided to take six of the wooden chairs. Trudi never really liked the carved wooden chairs, but her daughters loved the sculpted animals, making animal noises every time they sat in the chairs. They would like them in the new house.

Trudi found her mother staring at the large dining room table after the chairs had already been moved to the van. Trudi could see a tear rolling down her cheek. Trudi said, "Mama, I know it's hard to leave the house."

"It is hard. I love this house and I don't understand why everyone needs to leave. I don't understand why the French soldiers can't protect us from the Germans."

"I'm not sure I understand it myself. All I know is what I've read in the paper, that an evacuation plan was put into place for the cities near the Maginot Line if war was declared. Well, war was declared and everyone in Strasbourg and the surrounding municipalities must leave for our own protection. At least, that's what they say."

"This really makes no sense to me, but I'm not in charge. So here we are, packing up everything to leave for how long?"

"Mama, I don't think anyone really knows. I think we should plan to be gone at least a few months."

Her mother sighed loudly. "Mama, what's wrong now?"

"There is one valuable I know I can't take with us - the Matisse painting. That really makes me sad. I really do love this painting, but it's just too big to move."

"Mama, you'll see the painting again. Don't worry." Then Trudi hugged her mother.

By eleven a.m., the moving men had loaded everything and were on their way to Villeurbanne. By noon, after a quick lunch, the family was ready to leave the house. They said goodbye to Marie, who would be leaving by train to stay with a sister, and walked to the car. Once inside the car, Trudi took her mother's hand and said, "Don't worry Mama, we'll be back in the house before you know it." Her mother squeezed her hand, but Trudi worried what the future would bring.

Jacob had made the trip to Lyon on the N83 often and had told the family this road to Villeurbanne, a village just outside of Lyon, should take no more than five hours. As they were leaving the city, the road ahead looked clear, and Trudi assumed the drive would be easy and painless. But then the car slowed and soon stopped. Ahead was a cart being pulled by a horse. Military trucks and tanks were occupying the other side of the road heading north, and Georges had to wait until he was able to pass the cart. This continued for another three hours — horse-drawn carts heading south and clogged northbound lanes with military vehicles headed to the French border. Seeing the road teeming with military equipment and refugees, Trudi understood at once that France was at war. She also realized they would not arrive in Villeurbanne before dark.

•   •   •

Instead of five hours, the trip to Villeurbanne took more than ten hours. Georges had thought to bring extra gasoline, and they needed to use it along the way. As the car pulled up to the new house, Trudi saw the moving van parked in front and the men standing outside of the van, obviously angry. Her father immediately left the car and approached the men, handing them some francs, which seemed to help. Trudi let her daughters remain asleep in the car while she helped her mother instruct the movers where the furniture should go. For the next two hours, various pieces of furniture were moved into their correct positions in the house. While the house was a little small, most places would be small in comparison to the Strasbourg house, which had a smoking room next to the living room and a boudoir next to the master bedroom. But the three-bedroom house would serve its purpose for the short time they were expecting to be there.

It was nearly midnight when the movers were finished, and Trudi and Joseph carried the girls to their new bedroom. Georges then said goodbye to the family, wished them luck, and left. He was driving to Lyon to deliver the car to its new owner and Georges' new employer. His family knew Jacob was devastated to have to part with his car. Lili sometimes joked that the car was his one true love. But Jacob announced, just after they received the evacuation notice, that he had decided to sell the car. "It just makes sense," was how he concluded the discussion. Trudi assumed her father was worried about his finances, but he was too proud to say.

Trudi didn't even remember falling asleep that night but was awakened by the sunlight streaming into her bedroom. She turned over to Joseph and said, "I think the first thing we need to do today is buy shades for the windows." Joseph grunted, then turned over, facing away from the window.

Trudi got out of bed and looked at her watch. Six a.m. She had slept long enough and was not going back to sleep. She decided she would get to work, making their house a home. She would begin in the kitchen. Marie had sent them coffee, croissants, and jam for their breakfast. She would go out for groceries after everyone was fed. She walked down the stairs and saw her mother was already in the kitchen, unloading a box of dishes.

"Good morning, Mama. How did you sleep?"

"The sun woke me this morning. We need to buy shades today."

"I was thinking the same. We could take the tram into town after breakfast and find some of the things we need, including shades."

"It would be good to know what stores are here in Villeurbanne. We can go to Lyon another day."

"Right now, Mama, I think it would be nice to have a cup of coffee and enjoy the quiet before everyone wakes up."

"Trudi, that was just the invitation I needed. I actually found the coffeepot and cups. But it will need to be black, since we don't have any cream yet."

"Black will do, as long as I can have one of Marie's croissants." They both smiled and Lili began making the coffee. But before she finished, there was some noise and giggling on the stairs, and the girls soon joined their mother and grandmother. *So much for quiet time*, thought Trudi. Their husbands soon joined them.

After breakfast, the girls went back to their bedroom to play, and Trudi and Lili left to explore the shopping opportunities in the town. When they returned two hours later, they reported that they had found someone to come and measure the windows for shades and had found a grocer and a bakery. They arranged for most of the groceries to be delivered to their house, but carried home what they needed for lunch. The family sat at the table to eat their lunch and hear about the adventures around town.

As Trudi and Lili were clearing the table after lunch, they heard a knock at the door. Trudi opened the door and saw a telegram delivery man. He asked for Trudi Reich. No one liked receiving a telegram, but Trudi calmly announced that she was Trudi Reich, and the telegram was placed in her hand. She quickly opened the telegram, saw it was from Gertrud, found the Goethe poem, and sat down in a chair to decipher the code. After a minute, Trudi said, "Remember I told you Onkel David was fleeing to England and that the rest of the family was going to meet him a few weeks later. Well, now that England has declared war on Germany, the borders are closed. Tante Paula, Gustav and Alfred are stuck in Frankfurt. Gertrud wants us to try to get the family into France, although it looks like our borders are closed as well."

"Gertrud told you all of that in code? The four of you really are the sneakiest bunch. I don't want to know all the things you got away with when you were young. But is there no way they can get to England?"

"Apparently not."

"What about America? I know they were trying to get there as well."

"Gustav already told me they wouldn't be eligible for visas for several years."

"Trudi, write Cousin Gustav and tell him and his family to try to cross the French border and come stay with us here. Send him the letter today. Hopefully, it will reach him before they end mail service between our countries. I'm assuming that's why your cousin sent the telegram, although I don't know why Gustav didn't write you himself. But good thing you gave Gertrud the new address. Hopefully, Gustav and his family can find safety with us."

Munich
November 1939

Bettina could hear Gregor stirring in his crib as she finished preparing breakfast. Hans never liked waking before seven a.m., but once war was declared, his uncle announced that all daytime managers would need to report every morning by 7:30 am, so Hans needed to leave the apartment by seven. Now, breakfast was eaten by both of her men at 6:30 a.m. sharp. This new schedule was actually fine with Bettina since it gave her some extra time with her mother before she went off to the Community Center.

Hans sat down at the table, and Bettina brought him his coffee. While he read the morning headlines, Bettina went back to the kitchen to retrieve his eggs and toast. Then she attended to Gregor, feeding him his oatmeal. She then gave her son his morning bottle and, with everyone occupied, poured herself a cup of coffee and sat down at the table.

Hans looked up at Bettina and smiled. "The eggs are delicious. This morning schedule is hard on all of us, but it is important. We need to win this war, and we need to win it quickly. The quicker we're done with this, the faster things all go back to normal."

Bettina smiled at her husband, but she wasn't so sure that the war would be quick. And she wasn't sure what they would go back to. Hans chose to ignore everything happening to Munich's Jews, but Bettina was reminded of it every day by her mother. Fortunately, her mother never spoke with Hans about what she was doing, and neither did Bettina. They weren't purposely hiding it from Hans, but he stopped asking Henny what she did during the day and Henny wisely never volunteered. Bettina thought it was better this way.

"Hans, what time do you think you'll be home this evening? I was thinking about what to cook for dinner."

"I forgot to tell you my uncle wants me to attend a dinner with some of the local business leaders. Nothing very fancy, but he thinks it would be good for business and good for me. I shouldn't be home too late."

Bettina smiled at her husband and returned to her coffee. He was attending more of these business meetings, and she was hoping they were just meetings. She never asked for more details and was just as happy that Hans never shared. When Bettina first mentioned the meetings to her mother, Henny warned her daughter that Hans might be involved in the Nazi Party. Bettina dismissed those concerns but decided not to mention the meetings to her mother again. When Hans was not home for dinner, Bettina told her mother that he was working late because of the war. All these little lies reminded her of her cousin Gertrud.

After Hans finished his breakfast, he kissed his wife and son goodbye and left the apartment. Almost as soon as he left, her mother opened her bedroom door. Bettina knew that these days, her mother purposefully waited for Hans to leave. She once said that she wanted to give them privacy, but Bettina knew it was also because she wanted to avoid talking with Hans.

"Good morning, Bettina. I heard Hans just leave. Another early morning for him? And how is my golden boy?"

Bettina picked up Gregor and handed him to her mother. "Good morning, Mama. Gregi is as hungry as ever. I'm not sure there has ever been a child who could eat as much as this boy. Feel how heavy he is!"

Henny nuzzled her grandson, who started to giggle. "He's just a growing boy. And so cute! It's a good thing he has an appetite since I just want to eat him up!" She then started to nibble his toes, which caused Gregor to laugh. Bettina watched her mother and son and was so grateful Henny was living with them. She hoped Hans was right about the war and she hoped he was right about being able to protect them all.

"Mama, I just made Hans some eggs. Would you like some as well?"

"No, Liebling, just some toast and coffee. I didn't sleep very well last night, and I need to go over to the Community Center soon. Since Kristallnacht, we've been given almost total responsibility over the welfare system for the city's Jews, as well as the Jews in the neighboring towns. We're seeing increased needs but are still fighting with the Association over available funds." Bettina knew all about the Community Center's battles with the Reich Association of Jews in Germany. The Association had been established by the Nazi government in July and claimed that its mission was to facilitate the emigration of Jews from Germany. But it also was the entity responsible for distributing the funds to the Center, and it had become more and more stingy with those funds. Henny often complained that, while the need continued to increase, they had less money.

"We have a meeting this morning to determine where we should set up more soup kitchens and clothing distribution centers. It's harder and harder to find the necessary space. The city has taken almost all the property owned by the Jewish Community, and they're making us pay rent for the crappy space in the cigar factory. But let's not talk about any of this. All the problems will still be there when I get there. Let me enjoy some time with my grandson."

Suddenly, Bettina found herself crying and raced to the kitchen before her mother could see the first tear.

"Bettina, are you okay?"

"Yes, Mama, I just thought I left the stove on." She took some deep breaths, and the tears stopped. Why was she crying? Was it something her mother said? Or maybe she was just tired. Maybe she needed to take a stroll with Gregor after her mother went to work. *Yes*, she thought to herself, *that's all it is. I just need to get out of the apartment.*

After her mother left, Bettina washed the dishes and dressed Gregor. She put on her coat and hat, placed Gregor in the pram, and walked towards the old town. There was a chill in the air, but she was happy for the coolness. Maybe this would help her feel better. She soon found herself smiling. Yes, this was exactly what she needed.

As she turned the corner, Gregor began to yell with excitement. She hadn't been paying attention and she realized she was walking towards the old Uhlfelder department store. She had taken Gregor to the store numerous times when he was a little baby. The store had a petting zoo in the middle of the store, and sometimes it was the only thing that would quiet him. When she went to the store with her mother or Hans' aunt, she could spend some needed time on her own, trying on different outfits or sitting in the restaurant for a quiet cup of coffee. She couldn't believe Gregor still remembered the store. She hadn't walked past this store since Kristallnacht when the store was looted and damaged. That was nearly a year ago, when Gregor was just six months. How could he remember the store? She stopped in front of the old store – the windows were boarded up, defaced with swastikas, and nothing had replaced it. As she walked away, Gregor started to cry. And so did Bettina.

Frankfurt
December 1939

Gustav was sitting at the kitchen table eating his lunch and reading the letter from his cousin, Trudi. He looked at the postmark – September 4th. The day after England and France declared war on Germany. The day that began their new nightmare. It had taken nearly three months for him to receive the letter. Written in their "special" code, he was grateful to hear they were safe. He also appreciated the invitation to cross the border and live with them. Unfortunately, he knew his mother would reject the offer, still optimistic they would receive visas to America.

He was just finishing his lunch when his mother came back into the apartment. He put away the letter; he would tell his mother about the offer later when she was less tired and perhaps willing to consider the offer. Paula had been doing some sewing for some of their neighbors, earning a few Reichsmarks. Clothing ration cards had recently been issued to all Germans, but Jews were then required to surrender the cards, so no new clothing for Jews. Paula was helping to keep old clothing wearable and was paid a little for her help. Not enough for the long term, but it was helping the family to supplement the little savings they had left.

"Hello, Mama. How was your morning?"

"I hope I'm smelling coffee. I could really use a cup, even though it's that ersatz coffee." As she sat down at the table, Gustav went to get her some coffee. After he returned, she said, "The morning was okay. It's hard to get thread to mend the clothes, but I'm doing my best. I have enough food rations for a visit to the market this afternoon when it opens for Jews at four p.m. I even have enough in our rations book to buy a little butter, so I can make some cookies for us this evening. Hopefully, there will still be some butter left."

"Cookies sound wonderful. Is there anything you need me to do? I'm going to the Community offices to register for work this afternoon. I could stop at the market for you on the way home."

"Gustav, I know you're reluctant to get a forced labor position, but it might be something you like. Maybe in a tailor shop."

"If I'm lucky. And for a quarter of what I should be earning. But at least I would be bringing money into the family, and forced labor jobs are the only jobs Jews can get."

"I will go to the market today, but I need you to do something else. As I was leaving this morning, our landlord stopped me and told me he can no longer rent the apartment to Jews. But that's just as well, since we can't afford to stay in this apartment. Before I went to my jobs, I went to the Housing Advisory Board and they have a place for us, not far from here, and the place is available next month. I went to see it after I finished my work, and I think the place will be fine for us. But could you look at it on the way home and let me know what you think? With the restrictions on renting to Jews, I was told that it's one of the few places that would rent to us, since the building is owned by a Jew. The owner's name is Herr Neumaier."

"Mama, we both knew this would happen once they announced Jews could only live with other Jews. Oh, how I hate this government! They will not be satisfied until we are all living in the streets. But I would be happy to stop by the building. Just give me the address and I'll go after I register." His mother rose from her chair, kissed Gustav on his forehead, and walked into the kitchen to write down the address.

After he finished his coffee, Gustav reached for his scarf, coat, and hat, and left the apartment. The original Community office had been damaged during Kristallnacht, and the city took possession of the building. The city then leased to the Community a much smaller building in the West End, on Friedrichstrasse 29.

It took about thirty minutes to get to the Community office, and as Gustav opened the door, he was met by an unpleasant combination of smells and noise. The front door opened to a reception area, and there was a line just to get information on where to go. When he reached the front of the line, he requested the office for work registration and was told to go to the second floor. He walked up the stairs and opened the door marked "Labor Registration." Another line! But fortunately, a good friend was waiting at the back of the line.

"Heinrich, what a surprise seeing you here!"

"Gustav, great to see you! How have you been?"

"I imagine the same as you. I don't know if you I heard that my stepfather was able to get out just before the war started."

"I did hear that. Sorry the window closed for you. Are you and your family still on the waiting list for America?"

"We are. And you?"

"Still on the list. We've been having some trouble with some made-up taxes the Finance Office claims we owe, so we still haven't been able to get our tax clearance certificates, and as you know, no certificates, no passports."

"That sounds so frustrating. We finally received our tax clearance certificates, but only because my parents agreed to sell a building they owned for a ridiculously low price. But we still have high numbers on the waiting list, so who knows when we'll be called for the US visas."

"And so here we are, in line to register for a forced labor position. And you thought it couldn't get any worse." Heinrich laughed, but it sounded forced to Gustav.

"Well, Heinrich, maybe we'll get lucky. I know we won't get paid much, but maybe these will be decent jobs. Maybe we'll get a job in a candy factory where we can eat all the rejects."

"Or maybe we'll get a job in a bakery where we'll be forced to try all the recipes." At that, both laughed, and Gustav felt a little better.

"Heinrich, this is my first time in this building. It looks like everything the Jewish Community is doing has been consolidated into this one small building."

"That's my understanding, as well. And worse, they put the Reich Association in the building as well, although they're by themselves on the top floor. Jews acting as traitors against their own people!"

Gustav only knew that the Association was created at the beginning of the year to facilitate Jewish emigration and that it employed only Jews. But based on Heinrich's comments, he thought he needed to learn more. So, lowering his voice, Gustav asked his friend, "Why are they traitors? I guess I don't really know much about them."

"You know my father worked for the Jewish Community before he was dismissed. My father told me that, while the Nazis claimed they established the Reich Association of Jews in Germany to help Jews emigrate, what they're really doing is collecting information on where Jews live. Why do they need to collect this information?"

"Wow, I didn't know that. It's almost too much to think about, given everything else they're doing to us."

"And you probably don't know about an even worse problem. My mother is a nurse, or at least she used to be a nurse. She worked at the Jewish Hospital, which the city made the Jewish Community sell and then lease back. Then they fired almost all the nurses, including my mother. She has been volunteering her time, even though she's not supposed to, but she has complained to me she can't get enough medicine, and people are dying who shouldn't be."

"That's horrible. I've been so focused on trying to get out of Germany that I hadn't really seen what's happening to our people."

Heinrich lowered his voice and said, "Gustav, unfortunately, it sounds like you won't be leaving anytime soon. You need to open your eyes and see what's going on with your people. You should be helping us."

"Me help? What can I do? Sew clothes?

"There's more to you than sewing clothes. I know you and the fact that you have become very good at keeping secrets and not getting caught. By the way, how is that friend of yours?"

Gustav could feel the blood rush to his face. But Heinrich had asked the last question so quietly that he barely heard it. Gustav didn't respond.

"Gustav, I wouldn't be asking you to help if I didn't think you could do it. Our people really need help."

Gustav looked at his friend and knew he was right and he wanted to help. Finally, he answered in a voice only Heinrich could hear, "I always followed the rules when I was a kid, except when I was with you. But things have changed for all of us. I guess I could help if it's not too dangerous and doesn't put my family at risk."

"I have something in mind, but we can't talk here. Come to my apartment tonight at eight p.m. And trust me."

Gustav laughed. "Like I trusted you when we were kids?"

"I'm assuming you're talking about that night when we were fourteen and borrowed your uncle's giant car when he was visiting? We took it for a spin and returned it without anyone ever knowing."

"And I remember it was your idea, and I tried to stop you. But I never could figure out how no one found out."

Heinrich smiled and winked at his friend. "You remember the back way into my building through the alley?"

"How could I forget? Oh look, Heinrich, you're next. I'll see you tonight."

●   ●   ●

Gustav was at the Community Center for more than an hour, much longer than he expected. When it was his turn to register, they simply asked for his name, his address, and his date of birth. They asked him nothing about his skills or his interests. He thought that

was a bad sign. He bristled as he uttered his new middle name –
since the beginning of the year, all Jewish males were required to
use the middle name "Israel" and all Jewish women were required
to use the middle name "Sara." After he was finished at the Center,
he walked to the North End to see the apartment.

When he arrived at Friedbergerlandstrasse 27, he knocked on
the front door. As he waited, he looked up and saw there was a
ground floor plus four more floors. After a few more seconds, the
door opened, and an older gentleman stood at the threshold.

"May I help you?"

"Hello, my name is Gustav Heppenheimer. Are you Herr
Neumaier? My mother, Frau Zeydel, came to see you earlier today
about a place to live."

"Yes, come in, Herr Heppenheimer. Why don't you follow me,
and I'll show you the rooms."

Gustav was a little surprised when he said "rooms" and not
"apartment," but said nothing and followed the gentleman to the
stairs. He began climbing the stairs, and Gustav followed. They
didn't stop until they reach the attic level, and Herr Neumaier
turned to the right and unlocked a door.

"Herr Heppenheimer, there used to be just one family living in
the attic apartment. But since the passage of the new law earlier
this year that allows landlords to terminate the leases of Jewish
tenants, the city has made me increase the number of Jews in all my
apartments. Your family will have two rooms, and you will share
the rest of the apartment with another family."

Gustav walked into the apartment. It was dark, and the
wallpaper was peeling off the walls. The kitchen did have an
electric stove, which he knew his mother would like, but the living
room seemed to be heated with a coal stove. Herr Neumaier
showed Gustav the two rooms, which were smaller than their
current bedrooms and had a musty smell.

"Herr Heppenheimer, I know this is not where you want to live.
Between you and me, what the city is doing is criminal. It feels like

they're creating ghettos without the fences and barbed wire. I think it's likely they're going to make me cram as many people as possible into my apartments and all the other apartments owned by Jews."

Gustav's head was spinning, and he felt the need for fresh air. He thanked Herr Neumeier and rushed down the stairs and out of the building. He was grateful for the chill in the air. His mother knew the move would be a big change for the three of them. She had purposefully sent him on his own to look at the rooms because she knew he would need some time to accept the inevitable. He also knew she probably had little choice in where they could move. Knowing this was going to be hard on his mother, he decided he needed to support her. He also knew the move would be difficult for his brother, so he would do what he could to help her with Alfred.

By the time he arrived home, he was reconciled to the move. As he opened the door, he could smell dinner.

"Mmm, something smells delicious."

"My intrepid explorer, welcome home. And how was your journey?"

"The Community office was bedlam. Lots of people trying to do too many things. But I managed to register for work. I'm not optimistic about the options, but I'll just have to wait."

"And did you see the place?"

"I did."

"And?"

"We can make it work." At that, Paula hugged her son and simply said, "Thank you."

●　●　●

After dinner, Gustav got up from the table and put on his coat and hat. Paula looked up and asked him, "Where are you going?"

Gustav said, "Out to see a friend."

Paula stood up and approached her son. "Gustav, you know you have to be very careful seeing Gretel."

"I'm not seeing Gretel tonight. If I were, I would tell you. I forgot to mention that I saw Heinrich Cohen at the Community Center today. He asked me to stop by his place this evening."

"Heinrich Cohen. That boy was always getting you into mischief. When was the last time you saw him?"

"Gretel and I went out with Heinrich and a few others last year before Kristallnacht, when we could still go out to restaurants. I thought it would be nice to catch up."

"Well, be careful. Make sure the Gestapo is not in front of his apartment building and try not to steal any cars."

Gustav looked directly at his mother and smiled. Of course, she knew. He gave her a kiss on the cheek and said, "Don't wait up." But he knew she would, since she always did.

Gustav was used to sneaking around town. He was still seeing Gretel, although they both found it a challenge to spend any significant amount of time together. Gretel had told Gustav that she'd told her parents she had stopped seeing him so they wouldn't worry. She had also begun working at St. Marien's Hospital, a Catholic hospital near her apartment building. She was doing administrative work but sometimes was asked to help with the patients. With the start of the war, the hospital had been looking for additional staff. They tried to see each other when they could.

Gustav walked the ten blocks to his friend's building and checked the street to make sure the Gestapo was not spying on the building. He then entered at the back of the building and made his way to the third floor. Gustav knock softly and Heinrich quickly pulled Gustav into the apartment. Gustav looked around and saw five others—three men and two women. He knew none of them and was a little surprised to find them seated in the apartment.

"Hi, Heinrich. I thought you and I were meeting alone. If you're having company, I can come back another time."

"No need, Gustav. You're right on time. Have a seat."

So, this was intentional, thought Gustav. He should have known. This was just like Heinrich. But he was curious, so Gustav decided to stay. He sat in an empty chair and nodded to the group, who nodded back.

Heinrich sat in the last empty chair and said, "Gustav – no surname – is the friend I have been telling you about. I've known him since we were kids. Gustav was always someone I could count on, and he was always careful to make sure we were never caught doing the things we did."

"Doing the things *you* did," Gustav interrupted. Everyone laughed.

"True, I was the instigator, Gustav was the rules follower. And now we're doing something important, something for our people. Gustav, as I mentioned today, our people are having trouble getting medicine. Doctors lost their medical licenses after Kristallnacht and are not supposed to practice medicine. And they certainly can't prescribe medications. The only hospital Jews can go to is the Jewish Hospital on Gangerstrasse, and they can't obtain vital medicine for the patients that have been admitted. The only way the hospital and doctors can obtain most of their medicines is through the black market. And that's where everyone in this room comes in. You won't know each other's surnames, in case you're caught. We need you because each of you is good at avoiding detection. We need you to deliver the medicines to the doctors who need them. Is this something you can do? We're including a small delivery fee for your services, just to further entice you."

Heinrich no doubt knew that Gustav and his family needed the money, but Gustav was also angry that they had lost their window to escape Germany. He needed to do something with that anger. So, he would help his people and circumvent the Nazis. But he needed to make sure his mother didn't know. She would worry too much.

Finally, Gustav said, "Yes, I would like to help." The others in the room also agreed.

Heinrich smiled. "I knew that was exactly what each of you would say."

CHAPTER 10

Munich

May 1940

Bettina was in the back garden with Gregor, enjoying the warm spring day. Her hair was pulled back in a bun, and she was wearing one of her old cotton dresses. *What would Trudi say if she saw me now*, Bettina thought to herself and smiled.

Gregor was running up and down the rows but carefully avoiding stepping into the beds, as Tante Helga had taught him. To her surprise, Bettina found herself appreciating Tante Helga more. Initially, she had seemed mostly meddlesome, appearing in their apartment at the most inopportune times. But she had been a big help with Gregor, particularly in the beginning, when Gregor had been so colicky.

When food rations began at the start of the war, Tante Helga encouraged Bettina to plant a garden in the back of the building. They had prepared the garden beds in the fall and started planting a month ago. And now they were seeing seedlings sprouting up. Soon, they would be able to harvest turnips, carrots, potatoes and beets. The cabbages would come later. They did have access to other vegetables, but since they only received weekly rations of 500 grams of meat, 125 grams of butter, and a single egg, the garden would help them out.

Bettina was thinking how fortunate it was that her mother was living with them and able to take advantage of their rations.

Rations had been cut for all Jews, and friends of her mother's from the Community Center were struggling to put food on the table. Many did not have access to a plot of land to plant a garden.

When she thought about the Munich Jews, she thought about Gustav. She had heard from him recently by letter and knew that he had started a forced labor job. Because it was manual labor – shoveling coal all day into a boiler – he was actually able to receive some meat, although not nearly the quantity that Bettina received. The only manual labor she was doing was picking up Gregor, and so she felt guilty.

Gregor started to cry, and Bettina turned to her son. He had fallen into one of the beds. She couldn't tell if he was crying because he was hurt or because he knew he wasn't supposed to touch any of the beds. She started to laugh and picked him up. He stopped crying and also began to laugh.

"Looks like you're okay. But maybe we've spent enough time in the garden. I think it's time for lunch and a bath. What do you think?"

"Lunch, lunch, lunch," Gregor yelled.

"Okay, let's go upstairs."

After they entered the apartment, Bettina put Gregor in his highchair and began making his lunch. As she fed him oatmeal, the door opened, and her mother came in. Gregor yelled to be taken out of his chair, and his grandmother quickly came over. She lifted him up, gave him a kiss and hugged him tight. Perhaps a little too tight, since he yelled, "Ouchie, Oma!"

"Oh, I'm so sorry, my golden boy. I guess I was just so happy to see you." She put him back into his highchair and gave Bettina a hug. Bettina hugged her back, but Henny didn't let go.

Finally, she released her daughter and Bettina immediately asked, "Mama, what's wrong?"

Her mother took a deep breath, sat down in a chair, and said, "Remember when I told you last year that the Nazis had issued an edict that non-Jews are not supposed to rent apartments to Jews?

You told me Gustav and his family had to move to a tiny place. Well, the Munich government has finally decided to enforce that edict. We just found out, so I came home to tell you. Over the next few weeks, notices will be sent to Jews instructing them to move into houses and apartments owned by Jews. The government found out where all the Jews are living in Munich when Jews were required to register in April 1938 and when the Minority Census was conducted in May 1939. Now they're going to force Jews to live in a kind of ghetto."

"Mama, that shouldn't apply to you. Hans' uncle owns the building."

"It won't matter. And, unfortunately, it will also apply to you, even though you're married to a non-Jew. The only Jewish women it won't apply to are women who have had their children baptized."

With that last statement, Henny looked directly at her daughter, and Bettina immediately turned away, walking to the sink and pouring herself a glass of water. She drank the entire glass, returned to the living room, and said, "Mama, there's something I need to tell you. I wasn't sure when the right time would be to tell you, but it seems that this is the right time. When I was pregnant with Gregi, I promised Hans I would have the baby baptized Catholic. I was never very religious, and it was important to him. Plus, he thought it was important in order to protect us, and it turns out he was right. So, as you said, the order to move won't apply to us, because Gregi was baptized. I'm so sorry I didn't tell you earlier."

Bettina wasn't sure how her mother was going to react to the news. Her mother looked at her only child and said, "Bettina, when you decided not to have Gregi circumcised, I did wonder if Hans had convinced you to baptize the baby, so to be perfectly honest, I'm not surprised. But, at this point, all that matters is that you and Gregi are safe. You are my life. Whatever you need to do to keep the two of you safe, you need to do. Promise me you'll keep doing that.

I don't know what I would do if anything ever happened to you and my golden boy."

Bettina exhaled in relief and gave her mother a big hug. She must have squeezed too tight because her mother exclaimed, "Ouchie!"

Then Gregor yelled, "Ouchie, Ouchie, Ouchie," and all three began to laugh.

•   •   •

The notice for Henny to move came just a week later. She was to move into an apartment in a building located at Herzogstrasse 65. They were living just south of the old town, and the new place was far north of the old town. A tram or bus was out of the question, since Jews were no longer permitted to take the tram or the bus, except those in privileged marriages. Bettina suggested they take a taxi to visit the place, and her mother agreed. Tante Helga happily volunteered to watch Gregor.

The next day, Bettina and her mother telephoned for a taxi and when it arrived, Bettina gave the driver the address. He looked at her since he was given an address in a Jewish neighborhood. Bettina glared back at him, he shrugged his shoulders, said something under his breath, and began to drive. During the ride, Bettina could tell her mother was nervous and tried to keep the conversation light. But she soon found herself mostly talking to herself and stopped trying. Her mother didn't seem to notice. When they arrived, Bettina paid the fare, and the driver said something that she chose to ignore. She then turned to her mother, who was staring at the building. She took her mother's hand and walked up to the door. She rang the bell, and a woman came to the door.

"May I help you?"

Her mother said nothing, so Bettina said, "Hello, my name is Frau Schnitzler, and this is my mother, Frau Heppenheimer. She has received a notice to move into an apartment in this building."

"Yes, please come in. My name is Frau Gundersheimer. I own the building. Let me take you to my apartment, and we can talk."

The woman walked down the hall and opened the first door on the left. Her apartment was well-lit, but the furniture was worn and outdated. She walked with a slight limp and was rather stooped. Bettina thought she was at least seventy.

"Please sit anywhere, and I will get us some tea." She walked into the small kitchen and came back with a plate of cookies. Bettina knew the challenges faced by Jews with limited rations but took a cookie not to be rude. Her mother did the same. Frau Gundersheimer went into the kitchen and returned with the tea and sat down.

"Frau Gundersheimer, this cookie is very good. I know how hard it is to bake without eggs or butter. You must be a baking genius."

"Frau Schnitzler, that is so kind of you. Sometimes a little of this and a little of that produces a miracle. But I know you're not here to talk about my cookies. Frau Heppenheimer, you are here because the Munich government sent you a letter to move into my building. I know all about it. They came to me recently to ask how many units I had available for rent. A few of our tenants have been lucky enough to receive visas for America, and no non-Jew wants to move into a Jewish-owned building. We have sixteen apartments in total, and five units are available. They told me they would take care of filling the units. So here we are."

"Frau Gundersheimer, my letter says I am to take a unit on the second floor."

"Yes, that was the Baum's apartment. Lovely couple. No children. They left for America two months ago. It is a one-bedroom, but it has a nice kitchen. They even left all their furniture behind. Would you like to see it now?"

"Yes, I would."

Frau Gundersheimer stood up and said, "Please follow me." They left her apartment and climbed two flights of stairs. Her mother handled the stairs with ease, but Bettina worried about Frau Gundersheimer. But managed the stairs well, and they made their way to the end of the hall.

When Henny walked across the threshold, she let out a sigh that both ladies heard. Henny immediately said, "Frau Gundersheimer, I apologize for that. I didn't intend it to be so loud. It's certainly no reflection on the apartment. This will be a fine place to live. I guess I'm just sad I'm being forced to move away from my family."

"Frau Heppenheimer, there is no need to apologize. I'm glad my dear Moritz, may he rest in peace, did not live to see this. He died last year, before we were told that our building would become a Jewish House. I have four children, and three are already in America. My Olga still lives here with her husband and my granddaughter. I am hoping their visas will come soon so they can escape Germany."

Henny turned to her new landlady. "And what about you, Frau Gundersheimer? Are you planning to leave?"

"I am too old to leave. Besides, I can't leave until I know Olga and her family are safe."

Henny looked at her daughter, but Bettina purposefully looked away. Then Bettina asked, "Fran Gundersheimer, when can my mother move in?"

"She is welcomed to move in at any time. How about if we start the lease for the beginning of the month, June 1st?"

"Yes, Frau Gundersheimer. June 1st would be fine, right Mama?" Henny said nothing but stared out the window. Bettina was wondering what her mother was thinking, but assumed it wasn't anything good. Instead, she turned to Frau Gundersheimer and said, "Thank you again for showing us such hospitality. We'll move my mother things in on the 1st. Here's my telephone number, in case you need to speak with my mother."

Henny looked directly at Frau Gundersheimer and held out her hand to take the old woman's hand. "Frau Gundersheimer, thank you for your time. This apartment will be a fine place to live." She then walked out of the apartment and Bettina followed her mother out of the building.

Her mother said, "It's time to go home, as long as I still have a home. Let's find a taxicab."

•   •   •

On June 1st, Henny, Bettina, and Gregor walked out the front door and into a waiting taxicab. Henny and Bettina were each holding a suitcase. During the ride, Henny and Bettina were quiet, and Gregor slept. When they reached the apartment building, Gregor woke up and began to whimper. Henny picked up her grandson, left the taxicab, and stood in the front of 65 Herzogstrasse. Bettina paid the driver and carried both suitcases to the stairs of the building. Henny took a deep breath and opened the door. After Bettina retrieved the key from Frau Gundersheimer, all three walked up the two flights of stairs, and Henny used the key to open the door. Gregor raced into the apartment and ran in circles, but both Henny and Bettina remained in the hall. Bettina took her mother's hand, and the two walked into the apartment.

The previous tenants had left some plates, bowls and cups, as well as a teakettle. Bettina said, "Mama, I brought some tea with me. I'll make us some tea, then we can find a place to shop for some food. We can ask Frau Gundersheimer where the nearest store is."

"Bettina, I'm not hungry. And don't worry about the tea. Please sit down. I have a favor to ask of you."

Bettina sat down and her mother said, "Liebling, the Germans are gathering Jews throughout Germany and forcing them into these Jewish Houses. I'm worried this will end badly for us. I want you to do me a favor. I would like you to purchase sleeping pills for me. When the time comes, I want to have the option of ending it on my terms."

Bettina stared at her mother in disbelief, then said, "Mama, nothing is going to happen to you. Things will get better, I believe that. There's no need to talk about ending things."

Henny took her daughter's hand and said, "I hope you're right. But if things do get worse, I want you to get me those pills. Promise me."

Bettina knew her mother would not relent until she agreed, so Bettina said, "Okay, I promise."

"Thank you. And now, I have a special surprise for my golden boy. Gregi, come to Oma."

Gregor ran to Henny and Henny handed her grandson a small stuffed white bear. Gregor squealed with delight and hugged the bear. Both his mother and his grandmother smiled at him, then gave each other a sad smile.

Villeurbanne, France,
September 1940

Trudi opened the door, trying to juggle her grocery bundles and the mail. She closed the door with her foot and walked into the kitchen. Her mother was sitting at the small table in the kitchen, reading the newspaper and drinking coffee. Trudi put down her grocery bundles on the counter, reached for a cup and poured herself some coffee. Joining her mother at the table, she went through the mail. She immediately stopped when she reached an envelope.

Her mother looked up and knew to wait. It would take a little time for Trudi to decipher the code using Goethe's poem, which she kept handy in a kitchen drawer. After a few minutes, Lili couldn't wait any longer and asked, "Well, which one is it?"

"It's Gertrud. She wrote to tell me she and Franz are getting married next month. They need to wait for the honeymoon, since Franz's unit is leaving Germany. She thinks he's going east."

"Well, at least he's not going to France. Although it doesn't really matter since Germany basically controls the entire country now, anyway."

"Not quite, Mama. We live in the Free Zone." Trudi hoped that living in the Free Zone would keep them safe, but she wasn't so sure. When the Germans broke through the French lines earlier in the year and France agreed to an armistice, Germany divided the country into two zones: the Occupied Zone and the Free Zone. The Vichy government controlled the Free Zone, but all the recent anti-Jewish edicts imposed by the Vichy government were making Trudi worry about how safe they really were.

After they finished their coffee, Trudi and her mother began to prepare dinner. Throughout their lives, both had been fed by the family's cooks. Jacob had been successful in gaining access to his bank account, but Jacob and Lili decided it would be best to be careful with their spending, which included giving up a cook. Her mother was not a natural at cooking, but Trudi thought her own dishes were improving. At least her husband and father had stopped complaining about her meals, which she took as a good sign.

The Vichy government had just issued ration cards, allowing for the purchase of food equivalent to 1,800 calories a day per person. As this was not nearly enough for the family, Joseph was able to purchase additional food on the black market. Since everyone they knew was purchasing food on the black market, Trudi didn't worry.

As she was putting the casserole into the oven, Trudi could hear her older daughter enter the kitchen. She smiled as she looked up, but then noticed that her daughter was troubled.

"*Chérie*, is there something wrong?"

"Maman, Ruth is crying, and she won't stop. You need to come."

Trudi took off her apron and followed her daughter. Ruth was the more stoic of her daughters. She was only four years old but rarely cried. If she fell down, she would simply get up and resume what she was doing. Crying without stopping was not normal for Ruth.

As she climbed the stairs, Trudi could hear her daughter. It wasn't a loud cry but more like a whimper. She walked into the girls' bedroom and looked at her daughter. Her face was flushed, and when Trudi felt her forehead, she could tell her daughter had a fever.

"Ruth, tell me what's wrong."

Ruth whimpered louder and shook her head.

"Ruth, tell Maman where it hurts."

"Maman, it hurts everywhere," but she pointed to her throat and whimpered louder. Trudi noticed her daughter was having trouble breathing. She looked up and saw her mother standing in the doorway. Lili said, "Trudi, she never cries like this. Let me telephone Dr. Klein."

Trudi nodded, and she could hear her mother walk down the stairs to make the telephone call. She looked over at Laure, who looked worried. "Laure, see if you can help *Grand-mère*."

"No, Maman, I want to stay with you." Trudi was too worried about Ruth to argue with Laure.

Ten minutes later, Trudi heard the front door open and the doctor enter the house. She breathed a sigh of relief. The past ten minutes had been difficult. Ruth whimpered on and off, but didn't want to be held or comforted. Trudi sat on the bed next to her ailing daughter, holding her hand and feeling totally helpless. *But now the doctor is here, and Ruth will be fine*, Trudi said to herself.

As the doctor entered the room, Trudi said, "Dr. Klein, thank you so much for coming so quickly. Ruth, look who's here. Dr. Klein. Maybe he even brought a lollipop for you." When Ruth didn't react, Trudi started to worry again.

Dr. Klein could clearly see the anxiety on Trudi's face and said, "Madame Reich, of course I brought lollipops. But let me first take a look at Ruth. Madame Reich, maybe you and Laure can wait outside with your mother?" Trudi thought that was a strange request. She was always with her daughters when they were examined by the doctor. But she wasn't thinking very clearly and simply followed the instructions of the doctor and left the room. The doctor then closed the door.

Five minutes later, the doctor came out and closed the door behind him. He looked over at Laure, then said, "Madame Reich, could I speak with both you and your mother downstairs?" Trudi understood that Laure needed to be in another room.

"Of course, Dr. Klein. Laure, could you go into my bedroom and find a book to read?" Laure saw the look on her mother's face and knew not to object.

Trudi and Lili followed the doctor downstairs, and the three sat down at the dining room table.

"Madame Reich, Ruth has diphtheria. As soon as your mother described the symptoms on the telephone, I thought it might be diphtheria. I've been seeing such cases throughout the town. This disease is quite serious and highly contagious. Ruth needs to be taken to the hospital."

Trudi was listening very intently to the doctor, but when she heard the word "hospital," she started to cry. Lili touched her daughter's shoulder and said to the doctor, "Of course, she needs to go to the hospital. But she will be okay? Certainly, there are medicines that can be given to her."

"Madame Heppenheimer, there are several treatments that can be given to Ruth. But she is a very sick little girl and is having trouble breathing. I will telephone for an ambulance."

Trudi finally spoke up. "I will go with her to the hospital."

"Madame Reich, I really advise against that. Diphtheria is very contagious. You may already have it."

"I will not leave my baby alone."

The doctor could tell there was no use in arguing. "Very well, Madame Reich. Let me telephone for an ambulance now." When he returned from making the telephone call, he said to both women, "I must call the health department to alert them about the presence of diphtheria. They will post a sign outside the house and will send someone to fumigate the house. All of you will remain quarantined for as long as they require it."

•   •   •

Trudi felt like she was walking through quicksand. She had trouble moving her legs as she reached for her black dress. It was cold and rainy, so she decided to wear her long-sleeved wool dress. She picked up the dress and began to put her arms through the sleeves, but was having trouble doing this simple task. Everything seemed impossible today. Walking, dressing, even eating. She had no appetite. She felt like she would never eat again. How could she eat when she was about to bury her baby? She pulled her arms out of the sleeves, threw the dress on the floor, and dropped down on the bed in her slip. She could feel the tears falling down her cheeks. She thought she had no more tears left. She was wrong.

At that moment, her mother came into the room. She picked up the dress from the floor and said gently, "Trudi, let me help you with the dress." Trudi said nothing but stood up and let her mother first put one arm and then the other arm into the sleeves. Her mother then pulled down the dress. Just as she had done with Trudi when she was a child. Just as Trudi had done for Ruth until just two weeks ago. *Two weeks,* Trudi thought to herself. *The worst two weeks of my life. What a crazy disease! No one else in the house got sick and the one person who never gets sick dies.*

Her mother found stockings for her, as well as shoes, and handed both to Trudi. She finished getting dressed in silence, then hugged her mother tightly. The tears continued to flow down her cheeks, and Trudi wondered if she would ever stop crying. When she finally released her mother, the two descended the stairs. Everyone else was waiting for them. Trudi looked over at Laure, who was trying to be brave. Trudi wanted to walk over and hug her daughter but knew Laure would break down crying if she did anything other than help her put on her hat and coat, which is exactly what she did. Then they left the house to say goodbye to Ruth.

Frankfurt
October 1940

Gustav stood at the tram stop, waiting for the tram. He was exhausted from ten hours of shoveling coal into the blast furnace. Coal dust coated his clothing and hands. Gustav had always been meticulous in his dress and appearance and hated the idea of appearing in public this way. But this was the forced labor assignment he was given. RM 35 a week to shovel coal into a blast furnace to make iron. They didn't say what the iron was for, but Gustav knew – they were sending the iron to factories to make weapons for war. He hated he was part of the munitions-making process, but there was nothing he could do. Plus, it was the only steady money coming into the household, and they needed the money.

Gustav didn't have to wait long for the tram. As it pulled up, he waited for the others to board. Then he climbed up the two steps and walked to the back of the tram. There were a few empty seats, but he chose to stand. Gustav had a special pass to take the tram, but he had to give up his seat if someone else wanted to sit. He didn't want to take a chance of being accused of taking a seat away from an "Aryan" passenger. The ride back to his apartment was more than an hour, and he didn't relish the idea of standing the entire way back, but it was better than being bothered by the Gestapo. *At least they're not making me walk to work*, Gustav thought to himself. Jews were no longer permitted to use buses or trams, but because Gustav's factory was more than seven kilometers from his apartment, he received a special pass.

The day was unusually warm for fall, and Gustav got off the tram a few stops before his apartment. As tired as he was, he wanted to enjoy the day and chose to ignore the anti-Semitic posters seemingly everywhere. Besides, he wanted to walk by their spot, the place he and Gretel agreed to meet. Gretel worked different shifts and sometimes Gustav was forced to work late. But if they could, each would go to the bench behind a large tree in the small park at six p.m. Gustav would stand near the bench because Jews were forbidden to sit on the bench. If they were lucky, they would both be able to make it. And luck was with them on that warm day.

As Gustav walked up to the bench, he could see Gretel's blonde hair pulled up into a bun. His heart skipped a beat. To avoid startling her, he whistled a favorite tune of hers. She turned around and smiled at him and said, "Late, as usual." Gustav walked around the bench and pulled Gretel into his arms, careful to hide behind the large tree. No one could see them as they kissed. As tired as he was, Gustav wanted to stay behind the tree, kissing Gretel forever. But he knew they didn't have much time together, and they needed to be careful. So, he reluctantly stopped and simply held her for another minute.

Looking into her beautiful blue eyes, he said, "I tried to get here as quickly as I could. I hope you weren't waiting long and I hope I didn't get you dirty."

"I'm used to you being late. And as far as the coal dust on your clothing, that's why I wore my dark sweater. No one will be able to see coal dust on this sweater." They both giggled. Gretel looked at him with worried eyes and said, "Gustav, you look exhausted. Was it bad today?"

"It wasn't too bad. Herr Dieter actually said nothing to me today, which was a first. But I think it was because another Jew has joined our shift, and he was directing his taunts at the new guy."

"He really is an awful person. But I'm glad you had some relief from him today, although I feel bad for the new guy." Gretel then squeezed his arm and said, "The one good thing about this new job is that you're getting very muscular. I can hardly keep my hands off you now." They both giggled again, and Gustav kissed her, this time with such passion that he finally had to stop.

"Gretel, I wish there was a place we could go, but it's just too dangerous. But one day, you and I will be away from here and we'll be able to go where we want and with each other."

"Yes, that's what we need to think about. Not how bad it is now, but how wonderful it will be for us soon. But unfortunately, I need to leave for the hospital. I'm already a little late for my shift and you will need to get home before your mother starts to worry."

"Just one more kiss." They kissed one last time, and Gustav watched his girl walk towards the hospital. She turned around one last time, smiled at him, and then crossed the street. He stood watching her until she disappeared around the corner. Then he floated the four blocks to his apartment.

Gustav slowly climbed the four flights to the attic apartment. He could feel the exhaustion from the day's work and was grateful when he finally reached the top floor and took out his key to unlock the door. The main room was sparsely furnished – just a small couch, a table and chairs for eating, and a coal stove. They took three beds and two dressers from their old apartment for their two rooms. Everything else in their old apartment was sold at a steep discount. He could see his mother setting the table for dinner as he closed the door. The other family always ate first and were now in their one bedroom.

Gustav knew his mother struggled to feed the family. The Nazis had begun restricting where Jews could shop and limiting the amount of meat and butter they could buy. Since the beginning of 1940, Jews could no longer buy fruit or legumes and were restricted to a pound of sugar, half a pound of jam, and three eggs per month. But because Gustav was working in a blast furnace, he was allowed seven ounces of meat a week. With those rations, Paula could make simple stews for the family. Not very tasty, but filling, which was most important to Gustav, since he was always hungry.

"Hello, Mama. Dinner smells wonderful. It's a good thing since I'm starving."

"Gustav, before you do anything else, take off those dirty clothes and wash up. I'll wash your clothes later so you'll have them for work tomorrow. And I'll mend whatever you've torn, since you're always tearing something. Dinner will be ready in thirty minutes." Because Jews could no longer buy clothes, Paula had to mend all the family clothes and because Jews were banned from receiving voucher cards for textiles, she had to be creative with the larger clothing tears. Gustav smiled weakly at his mother and went into the bathroom to wash up and change.

Dressed in clean clothes, he sat on the couch and nearly fell asleep, awakened only by his brother's violin. It was one of the few normal things left for his brother, so Gustav said nothing as his brother continued to practice. It was the only music in the apartment since the family (like all Jews) had to turn in their radio the previous year. So, he closed his eyes and listened to the music. He actually fell into a light sleep and was awakened gently by his mother. He moved to the table. His mother placed the casserole in the center of the table and served him first. It was all he could do to wait until everyone else was served. Then he started to eat, saying nothing until his bowl was empty. He looked up to see both his mother and brother laughing.

"Were you hungry, Gustav?" his mother asked.

"I guess a little."

"It's a good thing I put away my violin, since you would have eaten that as well."

"Ha, ha. Alfred, you try shoveling coal for ten hours, then talk to me about hunger. Mama, is there any stew left?"

"Yes, Gustav, I saved a little for you." As she ladled the last of the stew into his bowl, Gustav felt a little guilty, since he knew his mother was giving him some of her own portion. But he was so hungry that he ate it. anyway.

When he finished the last of his stew, Gustav asked his mother, "Mama, how was your day?"

"Today was a little quiet. I had a little sewing work in the neighborhood, although the thread rations have limited my ability to do much work. I went to the Community Center to see if there is any work for me, but so far, nothing."

"Mama, I'm sure something will come through for you. And Alfred, how was school?"

"I hate that school. They have no music program, and hardly any teachers are left. I don't understand why I even have to go." Before Alfred was forced to leave his school in 1937, he attended a German school with a strong music program. Alfred was told he was gifted enough to one day become a professional violinist. After he was forced to leave his school, the only school he was allowed to attend was the Philanthropin, the Jewish school. With all the emigrations following Kristallnacht, the school had a small number of students and too few teachers. With each passing day, it was harder and harder for Paula to force Alfred to attend school. But she wasn't about to let her son languish at home.

Gustav, deciding to help his mother, said, "Alfred, every day you attend school is another day we say no to the Nazis. We all have a job to do, and your job is to say that Jews are entitled to an education." Gustav knew how his brother felt about the Nazis, and he was not disappointed.

"Okay, I'll continue to go. But only because the Nazis hate that I'm still in school. But I'm not going to feel any differently about the Philanthropin."

Gustav smiled and said, "Deal."

After dinner, as his mother was washing dishes, Gustav came into the kitchen and said, "Mama, I'm going out."

Paula wiped her hands on her apron and said, "Before you go out, there's something I want to ask you."

"Quickly, Mama. I need to be somewhere soon." Gustav knew his mother was aware of what he was doing, but she never said anything to him. He hoped she hadn't chosen that moment to tell him he needed to stop.

"Herr Wertheimer asked me if you would help them to make a minyan for the morning prayers. Your Papa was always available, but he's in England and they're having trouble finding ten men. You can do it on the way to work."

"Mama, the synagogue is gone. It was destroyed during Kristallnacht."

"They found a place not far from here. The morning prayers are over by seven a.m. You don't have to go every morning. Just when they're having trouble finding ten men."

"But I'm not religious anymore. I don't even know if I believe in God."

"You and I both know this isn't about belief. This is about helping your people. I know you're helping in one way. This is just another way of helping. This was important to your Papa, and this is important to me."

Gustav looked at his mother. She rarely attended services other than the high holidays – this was something that was important to his stepfather. But she wouldn't have asked him if it wasn't important to her. He didn't know why it was important, but it was, and so he told her he would do it.

She hugged him and said, "Thank you. And, Gustav, be careful tonight."

"I will, Mama."

As he reached for the door, his brother came up quickly from behind.

"Gustav, I want to go with you."

"Alfred, I'm only going for a walk."

"No, you're not. You're going to meet your friend and deliver medical supplies."

"What are you talking about? I'm just going out for a walk."

"Gustav, I'm not stupid. I know you've been doing this, and now I want to help. I'm small and fast, and I'm very good at avoiding detection. I can help and I want to help."

"Alfred, you're too smart for you own good. Okay, I'll try to find a way for you to help, but it can't be tonight. Promise me you'll stay home tonight, and I will find a way. But don't tell Mama. I don't want her to worry more than she already does."

"Okay, I promise to stay home tonight. But only because you have agreed to let me help. Be careful."

Gustav smiled at his brother and tousled his hair. As he left the building, he looked to the left and the right to make sure the Gestapo wasn't there. Then he walked to his friend's apartment. He knew a shipment of medicines had just come in, and it was his job to deliver them to the Jewish doctors who could no longer practice medicine. Without the medicine, Jews would die. So, he knew his task was important for his people. It also assuaged some of the guilt he felt at being forced to help the Nazis build their weapons. He also knew that he had no choice about the forced labor job – if he said no, the Gestapo would arrest him, and his family would starve.

•   •   •

The following week, Gertrud and Gustav were sitting at a small table in a smoke-filled room. The last time they met, Gustav admitted to his cousin that he was supplying doctors with black-market medicine. Now, Gertrud said to her cousin, "Gustav, I'm worried about you. You're going to get caught, and then you won't be able to help your mother or your brother."

"Gertrud, you always worry. You know how good I am at avoiding detection. Seeing Gretel after the Nuremburg Laws were passed made me an expert."

"Well, even an expert can make a mistake. You've been sneaking around for years and it's going to catch up to you. You need to think about your family first."

Gustav sighed, probably a bit too loud even for the crowded café. While Jews could no longer go to any cafés, this one was in a remote part of the city and filled with unsavory characters. The Gestapo never seemed to be anywhere near the place, perhaps purposefully.

"Gertrud, just understand that I need to do this. But let's talk about something else, like your wedding. I was so sorry I couldn't be there. That is one of the worst things about not being able to be with you in public, to miss all of your big events."

"The wedding was nice, but small. Just Mama, Karl, Franz's parents, a few friends from the bakery. But it felt incomplete since none of my cousins were there. And Papa wasn't there. But no one knew I was feeling sad since I am also a very good actress. Like you, I have had to hide things, but I have had to do it nearly my entire life."

"But you're happy, right?"

"I am happy. Franz is a wonderful man. No honeymoon, since he had to get back the next day to his unit. Mama has decided that the apartment is too small for all of us, so we're moving to Wolfsangstrasse in the Westend. It's a bigger apartment, but I can't help but think she's moving us again to make sure she and I are not caught."

"That probably makes sense. And I'm assuming Franz still doesn't know?"

Gertrud looked down at her coffee and said nothing at first. She finally said, "Gustav, I can't tell him. I promised Mama. I suppose I could have walked away from him. But I love him, and he loves me. And I don't see how he will ever find out. We've been really careful. The move to the new neighborhood will just protect us more. I'm sure I did the right thing."

Gustav suddenly felt bad that he raised the issue. They were practiced at hiding and were both good at it. He didn't want Gertrud to think that he was judging her. It wasn't his place. So, he said, "Gertrud, I'm sure everything will be fine. From what you've told me about Franz, he sounds like a fine man. I'm sure that, one day, we will meet."

Gertrud smiled at her cousin. "I'm sure, as well."

Gustav took a sip of his coffee and said quietly, "Gertrud, I know you're worried about your father."

Gertrud nodded her head. "I've been following the news. I never did before, but things changed, and the news suddenly became relevant to me. I know all the restrictions the Nazis imposed on Jews here have been imposed on the Czech Jews since Germany invaded. I just hope he's not doing anything political, but you know my father. Always trying to make the world a better place."

Gustav nodded his head and smiled.

When they were done with their coffees, the cousins got up from their back table, hugged goodbye, and left the café separately, walking in opposite directions. Gertrud had fifteen minutes to get back to the bakery and ran to catch the tram before it left the station. Four stops later, she left the tram and ran to the bakery. As she opened the door, she saw her mother standing at the register.

"You're ten minutes late. Where have you been?"

"They were having a sale on dresses at Schneider's shop. I went to see if there was anything in my size. I still have a ration coupon for a dress."

"And did you see anything you liked?"

"I did see one dress that fit me. Even though it was ugly, I still told the clerk to hold it and that I would think about it."

"Gertrud, you can't be so picky. You have a coupon for a dress, and so you need to buy a dress."

"But the new German designs are awful, so boxy and masculine looking. I would rather wear a paper bag."

"You just might end up wearing a paper bag if you don't buy that dress."

Gertrud knew her mother and knew a conversation about ugly German dresses would distract her from thinking about where Gertrud had really been. Gertrud laughed to herself, thinking, *I really could be a spy for the German government.*

As Gertrud was putting on her apron for work, her mother left the register and handed her the food rations book. "Gertrud, I need to work late, so I need you to go to the store after work. I have coupons for meat, butter, and an egg. Also, if they have soap, please buy a bar as well."

"Okay, Mama." Gertrud took the rations book and thought about a recent conversation she had with Gustav about his food rations. She felt a little guilty that her family was entitled to real butter and much more meat than Gustav's family. All because of a lie, her lie, her mother's lie.

CHAPTER 11

Frankfurt
June 1941

Gertrud was kept awake for most of the night by the moans of some of the patients in the ward. She had been here since yesterday and really wanted to go home. The doctor had just left, telling her she needed to remain in the hospital one more night. She just wanted to be by herself, in her own bed. But she had no energy to challenge the doctor.

When she first discovered she was pregnant, Franz was away, fighting. She didn't want her mother hovering over her, so she didn't tell her. Franz came home from leave just a month after she found out she was pregnant, and she told him. He was so excited that the excitement rubbed off on Gertrud, and they both told her mother and Karl. Her mother was also excited but angry at Gertrud for hiding her pregnancy. "I don't understand why you didn't tell me immediately. You've always kept secrets from me!"

Franz looked quizzically at Gertrud and asked, "What secrets have you kept from your mother?"

Gertrud glared at her mother, then answered, "You were a secret when we first started dating, don't you remember?" She smiled at him, and he nodded and smiled back.

Her mother then said, "We should celebrate! We'll go out to a restaurant for dinner. Gertrud, you pick the place. Any place you want."

Gertrud was lying in the hospital bed, remembering that night well. Everyone was happy and everyone was laughing. Over the next few months, she continued to feel fine – in fact, not at all pregnant – but last month, the doctor expressed some concern that the baby was not growing fast enough. At five months, the baby should have been bigger, she was told. And then she started to spot. The doctor told her that spotting was not uncommon. Finally, yesterday, she started to bleed. When she arrived at the hospital, a doctor told her she was miscarrying. Gertrud was devastated.

She was thinking about that previous day when she heard someone call her name. She looked up and saw a familiar woman walking towards her. The woman said, "Gertrud, I don't know if you remember me. I'm Gustav's friend, Gretel." Gertrud then knew who she was and started to cry. Gretel hugged her until Gertrud finally stopped crying.

"Gretel, of course I remember you. We may have met only a few times, but I could never forget Gustav's special friend. But what are you doing here? How did you know I was here?"

"I've been working here for the past year. I work in administration. I saw you come in yesterday and looked at the register to confirm it was you. Gertrud, I am so sorry you lost your baby. I heard from Gustav you were pregnant."

Gertrud was quiet at first, then said, "I knew something was wrong with the pregnancy. I never felt the baby. It was stillborn, and the doctor thinks it might have stopped growing a few weeks ago. It was a boy. I wanted to remember him, so I gave him a name. Wolf."

"Gertrud, Wolf is a wonderful name."

"My mother didn't want me to name the baby, but I insisted. She's filling out the death certificate now, and I told her to make sure to include his name. But I see her coming now. Gretel, I'm sorry, but my mother can't know that I know you."

"Gertrud, I completely understand. I'll let Gustav know what has happened. I'm actually hoping to see him later today."

"Gretel, thank you so much for coming. And thank you for the hug."

As her mother neared her daughter's bed, she glanced at Gretel and asked her daughter, "Why was that woman talking to you?"

"She was someone from administration. She wanted to make sure I filled out all the required forms before I left. I told her you were taking care of them."

"Well, if I didn't do them, they wouldn't get done. Your stepfather is on his way. He stopped to buy newspapers downstairs. He thinks the world will end if he doesn't read the paper." At that moment, her stepfather appeared, carrying two newspapers, and sat in the chair next to the bed.

Gertrud decided to be nice to her stepfather, engaging in his favorite topic of conversation. "Good morning, Papa. How is the war going?"

Her stepfather was clearly excited by what he had been reading. "Gertrud, the war is going very well for us. Before you know it, Germany will control all of Europe."

"I assume that's a good thing?"

"What a silly question! Of course, that's a good thing. Certainly your husband agrees with me. Germany is a great country, and now the world will understand why. We just need to finish off England, and we'll control all of Europe." Karl's voice softened a little at the end of that statement, and Gertrud wondered why.

"Is everything okay, Papa? Anything in the paper?"

"Do you really want to know what's in the paper? You must be tired from everything that happened yesterday."

"Believe it or not, I want to know. I want to talk about anything other than what happened yesterday."

"Well, there is one thing I am a little concerned about. Do you remember when I told you about the agreement between Germany and the Soviet Union in 1939 that essentially divided Poland without us going to war? Germany has now invaded the Soviet Union, and I am a little worried about going to war with the Soviet

Union. But I'm sure the Fuhrer knows what he's doing. Hopefully, it will be quick and then we really will control everything, just as the Fuhrer has promised."

Karl continued to talk about the greatness of Germany, and Gertrud stopped listening. In her years with Karl, she understood that Karl never expected engagement; he simply liked to lecture. Usually, she found the lectures boring and sometimes troubling, but today, she was happy to have him drone on and on. Besides, it prevented her mother from speaking with Gertrud about the miscarriage.

At some point, she fell asleep, and when she awoke, she was alone. She wasn't sure how long she had slept, but it must have been many hours since it was dark outside. When she looked at her side table, she saw a piece of paper. She picked it up and saw a drawing of a sparrow cradling a small wolf. Gustav! She was the spätz, holding the baby she had lost! And then she saw a butterfly in the picture's corner, the butterfly from Pandora's box. Hope! It was beautiful! Had he been here while she was sleeping or had Gretel brought it by? She couldn't know, but she was so happy to have the drawing. She held to her chest and smiled as a tear fell down her cheek.

Frankfurt
November 1941

Gustav was late leaving work. The furnace needed maintenance several times, and they still had a quota that needed to be filled. Ten hours soon became twelve hours, and by the time he walked through the door of the apartment, it was nearly eight p.m. His mother was sitting at the kitchen table, bundled in a sweater and hat. Their coal rations had been reduced to almost nothing, and most days, they sat in the cold apartment in several layers. His mother was staring into space, and he wondered if she had worried about him. Things had not been the same since the deportation last month, when about a thousand Frankfurt Jews had been put into rail cars and sent away to who knows where, including the family who shared their apartment. That deportation also included his friend Heinrich and Heinrich's family. The rumors were that the train was headed to the Soviet Union, to areas now controlled by Germany. But no one really knew for sure. The only thing they knew was that it was more and more dangerous to be a Jew. And now that Jews were required to wear bright yellow Jewish stars on their outside clothing, it was impossible to sneak around. That had also made it harder to meet with Gretel in their usual spot.

Gustav had also not seen Gertrud since Jews were required to wear Jewish stars. She was pregnant again and having morning sickness, so the doctor was not worried about the pregnancy. But Gertrud was worried, and Gustav wished he could give her support.

As he walked towards his mother, he could see she was holding a piece of paper. When he was close enough, she handed him the paper and said, "Read it." The paper was a notice of deportation for his family. They were to leave on November 12th, in three days.

"Mama, when did you get this?"

"A Gestapo officer came to the door this afternoon. He handed me the paper, told me to read it, then left."

Gustav re-read the notice. He looked up at his mother and said, "For the last deportation, they just came to the door, told the families to pack, and the families left with the officers. So, they're now giving us three days to get ready? Although they are telling us to pay for our own transportation, so maybe this is a way of getting more of our money."

"They'll get our money either way."

"So, what should we do? Should we start packing? We have little left, so it will be easy enough."

"No."

"Mama, what do you mean by no?"

"I mean, no, we're not packing because we're not going."

Gustav stared at this mother in disbelief and said, "What do you mean we're not going? We have to go. We don't have a choice. We tried to emigrate. Germany shut that down for good last month when they closed the borders to all emigration. Now, no Jew can emigrate, even with a visa."

"If we follow their orders and get on that train, we will die. I'm sure of it. We need to escape!"

"Mama, how are we going to escape?"

"Gustav, we have three days to figure that out." Gustav looked at his mother, nodded, and said, "Mama, you have hope."

She got up from the chair, touched Gustav's arm, and said, "Yes, I do. But you must be hungry. Let me get you something to eat." At that moment, Gustav heard his brother practicing the violin. He wondered whether Alfred had been playing the entire time he had been home.

•   •   •

The next day, Gustav decided he had to see Gretel. He wasn't supposed to see her for several days, but this was an emergency. He waited outside the hospital, hoping her schedule had not changed at the last minute. Gustav left work early, complaining of a migraine. His supervisor told him he would have to make up the time. The weather had grown colder, and it felt like it might rain soon. He hoped Gretel would come outside before any rain began. Just as it began to drizzle, Gretel walked through the front doors. She immediately saw Gustav and walked to their usual spot. He followed her.

Once they were alone, they kissed, then she asked him what was wrong.

"We received a notice of deportation yesterday. The notice says we will be taken by the Gestapo to the Grossmarkt Hall in two days and put on a train. But we're not going. We have decided to ignore the order and try to leave Germany." Gustav waited for Gretel to digest what he had just told her.

Finally, she spoke up. "You're leaving your apartment tomorrow night and coming to our place. Then you can take my papa's car and drive to the border."

"We can't go to your parent's apartment. I can't put you in that kind of danger. Plus, how do you know your parents would even let us stay? They think we ended our relationship. No, it's just too dangerous."

Gretel took Gustav's hands. "Schatzi, my parents have known I've been seeing you all along. I just didn't want you to worry. See, even I'm good at lying. I'll leave right now to ask my parents, but I'm sure they'll say yes. They know I love you and want to be with you, and they approve. So, you go home and talk to your mother, and I'll go home to talk to my parents. Meet me here tomorrow at six p.m. Then we can move you in the middle of the night, before the Gestapo shows up."

"Gretel, do you really think your parents would do that for us?"

"I know they will. Now go home, and I'll see you tomorrow night with the good news."

•   •   •

The following evening, Gustav was waiting at their usual spot. He got there a little early, eager to know what the news would be. When he saw Gretel walking over to him, smiling, he knew. They hugged, and he hurried home to pack.

At midnight, Gustav walked out of the building and down the street to the side alley. The car was waiting there, with Gretel behind the wheel. *Of course, she would be driving,* he said to himself. He told her no one was outside watching the building and they would be back in a few minutes. He left the alley and began walking back to his building. As he approached the stairs to his building, he heard someone across the street yell, "Good evening, Herr Heppenheimer." When he turned toward the voice, he saw Herr

Rolf, a long-time customer of his stepfather, who was also a police officer. Gustav crossed the street.

"Good evening, Herr Rolf. It has been a long time since I've seen you."

"Yes, it has. I've been unable to find a decent tailor since I had to stop patronizing your stepfather's shop. He always did great work and for a fair price. I hope he is doing well."

"He actually was able to emigrate to England."

"And not the rest of your family?"

"Unfortunately, no." Gustav was getting nervous, but he couldn't show his nervousness. He knew he needed to remain calm and he hoped his mother was seeing him talking to a police officer and would wait inside.

"It's rather late to be outside. And I don't see the Jewish star on your coat."

"I thought I heard a noise in the alley and wanted to make sure there wasn't a prowler. I must have forgotten my star. But I didn't find anyone in the alley, and I was just returning to my apartment."

Herr Rolf looked down at Gustav's feet. "You're wearing very nice shoes, too nice to simply check out the alley. If I were a suspicious man, I would think you're wearing traveling clothes and that you're leaving Frankfurt in the middle of the night."

Gustav was working hard to control his breathing. "I assure you, Herr Rolf, the only place I'm traveling to is bed."

The police officer nodded his head and said, "Okay, I believe you. But if anyone were trying to leave the city, I've heard there are roadblocks on the roads leading south and west of the city and they intend to keep these roadblocks in place for several days. But nothing on the roads heading north or east. Herr Heppenheimer, it was nice to see you, and please give my best to your mother."

"I will certainly do that. Good night, Herr Rolf." Gustav hastily re-crossed the street and walked into his building. His mother and brother were waiting on the other side of the door, along with their suitcases.

"Gustav, why were you speaking with that police officer?"

"That was Herr Rolf. I thought for a minute he was going to arrest me. Instead, I think he just saved our lives. He told me there are roadblocks on the main roads leading south and west of the city for the next few days. We'll need to figure out another route."

"You told him we were leaving?"

"No, but I think he guessed."

"How unexpected, but your papa always treated his customers fairly. Herr Rolf was always a nice man and a good customer. But let's leave before we run into any more police officers." They left the building quickly, got into the car and drove to Gretel's apartment.

As they crossed the threshold, Gretel's mother stood up from the dining room table and welcomed them all with a hug. Gretel's father shook Gustav's hand and told him how much he missed seeing him. He then said, "Welcome to our home. Now, what is the plan to escape?"

"Herr Weber, first, thank you so much for taking us in. I don't know how we will ever be able to repay you."

"Please, Frau Zeydel, you and Herr Zeydel helped me out more times than I can count when you purchased fabric from me over the years. And because of Gustav, you are now family. It would be wrong not to help you. And because you are family, please call us Herman and Erna."

"And please call me Paula."

Herman invited everyone to the table, and Gretel's mother brought out coffee and cake.

Paula took a sip of her coffee and said, "You have asked about our plan to escape. We have family who used to live in Strasbourg and now live just outside of Lyon in the Free Zone. Gretel told Gustav we could borrow your car to drive to Metz and so we thought we would leave the car there and walk across the Moselle River into Occupied France. Once we're in France, we could go south until we reached the Free Zone. If we stay off the main roads, we could make it to Metz in a few hours. We thought we would travel once it's dark, maybe tomorrow night. I know it will be risky once we're in Occupied France, but it seems the best option."

"Paula, it sounds like you have thought a lot about this plan. The bridges in Metz may be heavily guarded, but you won't know until you're there. It's late and my suggestion is that everyone get some sleep. If you want to leave tomorrow night, it's especially important that you sleep now."

Gretel's mother walked them to the spare bedroom where bedding was set up on the floor. "It is not the most comfortable of arrangements, but you should be fine for one evening." Paula looked at the room and started to cry. Between sobs, Paula said, "Erna, I can't tell you how grateful I am that you are putting yourselves at risk to save us." She then took some deep breaths to stop crying and pulled her sons into the bedroom.

The next day was spent getting organized for the trip. Because the Zeydels were not at home when the Gestapo appeared, the Gestapo was now looking for them. Gretel went out to fill up the gas tank and even filled up a spare can of gas, just in case. Gretel's mother made the family sandwiches for the trip. At six p.m., as the sun was setting, the family said their goodbyes to Gretel and her family and left. Gustav's heart was breaking as he put the car in gear for their ride to Metz.

Gustav was driving especially carefully, and his mother was navigating based on the map Herr Weber provided them. They first took a road that took them north of the city, then quickly turned west and then south. They encountered no roadblocks out of the city and Gustav said a silent thank you to Herr Rolf. Gustav knew that if they were stopped, they would be immediately arrested. They had no identification papers on them and Gustav had no drivers' license – Jews had lost their driving privileges even before Kristallnacht. It took them about five hours, but they finally pulled into Metz around eleven p.m. They parked the car near the river in the agreed-upon place and left the bags in the car while they inspected the bridges. As they walked along the river, they could see that each bridge was heavily guarded. These were the only bridges across the Moselle.

They returned to the car to talk about their options.

Gustav sighed and said, "Mama, there's no way we can cross the river. We can't cross on any of the bridges, and we'll drown if we try to swim across the river. I hate to say this, but I think we need a new plan. And we need to go back to Frankfurt to come up with that plan."

Paula said nothing, staring out the window at the river, almost willing the river to disappear. Finally, she nodded her head and said, "Okay, let's go back and come up with a better plan."

• • •

They were back in Frankfurt before the sun rose, helped by the extra can of gas. Gretel was shocked to see them, but her father didn't seem especially surprised. He said, "I must admit I was a little worried about your being able to cross the Moselle. Please sit down for breakfast and let's try to figure out a new plan."

As they talked through their options, Gustav remembered friends telling him about others who had crossed into Belgium, even after Germany had invaded Belgium in 1940. While the Nazis occupied Belgium, Gustav had heard that life in Belgium was better for Jews, and so he offered the suggestion. He also reminded his mother that her best friend and cousin, Lina Rohr, had escaped to Belgium and was now living with her husband in Brussels.

Gustav said, "We could cross the border into Belgium. It doesn't have a river, just a large forest. And we could find Tante Lina. She would take us in. I could drive to the border by myself and try to find someone who could help up across the border."

Paula looked down for a moment, then said to her son, "Gustav, I think this may be the only choice we have. I'm glad you thought of it. But you can't go by yourself. Alfred and I will go with you."

"No, Mama, you stay here. From what Herr Rolf told me, there will be no roadblocks traveling north. But once I am out of the city, I don't know how dangerous the drive will be. I don't want to risk all of us getting caught. I'll sleep today and leave tonight. If all goes well, I'll be back tomorrow with good news."

Paula knew better than to try to challenge Gustav once he had made up his mind. So, she simply shook her head, and the three returned to the spare bedroom to sleep. While Gustav slept, Gretel repeated the preparations of the previous day, so that when he woke, he was ready to leave.

The drive to Aachen, a city along the Belgian border, was uneventful. He drove back carefully, along back roads, and was back by morning. Gretel answered the door, and they hugged for a long time. He then told everyone both the good news and the bad news. The good news was that he had found someone who would take them across the border. The bad news was that they would need to stay in Frankfurt until Gustav was contacted, and there was no way of knowing how long that would take.

His mother was the first to speak up. "Gustav, you did very well. I am so proud of you. As you like to say, we have hope, and we didn't have that yesterday. We will simply wait until it's time to leave."

Gretel smiled and took Gustav's hand. "I actually don't think that this is such bad news, since we'll have more time together."

Munich
November 1941

Bettina was running late for work, even with Tante Helga helping to watch Gregor. She had been making Hans' breakfast when Gregor fell down and wouldn't stop crying. It took both her and Tante Helga to calm Gregor, and then Tante Helga volunteered to feed him. Bettina picked up her purse but struggled to find her coat, hat, and gloves. Finally ready, she bounded down the stair and caught the tram just as it was about to leave the stop. *Maybe I'll be on time after all,* she thought and smiled.

Hans' uncle had warned Bettina several times that she would be required to take a forced labor position, which might require that she live at the job site and away from her family. "You are a Jew, and all Jews must work," he said rather dismissively. She desperately wanted to remain home to care for Gregor. Fortunately, Tante Helga had a friend who owned a hat factory and had received permission to hire Jews as forced laborers. The owner, Frau Brettschneider, treated Bettina well and did not tell any of her fellow laborers that she was Jewish. And because Bettina was in a privileged marriage, she was not required to wear the Jewish star. She chose not to engage much with her fellow workers, to keep them from finding out the truth, and hoped they thought she was just shy. This way, she avoided the taunts directed at the other Jewish laborers.

The work was hard, but not terrible, based on what she had heard from Gustav about his own forced labor position. Her factory made the hat bodies for the millinery shops. For some reason, while every other piece of clothing in Germany was being rationed, hats were not. In fact, the Nazi government encouraged women to buy hats, as long as they weren't too fancy. The felt for the hats (which was made from rabbit pelts) was delivered to the factory, which was located in the old part of town. To make the hats, the workers first placed the felt over wooden blocks to shape the hats. After the hats were shaped, the brims were trimmed, and the hats were steamed and ironed. Bettina's job was to inspect the finished hat bodies to make sure there were no mistakes. The hat bodies were then moved to a warehouse just a few blocks away and shipped around the country. Bettina was earning 75 RM, which she discovered was twice what the other forced laborers were earning. She said nothing to Tante Helga, but knew she was probably responsible.

As she opened the door to the factory, she noticed several of the Jewish workers standing in a corner, speaking in an animated fashion. When she approached them, they stopped talking and went to their stations to begin working. Later in the morning, Frau Brettschneider's assistant asked Bettina to come to the front office. When Bettina arrived, Frau Brettschneider got up from her chair, walked to the door, closed it, and told Bettina to sit down. Bettina was sure she was about to be fired.

"Bettina, I want to tell you something, but I don't want others to overhear it. I know you have kept quiet about being Jewish and I understand why. I wanted to let you know that several of the workers have told me they have received deportation notices. They will be leaving in three days. I know from Helga that your mother lives in a Jewish House in the Jewish neighborhood. I thought you would want to know."

"Frau Brettschneider, thank you for letting me know."

"Bettina, I understand you may be worried, but I expect you to finish your shift. You can see your mother after work."

"Yes, Frau Brettschneider, I completely understand."

Bettina left the office and almost knocked over an umbrella stand. She walked back to her station and told herself to take a deep breath. She knew Frau Brettschneider was behaving better than most of the factory owners employing forced laborers, but she was still happy to exploit Jewish labor, and she wasn't going to let Bettina off early, even if Bettina was about to lose her mother.

As soon as her shift was over, Bettina raced out of the factory and took a tram to her mother's house. She had called Tante Helga earlier to let her know she would be late. Bettina was feeling grateful she had this woman in her life.

When she reached the tram stop, Bettina hopped off the tram and practically ran to her mother's building. She climbed the stairs and knocked on the door. No one answered, and Bettina used the key her mother gave her to let herself in. Her mother was sitting in a chair in the small living room, staring at a piece of paper and seemingly unaware that her daughter was even there. But then her mother looked up with surprise and said, "Bettina, you're here. I guess you heard that I'll be leaving."

Bettina was stunned. "You're leaving? I didn't hear that! All I heard at work was that a deportation notice had been issued to some of the Jews in Munich. But I didn't hear it was you. Not you! Oh Mama, not you!" Bettina began to cry. Henny stood up from her chair, took her daughter's hand, and led her to one of the chairs.

Henny waited for her daughter to stop crying. She finally said, "I received the notice this morning. In fact, everyone in the building received a notice. There's a list of items we need to take, and a list of valuables we cannot take. As if I have any valuables. They were already handed over to the Nazis. In three days, we need to walk with our things to the Milbertshofen barracks. I had heard they were building barracks to house Jews, but I didn't really know the reason. Now we know — it's to house us until they're ready to deport us. I also have to take money with me to pay for my accommodations and for my transportation. The notice says I will need to take enough money for a stay of at least a few weeks. I'm sure the Nazis will find a way to get more of my money if I run out, since they control my bank account, anyway."

"They're making you walk to these barracks? How far is it?"

"A little over three kilometers. Not far. Just up Knorrstrasse."

"Mama, I need to come with you to help you in the move."

"Absolutely not. Every time you visit me, you put yourself at risk. We cannot run the risk that some Nazi thug will assume you are also being deported. It may take months or even years for the deportation to actually happen. I need you to promise that you will not try to see me for a few weeks after the move. Once we're settled in and I know better what will be happening to me, you can come and bring my golden boy."

Bettina knew her mother was right, that trying to do anything right now would be foolish. But she felt guilty that her mother had to shoulder this burden on her own. "Okay, Mama. I promise." She then took her mother's hand and said, "Mama, I'm sorry I didn't get you the sleeping pills. I just couldn't do it. I guess I didn't think they would actually deport you. I could try to get them now and bring them to the barracks."

Henny shook her head and said, "No, not until it's safe. But as long as you're here, you can help me go through the list of things I can take."

Bettina smiled a sad smile, and said, "Yes, I would love to help."

Over the next week, Bettina thought a lot about her mother, hoping the move to the barracks had not been too taxing. She overheard the conversations of the Jewish workers who had not been moved to the barracks on November 11th, about how Gestapo officers came to the homes of Jews who had received notices, told them to put their identification information on cardboard signs, and to wear the signs around their necks. Bettina thought about how humiliating that must have been for her mother. But she heard no more conversations about the barracks, so she began to worry less. Perhaps nothing would happen to her mother and the other Jews – maybe they would even be allowed to return home at some point.

•   •   •

Bettina woke up on November 20th to a pouring rain. She was grateful she could take a tram to work, unlike other Jews, who were forbidden from using the trams. She wondered how long she would benefit from being in a privileged marriage. And that made her think about her mother, and she wondered how her mother was doing. Most of her thoughts eventually returned to her mother. She had promised her mother she would wait to see her but had decided she would see her at the beginning of December. On her first day off next month, she would bundle up Gregor and the two of them would take the tram to see her mother. She wouldn't take Hans. He was working long hours at the munitions factory and would not want to use any free time he had to visit her mother. Besides, he would not want to risk anyone of importance seeing him among Jews.

Gregor was still asleep, and Hans had left early for work, so Bettina took advantage of the quiet and made herself some toast and coffee. She decided to let Gregor sleep and have Tante Helga feed him. Bettina finished the last of her coffee, then dressed quickly. She put on her coat, hat and gloves, and took one of the umbrellas from the umbrella stand. She called up to Tante Helga, who came down quickly. The tram stop was just a block from their apartment, and if she was lucky, the tram would be waiting when she arrived. And she was lucky!

Twenty minutes later, she was at the factory and ready to start the day. As she hung up her coat, she noticed a group of Jewish workers talking in the corner. Several were crying. She walked up near the group, pretending to read a notice on the board. The group was speaking loud enough that Bettina didn't have to strain to hear what they were saying. She knew one of the women talking, Bertha, who said, "The train has already left. They made them walk in the pouring rain to the station."

"My Tante Johanna! My Onkel Maier! Does anyone know where they're going?"

"No one knows for sure, but there's talk they're sending them to Riga in the Soviet Union."

"The Soviet Union! Why would they send them there?"

"I don't know. All I know is they want all of us gone, and the Jews at the barracks were the first to go."

The Jews at the barracks! Her mother! She needed to find out more. Even though they didn't know she was Jewish, she needed to ask them. But she needed to be calm, to only seem curious. So, she asked the woman she knew, "Bertha, is something wrong?"

"Yes, Frau Schnitzler, they just deported Jews from the Milbertshofen barracks, including some of my family."

"Were all the Jews deported?"

"I don't know. But we should all get back to work." Then they all dispersed. Bettina hoped it wasn't because she had spoken to them. But she stopped worrying about that and began to worry about her mother. She needed to find out about her mother. She knew going to the barracks now would be a bad idea, since she could be arrested. She decided to telephone her husband, and walked to the front office to make the call.

Hans was out on the assembly floor, but Bettina told his assistant that it was an emergency. She waited anxiously for about five minutes until Hans picked up the receiver.

"Bettina, is everything okay? My assistant told me it was an emergency. Is something wrong with Gregi."

"Gregi is fine. But something happened at the Milbertshofen barracks this morning. Some of the Jewish workers here said the Jews were put on trains this morning and deported."

Hans interrupted his wife. "Bettina, you cannot go there. It's not safe."

"Hans, I know that. But I need you to find out what happened to my mother."

"I know someone who can find out for me. But Bettina, you need to promise me you won't go to the barracks."

"I promise. But Hans, hurry. I'm just sick with worry."

"Bettina, it may take a little time. You need to get back to work and try not to worry. I'll be home for dinner and hopefully will have news by then."

"Hans, please call me here if you find out anything."

"Bettina, I don't want to put you at risk at work. I'll let you know what I find out when I get home." Then he hung up.

Bettina knew Hans was probably right, that Frau Brettschneider would not want Bettina to take personal calls at work. Even if it involved her mother. Frau Brettschneider had been nice to Bettina, but she was still using forced laborers, and Bettina was still a Jew. So Bettina grabbed her clipboard and began her workday. *Perhaps the work will distract me*, she thought to herself as she began to inspect the hats for shipment.

She had been able to put aside her worries about her mother until she left the factory. But as she approached the door of her apartment, her anxiety returned. She realized she hugged her son a little too hard when he cried out, "Mama, you're hurting me."

"Sorry, my dear boy. I guess I'm just so happy to see you. Come and help Mama make dinner. Let's say goodbye to Tante Helga."

Bettina took out the chicken from the refrigerator to make the schnitzel, while Gregor prattled on about going to the playground with Tante Helga. When he tired of talking, he went into the other room to play with his trucks. Just as she placed the chicken in the oven, Bettina heard the door open. She walked into the living room to hear the news.

Hans gave his son a hug, and Gregor then showed him one of his trucks. He looked at Bettina and said, "Gregi, I'm going to speak with Mama first, then you can show me the rest of your trucks, okay?"

"Yes, Papa, but come right back."

Hans took Bettina's hand and walked her into the dining room. They both sat down. Bettina looked at her husband and said, "Tell me."

"Your mother was on the list of Jews scheduled to be deported today. My friend said everyone on the list was on the train this morning. He didn't know where they were going, although he thought it might be Riga. Bettina, I'm so sorry."

Bettina stared off into space. Gustav had written to Bettina when the first deportation of Jews in Frankfurt occurred in October. When she spoke about this with her mother, Henny reminded her that Munich was the birthplace of the Nazi Party, and said, "I am surprised it didn't happen here first." Then her mother said, "Bettina, whatever happens to me, I want you to do everything you can to protect yourself and my grandson and if

there is a way for you to leave Germany, I want you both to leave."
She said nothing about Hans.

As Bettina was getting ready for bed that night, she went into
Gregor's room. He was sound asleep and hugging his white bear,
the one her mother gave him. He slept with it every night. She sat
down on the bed next to her son and thought about what had
happened to her mother. She was devastated by the news. But, in
truth, she knew it was coming. Maybe sooner than she had hoped,
but she knew, once she received that letter from Gustav, that her
mother would be deported at some point. She hoped it would be
different in Munich, that her mother would simply remain at the
barracks and not be deported. But the move to the barracks had
simply delayed the inevitable. Not all the Jews had been taken to
the barracks, and she wondered if her mother's involvement with
the Jewish Community had made her a target because the Nazis
knew everything the Jews were doing. Not surprisingly, having
Hans as a son-in-law made no difference. Still, Bettina had to
believe she would see her again. That it was good she hadn't given
her mother the pills she had asked for. But she also knew she had
to keep her son and herself safe. And maybe her mother was right.
Maybe she needed to think about trying to leave Germany.

Frankfurt
December 1941

Gustav moved the last of the luggage to the living room. His mother
had said that each could only take what they could carry. Gustav
packed warm sweaters, lots of socks and underwear, and a few nice
scarves, just in case he went out to the theater. He hoped Jews were
still permitted to attend the theater in Brussels. When he saw his
brother packing only a single suitcase earlier in the day, Gustav had
asked him why he was only packing the one suitcase, and his
brother had said, "I need the other hand to carry my violin." Gustav
knew not to challenge his brother. Instead, he remembered seeing

an old rucksack in Gretel's hall closet, and he stuffed more of his brother's clothing into the rucksack.

Five suitcases, one rucksack, and one violin. They would leave the apartment after dinner, when it was dark. Gustav joined his brother at the dining room table. His mother was helping Gretel's mother put the food on the table. This was the last meal the families would have together, and Gretel's mother used much of the family's rations to make it special. Goose with apple stuffing, spätzle, and a strudel for dessert. During the last month, the three had always remained inside. Fortunately, no one came to the door. Gretel's parents were also being careful, but never made Gustav or his family feel like a burden. Gustav had always liked them, but he formed a special bond with them this last month. He knew he would miss them and he knew he would really miss Gretel.

As best as they could, the two families enjoyed this last meal. After the ladies washed the dishes, everyone sat down in the living room. Gretel's father was the first to speak.

"Gretel, are you sure you know all the roads you need to take?"

"Yes, Papa. We've been through this twice already."

"I know, but I just want to make sure."

"Don't worry. I'll be back tomorrow."

Gretel's mother asked, "Paula, do you have everything you need? And enough money?"

"Yes, Erna. I have everything I need. Because the directive from the Gestapo ordered that I withdraw RM 50 for each of us to pay for our deportation, I have the money to pay the farmer who will lead us across the border. You and Herman have been so generous. I don't know how I will ever be able to repay you for what you've done for us."

"Paula, this is what we do for family," Gretel's father said. "The next time we see each other, it will be at the children's wedding." At that, Paula began to cry, and Gretel hugged her, as a daughter-in-law would.

• • •

The drive to Aachen was long and tedious, taking nearly eight hours. Paula and Alfred slept in the back seat, but Gustav remained awake to make sure Gretel stayed awake. As the sun was rising, the car pulled up to the farmhouse. The farmer who was to help them escape came out of the house quickly and instructed Gretel to drive to the back of the house. He then pointed to the barn and told them to enter through a side door. Once inside, Gustav could see three small cots against the wall and a small table with three chairs. He told Gretel to sleep while he and his mother spoke to the farmer.

Gustav shook the farmer's hand and said, "Herr Schmidt, good to see you again. This is my mother, Frau Zeydel."

Herr Schmidt shook Paula's hand and said, "Welcome to my farm. I am happy to help you and your family cross the border. There is food in the barn. I see there are four of you, but I can only take three across the border. And someone needs to take care of the car."

"Herr Schmidt, you are only taking three of us. The woman who was driving will be driving the car back to Frankfurt."

"Okay. She'll need to leave by the early afternoon. We're leaving when it gets dark. I have arranged for a friend to drive us to a place near the border. But we'll need to walk through the forest on foot. Get some rest because we'll be walking through the night. Before dawn, we need to get to the farm where we'll be staying for the day."

Gustav returned to the barn, opened the door, and saw Gretel asleep in one of the beds. The room was dark, but he could see a loaf of bread and cheese on the table. He cut a slice of bread and broke off a hunk of cheese and ate quickly. He then walked to the bed next to Gretel and fell into a deep sleep.

He felt a gentle nudge on his shoulder and opened his eyes to see Gretel sitting next to him on the bed. Gustav pulled her down next to him and they hugged. He looked into her eyes and gave her a passionate kiss. As she pulled away, he could see tears welling up in her eyes.

Gustav said quietly, "Gretel, let's go outside so we don't wake my mother and Alfred." They climbed over Alfred, who was sleeping on the floor, and quietly opened the door. It was still light outside, but Gustav could tell the sun would be setting soon. He knew Gretel would need to leave in the next few minutes. The love of his life would soon be gone, and who knew when they would see each other again.

"Gretel, you need to leave now, before it gets dark. As soon as we get to Brussels, I'll write to you. I left behind a copy of the Goethe poem and I already taught you how to use the cousin's code. I know we will see each other soon, so this is not goodbye." Before Gretel could respond, Gustav kissed her. The kiss lasted as long as they were able to hold their breaths.

"Gretel, I love you more than I can say." He took a folded paper out of his pocket and handed it to Gretel.

She unfolded the paper and gasped. Looking up at Gustav, she said, "A butterfly! It's so beautiful!"

"I've told you about the myth of Pandora's box and what remained in the box after she first opened it. The butterfly of hope. I have hope that I will survive these dark times and that we will see each other again."

"Gustav, I have hope as well. I'll keep this butterfly with me always and think of how our life together will be every time I look at it. I love you more than I can say."

They kissed one last time. Then Gretel got into the car and drove back to Frankfurt.

•   •   •

At nine p.m., Herr Schmidt knocked on the door of the barn. Gustav, Paula, and Alfred were ready and walked out of the barn with their things. The four walked to the waiting car and got in. The driver said nothing, and the passengers were too nervous to talk. After thirty minutes, the car slowed and pulled over to the side of the road. Herr Schmidt told the family to take their things and walk toward the trees.

Standing among the trees, Herr Schmidt provided the family with instructions for the journey. "We will be walking through the night. The moon is full, so it will provide us with some light, but it also makes it easier for the German border guards to see us, so we need to be careful. We'll begin our journey in the woods, but at times we'll need to walk on the road. If we hear any cars while we're on the road, jump to the side of the road and hide. And if we hear anything while we're on the trails, just fall where you are and stay down until I tell you it's safe to get up. Once we reach the farm around sunrise, you can rest until the sun goes down, then we'll resume our journey. If all goes well, you will be in Brussels in two days. Let's get going."

The beginning of the trail was flat, and the moonlight made for an easy journey. But they soon found themselves climbing and Gustav could feel the bags becoming heavier. After an hour, they stopped for a rest, and Gustav was happy to sit. He could tell that his mother was struggling with her bags, and he switched her heavier bag for his lighter one. His mother did not resist.

After another hour of walking, they reached a road, and Herr Schmidt reminded them to be cautious. They were on the road only about ten minutes when they heard the sound of a car. Herr Schmidt pointed to a grove of trees, and the four rushed to the trees. Gustav hid behind one of the trees, but could still see the back of a police car as it passed. He had a momentary rush of adrenaline but took a deep breath, thankful they had not been seen. About a minute later, Herr Schmidt signaled for them to continue.

They arrived at the designated farmhouse just as the sun was rising. Herr Schmidt instructed them to remain in the woods, and he walked to the farmhouse door to make sure it was safe. Gustav understood that, while they were closer to the border, they were still in Germany. Herr Schmidt returned almost immediately and told them to follow him to the barn. As they opened the barn door, Gustav could see blankets arranged in the corner and food on a table. The barn was as cold as the outside, and the four ate their food under the blankets. Once Gustav finished his breakfast, he fell fast asleep.

His mother gently woke up Gustav. He had no idea what time it was, but he was starving. He walked to the outhouse to relieve himself. When he returned, Herr Schmidt told them they all needed to eat. There was no conversation as the four ate. Then Herr Schmidt said, "We still have a few hours before the sun sets. I would suggest you try to limit your activity. Once we leave, we will re-enter the forest. As we get closer to the border, the trail will also move closer to the road. The most dangerous part of our trip will be at the actual border, since a guard house will be approximately a kilometer from where we will be. At that point, we'll need to be as quiet as possible. Everyone understand?" Gustav, Alfred and Paula nodded their heads at the same time.

Gustav took a pad out of his suitcase and began to sketch. He looked up at his brother, who was practicing a piece of music with his fingers on an imaginary violin. His mother's eyes were closed, and Gustav was wondering what she was thinking. Maybe about the journey. Maybe about his stepfather. The three remained quiet the rest of the afternoon, saving their energy.

At eight p.m., Herr Schmidt told them it was time to leave. They grabbed their bags and followed him. Gustav took his brother's rucksack and put it on his back. His brother smiled in appreciation. As they entered the woods, everything became darker. While the moon was out again, the forest was thicker, and the trail was more overgrown. They soon began to climb, and Gustav hoped it wouldn't last long. Several times, Herr Schmidt stopped them, worried that he had heard something. But each time was a false alarm, and they continued their journey. The temperature was near freezing, and even with his several layers of warm clothing, Gustav started to shiver. He tried to ignore his discomfort and focus on the fact that they would soon be across the border.

As they were descending a hill, Herr Schmidt told them they were nearing the border and needed to be especially careful. They continued their walk in silence, and Gustav could see a road through the trees. They heard a car stop and then men talking. Herr Schmidt signaled for them to fall where they were standing. They were next to a small brook, and as Gustav dropped down, he slipped and fell into the brook. It was shallow, but his face hit the water. He lifted his face out of the water but dared not lift the rest of his body. His fall must have made a noise since he could hear shouting and then saw flashing lights. Hearing what they were saying, he could tell that they were border guards. He didn't dare move.

The first guard yelled, "Hello! Is someone there?"

The second guard said, "I thought I heard a noise over there. Flash the light there, near the water."

Gustav prayed, "Please don't flash the light by me." He could see the light to his left and then to his right. He was hoping his dark clothes would blend in with the rest of the rocks in the brook.

After what seemed like an eternity, the first guard said, "It was probably a deer. Let's get back to the barracks. I'm hungry."

Gustav could hear them walking away, but then one of the guards said, "Wait, let me flash the light one more time." Gustav held his breath as he saw the light again. This time, the light seemed to be shining right at him. Gustav continued to hold his breath. But then the light was gone, and he heard the guards walk away. Gustav finally breathed. He waited until Herr Schmidt said it was okay to stand. When he finally stood, he realized his clothes were wet. He looked over at his brother, who had also fallen in the brook. His mother was dirty, but had avoided the water.

Herr Schmidt said, "I know you're wet and dirty, but we need to leave now. If those guards talk to other guards about hearing things, they might come back. These two were young and may not know this is an area known for illegal crossings. I know you don't want to hear this, but we need to walk even faster. Let's go."

Herr Schmidt didn't wait for a response, but began to walk. The family picked up their things and followed him. Herr Schmidt stopped them two more times, but they saw no more guards that night. They crossed several streams, and Gustav noticed at some point that the bottoms of his pants were dripping wet, but he said nothing. He knew Herr Schmidt would not stop.

As the sun was rising, they could see a farmhouse. Herr Schmidt turned to the family and said, "Welcome to Belgium. You are safe."

Gustav exhaled and said, "Thank you, Herr Schmidt. You saved my family."

Gustav looked over at his mother and saw tears streaming down her cheeks. He could feel tears falling, as well. He put down his bags and took his mother's hand. She squeezed his hand and said, "We made it. We're not finished with our journey to safety, but at least we've escaped Germany!" Gustav smiled back at his mother. He knew they would never be truly safe until they were out of Europe, but this was a good day. He hugged his brother and his mother immediately joined the hug.

The owner of the farm came out to greet the family. He escorted them into the house and invited them to use two separate rooms to change. Gustav and Alfred walked into one of the rooms and saw a basin of warm water for them to clean themselves. They quickly changed into dry clothes. The farmer's wife served them a hot breakfast, then a taxicab arrived to take them to Brussels.

•　　•　　•

The drive to Brussels took about three hours, but Gustav could have stayed in the car for days. He was so tired he thought he could never take another step. He dozed a little but mostly looked out the window, enjoying the fact that he was out of Germany. Out of

Germany! He kept repeating it to himself. At some point, he turned to his mother and could see her smiling. He knew she was also enjoying the feeling of having escaped.

They had given the driver the address of Paula's cousin, Lina Rohr, on Boulevard de Waterloo. Lina and her husband Friedrich had owned a women's dress shop in Frankfurt, but moved to Belgium in 1936. He had always liked Tante Lina, who came from the same small village in Poland as his mother and left around the same time, just before the Great War. The cousin had married around the same time as Paula, but she and her husband had no children. Just before Belgium was invaded by Germany, Lina had offered her cousin a place to live. Paula had thanked her cousin but told her they were trying to emigrate to America. Paula had not communicated with her cousin in recent months and hoped they were still living at the same address. Paula told Gustav that she didn't dare risk telling her cousin about her family's plan to escape Germany.

As the driver navigated the streets of Brussels, Gustav thought about Gretel and that last kiss. He was already missing her, wondering if there would be any way for her to visit him in Brussels. As the car turned onto Boulevard de Waterloo, Gustav suddenly noticed the grandeur of the buildings. *This is a fancy neighborhood*, he thought to himself. As the car pulled up to Lina's building, Gustav could see that his mother's cousin must have brought money out of Germany. The building was elegant, with three stories. Looking at the building, he asked his mother how Tante Lina could live in such a fancy neighborhood. His mother just shrugged as she paid the driver.

Standing on the sidewalk, Paula looked at a piece of paper and said, "Lina and Fredrich live on the first floor. Why don't the two of you stay here with our things and I'll go up and see if they still live here." Paula didn't wait for an answer but immediately opened the door and left her sons to wait on the sidewalk. Their mother was gone for a few minutes, then Gustav could hear footsteps from inside the building. The door opened, and Paula stepped out first, followed by Lina. Lina ran over to Gustav and immediately hugged him, then hugged Alfred. "Gustav, Alfred, I am so happy to see you!" Gustav found himself smiling, so happy to see Tante Lina. She was one of the most cheerful persons he knew, and nothing had changed since her move to Brussels.

"Please, take your things and come up to our place. I telephoned Onkel Friedrich, and he should be here shortly." Gustav was relieved that Lina was so welcoming. He remembered hearing stories from his mother about growing up with Lina, about how Lina felt like a sister to her. That sisterly bond strengthened in their years together in Frankfurt and would continue in Brussels, Gustav thought to himself.

As Gustav stepped into the apartment, he nearly gasped as he looked around. He walked into the large and well-furnished living room and could see a modern kitchen and a separate dining room to the right. He couldn't tell how many bedrooms were in the apartment, but the living room was nearly as large as the one in Onkel Jacob's home in Strasbourg. What a difference from the place he had just lived in with his mother and brother in Frankfurt.

Lina told the family to follow her, and Gustav walked past what he assumed was Lina's bedroom – very large and well-lit – and continued down the hall until she stopped at a closed door. She opened it and he saw two beds. *This will do,* he thought to himself as he and Alfred carried their bags into the room. He took off his coat and draped it over a chair and placed his hat on its seat. Lina reappeared at the door and told them to follow her. As they approached the dining room, Gustav saw a large radio in the living room. He hadn't listened to a radio since the family was required to turn over theirs to the Nazi government in 1939.

"Tante Lina, can I turn on the radio?"

"Of course you can, Gustav. And you can listen to anything you want."

Gustav turned on the radio, and as soon as it warmed up, classical music filled the room. He turned the dial and found a station playing swing music. He had not heard swing music in so long! Even before they had to turn in their radio, the Nazi government was discouraging radio stations from playing swing music. Gustav closed his eyes and began to sway to the music. He then heard his mother calling to him and walked to the table, smiling and singing along to "It Don't Mean a Thing If It Ain't Got That Swing."

After they all sat down, Fredrich came bursting through the door. In no time at all, he was embracing Paula and shaking hands warmly with her sons. As they spoke, Lina filled the table with bread, cheese, and nuts. She poured everyone coffee and sat down. She asked Paula to describe their journey, and they spoke for the next hour about how Paula and her sons had escaped from Germany.

When Paula was finished, Fredrich said, "Paula, that was quite a harrowing journey. I am so happy you and the boys are safe. Thank goodness David is in England, although German occupation means you still can't communicate with him. But I want to talk to you about some things you must do tomorrow. Rest today and don't worry about anything, but in the morning, you will need to register in two different places." Paula shuddered and he immediately said, "You don't need to worry about registering, Paula. This is not Germany. All the Jews in Belgium must enroll in the Jewish Register. And because you're a foreigner, you also need to register with the police department. Many Jews have crossed the border over the past few years and registered, and nothing has happened to them. Of course, since they closed the border in October, we have seen almost no Jews arriving in Brussels from Germany. So, you three are a bit unusual. But there's nothing to worry about."

Paula exhaled and said, "I'm sorry, it's just that registering in Germany meant they knew where the Jews lived, which made it easier for them to issue the deportation notices. I just don't want to go through that again."

Fredrich waited a moment and said, "Paula, I can't promise you that you won't be served a deportation notice at some point. I can just tell you that, so far, we're safe. And that is really the best we can hope for now. There is one other thing. Jews in Belgium no longer receive ration coupons, but that's not as dire as it sounds. We can purchase fake ration coupons from several underground organizations, and plenty of food is available on the black market, as you can see from our table."

Paula smiled. "Thank goodness for the black market! Lina, Fredrich, I can't tell you how grateful we are that you are so welcoming to us. I was able to leave with a little money and I would like to pay you something for taking care of us."

Lina snorted and said to her cousin, "Paula, put away that money. You are family and your money is no good here. But I could use your help in shopping for your family for dinner. When you're ready, let me know and we can go to the store. Plus, it will give us a chance to catch up, and we don't want to bore the men."

As Fredrich poured himself another cup of coffee, he said, "There's one more thing you should know, although I think it may be good news. While you were crossing the border, the Japanese bombed an American naval base in Hawaii, and the Americans are now in the war, on the side of the Allies. Hopefully, that will mean a quicker end to the war." Everyone nodded their heads.

An hour later, his mother and cousin left the apartment, and Fredrich excused himself to return to his shop. He had explained that he had found work with a local tailor and suggested that Paula and Gustav might also find some work with the tailor. Gustav knew he should join his brother for a nap, but he was too excited to sleep.

He needed to leave the apartment, and so he put on his hat and coat and walked down the stairs and out the door.

The weather was typical of a December day at home, but the sun made the walk pleasant. Boulevard de Waterloo was a wide street with generous sidewalks. The buildings suggested old money. Some newer restaurants and tea rooms were sprinkled among the buildings, along with a few modern cinemas. Gustav marveled that Lina and Friedrich could afford to live in such a fancy neighborhood. Gustav was feeling a sense of freedom he had not felt for a long time, and he was loving the feeling. He just wished he could share this moment with Gretel.

CHAPTER 12

Frankfurt
June 1942

Gertrud was enjoying the quiet in bed. Her mother was working the early shift at the bakery, and Karl was working the early shift at the munitions factory. No one was home, and the baby was still asleep. This was the first time Heidi had slept through the night. She was three months old but had been having trouble sleeping. At least at night. She was having no troubling sleeping during the day. Gertrud decided to stay in bed until the baby stirred.

Gertrud was thinking about the two letters she had received during the last week, one from Trudi in France and one from Gustav in Brussels. When her mother first saw letters arriving from abroad, Gertrud said she had friends from school now living in France and in Belgium. Her mother didn't ask for details. Gertrud didn't know if her mother believed her or not, but Gertrud was happy she didn't ask again. And Gertrud was so happy to hear from her cousins.

It seemed to Gertrud that Trudi was adjusting to her life in Villeurbanne. Trudi didn't mention her daughter in any of her recent letters, but Gertrud knew her cousin and knew that Trudi was likely struggling with the loss. But also knowing her cousin, Trudi was likely struggling in silence, trying to stay strong for the family. The Vichy government still controlled the Lyon region, which Trudi said made it easier for her family, although Jews were now required to wear the Jewish star on their outer clothing. From previous letters, Gertrud knew the family had obtained forged documents – just in case they needed to leave quickly – and wondered how often they now used the forged documents to avoid wearing the star.

Gertrud was more concerned about Gustav and his family. When she received his first letter from Brussels in January, she was so relieved. She knew the deportation of Jews had started last October, but she couldn't contact Gustav at the time in a way that wouldn't put them both at risk. She worried when she heard about the second deportation in November. When she received his letter letting her know the family was safe in Brussels, she cried. Fortunately, she was the only one home. The next letter spoke of their move from a spacious apartment to a much smaller apartment in the Jewish quarter of Brussels and their efforts to find work. He didn't say it directly, but Gertrud knew her cousin was worried about how they would live without work.

In a letter from Gustav in April, he told her that Alfred had been forced to leave school because he was Jewish, then spoke about the jobs he and Alfred were able to find at a small hotel. Gustav's Onkel Fredrich had lost his job as a tailor because he was Jewish, but his boss had a friend who owned a hotel and was willing to hire Jews, and so he hired Gustav and Alfred; he said Fredrich was too old. They were not making much, but they were making enough to survive.

Gertrud heard her daughter making gurgling noises. She got out of bed and walked over to the bassinet. Her baby looked at her and started to cry.

"There, there, my little Heidi. Mama is here. I'm sure you're hungry. You slept so long. What a good baby!" Gertrud lifted her daughter, placed her on the changing table, and changed her diaper. She then brought the baby back to bed and started to breastfeed her. Gertrud knew the Nazis were encouraging women to breastfeed their babies, but she was happy to do it. She loved the connection she felt with this baby, this little miracle.

After the stillborn birth of her son, Gertrud was worried about getting pregnant, going through that nightmare again. But Franz was insistent they have a baby and she gave in. She became pregnant almost immediately and worried through her entire pregnancy about the health of the baby. But when she finally went into labor, everything turned out fine. Her husband was away at war, but her mother was there to help and actually had been a great support. Gertrud brought the baby home after two days. Since that time, Gertrud was mostly home with the baby, feeding her, bathing her, and changing her.

Because the two had slept so well, Gertrud decided to take the baby for a long walk around the city. The weather was warm, but not too warm, and she could see from the window the sun was shining. "Okay, my little spätz, are you ready for a nice walk? Mama is certainly ready for one."

Gertrud bundled up the baby, put on her own sweater and a hat, and walked down the two flights of stairs. Her mother had left the pram on the side of the outside door. After placing the baby in the pram, Gertrud thought about where they would go. To the left would take her to the zoo, and to the right would take her to the Main River. She decided the zoo would be a better walk, so she turned to the left.

The morning sun was warming the air, but it was still cool enough to enjoy her walk, and Gertrud decided to take the long way to the zoo, going up streets she had not been on in years. As she was walking, she heard Heidi fussing and thought she had probably overdressed the baby, just like her mother had overdressed her when she was young. She took off one of the sweaters, and the baby stopped fussing and drifted off to sleep.

Gertrud was walking on the Zeil, the main shopping street of Frankfurt, window shopping and humming a tune she had recently heard on the radio when she heard what sounded like her name.

But her old name. The name she hadn't used in years. Heidi had just fallen asleep, and she didn't want to stop walking. Besides, who would be calling her by her old name? She must have been hearing things, and so she continued on. Then she heard the name again, this time louder – "Gertrud Heppenheimer!" Her instincts told her to keep walking and not turn around. She could hear the woman getting closer and then the woman was in front of her, requiring her to stop the pram.

The woman glared at Gertrud. "Didn't you hear me calling you? It's Frau Müller. And I know it's you. I would know that face anywhere. You look exactly like you did when you were a child. And you look just like your father, the socialist Jew. Don't pretend it isn't you." Gertrud remembered this woman, mostly remembering that her father said that she hated Jews. She needed to get away from her, and fast. She walked around the woman, replying, "I don't know who you are."

"You certainly do. I used to give you candies all the time when you were little. I saw you with your father and now you have a baby, polluting our German blood. Trying to hide who you really are! Are you also trying to hide your father? I'm going to find a police officer and then everyone will know you are a Jew."

At that moment, the baby woke up and started to wail. Gertrud wanted to hug her daughter at that moment, to thank her for crying. Instead, she turned to the woman and said, "Look what you've done! You just woke up my daughter! Now go away and leave us alone." Gertrud didn't wait for a response but dashed down the Zeil, then turned onto a side street. But before she turned, she could hear the woman yell, "I will find you, Gertrud Heppenheimer! And then you will be sent east with the rest of the vermin!"

Gertrud didn't slow down until she reached the zoo. She turned around to make certain the woman hadn't followed her. How could that woman still recognize her? What if a policeman had been nearby? And what if they believed this woman? Gertrud would be deported, her mother would be sent to a concentration camp, and what would happen to her baby? Gertrud found a bench and sat down. The baby was back asleep, and Gertrud waited until her heart stopped racing. She thought, *At least the Zeil is far enough from my apartment. I'll just have to avoid that street. And the zoo.*

Munich
September 1942

"Mama, I think these carrots need to come out of the ground." Before Bettina could tell Gregor to leave the carrots alone, he had already pulled out a bunch and was walking over to the basket. She started to laugh. "Gregi, I think we have enough carrots for tonight's dinner. Why don't you hold these carrots, and we can take them to Tante Helga. She would love that you picked carrots just for her."

"Yes, Mama. Tante Helga loves carrots. We can pick some more."

"No, Gregi. We have plenty of carrots. We can pick more vegetables tomorrow. Let's take everything inside and you can help me start dinner." Bettina picked up the basket of cabbages, beets, onions and carrots and began walking to the front of the building, with Gregor following behind her. They climbed the stairs to Tante Helga's apartment and knocked on the door. She opened the door, and Gregor immediately handed her the carrots.

"Gregi, did you pick those carrots for me?"

"Yes, I did. And Mama picked some other stuff."

"Gregi, thank you so much. All of these vegetables will make my stew especially delicious. We can have it for lunch tomorrow while your mama is working." Gregor smiled, then ran down the stairs to their apartment.

Bettina smiled. "I guess Gregi is ready to help me make dinner. I hope he behaved himself today."

"He was perfect, as always. And I hope work wasn't too hard for you?"

"Work was fine. Busy, but Frau Brettschneider is very good to me." Her last comment was mostly true, but Bettina made sure that Tante Helga never thought her good friend was anything but wonderful to Bettina. Tante Helga didn't need to know about the snide comments about Jews (knowing that Bettina was Jewish), nor did she need to know that Bettina could barely take time for lunch. And lately, Bettina needed to substitute for some of the workers who had been deported, so that she was now required to work with the dangerous boiling water used to shape the hats. Still, it was worth it. Her forced labor position was in Munich, and she was able to live at home with her son. She gave Tante Helga a quick hug and went downstairs to join her son.

Dinner was going to be a quick stew. Their rations still allowed for some meat, but not as much as earlier in the war. Thankfully, the garden in the back helped to supplement what she could find at the market. Hans would be home from work in an hour, which was plenty of time for the stew to cook. He was not demanding in terms of meals and often complemented Bettina on the simple things she cooked. Once the stew was on the stove, Bettina sat down in a chair to read the paper with Gregor playing with a truck at her feet. She must have fallen asleep since the next thing she heard was Gregor yelling, "Papa! Papa!" She opened her eyes and saw her husband lifting her son and giving him a hug.

He then looked down at her and laughed. "That must have been a very boring article." She smiled, stood up, gave him a kiss, and walked into the kitchen to check on dinner. She could hear Hans and Gregor go into the bedroom so that Hans could change, and Gregor could watch.

This was their routine most days. She brought Gregor up to Tante Helga in the morning or Tante Helga came down, Bettina took the tram to the hat factory, then came home and made dinner. Hans was usually home for dinner. But on the evenings he had to work late or went to one of his mysterious dinners, Bettina usually had bread and jam (when she was able to find jam). Or just bread.

As she stirred the stew, Bettina could hear Hans and Gregor giggling. She was happy Hans enjoyed playing with their son. Gregor would insist they sit on the floor and move the trucks along the edge of the rug. She knew Hans was tired, and probably enjoyed sitting on the floor, resting from his day at work. As they played, she set the table, then brought out the stew and bread. She called her family to the table, and they sat down to eat. Hans asked Gregor to tell him about his day, and Gregor spent the rest of dinner going into great detail about everything he did with Tante Helga. He was four years old and would soon be ready for school. Bettina was happy that, for now, he enjoyed being with Tante Helga and that Tante Helga took such good care of her son.

After dinner, Bettina took the plates into the kitchen and began washing up. This time of the evening, when Hans was reading and Gregor was playing, was the hardest for Bettina. Because this was when she most often thought about her mother. She had heard nothing about what had happened to her mother since she was deported last November. There had been rumors that the train had been diverted to Kaunas in Lithuania and that everyone had been shot. She found this hard to accept and so chose not to believe the rumor. Hans had tried to find out what had happened, but he could learn nothing. Or, at least, that's what he told her. So, Bettina decided to remain hopeful and assume that her mother was living some place in the east. Still, she missed her. And she missed her mother seeing her son grow. He was so smart, and she would have loved seeing how handsome he had become. She could feel a tear rolling down her cheek and shook her head to stop herself from crying.

After she finished the last of the dishes, she wiped her hands, took off her apron, and went into the living room. Hans was asleep in the chair and Gregor was asleep on the floor. She picked up her son and put him to bed. Then she came back into the living room, took her husband's hand, and walked him into the bedroom. They were all in bed before nine p.m.

A loud bang woke up Bettina. Then she heard a second bang, which woke her husband. A third bang woke up her son, and he began to cry. Then they heard the air raid siren. Bettina said, "I'll dress quickly while you dress Gregi. Then you can dress, and we'll go to the shelter." Her husband nodded. They were out the door in five minutes. Once they left the building, they could see neighbors hurrying to the shelter. It was only a few blocks away, but Bettina felt like it was taking forever. She could hear bombs exploding as they walked quickly. At some point, Hans picked up Gregor, who was lagging behind.

They soon arrived at the four-story concrete and windowless structure. Bettina had never been in one of the towers before. It felt like she was walking into a mausoleum. They were built last year and were supposed to be as safe as underground bunkers. Bettina wasn't so sure, but they had no choice. She took Hans' hand and the two of them walked with Gregor to a bench against one of the walls on the first floor. They sat down as the bunker began to fill with people. There were stairs leading to other floors, and people were climbing them. There was a lot of animated talking and what seemed like high levels of anxiety. At some point, it occurred to Bettina that she had no idea what time it was. She asked Hans, and he didn't know. He forgot his watch.

After about two hours, the "all clear" signal was given and everyone could return to their homes. As they were leaving the shelter, Bettina looked toward the old town and saw fire and smoke.

Gregor was sleeping in Hans' arms when they opened the door to the apartment, and Hans put him in his bed and returned to the living room. Bettina looked at the clock and saw it was two a.m. She worried about whether either of them would be able to go back to sleep, so she made them both coffee. Hans was already sitting at the dining room table when she brought them two steaming cups. After she handed a cup to him, he said, "So I guess it has started.

The Allies will be bombing our cities. Just like we bombed London during the Blitzkrieg."

"Do you really think that's true?"

"I don't really know. Maybe my uncle will know more. Did you see him or Tante Helga? I forgot to check on them."

"No, I forgot as well. I was so worried about Gregi and just wanted to make sure he was safe. Maybe I should go up now." Just then, there was a knock at the door. Hans' aunt and uncle were standing at the threshold. Bettina moved to Tante Helga and hugged her. "I am so glad the two of you are safe. We were in such a rush to get Gregi to safety that we forgot to check on the two of you."

Tante Helga said, "And I wanted to check and make sure Gregi is all right."

"Gregi's fine. He's already back asleep."

Hans' uncle grunted and said, "You see, I told you he was fine. Now let's go back to sleep." He immediately walked up the stairs. Tante Helga smiled at Bettina, squeezed her arm, and followed her husband.

Hans closed the door and said, "Bettina, maybe we should also try to get some sleep." Bettina nodded and turned the lights off in the kitchen and dining room. She joined her husband, but doubted she would get any sleep. And she was right.

In the morning, Bettina hurried off to work. The morning tram was unusually crowded, beyond just the normal workers. It was filled with people who seemed curious about the damage the bombing had caused. She wanted to tell them to go home, that this was not a tourist attraction. But she understood people were probably worried, knowing the war had come to Germany. There had been minor attacks which had caused minimal damage, but this was different. This was the first time the air raid sirens had sounded.

Bettina had to push her way through the crowd to exit the tram once it reached her stop. She looked around and saw no evidence of damage. She walked further and still saw nothing. Then she turned a corner and saw the destruction – huge craters and buildings on fire. The fire department was working to put out the flames. She couldn't look anymore. She turned around and walked to the factory. At least her factory wasn't damaged by the bombs. But what about next time?

Brussels
September 1942

Gustav was sitting at the small table, eating the last of his breakfast. He looked at his watch. Seven a.m. He yelled to his brother, "Alfred, we have five minutes before we need to leave. I'll slice some bread and bring it with us." No response, but he knew his brother had heard him. He drank the last of his ersatz coffee and put the cup and plate in the sink. He would do the dishes after work.

While his mother was living with them, he wouldn't dream of leaving the dishes in the sink all day. But there was no reason to do them now. They would stay where they were until he and Alfred returned from work. Whenever that was. Because foreign Jews were not permitted to hold jobs, their boss often took advantage of them, forcing one or both to work through the night. But he always paid them and often allowed them to take the food that could not be served to guests or the leftover scraps. In fact, their breakfast this morning included a very bruised apple he took home the previous day.

He could hear his brother in the bedroom, and he yelled again. This time, his brother appeared and grabbed the two slices of bread on the table, and said, "I liked you better when you didn't care about being late." Both put on their coats and hats and left the apartment. They raced down the four flights of stairs and bounded out the door. The hotel was a three-kilometer walk, and they had about thirty minutes to get there. As Alfred ate, he turned to his brother and said, "I was thinking this morning how nice it would be if we were still living in Tante Lina's apartment. The place was so large, and she always had such delicious meals. If we were still living there, I would have had pancakes this morning."

"It was a nice contrast from our last place in Frankfurt."

"Then they made us move to the Jewish quarter to an apartment even smaller than the one in Frankfurt. And with holes in the mattresses."

"Well, Alfred, we didn't have a choice. When the Jewish Community office tells you to move, you move."

"I can't believe they even made Tante Lina and Onkel Friedrich move. Their current place is even smaller than ours."

"Mama warned us they would do to Jews in Brussels what they did to Jews in Frankfurt, moving us into places where it would be easier to deport us. I told Mama at the time that she was overreacting, that the Jewish Community was just trying to better manage the limited housing. I was wrong and Mama was right."

"Gustav, there's nothing you could have done about it. Even if we took her concerns seriously, where would we have gone?"

"We could have gone underground, but then we wouldn't have a place to live. So, I guess we are stuck here. I'm just worried about Mama."

"For now, she's safe. It was a good idea having her move in with Tante Lina once she received the notice. The police know she's no longer living with us, and they don't know where she is. Gustav, it's good that you answered the door when they came last week. I don't know what I would have said. You really are a good liar."

"Well, I've had years of practice."

•   •   •

Work was hard and long that day and the owner didn't let them leave until nearly seven. The eight o'clock curfew meant they had to hurry in order to spend a little time with their mother. Fortunately, Tante Lina's apartment was just a few blocks from their own. They brought a stale loaf of bread and some moldy cheese, but Gustav knew his mother would be grateful for the food. They arrived at 7:30, which gave them about twenty minutes to spend with her.

Their mother answered the door and showed her boys into the small living room. Tante Lina and Onkel Friedrich were already sitting on the one couch, and the boys pulled up chairs from the dining table. Their mother started the conversation by asking about work. Alfred immediately said, "Work was very hard today, Mama. Monsieur Jacques worked us harder than normal. My finger started to hurt again, and he wouldn't even let me rest it."

"Liebling, let me look at your finger." Paula took her son's hand and examined the finger. Then she said, "It does look a little swollen. When you get home, soak it. The doctor told you it was good to use it so it wouldn't stiffen up, but that you still need to let it heal."

Alfred shook his head and said, "I try, but I still need to do what the boss says. He's always saying we're lucky that he's risking his neck to give us work. All he's doing is taking advantage of us."

Gustav didn't want to listen to his brother complain. He heard enough of this at work. Alfred had cut his finger at work earlier in the year, and the finger had become infected. It took some time to find a doctor and the damage from the infection likely meant he could no longer play his violin, at least not professionally. Gustav felt sympathy for his brother, but he still wanted some time with his mother and so spoke up. "Mama, they've stopped coming to the apartment looking for you. Perhaps in a week or two, you might be able to come back home."

"Gustav, I would love that more than anything. Let's see how things are in a few weeks. Tante Lina has heard from neighbors that they're still sending out those ridiculous letters ordering us to report to the Dossin Barracks, that a great job awaits us. Such lies. We shouldn't have registered when we arrived here. They did it just so they could easily deport us. Maybe when they get enough Jews to fill a train, they will stop looking for me. For now, I need to

stay here. As long as Tante Lina and Onkel Friedrich will have me."
She smiled at the two of them.

"Okay, Mama. So far, you've been right about how to avoid
arrest. But, unfortunately, it's nearly eight and we need to leave."
Gustav got up from the chair and hugged his mother and Tante Lina
and shook hands with Onkel Friedrich. Gustav and Alfred then
raced down the stairs and ran to their apartment building. They
reached the building with sixty seconds to spare.

• • •

Gustav slept badly that night and woke with a headache. He got out
of bed, careful not to wake his brother, and walked into the small
kitchen to heat up some water. He didn't like the ersatz coffee, but
he liked the routine of a hot drink in the morning. His headache was
making him a little nauseous, but he knew he needed to eat
something and so sliced himself some bread. Gustav heard a bit of
commotion in the street below and took his cup of coffee to the
window. He could see people in the street and could hear a little
yelling. He still had an hour before they needed to leave for work
and thought it would be prudent to see what the commotion was
about.

As he left the building, he saw a man he knew from the
neighborhood, a fellow German Jew. He walked up to him and said,
"Herr Frank, there seems to be a lot of noise so early in the
morning. Did something happen?"

"Did something happen? I should say something happened! The
Gestapo came in the early morning hours, went into a few
buildings, and took out every Jewish family. Someone said the
Brussels police had refused to follow the German orders to arrest
Jews, so they did it themselves."

Gustav could feel blood leave his face. "They arrested Jews?"

"Apparently, few Jews responded to the directive that Jews report to the Dossin Barracks. Like anyone would believe great jobs are waiting for us. So, the Gestapo lost patience."

Gustav didn't need to ask anything more. He needed to find his mother. He said a quick goodbye and ran to her building. As he reached the building, he saw a large truck pull away. Several of the people in the street were crying. He ran to the door, raced up the four flights of stairs and stood before an opened door, Tante Lina's door. He went inside, but he already knew that no one was there. As he left the apartment, he could see all the doors in the building were open. Everyone had been taken!

He walked outside and sat down on the front stoop to catch his breath. He thought he was going to faint, and an old woman came up to him and asked if he was okay.

"My mama was taken."

"Oh, dear, I'm so sorry. They came about an hour ago and took every family out of this building and the one next door. They knew where to look since every family in these two buildings had registered. My cousin's family was in the second building. They took them all away. When I heard what was happening, I came right over, but they had already been taken. I didn't even get to say goodbye."

"My mama warned me they were moving us all together so it would be easier to deport us and now they've taken her away." Gustav began to cry. He couldn't remember the last time he had cried, and now he was crying in front of a total stranger. Only she wasn't really a stranger. She was a Jew, just like him, who had lost family, just like him. She sat down next to him on the stoop and handed him a handkerchief she had in her pocket. "If you have a place to stay outside of our neighborhood for a few days, I would go there. I'm going to stay with a cousin who lives just outside of Brussels. Stay safe." And with that, she left Gustav on the stoop.

Gustav stood up and began walking back to his apartment. When he got inside, his brother was standing at the window, eating. He asked Gustav, "What's happening outside?"

Gustav walked up to his brother and hugged him and said, "Alfred, they've taken Mama. And Tante Lina and Onkel Friedrich. They took everyone in their building."

Alfred pushed himself away from his brother. "What do you mean? We just saw her last night!" Alfred began to cry, and Gustav handed him the handkerchief he had been given by the old woman.

Gustav and Alfred began to pack enough clothes for a week. When Alfred finished packing, he looked at his older brother and asked, "Gustav, do you regret registering with the Brussels police every six months? Maybe we should go underground."

Gustav stopped packing, took a deep breath, and said, "Let's think about it. It may make sense, at some point."

They knew their boss would be fine with them staying in the back room of the kitchen for a few days, since it would mean they could work longer hours. He would also want them safe, but mostly because he liked the cheap labor. They both took their identification cards, but Gustav told his brother to take off the Jewish star. He had worn it every time he went out, ever since they were required beginning in June. But he would not give the Gestapo the advantage, not anymore. If they wanted to know he was a Jew, they would have to stop him and look at his identification card. They had no money for false identification cards, so he had to hope they would not be stopped.

CHAPTER 13

Villeurbanne
January 1943
Trudi walked downstairs and into the dining room, hoping to have a quiet moment before her daughter woke from her afternoon nap. Her father was at the table, drinking some ersatz coffee and reading the paper. Trudi looked at her father and frowned. He was hunched over, and his face was paler than normal. Her mother had told her the day before that the doctor was worried about his diabetes. He had always been healthy in Strasbourg, but the last three years had been hard on his health, and he had developed diabetes last year.

"Anything new in the paper, Papa?"

"Nothing new. At least, nothing true. Every article is about how wonderful the Germans are. It was bad enough when the Vichy government was in power. Now that the Germans have taken control of the Free Zone, the paper is nothing but Nazi propaganda."

"Then why read the paper, Papa? Maybe a good book instead."

"Even the propaganda contains kernels of truth. And I hear that things have been going well for the Allies in North Africa. I need to believe that the Allies will win this war. The world will be lost if the Nazis win."

Trudi could see that reading the paper was doing her father no good, so she lifted it out of his hands and moved it to the kitchen.

She returned with the coffeepot and another coffee cup and poured each of them some.

"Thanks for the coffee. Where is your husband? I was napping on the couch and woke up to find no one on the first floor. I know your mother went to see a sick friend down the block."

"We heard potatoes and bread would be available this afternoon, so Joseph volunteered to stand in line. Since Jews can now only shop between four and five p.m., he thought he would get in line early. With the Gestapo in charge and new deportations having been ordered, he worries that Mama and I would not be careful enough to avoid being stopped."

"They said they are only arresting foreign Jews and both you and Mama were born in France. So, Joseph is actually more at risk as a foreign Jew."

"Joseph took both his real identification card and his forged card. He should be fine." But Trudi worried. They needed food, and they could only purchase food with the French identification card, the one with "Jew" prominently stamped on the front. Joseph had already been stopped once since the Germans took charge in November 1942, and the forged card fooled the Gestapo officer. But Joseph, who spoke French with a slight German accent, wasn't sure how much longer it would work, and neither was Trudi. She always breathed a sigh of relief when he returned home.

At that moment, Trudi remembered the letters she received in the morning, one from Gustav and one from Gertrud. This would be a good distraction for Papa, she thought, as she pulled them out of the pocket of her housedress. "Papa, I forgot to tell you I have two letters to share with you. In code, of course!"

Her father laughed. "When you first told me about the code, I thought it was just youthful nonsense, using a Goethe poem to send secret messages. But it's the only way we can get real information from the family, and still keep them – and us – safe."

She had already read both letters and knew there was nothing troubling in either letter. Not like Gustav's last letter when he told her that his mother had been arrested. Gustav had not heard from her since. "Let's start with Gustav's letter. Remember I told you that Gustav and his brother were staying at the hotel where they were working, worried they would be arrested if they went back to their neighborhood. Well, apparently, the arrests have stopped, and Gustav felt it was safe enough to return to his apartment. They were relieved that nothing had been taken, including Alfred's violin. Which was important, since it was their last thing of value, and Alfred agreed to sell it. But poor Alfred is heartbroken. But otherwise, they seem to be okay."

"Gustav said all of that in a coded letter?"

Trudi smiled and said, "Papa, the code works! He also said they no longer have to wear their Jewish stars, which he had already stopped wearing, and this has made it easier to walk around without being stopped. Can you imagine not having to wear these silly stars?"

"That would be nice. And what about my niece?"

"Gertrud is fine, and little Heidi is doing well. She is crawling all over the apartment and sleeping through the night. Gertrud still worries about her father, but has no way of contacting him. She's not sure where her husband is but doesn't seem to be worried about him."

"It's good to know that both Gustav and Gertrud are safe. I thought our family would be safe in Strasbourg and then would be safe here. And now the Nazis control all of France. Maybe I should have tried to emigrate to America."

"Papa, stop. No one could have known we wouldn't be safe here."

"I should have known." Jacob shook his head and grew quiet. Trudi was trying to think of a reassuring thing to say when the door opened and Joseph walked in. She looked up at her husband and knew something was wrong from the expression on his face. "What is it?"

"They just arrested people, right in front of me as I was waiting in line. The Gestapo came up to several couples and demanded to see their identification cards. I walked backwards out of the line and darted into an alley and hid. But I could still see the Gestapo shoving people into a truck. I waited until they left and came straight home." Trudi grabbed Joseph and hugged him hard. She could feel his heart beating fast and thought she would hold him until his heart slowed. But he pushed back from his wife and said, "I never got the groceries!"

"It doesn't matter. You're staying here. I'm going down the street to get Mama, then we are staying in for the rest of the day, just in case the Gestapo is still roaming the streets. We have enough food for today, thanks to Monsieur Peltier. I don't know what we would do without your farmer friend, Papa. The ration cards are never enough for us anyway, but the milk, jams and cheese we got last week will be enough for us for the next few days. So, no need for you to go back to the line, right Papa?"

"Right. No one is going anywhere."

•　　•　　•

The next day, Trudi told her family she would be the one to wait in line for food. She put on her coat with the Jewish star but took both of her identification cards, the real one and the forged one. She could always take off her coat if she needed to. Familiar faces were already in line when she arrived, and she found herself behind a woman she knew from her neighborhood. Madame Klein seemed to know everything going on, and Trudi thought it was fortuitous that she would find herself in line with this woman.

"Good afternoon, Madame Klein. I hope you are well."

"Good afternoon, Madame Reich. I am as good as I can be, given the times we live in."

"It's good to hear you're doing well. But I agree these are scary times. My husband came home yesterday after seeing several families being arrested. Did you hear about the arrests?"

"Yes, what a horrible day yesterday was! I heard they arrested Jews all over town. Before the Gestapo took control, they mostly left us alone. But now that the Nazis are in charge, I guess things are changing. Nothing so far has happened today, or at least that's what I've heard. Maybe they just wanted to scare us a little. But we need to eat, so here I am today, in line for food."

"Yes, we need to eat. But thank you for the information."

"I'm happy to help. We need to look out for each other, since who else will? Am I right?"

"Yes, Madame Klein, you're right."

Trudi looked around and saw more people she knew lining up for food. She took that as a good sign. Or maybe it was just desperation – for food or for information. But the one thing she knew was things had changed for the Jews in Villeurbanne. They may have felt safe – or relatively safe – when the Vichy government was in charge. But now that the Germans were in control, things were changing, and not for the better. She knew her Cousin Gustav was constantly worried about being arrested and deported. She had been worried about her father or Joseph being picked up as foreign Jews, since the Vichy government had already revoked the citizenship of Jews born outside of France, but arrests were not common. But now, all of them were vulnerable. She knew, from now on, they needed to be careful. And she now thought, probably for the first time, that maybe they needed to escape France.

Munich
March 1943

A knock came at the door, and Gregor answered it. He knew Tante Helga was coming to watch him this evening, and he was excited to have his Tante all to himself. Bettina smiled as she heard her son chattering with his Tante about all the things they would do that evening. At that moment, she was thankful she had Tante Helga. But then she thought about her mother and worried about where she was. She had to remain hopeful she would eventually see her mother again.

Bettina decided to wear her blue dress, one of the few dresses she had from her life in Frankfurt. The dress had a beaded bodice, and it showed off her still-trim figure. She could no longer get a permanent for her hair, but the curlers she put in her hair the previous night gave her the wave she wanted, and looking in the mirror, she liked what she saw. Maybe not as fancy as Trudi but more than presentable. She could almost pretend this was just any night out with her husband, just one more anniversary to celebrate. As she slipped into her dress, the Beethoven symphony on the radio ended and German military music began. Bettina hated military music and moved the dial. She heard Hitler speeches, then German folk music, more military music, and finally landing on a Mozart opera. She thought about how Gustav would have hated such limited choices.

When Hans had suggested they go out to a restaurant to celebrate their tenth anniversary, she told him he was crazy. How could they go out to dinner to celebrate in the middle of a war? But Hans had said, "That is exactly why we need to go out. We can use our ration coupons for the meal and have a nice time." Bettina knew the dinner was important to Hans. She felt a bit guilty about going out to a restaurant when others were struggling for enough to eat, but she agreed to the dinner.

Then she thought about the Jews left in Munich. Like her, the only Jews left were Jews in privileged marriages – those who were married to non-Jews. And she knew she had been lucky. She hadn't been forced to leave her home and live in a horrible labor camp in wretched conditions with meager rations. So far, she could live in her own apartment, and they had enough to eat. And because Tante Helga had taught her how to can vegetables, their backyard garden provided them with additional help over the winter months.

Bettina heard the door open and Gregor squeal with delight. Hans was home. He needed to change his suit, but she knew he would want to leave soon. He was always hungry when he came home from work, and a hungry Hans was generally a cranky Hans. She walked over to him, gave him a kiss, and said, "Happy Anniversary, darling. I'm ready to go whenever you are."

"Happy Anniversary to you. I'll change and we can leave." About ten minutes later, they were out the door of the building. He said nothing about her dress or hair, and she was a little disappointed, but said nothing. They were going to a restaurant in their neighborhood. When they opened the door to the restaurant, the owner came over and greeted them warmly. Hans must have said something to him since he said, "Happy Anniversary, Herr and Frau Schnitzler. It is nice to see you again after such a long time and on such a wonderful occasion. I have a quiet table in the back for you. Please follow me."

When Bettina first moved to Munich, she and Hans were frequent patrons of the restaurant. Unlike many restaurants, this restaurant never posted a sign forbidding Jews from dining in the establishment when Jews were still permitted in restaurants. And while Jews could no longer dine in restaurants, Hans thought they were safe because Bettina was in a privileged marriage. Bettina wasn't so sure, but she agreed because Hans really wanted to dine out. She also wondered if the owner was putting them in the back of the restaurant to avoid any problems.

As they sat down, a waiter came over. He was fairly old, maybe sixty-five, but Bettina understood the younger waiters were now fighting in the war. He didn't have any menus, instead speaking even before Bettina had a chance to put her napkin in her lap. "Good evening, Herr and Frau. My name is Alfred, and I will be serving you this evening. As you can imagine, we serve what is available, and this evening, we have rabbit with spätzle and carrots. We also have a very nice potato soup to start. I hope that is to your liking?"

"Alfred, that sounds perfect. We would also like some white wine, whatever you have. Here are our ration coupons. Please take what is necessary."

"Very good, mein Herr. I will bring the wine right away."

Bettina smiled at her husband. "Lucky you, Hans. Rabbit. Your favorite!"

"And you hate rabbit."

"That's okay. I'll eat all of your spätzle, which I love and you hate, and you can eat all of my rabbit."

"This date keeps getting better and better." They both laughed. Hans then took her hand and said, "Bettina, thanks for agreeing to come out to a restaurant with me. I know you were a little nervous, but we're fine and not in any danger."

"I'm sorry. I can't help but worry. I guess I'm just getting more worried about everything. I worry about how safe I am and what might happen to you or Gregi. The German government is not deporting privileged Jews now, but will that change? And how safe will our son be then? Every time there's a knock at the door, every time I see the Gestapo walk down the street, I worry. Sometimes I think they can see right through me, that they know I'm a Jew. Even with my blue eyes, they still know."

"Bettina, how many times do I need to tell you that you are safe, that our son is safe? You'll see - Germany will win the war and you'll be fine."

Bettina smiled at her husband and squeezed his hand. But in recent weeks, Bettina started to doubt Germany's ability to win the war. After years of non-stop propaganda about the superiority of Germany, Bettina was surprised by a speech last month on the radio given by Joseph Goebbels, the German Propaganda Minister. During the speech, Goebbels actually admitted that Germany lost the Battle of Stalingrad. Bettina had never heard any Nazi admit to anything but victory. He then said that losing to the Jewish Bolsheviks was not an option and that Germany needed to increase its war efforts.

But Bettina was also troubled by another part of the speech, something that made her blood turn to ice. Goebbels said that Germany intended to take the most radical measures against the Reich's Jews. Hearing those words, Bettina understood that Germany winning the war would be the worst thing for her and her son, if they were to survive the war. But she knew she couldn't say anything to Hans. Maybe it was working in a munitions factory or going to those dinners with his uncle, but Hans believed in the German cause. He knew she was worried about her mother but believed that all would work out in the end. In fact, that was the phrase he kept repeating – "Bettina, you'll see, it will all work out in the end." Maybe it was his need to believe it, his need to think that moving his family to Munich was the right thing, the thing that would keep them safe. She didn't blame Hans for her mother's deportation. The same thing would have happened had they remained in Frankfurt. And her mother had refused to consider leaving Germany without Bettina. But she was worried that he had a blind spot when it came to her "privileged marriage" status. He believed the Nazi government when they said that his wife and child would be safe. But she decided not to think about this, to enjoy this night out instead.

"Hans, I can't believe how busy we are at the factory. I understand why you're so busy. Germany needs munitions. But hats? We can't make hats fast enough."

"It is a little crazy, but I am happy you're busy. That means they can't send you someplace else."

"I agree. But of all the things for the German government to promote, women's hats? We're in the middle of a war, but the government wants women to stay fashionable. But, of course, not too fashionable. And not too showy. A simple hat, but with some feathers and bows. When I'm at work, I sometimes forget there's a war on. It doesn't seem to make much sense, with families struggling to find enough food. But women still want their hats, the government wants us to make hats, and so we make hats."

"Well, you're doing a good job. The hat you wore tonight is nice."

Bettina giggled. "It was one of our rejects. But I added a nice bow, and you can't really tell."

"And no one at work has ever suspected that you're Jewish?"

"Maybe at times when I first started to work there. But now that almost all the Jews in Munich are gone, I think my fellow workers assume that I'm like them. I imagine there are others from privileged marriages who are also working there, but none of us share our status, so I wouldn't know. Which is just as well. I don't want anyone to know anything about me, and I don't want to know anything about them. My fellow workers just think I'm shy or unfriendly. But I don't care. They leave me alone, I get my work done, and I get to come back to my apartment."

"And home to me." Hans kissed his wife's hand. He then took out a small box from his pocket. "Bettina, we don't have much money and there's not much to buy, but I found this in a jewelry store and thought you would like it." He then handed the box to his wife.

Bettina opened the box and saw a lovely locket on a gold chain. She could see it had been owned by someone else –the back of the locket had a few scratches. She took it out of the box and put it on. It felt heavy on her neck, and she wondered if it was really that heavy or if she was imagining the weight of its past owner. Was that owner a Jew, someone who had been deported, like her mother? It never would have occurred to Hans to wonder about the previous owner. But Bettina couldn't help herself. And she knew. She also knew she would never wear the locket again.

•   •   •

Bettina was sound asleep when she became aware of someone shaking her. She had had little alcohol over the last few years, but she and Hans had finished the bottle of wine during their anniversary dinner. She had trouble opening her eyes, but soon became aware that the building was shaking. Hans was yelling, "Bettina, wake up! We need to get to the air raid shelter. Now! I'll get Gregi." Bettina quickly got out of bed, put on her housedress, and then her socks and shoes. She left the bedroom and saw Hans putting on Gregor's jacket. She put on her own coat and hat, and the three left the building and hurried to the shelter. The street was filled with people, and Bettina and Hans had a hard time getting into the shelter. When they were finally inside, they found an empty bench in the back and Bettina took the blanket she had grabbed before she left and wrapped it around the three of them.

"Hans, what time is it?"

He looked at his watch, which he had remembered to take. "It's just after one in the morning. It has been months since the last bombing, but this one seems different. Louder and bigger. Just wait here. I am going to walk around to see what other people know."

Gregor fell back asleep almost immediately, and Bettina was dozing when Hans returned. "No one knows much, but everyone seems to agree they're hitting us harder. I don't think we're getting out of here anytime soon. I think you have the right idea. Let's try to get some sleep." Almost as soon as he sat down, Hans was asleep, but now Bettina was wide awake. She stayed on the bench for as long as she could, then got up and walked around the shelter. Bettina heard much talk around her, mostly in whispers. She could hear someone crying, but couldn't tell if it was coming from a child or an adult. But she could also feel fear. She never thought fear could have a physical presence, but it was here, all around her. It felt as if it could swallow her up, so she quickly returned to her family. Bettina felt safer with them. At some point, she must have fallen asleep because she could feel the gentle shaking of her husband.

"Bettina, they have sounded the 'all clear.' I'm surprised it didn't wake you." Still groggy, Bettina grabbed the blanket, stood up, and took Gregor's hand. All she wanted to do was get out of the shelter and get home. She thought they still might get a few hours of sleep before work. But as she stepped outside, she could see it was already light outside. It hadn't occurred to her it would be morning. Hans must have seen her face and knew what she was thinking since he said to her, "It's seven a.m. Time for breakfast."

Bettina looked toward the town center and saw plumes of black smoke and fire in multiple places. She looked at Hans, who was seeing the same thing. Then she felt Hans' hand in hers. He said, "Bettina, let's go home. We'll find out what's happened later."

Frankfurt
June 1943

Gertrud loved her daughter, but there were times when she would have gladly traded her in for a good night's sleep. Heidi had been sleeping badly all week and was now crying non-stop. Her mother said that she was teething and that it would end as soon as the first tooth came in. So far, nothing was working to soothe the ache, and Gertrud thought she was going to lose her mind. Plus, she was hungry. She felt like she was hungry all the time, but she knew it was mostly because she hated all the imitation food and drink – imitation meat, imitation eggs, imitation coffee. She especially hated the imitation coffee. Whose idea was it to take barley, oats, chicory and acorns, add hot water, and call it coffee? That was not coffee! Maybe drinking this muck was making her cranky. Maybe a good walk around the neighborhood would do her some good.

Since she ran into that scary Frau Müller, the woman who threatened to turn her in, she had been avoiding the zoo. But a walk down to the Main River might be just the thing she and Heidi needed. She struggled to dress her screaming child, but once they were outside, Heidi stopped crying. The morning was still cool, although Gertrud could tell it was going to be a warm day. She was glad she decided to walk before it got too hot. She was also glad she checked the mailbox before she left, since a letter from Bettina was waiting for her. What fun to sit by the Main River and decipher the code. Although, like every time she received a letter from a cousin, she worried the letter might bring bad news. But it couldn't be too bad if the letter was actually sent.

Gertrud walked to a park along the river. Since Heidi was still asleep, Gertrud sat down on an empty bench and took out the letter. Gertrud had always been good at puzzles and could now decipher the letter without the poem.

Her cousin wrote that the family was safe. Gertrud let out a sigh of relief and returned to the letter. Bettina started with that good news, but then the letter got dark. Bettina and her family had been spending a lot of time in the shelter, as the Allies had been pummeling Munich. She wrote that night had become day since the bombs were dropped at night and lit up the sky. So far, neither Bettina's nor Hans' factory had been hit, but they had bombed many of the rail lines, so it had been harder to find food. Electricity had been out more than it had been on. The gasworks were damaged, so the gas stove no longer worked. There were also no more coal shipments, so they would need wood for the stove once the weather turned cold. Since the water mains had also been bombed, water was now being delivered by truck. The air was constantly filled with dust and there was always a smell of burning. People were leaving, but Hans thought it was better to stay. Bettina was not one to complain, so Gertrud assumed her cousin's life was harder than she described in the letter.

Gertrud put the letter down, looked out over the water, and sighed. A few bombings had occurred in the inner city of Frankfurt, but nothing major. Certainly, nothing to compare with Munich. There were food rations, but so far, they seemed to have plenty to eat, even if much of it was imitation. They weren't experiencing food shortages like her cousin Bettina. Gertrud felt fortunate to be living in Frankfurt and away from the worst of the war. She did worry about Franz, but so far, her husband had avoided any dangerous assignments. He couldn't tell her what he was doing, but wrote it was something that didn't put him in direct danger. But she hadn't seen him in a few months and missed him.

The biggest challenge Gertrud had was having to listen to Karl, her stepfather, rant on about the war. Through 1942, Germany had been doing well against the Allied forces, at least according to Karl. But it sounded like the Allies were doing better in the Pacific, and Karl seemed a little concerned about the Allies' decision to begin bombing German cities. Still, Karl always ended his lectures to Gertrud the same way - no one can defeat the German military.

Gertrud looked away from the water and saw two Gestapo officers in the distance. She saw one of them looking at a piece of paper and pointing at her. They started to walk towards her, and she immediately put away Bettina's letter. Why had one of the officers pointed at her? And why were they walking towards her? Gertrud wondered whether that horrible Frau Müller had actually alerted the Gestapo about her, and they were now looking for a woman hiding her Jewish identity. But there was nothing she could do now. As they continued to approach, she told herself to remain calm. They soon stopped in front of the pram, and one of the officers looked inside the pram, then looked at Gertrud. He said, "Papers, please."

Gertrud opened her bag and retrieved her identification card, hoping the officers couldn't see the letter in the bag. She handed her card to the officer, who looked at it carefully, then back at her. He looked in the pram again, then under the pram. Finally, he handed the card back to Gertrud and said, "Sorry to bother you. We've heard the resistance has been operating in the park, hiding contraband in baby carriages. But I can see you only have a baby in the carriage, and a beautiful Aryan baby at that." Gertrud was so relieved that all she could say was, "Thank you."

As the officers walked away, she could hear one say to the other, "At least that baby doesn't look like my sister's baby. If I didn't know better, I would swear the father was a Jew." They both laughed.

Every time Gertrud saw a Gestapo officer, her heart quickened a little, and this time was no different. But she had her identification papers identifying herself as an Aryan, and her blond-haired child did look like the perfect Aryan baby. She had nothing to worry about. At least, that's what she told herself. Except that Frau Müller was still out there somewhere and had promised to find her. Gertrud got up and walked back to her apartment. As she approached her building, she thought about the letter from Bettina and wondered how long before Frankfurt would become a target for the Allies. *Which will happen first?*, she wondered. *Will I be discovered by the Gestapo or will I be bombed by the Allies?*

Brussels
October 1943

It was Alfred's night to cook dinner. They were able to buy some very fatty meat on the black market, which Alfred turned into a tolerable stew. Their mother had taught her sons how to cook when they first came to Brussels, but neither was very skilled at it. Mostly, each made a stew in which they tossed in whatever they were able to purchase or whatever they were able to take from the hotel. As Alfred carried dinner to the table, he could see Gustav reading and asked, "Another letter? Who is this one from?"

"This one is from Gertrud. They had avoided much of the Allies' bombing, but the city was just hit with a bombing raid and over 500 people were killed. The East End of the city was badly damaged, but Gertrud's apartment building was not hit. I heard from Bettina that bombing has continued non-stop in Munich. I worry about them both, but I have to confess I'm cheering on the Allies to keep bombing these cities until Germany surrenders. Just don't hurt the cousins."

"And when do you think Germany will surrender? Hopefully, soon. I really hate this food."

"Alfred, let's try to be positive. The Allies will soon win, and we are about to eat a delicious dinner."

"Agreed. Let's sit down and enjoy our feast. Oh, I forgot to ask, did Monsieur Jacques tell you to come in early tomorrow? He said a large family was coming and all the rooms will be in use."

"He said nothing to me, but I'll go in with you. These days, I don't want us to be separated."

Since his brother cooked, Gustav washed the dishes, then told his brother to bring him his work clothes. They each had a single white shirt and a single pair of black pants, and replacement of either garment would come out of their pay. So, every few days, Gustav the tailor repaired their clothes. So far, they only had to replace a single shirt. After Gustav was finished with the repairs, he looked up and saw that his brother was fast asleep. He shook him awake and each of them walked down the hall to brush their teeth and were asleep almost as soon as their heads hit the pillows.

• • •

Alfred needed to be at work by eight a.m., so Gustav woke at 6:30 and made them both breakfast, which consisted of stale bread and some jam they took from the hotel. But it was filling, and it was fast. After breakfast, they got dressed quickly and were out of the building by 7:15. The walk to work would take them about thirty minutes, but they added extra time, just in case. The sidewalk was relatively empty this time of morning, particularly since this was the Jewish part of Brussels. Few Jews had jobs or any other reason to be out this early.

As they moved up the main street, Gustav noticed a man walking towards them. At the same time, he saw a truck driving towards them very slowly. Two German officers were walking behind the man. The man lifted his arm and pointed at Gustav. Gustav noticed an alley to his left, turned to his brother, and said, "Run down the alley. Now!" At the same time, Gustav ran in the opposite direction, across the street. Both officers followed Gustav, which was what he had hoped. He continued to run down the street, but one of the officers caught up to him and threw him down to the ground. Gustav could feel his lip bleeding, but stayed on the ground and didn't move until the officer told him to get up, and then he got off the ground slowly.

"Papers." Gustav handed the officer his identification card, with "Jew" prominently displayed. The officer grinned and looked over at the man who had pointed to Gustav. He was an older man with a beard and glasses. The officer said, "Right again. Another Jew. I don't think you've been wrong once since you've started working for us."

The other officer said, "Maybe Jews have radar. One Jew can always spot another Jew." Then the officers grabbed each of Gustav's arms and shoved him into the back of the truck.

Five people were already in the truck. As it picked up speed, Gustav was thrown to the floor. He sat up and touched his lip, which had stopped bleeding but was beginning to swell. He looked up at the others in the truck and asked no one in particular, "Do you know where they are taking us?"

One of the men said, "Probably to hell."

Gustav didn't respond, but a minute later, one of the other men moved next to Gustav and said, "I can hear your German accent. I am also German, and it is a relief to speak German. I heard yesterday they had started arresting Jews again and were taking them to the Dossin Barracks. I assume that's where we're going. By the way, my name is Julius."

Gustav nodded and said, "And I'm Gustav. My mother was arrested last year, and I heard she was taken to the Dossin Barracks. I haven't been able to find out anything about what happened to her – whether she is still there or whether they have moved her somewhere else."

"What I just told you is all I know. I'm sorry about your mother. I'm the first in my family to be taken. My wife will be so worried about me. I hope she leaves our apartment and goes into hiding. It's what we talked about, in case one of us was taken."

"My brother and I had the same conversation. I told him to run when I was being taken this morning. I hope he made it out of the neighborhood."

Just the previous night, Gustav asked his brother, "You know what you need to do if I'm ever taken?"

"I know, I know. We've gone through this a million times."

"Well, let's go through this a million and one times."

"Fine. If you're ever taken, you have four postcards already filled out, and I need to mail them – to the cousins and to Gretel. I'm to pack up all my things and never go back to the apartment again. Did I get that right?"

"Yes, you got that right. I don't know why I worry, but I do." But he worried now. *Alfred*, he said to himself, *I hope you did as I asked.*

Gustav then thought about how he rushed his brother to get out of the apartment, so he wouldn't be late for work. The old Gustav was always late. Why couldn't he have been like the old Gustav this morning!

They had been traveling about an hour when the truck stopped, and the back door opened. A German officer yelled to get out of the truck, and they immediately complied. As Gustav's eyes adjusted to the bright light, he saw a large U-shaped building with a center courtyard and barbed wire fencing all around the perimeter of the camp. The officer ordered them to follow him. They walked through a door into the building and the officer sat behind a desk. He told the group to form a line in front of the desk. Gustav needed to go to the bathroom and was also getting hungry, but was reluctant to say anything. His lip hurt and he was worried any requests would result in further punishment.

Gustav was first in line. The officer told him to turn in his identification card. The officer then asked what his occupation was. When Gustav told him, he said, "You will work in the clothing workshop, beginning tomorrow." He then handed Gustav a piece of paper to sign. Gustav looked at the paper, which authorized the Gestapo to take possession of all items in his apartment. *I really hope Alfred did not return home*, he said to himself as he signed the paper. The officer then filled out a card with a string attached and handed it to Gustav. He said, "On the card is your number and transport– you are number 214 and the transport is 23. Wear this card around your neck at all times. Never take it off except when you're showering or sleeping. If you are found without the card, there will be severe consequences."

When the six of them were registered, the officer stood and walked the group to a room where another guard handed each a striped prison uniform, a blanket, a bowl and a spoon. A woman officer took the two women with her, and Gustav and the other men were instructed to follow the officer.

They walked across the courtyard, and the officer opened a door. There were rows of bunk beds in the large room. The officer assigned each of the four men a bed and told them to put down their bowl and spoon on the bed. They were then told to change into the prison uniforms and to put their old clothes in the basket near the door.

After they changed, the officer took them to the latrine. Gustav was so relieved he almost started to cry. When they finished, the officer said, "You need to remain in the courtyard for the rest of the day. When the other prisoners are finished with work, they will join you for roll call, and then you will return to your bunk to retrieve your bowl and spoon for dinner. If you leave the courtyard, you will be shot." He then turned and walked away.

Gustav sat down on the ground next to Julius. Neither spoke for a minute, then Julius asked, "Gustav, where are you from?"

"Frankfurt. And you?"

"Berlin. We came to Brussels just before Germany invaded, although both my parents died soon after we arrived. When did you come?"

"At the end of 1941."

"At the end of 1941? How is that possible?"

"We paid someone to sneak us across the border. We had received a deportation notice and my mother said we would escape instead. We tried to cross the French border, but that proved impossible. So, we went across the Belgium border. We thought we would be safer here than in Germany."

"You were right about that. You made it until 1943."

"Yes, I guess my luck ran out. My brother and I had started to discuss going underground, but that never happened."

"And what about your father?"

"My father died in the Great War. We were supposed to emigrate to England, but only my stepfather made it out. I am hoping to find my mother. I'm assuming the women are being held in a different part of this place."

As it began to get dark, two doors opened at the far end of the courtyard, and men and women came out of the two buildings. Gustav looked around to see if he could see his mother. He was surprised to see only a few hundred people in the courtyard. He turned to Julius and said, "I was expecting to see thousands of prisoners here, but there are just a few hundred. And I don't see my mother among the women prisoners."

"I'm a little surprised, as well. Maybe we'll find out more from the other prisoners."

An SS officer told everyone to get into lines for roll call, based on their numbers. Then Gustav understood the significance of his number. A little over two hundred prisoners were in the Dossin Barracks – he was number 214. *Where are the other prisoners?* Gustav wondered to himself.

After the counting was done, the prisoners were instructed to retrieve their bowls and spoons and return to the courtyard. Gustav and Julius did as instructed, then quickly returned, only to see that a long line had already formed for food. When Gustav reached the front of the line, he put out his bowl and a ladle of soup was poured into it. He also took a roll, and he and Julius found a place to sit on the ground and ate. Gustav was so hungry that he was nearly finished with his soup before he realized it was tasteless and almost unrecognizable. Maybe there were pieces of meat. He could identify a potato. But he didn't care. He was just happy to eat. The roll was less offensive, and he finished it in three bites.

Gustav had just finished his roll when one of the German officers yelled for everyone to return to their barracks. *I guess we don't clean our bowls,* Gustav thought to himself. But he was anxious to speak to some of the other prisoners, and he and Julius walked quickly back to their barracks. As he walked through the door, Gustav could hear a lot of talking and the empty room of just a few hours ago was now nearly filled with other men. Gustav put his bowl and spoon down on his bed, and he and Julius joined a group of three men who were talking.

"Excuse me. We were brought here today. I am Gustav and this is Julius. Could we ask you a few questions?"

The most animated of the trio answered first. "I am Chaim, this is Lazer, and this is Joseph. How many of you were in your truck?"

Julius said, "There were six of us. Four men and two women."

Chaim shook his head. "Just six today. The last truck came three days ago and only had seven. It will take them a long time to fill up the train. Which is good for us." The other two men nodded their heads in agreement. Chaim turned to Gustav and Julius and said, "I can see the two of you are confused. Let me explain. I was arrested two weeks ago with ten others. When we arrived, Dossin Barracks was empty. No prisoners. As you can imagine, I was confused, but one of the officers - one of the Belgium officers since none of the German officers will talk to us - explained to me that all the prisoners had already been deported a few days earlier and they were starting again. He told me they would wait until they were able to fill the cars, which he said holds about a thousand. During the first week, trucks arrived nearly every day. But this week, only two trucks came and only brought twelve people. Let's hope it means they're having trouble finding Jews and that our deportation will be delayed."

Gustav was reluctant to ask the next question, worrying about the answer, but he took a breath and asked anyway. "Where did they take the prisoners? My mother was arrested almost a year ago, and I had heard that she was taken here."

"Somewhere east is all I was told. I'm sorry I don't know more." Chaim then turned back to the other men. Gustav and Julius walked around the barracks, but didn't speak to anyone else. At nine p.m., the lights were turned off, and everyone climbed into their beds.

Gustav's bed had a straw mattress that made noises when he moved. He wasn't looking forward to sleeping in this bed tonight with all of these strangers. He touched his lip. It was inflamed and sore. But it could have been worse. At the moment, all he wanted to do was sleep. He would think about everything that had happened to him tomorrow. So he closed his eyes and went right to sleep.

•   •   •

Gustav was startled awake by shouting. He opened his eyes and saw a man trying to leave the room. The door was locked, and he was banging for someone to open it up. People were yelling at him to be quiet, to go back to bed. But he wasn't listening to anyone. He just kept banging and yelling. At some point, the door opened, and an officer walked in and asked what the problem was. The man said he wanted to leave, that he wanted to go home. The officer grabbed him by the collar and dragged him out of the room. The door was then locked. The room became quiet, but Gustav was fully awake. He had no idea what time it was, but he knew he wasn't going back to sleep.

As he lay in bed, he thought about his arrest. As careful as he had been, he knew the dangers every time he stepped outside. He also knew the dangers of continuing to live in the Jewish quarter and to be registered. His thoughts drifted to his mother and how disappointed he was that she wasn't here. *But if she's not here, where is she?* And then he began to worry about her.

It was still dark when the lights came on in the room. They were told to go to the latrine across the courtyard, twenty at a time, taking their bowl and spoon, and then to line up for roll call. When Gustav returned to the courtyard, he noticed for the first time that it was cold, and he began to shiver. Someone said it was six a.m. They stood until seven, when breakfast was brought out. Gustav got into a line and was served what he believed was the same soup he had been served the day before. He ate quickly.

After breakfast, everyone took their bowls and spoons to their barracks and returned immediately to the courtyard. Gustav followed the men assigned to the clothing workshop. Julius had been assigned to the leather goods workshop.

The work in the clothing workshop was tedious, hand-sewing clothing. Gustav was given a needle and some thread and simple instructions. He spent the morning sewing. At noon, they stopped for a lunch of watery soup, then returned to their sewing. The work stopped at six p.m., and they returned to the courtyard for roll call, then dinner. Dinner was the same soup and roll as the previous night. Gustav assumed this was to be their daily meals.

After dinner, Gustav sat on his bed and spoke to Julius about conversations Julius had heard during the day about when the next transport would leave. Julius said, "It's like a ticking time bomb, counting down until a thousand Jews are in the camp. Sending us east cannot be a good thing. Maybe we need to find a way to get out of here."

Gustav was surprised. "And how would we do that? With barbed wired fences and guards with guns?"

"I heard from someone in the leather shop that one of the transports out of Dossin was stopped by partisans, and some of those on the train escaped. Since they're trying to gather a thousand of us for the next train, we have some time. We'll find a way."

Gustav looked at his new friend and smiled for the first time since he had been arrested by the German police. He liked that Julius had hope.

CHAPTER 14

Munich

January 1944

"Gregi, get away from that building! You need to stay by me!" Gregor reluctantly walked over to his mother. Bettina knew, from a six-year-old's perspective, this was like a giant playground. But too many children were getting hurt by the broken glass and exposed metal, and she didn't want to have to try to find a doctor. Or medicine, for that matter. "I know playing with your friends is fun, but you could get hurt. Once we're finished helping, you and I can go for a nice walk, okay?"

Gregor kicked a stone and said, "Okay, Mama."

"And you can help me now. Take the smaller broom and help me clear this mess." Gregor's face brightened at the prospect of pushing the broom. "Okay, Mama. You go first, and I'll follow you."

The previous night's bombing had been close to their apartment building and had left destruction for multiple blocks. Bettina had joined a group of neighborhood women who were helping to sweep up the rubble left behind following the bombings. There was little traffic in the streets, but it was still important to have the streets cleared of debris. And it was also important for Bettina to do something. Staying in her apartment all day, waiting for the bombs to fall, would drive her crazy. Besides, it was also cold in the apartment - and dark. While there were no more coal deliveries, Hans had located some coal for the stove, but they used it sparingly. And no electricity meant no lights. As cold as it was outside, it was worse inside.

Bettina hated the bombs, but she was more afraid of the fire. The Allies were now using firebombs to terrorize the city. More and more of her friends were leaving Munich, although some had returned, finding no food or shelter outside of the city. They might as well stay, Hans often said whenever she asked whether they should think about leaving.

And now he was leaving. He had been drafted into the army. They both knew this would happen after his munitions factory was bombed in October. Bettina also lost her job in November when her factory was destroyed. She had been waiting for a notice for a new forced labor position but, so far, had not been contacted. She wondered if Germany was simply running out of forced labor jobs given all the recent factory bombings, although she had heard rumors that some of those jobs were now held by slave laborers from the east. But she was happy to be home with her son, particularly now that Hans was about to leave.

"Mama, you need to go faster." Bettina realized she had stopped to stare towards the old town. The smoke was everywhere, and she could see fires raging. "Sorry, Gregi, I will work harder." She resumed her sweeping. After an hour, she could see that her son was tired, so they returned the brooms to the shed. She smiled at her son and said, "Let's go see if Tante Helga wants to take a walk with us. Then the three of us can have lunch with Papa."

Bettina knew that the bombing had been especially hard on her husband's aunt. Because all German men under sixty were now being drafted, Hans' uncle was in the army and his aunt was both frightened and lonely. As much as she could, Bettina included Tante Helga in her activities with Gregor. Certainly, a walk away from the neighborhood and to a park would be good for everyone.

As they reached their building, Gregor told his mother to wait outside, and he would get Tante Helga. She agreed, thinking how much he was becoming his own person. She watched neighbors walking in the street. Everyone seemed hunched over, seemingly feeling all the stresses of the past few months. One of her neighbors was carrying a water jug, and she remembered she needed to go this afternoon to refill their water bottles. Gregor soon opened the door, announcing, "Here we are, ready for our walk!" Both Bettina and Tante Helga laughed as they each took one of Gregor's hands and walked toward the park.

In past years, the park had been a favorite of Bettina's. It was wonderful to visit on a warm summer afternoon, sitting under one of the enormous trees. As they approached the park, each gasped. It had been a couple of weeks since Bettina had been to the park, and she knew Tante Helga hadn't been here since last fall. Nearly every tree was gone.

"What happened to all the trees? All the beautiful trees?"

"Tante Helga, when I came here with Gregor a few weeks ago, some of the trees were gone. But most were still standing. How could this happen in just a few short weeks?"

A woman standing near them heard their conversation and said, "Winter happened. With no coal or gas, the only thing we have left to heat our homes or cook our meals is wood." Bettina saw that the woman was carrying tree limbs. The woman continued, "If I were you, I would take what I could carry. That's what I'm doing. Pretty soon, all the trees will be completely gone." Then she walked away.

Gregor watched her go and turned to his mother and said, "Mama, let's go find some wood and take it home, too." Bettina could see that her son thought this was a new game. But he was right, and so was that woman. If she didn't take what was there, someone else would. She said to Gregor, "Darling, that is such a good idea. Let's try to get as much wood as we can. We don't have an ax, so we'll pick up whatever is on the ground. Tante Helga can sit on this bench and we'll bring the wood to her. Once we have enough, we'll carry it home." Tante Helga nodded her head, giving

Bettina the permission she might have needed to further destroy this beautiful park.

As they carried the wood home, some of their neighbors stared at them. But Bettina didn't care. At one time, she would have. At one time, she might even have yelled at anyone who had damaged the park. But not now, not today. The most important thing was to keep her family safe. She would do anything she had to do to make that happen.

As she entered the apartment, Hans stood up from the table and laughed. "It looks like the three of you were on an adventure."

"We were, Papa! We went to the park and all the trees were gone, but there were sticks everywhere and we picked them up to bring them home."

"I see that."

"We're going to use them in the stove to heat up the apartment and make our dinner. Isn't that great?"

"That's wonderful, son. You can help me heat up the stove when Mama is ready to make dinner. This way, you'll be a big help to Mama." With that last statement, Gregor beamed with pride. *He is really going to miss his father*, Bettina thought to herself.

As she walked into the kitchen, Bettina was thinking that she wasn't so sure that she would miss Hans. The last few months had been the hardest in their marriage. When they first married, they were living with her parents, and her father was sick. Most of the focus was on keeping the business going and keeping her father alive. Then the Nazis took power, her father died, they moved to Munich, her son was born, and her mother was deported. She had no time to think about anything other than keeping one foot in front of the other. When they were both working, they were both working long days and any free time was mostly spent with Gregor. But for the last few months, they were spending all their time together. She was happy that Gregor had more time with his father and he was a good father to Gregor, but she was having a hard time spending any time alone with him.

Bettina understood that the stress from the constant bombing, the lack of basic comforts, or the limited food could certainly influence how she felt about Hans. Still, she had noticed a change in him. When they first moved to Munich and she had expressed concern that eventually the German government would deport her, Hans had said that it would never happen, then added that he would never let that happen. Recently, after she shared her worries with Hans, he responded that the worst that would happen is they would send her to a nearby camp. He also began to rant about how the Allies had started the war, and it was up to Hitler to finish it. He was not a big supporter of Hitler when she first met him, or at least that was what he had said. But when she received the postcard from Gustav's brother about his arrest, Han's response was chilling—he said that he shouldn't have gone to Belgium in the first place. When a letter came last month from Trudi, she didn't tell Hans.

Maybe the war was changing him. Or maybe he had always been this way, and she had just missed the signs. But it didn't matter. He was leaving in a few days and would likely be gone for months. She thought she needed some separation from him. Maybe leaving would be good for him, to realize how much she meant to him and how he needed to protect her.

Gregor was crying and Bettina heard Hans say, "I bet you're hungry. Let's see if there's anything in the kitchen for you to eat. Then we can take the wood and light a fire for Mama so she can cook dinner for us." *Yes,* she said to herself, *I will make dinner. I will go out to the water truck when it comes. And I will think about other ways of keeping my son safe.*

Dossin Barracks, Belgium
January 1944

The lights turned on exactly at 5:30 a.m., and Gustav grabbed his blanket and left the barracks, waiting in line until it was his turn to use the toilet. He was getting into the rhythm of the place.

Bathroom. Watery soup. Work. Watery soup. Work. Watery soup with a roll. Boredom. Bed. The same thing every day. The drudgery was broken by periodic beatings of fellow prisoners, sometimes for no apparent reason. The only good thing was that the prisoners could receive occasional packages to help supplement their rations. Gustav was relieved to receive a package from the hotel where Gustav and Alfred had work, which meant Alfred was living there. In the package was food from the restaurant, which he shared with Julius, as well as a pencil and a small pad. Gustav drew in the pad until the pencil was worn to the nub. Julius also received a package of food from an unidentified person who Julius knew was his wife, and he shared the food with Gustav.

Over the past four months, prisoners continued to arrive, including some children, but the numbers remained below what the Germans wanted, at least from what Julius had heard in the leather workshop. Gustav was hoping the deportation would be delayed, but he continued to worry about his mother. Recently, Gustav had been thinking about the last day he and his mother had been together. He wondered how she was and whether he would ever see her again. Maybe when he was finally deported, he would see her again. And when he thought about his mother, he thought about Gretel. He really missed her. But he was worried that he was forgetting what she looked like, forgetting what she sounded like, forgetting what she felt like. They had written frequently before his arrest, but writing was not the same. It had been over two years since they had held each other. *What is she doing now?*, he wondered? He imagined she was still working at the hospital, perhaps helping wounded soldiers. The soldiers who wanted him dead. *Ah, this war is so complicated,* he thought.

As he stood in line for his breakfast, Julius came up beside him. "Did you hear? A train came in last night. Ten cars long – all cattle cars. The rumor is that we'll be deported tomorrow."

"Tomorrow? Where did you hear that?"

"Someone in the latrine. But, of course, it's just a rumor. But it is the first time we've seen a train."

"True. But I thought they were going to wait until there are a thousand of us. We can't be more than half that."

"I guess they couldn't wait. I'm still thinking about that thing you and I discussed. Remember?"

"I do." Gustav lowered his voice. "But a cattle car is almost impossible to get out of."

"Perhaps. But maybe it can be done."

"And how would you do it?"

"We'll talk this evening."

The camp was buzzing the entire day with rumors until the entire camp was ordered to report to the courtyard after dinner. One of the officers addressed the camp. "I am sure a number of you are aware that a train has arrived at our camp. We have decided to move all of you to a camp where you will have better facilities and better food. There will, of course, be work for you there. You will report to the courtyard after breakfast to board the trains. Go back to your barracks to prepare."

•   •   •

There was not much to do to prepare. Gustav had nothing that belonged to him other than his prison uniform, his bowl and spoon, and his blanket. Still, after the men in the barracks were told they would be on the first transport in months, they all sat together around the barracks' stove and began to talk. For Gustav, it was the first time he had spoken to a number of the men in his barracks. He was never very interested in making friends, expecting to be deported at any moment. Julius was his friend – he might even say his best friend – but even with Julius, he kept a bit of a distance. Why get close to someone who you would probably never see again? But that evening, until the lights went out, all the men in the barracks talked to each other – about where they came from, what they did, their wives or sweethearts. It almost seemed a little magical to Gustav, having this moment where it almost felt normal and where he could speak about Gretel.

After the lights went out, Gustav had trouble falling asleep. Even when he did drift off, it was a restless sleep. For the first time in a long time, he dreamt about Gretel. When he awoke, he found himself crying. He shook himself to stop the tears and waited in bed until the lights were turned on. He quickly got out of bed and was first in line for the bathroom. He sat next to Julius at breakfast, but both men were silent. The magic of the night before was gone, and they were only feeling the weight of the upcoming deportation. As they walked back to their barracks, Julius pulled Gustav aside and said quietly, "I have a metal bar from our workshop. It's stuffed in my sock. Once we're on the train, I'm going to cut a hole in the car and jump to freedom. And then I'll find my wife. Make sure you're in my car." He didn't wait for Gustav to respond, but instead walked to his bed to retrieve his blanket.

When they reported for roll call, they were joined by men from the other barracks, as well as the women and children. Then a large group of men, women, and children walked out of a door at the far back corner of the building and joined the rest in the courtyard. Gustav turned to Julius and asked, "Who are those people?"

Julius didn't respond, but another man near them said, "Those are the Roma and the Sinti, the ones the Nazis call Gypsies. They've been arriving over the past few weeks while we were working and were put in the basement. As bad as the Nazis have treated us, those people have been treated far worse."

Gustav said, "I guess that's how our total number reached a thousand."

After everyone was assembled, they were directed to march to the train cars and form two lines before the doors of each car. Gustav and Julius stayed together, getting into a line for one of the middle cars. As the lines were forming, Gestapo officers walked up and down the lines. At some point, they started to move people out of one line and into another. Gustav felt a hand on his arm and was suddenly pulled to a different line for a different car. He knew not to say anything, and he knew he couldn't leave the line. He was separated from Julius and his plan to escape. Gustav thought it was a crazy plan, destined to fail. But he liked the idea of a plan, any plan, and now he had no hope except the hope that this new camp would be better than the Dossin Barracks. As he walked to the door of his car, Gustav looked over to his friend and gave him a discrete wave. Julius shrugged and returned the wave.

As Gustav climbed the stairs of the car, he could see straw on the floor. The only light was coming from the cracks between the slats of the train's walls. People were already finding places to sit along the walls, and he quickly found a place for himself. Two large buckets sat in the corner - one contained water, and Gustav assumed the other would be used as a toilet. *So, they're not going to stop the train even for us to relieve ourselves,* he thought to himself. *What barbarians!* He bundled himself in his blanket and closed his eyes. He was always good at falling asleep in random places. He would try to do that here, in the worst place he had ever been.

●   ●   ●

For the next two days, the train moved, never stopping. About a hundred people were crammed into the car. The water bucket was empty by the end of the first day, and Gustav tried to ignore both his hunger and thirst by sketching in his mind. At times, the train sped along, while at other times, it crawled. Gustav knew the difference between day and night only through the spaces in the car walls. The floor was cold, and the car smelled from the bucket, which began to overflow on the second day. Gustav could hear people crying and sometimes banging on the walls. Mostly, Gustav could sense the terror all around him.

During the night following the second day of travelling, the train stopped. Gustav opened his eyes, and the door to the car soon opened. Someone yelled in German, "Jews, get out of the car. Now!" Gustav immediately stood up and walked to the doors. Others saw him and followed. The German yelled again, and this time, started to hit people with his baton. Gustav quickly left the car and stood on the wooden platform. The platform was so well lit, it was almost like day. SS officers stood all along the ramp, holding guns and yelling. Gustav looked around him as people were exiting the other cars, trying to find Julius. But there were too many people. He wondered if Julius had succeeded, if he had managed to cut a hole in the train. He hoped he had. He hoped Julius was on his way to finding his wife.

One of the officers yelled for everyone to begin moving and Gustav walked to the end of the platform, down some wooden stairs, and onto a road. They were all walking towards a group of officers. As Gustav passed one of the officers, he yelled for Gustav to join a line to the left. Gustav saw two lines ahead of him and moved to the left. The line to the right had mostly older men, as well as women and children. No women or children were in his line. He didn't understand the significance of either line. At the end of the road stood a number of trucks. He looked around – it looked like they were in the middle of a freight station. As he waited in the line, Gustav began to feel dizzy. He knew it was probably from hunger, so he took several deep breaths and the dizziness passed. After about an hour, one of the officers yelled for Gustav's line to follow him. As he began to walk, Gustav looked back at the second line and saw the people in the line walking towards the trucks. He envied those people.

Gustav wondered where he was. He knew he was far east of Belgium. It was colder, and he could see snow on the ground. Gustav was thirsty, and he reached down to grab some snow. An officer smacked his hand with a baton, and Gustav dropped the snow. He wrapped his blanket around himself but was still feeling the cold. Any person who lagged behind was hit with a baton, so Gustav just focused on walking forward.

They walked until they reached a line of trucks and an SS officer ordered them inside. Gustav pulled himself into one of the trucks and found a place to sit on the floor, and they rode for about ten minutes. When it stopped, they were told to quickly climb out, and when Gustav did so, he could see they were in some kind of camp, with many barracks and a barbed wire fence surrounding it. They were walked to a latrine and were told to go quickly. Then they were all walked into one of the larger buildings.

Once inside, Gustav was told to take off his clothing. He walked into a room, where he was sprayed with what he was told was a delousing powder, then directed to the showers in an adjoining room. Gustav stood under the cold shower and opened his mouth to drink the water, but the water was brackish and he immediately spit it out. When everyone was finished with the shower, they were directed into a large room where he saw men in striped uniforms holding scissors and razors. Gustav's hair was cut, and every part of him was shaved. Gustav asked the man who was shaving him where they were and why they were being shaved. The man answered quickly that they were being shaved to avoid a lice epidemic and that they were in a camp called Auschwitz III. "What is this camp? Are we to work here?" The man said nothing more.

Naked, Gustav was directed into another room where he received a set of prison clothing: blue and white-striped pants and jacket, a shirt, a pair of underpants, a cap and a pair of wooden shoes. Gustav put on the clothes and was told to stand in a line in front of a desk. When he reached the front of the line, he provided his name, date of birth and city of birth, and then was told to sit in a chair at a table where a man was waiting. The man held a needle and said, "I am going to tattoo a number on your arm. Do not cry out or the SS will beat you." He then tattooed the number "172331" on Gustav's left forearm. Gustav was then handed two pieces of cloth, each containing his number and a downward-pointing red triangle over a yellow triangle pointing up, forming a Jewish star. He was told by the man to sew one on the left breast of his jacket and the other on the right leg of his pants – to identify him by his number and by the fact that he was a political prisoner and a Jew.

Gustav gathered with others in the corner of the room. An SS officer then came up to the group and said, "Follow me. Anyone talking will regret it." He said it in German, but everyone seemed to understand and followed the officer. When they reached one of the barracks, he said, "Walk in slowly, and wait inside."

Once everyone was inside, a prisoner spoke. "This is Barracks 20. Remember that. My name is Aaron, and I am the bunk elder. That means I'm in charge of everyone in this barracks. I will let you know when it's time to wake up and when it's time to go to sleep. In the morning, you will be assigned to a Kommando, which will be your work detail. As long as you work hard and follow the rules, we will get along fine. You missed dinner, but you will be given a piece of bread and coffee in the morning. Mendel is my assistant, and he will assign each of you to a bunk. It's too late to go to the latrine, so if you need to go, there's a bucket near the door."

Gustav followed Mendel into the main room of the barracks. The room was warm – there were pipes near the ceiling, which Gustav assumed was bringing heat to the barracks. Gustav followed the group until Mendel pointed to a bunk and said, "You will share this bed with one other. Take off all your clothes before you get into bed." When Gustav thanked him, Mendel looked at him and asked, "Are you German?"

Gustav answered, "Yes, I was born in Frankfurt." Mendel nodded and then continued assigning beds to the other prisoners.

Gustav looked at the three-tiered bunk and was happy he was in the middle bunk – he would be away from any rats at the lower level, but he also wouldn't have to work too hard to get to the top. It was the middle of the night, and the occupant was already taking up the entire bed, so Gustav pushed him a little. He didn't move at all. Gustav pushed him again a little harder and still no response.

Gustav was too tired to do battle with this person, but he needed the sleep, so he poked the man hard. This did the trick, and the man started to complain in a language Gustav couldn't understand. But he moved over, and Gustav climbed into the bed. The bedding was made of straw and poked Gustav when he laid down. Gustav's arm was itchy from the tattoo, but he was so exhausted that he was soon asleep.

A loud gong woke up Gustav. He was initially disoriented, thinking he was still at the Dossin Barracks. The grunting man next to him reminded him he was somewhere else. Mendel walked into the room and yelled, "Out of bed, out of bed." Gustav immediately left the bed, hoping to use the latrine. Mendel then yelled. "First, everyone must make their beds. New people, ask someone to help you. You then may use the washrooms." Gustav dressed, helped his bunkmate make the bed, then immediately left the barracks. He soon found the latrine and stood in line. It didn't take long before he reached the front of the line and entered the room. There were maybe twenty or thirty toilets, which were actually holes cut in a piece of metal, resting on a long wooden bench. Gustav found a free hole and sat down. He could tell almost immediately that he had diarrhea. He had diarrhea periodically in the Dossin Barracks, and he was hoping this would go away once he settled into the camp. Gustav returned to his barracks, and bread and ersatz coffee were waiting for him and the others, brought by some prisoners from the kitchen. He was so thirsty that he quickly drank the tepid coffee and gobbled down the bread.

The sun was rising as they reported for roll call. Their bunk elder told the new prisoners to bring their bowls and form a separate line. Another prisoner came over to this group and took the first twenty men, including Gustav, and told them to follow him. Their group was soon joined by about fifty others, and they walked as a group to the gates of the camp with a band of prisoners playing a military march. When they stopped at the gates, the prisoner announced to the guard, "This is Kommando Ten. We have seventy men in this Kommando." He then turned to the group and said, "Remember the number of the group, and remember me. I am your Kapo. That means I am in charge of this Kommando. My name is Ivan. Your job is to unload goods from a train. You will either do your job well, or you will be beaten. Now let's move."

When he had arrived the previous night, it was too dark for Gustav to see much other than the camp itself. But as he left the camp, he could see the vast complex across the road. There were large factories and a number of smokestacks. He didn't know what they were manufacturing, but whatever it was, they were making a lot of it, and he saw civilian workers all over the complex. As he continued to walk, he saw several construction sites with large cranes and multiple trucks. They walked about a kilometer until they reached the rail yard. They stopped, and the Kapo told them they would be unloading bags of cement from one of the train cars. The Kapo said that he expected the entire car to be emptied by the end of the day, then sat down in a chair.

Gustav wasn't sure what to do, but he saw a prisoner walk up to the car and followed him. The man picked up a bag of cement and carried it to one of the waiting trucks across the road. Gustav walked over to the bags and started to pick one up. He couldn't budge it. He tried a second time; still nothing.

Another prisoner laughed and said, "Here, I'll help you." He then picked up the bag and handed it to Gustav. Gustav nearly dropped it, and the prisoner laughed again. Gustav better positioned the bag on his shoulder and walked toward one of the trucks. As he dropped the bag, the prisoner clapped him on the back and said, "Don't worry, you'll get the hang of it. My name is Isaac. I heard you speaking to Mendel in German last night when you arrived. I am also in Barracks 20. I'm assuming you can understand my Yiddish."

Gustav smiled, happy that someone was speaking to him. "Yes, I can. I have spoken to others who spoke only Yiddish, but you are much easier to understand. Your accent sounds Polish, and I also speak Polish."

"I've actually learned some German since I've been here. And it's better if we speak German – if we speak Polish, we will be hit. But let's walk back to the train, or Ivan will take out his stick and beat us."

"Isaac, it's nice to meet you. My name is Gustav. Your German is pretty good. How long have you been here?"

"About four months. That's a long time for this place. I come from a small village in Poland, and I was the only one selected for work. The rest who came from my village were gone the first day we arrived."

"Gone where?" Gustav was remembering the others who were put into trucks and driven away. The older men. The women and children.

Isaac pointed to the sky.

"I don't understand."

"I suppose you wouldn't. I will explain it to you when we stop for lunch. But for now, let's get these bags moved." Isaac then handed Gustav a bag of cement, grabbed a bag for himself, and the two walked down to the truck.

At noon, the Kapo yelled for everyone to stop working, and a few prisoners came up with two large pots. They took off the lids. The Kapo then said, "You have thirty minutes to eat."

After they were served, Isaac signaled for Gustav to sit on the ground next to him. Isaac said, "Eat while I talk, and I will tell you everything I know about this place. You are in Auschwitz III. This camp was built in a town called Monowitz. Originally, the people who lived in our barracks were the civilian workers who built the first factory where they make synthetic fuel, but then they moved them out into nicer places, and we replaced them. That's why we have heat in our barracks. Auschwitz I is a prison and Auschwitz II, which is also called Birkenau, is the death camp. The people on your train who were not selected for Auschwitz III were taken to

Birkenau. A few of them may have been selected for work at that camp, but most went to the gas chambers and then into the ovens."

Gustav stopped eating after he heard that last statement. "What do you mean, they went to the gas chambers?"

"From what I have heard, they put them in a large room and turn on some type of gas. Then they die."

"All of them?"

"Yes, all of them."

"I still don't understand. How could they kill all of them?"

"I don't know how to answer your question except that's what they're doing. Birkenau is about five kilometers away, but sometimes you can actually smell the burning flesh. And if you can't do the work here, they will send you to Birkenau. If you get too sick, they will send you there. If you are too injured, they will send you there. That is, if you don't die here first."

Gustav just stared at the ground. He finally said, "My mother was deported last year. What would have happened to her?"

"If her train went to Auschwitz, she might have been selected at the main camp for work. But otherwise…"

Gustav looked at his feet and said quietly, almost to himself, "Maybe the train went somewhere else."

"Maybe. But to do your work, you need to finish your buna soup before we go back to work."

Gustav returned to his soup again and asked, "Why do you call it buna soup?"

"The work we are doing is to build a buna factory. I was told that buna is rubber in German and the factory we are building is for the giant German company IG Farben, to make synthetic rubber. But the soup also tastes like rubber, don't you think?"

"It is pretty bad."

"Well, believe it or not, it's the best meal you will have today. Probably the only one that has any real food in it."

Gustav stopped eating, sighed, and asked, "What's the point? You said it yourself. Everyone comes here to die."

Isaac's face grew dark, and he said, "That may be true, but you are alive today. If you have that attitude, you won't be alive tomorrow." Isaac said nothing more. Gustav remained quiet and finished the rest of his soup. The two then returned to work.

As the sun was beginning to set, the Kapo approached and told them they were done for the day. But before they left, the Kapo announced one man had not met his quota for the day. Gustav worried it was him, but the Kapo called out the tattooed number of another prisoner. The man was told to bend over a sawhorse and then was given twenty blows with a cane to his back. Gustav gasped, and Isaac looked over at him and shook his head. Gustav closed his mouth and looked down at his hands, noticing the blisters that had formed. They then walked back to the camp. As they walked through the gates, the Kapo yelled, "Seventy" to the guard. The band was playing another march. The Kapo led them to the square where others were forming lines for roll call.

As his Kommando was forming their line to be counted, Gustav looked ahead and saw two men lying on the ground. Isaac turned to him and whispered, "Anyone who dies is carried back by the other prisoners. Everyone must be counted for roll call, even the dead." Gustav shuddered, but said nothing in response.

After roll call, they were told to use the toilet and the washroom, and to return to their barracks for dinner. Dinner was brought by a few prisoners and consisted of a watery soup, a piece of bread, a small piece of cheese, and a small chunk of something that might have been sausage. Gustav ate his dinner quickly, then laid down in his bed. He saw Isaac speaking with a few other prisoners, but he was too tired to engage with them. Plus, he was thinking about his mother, wondering where she could be. Obviously, she was not in their camp because only men were in this camp. He hoped she hadn't been sent to Birkenau. Perhaps she was sent somewhere else. But he was too tired to think. When the gong sounded at nine p.m., the lights were turned off and Gustav closed his eyes, ready for sleep.

He rarely had trouble falling asleep, and there were many days during the past few years when sleep had been a welcomed respite. He was counting on his ability to fall asleep anywhere, but sleep now eluded him. He was thinking about what Isaac had told him, about how most Jews who came here were murdered – maybe even his mother. How was this also not the end for him? Gustav soon found himself crying. He tried to stop himself, but he couldn't. He tried to cry as quietly as possible, but could still hear his own sobs. He wanted Gretel at that moment. And he wanted his mother. So, he imagined what each would say to him. Gretel would tell him, "We will see each other soon." And his mother would say, "Everything will be okay." He had each repeat the phrases over and over again. "We will see each other soon." "Everything will be okay." "We will see each other soon." "Everything will be okay." But nothing was working. And then he thought of the butterfly, the butterfly of hope. He could actually see the butterfly – it was blue and shiny. He reached out to the butterfly, and it rested on the palm of his hand. The butterfly soon disappeared, but his hand felt warm and tingly. He actually felt better. He stopped crying, and he gently fell into a deep sleep.

Monowitz
February – March 1944

Gustav was adjusting to his life in Auschwitz III. Isaac had become a friend and helped him avoid the wrath of the Kapo while he was still in his first Kommando. And several other things happened that he hoped would help him survive the camp. First, when the bunk elder, one of the few decent bunk elders in the camp, learned that Gustav spoke fluent German, as well as French and Polish, Gustav was appointed the unofficial translator for the barracks, given that there were no other Germans in the barracks, and only German was supposed to be spoken in the camp. And because of that, the bunk elder was able to move Gustav to the painting Kommando, which was much easier work. Gustav had his friend Isaac moved to that Kommando as well. Additionally, when the bunk elder discovered Gustav was a tailor, the bunk elder found Gustav a needle and thread to repair the clothing of the bunk elder and his friends, which brought Gustav some additional scraps of food.

While Gustav was able to take advantage of these modest privileges, life in Auschwitz III was still brutal and made worse by the arbitrary requirements imposed on the prisoners. While they lived in filth through much of the day, the entire barracks would suffer if someone left their bed unmade. Once a week, they were required to shower, but with no soap, and leave the showers naked and in the freezing cold. And each Sunday, they were subject to lice inspection. While it was a day off for all workers at the construction site, only those living outside Auschwitz III were able to enjoy the day. Those civilian workers lived in comfortable apartments and were well-fed. The prisoners of Auschwitz III, on the other hand, had to show up for inspection naked, and if any lice were found in the barracks, all the clothing was taken to be steamed, and the entire barracks remained naked for the rest of the day and through the night. That had happened to Gustav and his barracks the previous week.

The diarrhea that Gustav experienced when he first arrived at Auschwitz III had improved, although he still had periodic issues. That was generally the case for most of the prisoners, and it was often a topic of conversation, so he knew he was not alone. But one morning, after having been in the camp about a month, he woke up and his stomach felt queasy. He went to the latrine, and his diarrhea had returned. He thought he could suffer through the day, assuming it would improve. But as the day wore on, his diarrhea worsened. It was even worse the next morning, so by the time he reached the camp gates after work, he knew he would not survive another day without some help.

Gustav knew too well that he was taking a chance by going to the infirmary. He knew that a visit to the infirmary could result in removal to Birkenau, depending on the prognosis. But he also knew he had no choice. When he returned to his barracks, he informed the bunk elder that his diarrhea was bad and that he needed to go to the infirmary. The bunk elder looked at him in disbelief, but he shrugged his shoulders, and said, "Go wait in that line," pointing towards the infirmary barracks. Gustav walked out of the barracks and to the line. When Gustav reached the front of the line, he provided his tattoo number, his temperature was taken, and because he had no fever, he was then examined by a doctor. The doctor told him he would be admitted to the infirmary but that he needed to return in the morning before roll call.

The following morning, Gustav felt even worse. He informed his bunk elder that he was returning to the infirmary, and then handed his bowl to Isaac for safekeeping, since it would have been taken if he brought it to the infirmary. Gustav walked to the infirmary and waited to be examined by a doctor. After he was seen and his hospitalization was approved, Gustav was shaved and told to shower. He was then assigned to the diarrhea barracks, which required that he go outside, naked, and walk to another barracks. Once inside, Gustav was given a hospital shirt and underwear, assigned a bed that was already occupied by another patient, and told to wait on the bed. After an hour, one of the nurses came to get him, and he was brought to a doctor. The doctor asked if he spoke German, and when Gustav nodded, the doctor smiled and said, "Good. This will make it easier to communicate. According to the records, you have diarrhea. We don't test for the cause, but we will give you a standardized treatment approved by the SS. You will fast for twenty-four hours, and then we will give you a special diet of white bread and a milky soup. We will also be giving you some tablets to help with the stools. Hopefully, you will get better in a few days."

Gustav walked back to his bed and laid down next to his coughing bedmate. He was told this barracks was only for patients being treated for diarrhea, but he thought this man had more problems than just diarrhea. He thought about what Isaac had said to him just before he left for the infirmary: "I will save a paint brush for you. And don't stay for more than two weeks. Otherwise, they will send you to Birkenau."

• • •

Gustav was awakened by the hacking cough of his bedmate, Levi. He pushed Levi, who stopped coughing and went back to sleep. Gustav knew he wasn't going back to sleep. He got up from his bed and walked to the toilet at the end of the floor. He was fortunate that this part of the infirmary had a toilet in the building. The other infirmary barracks had buckets in a corner. Still, he was worried. His diarrhea was as bad as ever. When he was finished, he returned to his bed. They would be serving breakfast soon. The same milky soup for every meal.

Before breakfast was served, all the patients were told to form a line to speak with the doctor. Gustav liked this doctor, who was from Warsaw and had been arrested for anti-Nazi activities. And he spoke German.

When it was Gustav's turn, the doctor asked, "So, Gustav, how are you feeling today?"

"About the same, doctor. The diarrhea doesn't seem to be getting better."

The doctor looked at Gustav's chart, then said, more quietly, "Yes, I was afraid of that. It's probably the food. Or the lack of it. Your problem is that today is your fourteenth day in the infirmary. I'm assuming you know that any patient who cannot be cured within fourteen days gets sent to the main camp. You understand what that means?"

Birkenau. And the gas chamber. The doctor continued, even more quietly, "But you don't want to go to the main camp, do you?" Gustav shook his head no. "I didn't think so. I am going to discharge you from the infirmary. But if you have a relapse overnight, you are to report back here. You don't have to wait in line to be approved for admission as you did the first time. I'm going to give you a slip of paper to release you so you can return to your bunk. You will need to work a full day, but if the diarrhea has not improved, you are to report back here after work. Hopefully, we will then be able to cure you within that fourteen-day period. Do you understand what I am saying, Gustav?"

"I do, doctor. And thank you." After his breakfast of milky soup, Gustav got out of bed and took off his hospital shirt and underwear. He left the diarrhea barracks, naked, and walked to the main building. He handed his paper to an officer and was told to wait in line for a new prison uniform, then return to his old barracks. When he entered his barracks, the bunk elder said, "I'm surprised to see you back, Gustav. You can return to your old bed. The person who replaced you has already died. If you need to wash up, do it now."

"I did that before I left the infirmary. I'll just go to my bed." Gustav walked down the rows of beds until he found his bunk. The person he had shared the bed with recognized him and mumbled something unrecognizable. Something in Greek. He sat on the bed and waited for Isaac to find out he was back. It didn't take long for his friend to hear that he had returned.

"Gustav, you're back! Here's your bowl. I assume you are better?"

Gustav signaled for his friend to come closer. "Actually, I'm not. The doctor discharged me but told me to return after work this evening."

"He wants you to come back? Why?"

"He told me if I work a full day and then return to the infirmary, it would re-start the two-week clock and hopefully you will be better."

"And you believed him? Gustav, you can't return."

"Isaac, I have to. If I don't, I will surely die. It will be hard enough to work today. I barely have the strength for that. Knowing

I can go back to the infirmary today is the only thing that is giving me any hope."

Isaac smiled at his friend and said, "Okay, Gustav. I'll make sure nothing happens to you today."

Gustav struggled to make it through work with his paint Kommando but was feeling better as he walked back into camp, thinking that maybe two weeks was all he would need to get rid of the diarrhea. When he reached his barracks after roll call, he told the bunk elder that he needed to return to the infirmary because his diarrhea had returned. The bunk elder asked, "Are you sure, Gustav? You know what it means to return to the infirmary?" Gustav nodded, and the bunk elder said, "Very well. And good luck."

He shook Isaac's hand, who took Gustav's bowl and said, "I will hold this for you again." Then Gustav walked to the infirmary, hoping what the doctor had told him was true, that he wouldn't be sent to Birkenau.

As he walked to the infirmary, Gustav glanced over at the courtyard and saw a prisoner standing on a box, about to be hung. The rest of the man's barracks were standing to watch the hanging. Gustav understood that the man was being hung because he had tried to escape and the remainder of his barracks would be forced to stand for twenty-four hours as punishment for allowing the man to try to escape. This was not the first hanging Gustav had witnessed, and notwithstanding all the constant death around him, he was always horrified when he saw a hanging. And so, he turned away, forcing himself not to think about it because he had to remain focused on what he must do - get healthy.

When he reached the infirmary, he told the clerk at the intake desk that he was number 172331 and that he was returning to the infirmary because his diarrhea had returned. Gustav was shaved and told to shower, and then he walked naked to the diarrhea barracks. He was given a hospital shirt and underwear and escorted to a bed, sharing it with a different patient this time.

The next morning, two SS officers appeared in the barracks and began to walk up the aisle. One had a clipboard in his hand, looking first at the patient and then his clipboard. The SS officer with the clipboard looked at Gustav with cold eyes and then continued up the row of beds. When he finished, he called out the tattooed numbers of patients. Gustav held his breath as the numbers were read. After the tenth number was called, the officer instructed those prisoners whose numbers were called to follow him. Everyone knew this was the end, that they had been selected for the gas chamber. But Gustav's number had not been called. He was safe, at least until the next selection occurred. He felt a relief he had not felt in a long time. Had Gustav found a guardian angel in this hellhole? He knew this doctor couldn't keep him safe forever. He would need to get better.

Villeurbanne,
March 1944

Trudi woke up nauseous. She ran to the bathroom and threw up more of last night's stew. She had to admit it was an awful stew. Food rations were making it hard to find any fresh meat, and they had finished the last of the winter vegetables. The mutton didn't taste very good but may have actually gone bad. But Joseph seemed fine, and she had an iron stomach. She walked back to bed and Joseph rolled over, looked at her, and asked, "Is everything okay? This is the third time you've gone to the bathroom this morning."

"It must have been the stew."

"Maybe. I guess I need to watch out for my own stomach." They both laughed, but then she ran back to the bathroom.

This was not normal, not for her. And the nausea felt familiar. She had had the same feeling two times before. But was it possible? Could she be pregnant? She counted the days from her last menstrual cycle and realized that she could, in fact, be pregnant. Pregnant? Now? With everything going on? She went back to their bed, smiled, and said, "It might not have been the mutton."

"I was thinking the same thing." He then hugged her and said, "How wonderful! In the middle of all this sadness to bring some joy into our world!"

"Are you really happy, Joseph? Is it really okay for us to have another child? Now?"

"I honestly don't know if it's the right thing to do, but I'm happy to have another child. We'll never be able to replace our beautiful little Ruth, but I'll be happy to have another little Trudi."

Trudi started thinking about Ruth, then shook her head to stop the thoughts. Smiling, she said, "Or another little Joseph."

"Yes, a boy would also be wonderful. We just have to find a way to keep us all safe."

"Joseph, that's exactly what I'm worried about."

"I am, as well, which is why your father and I are going out this morning to speak with someone about leaving this neighborhood, to find a better place to survive. We spoke about how it's likely that we'll all be picked up at some point by the Gestapo. And who knows what happens after you're picked up or where you're sent! We've heard rumors, and none of them are good. Your French citizenship now makes no difference to the Germans. If you are a Jew, they will arrest you. And our forged identification papers are not as good as they need to be."

Trudi nodded sadly and said, "Joseph, I agree with you we need to leave. Now, more than ever. But I'm still frightened about what could happen even after we leave." Trudi was quiet for a moment, then said, "I'm feeling a little better, so I'll get up and talk to my parents about the possibility of the new arrival. I can hear all of them downstairs, anyway."

As Trudi walked down the stairs, she felt a new wave of nausea. She looked up and saw her mother, who smiled and said, "The walls in this house are a bit too thin at times. I could hear you in the bathroom. Are you alright? Is there something you would like to share with us?"

"Mama, how did you guess when Joseph and I just figured it out ourselves?"

"I have been through this before. And I know my daughter."

"You're both happy about this?"

"We are." Lili got up from her chair and gave Trudi a big hug. Then Lili quietly said, "But we will never forget our little Ruth."

Laure looked at her mother and grandmother and asked, "Why is everyone so happy?"

Trudi sat down next to her daughter and said, "Chérie, I think I am going to have another baby. I'll have to go to the doctor to make sure. Would you like another brother or sister?"

Laure began to cry and said, "No," then ran out of the room. Trudi was about to follow her when her mother put her hand up to stop her.

"Trudi, she'll be fine. She really misses her sister, and I think this was just a reminder. But she will be so happy when the baby comes."

"Assuming we aren't deported first."

"And that is why Papa and Joseph are going out this morning. I made breakfast, so let's all eat first. And Trudi, you now need to eat for two."

•   •   •

Jacob and Joseph returned in the afternoon and reported that they had made a lot of progress. They had met with someone who knew of a small village where Jews were being hidden. They could take Trudi, Joseph, and Laure.

Trudi seemed skeptical. "Really, an entire village is helping Jews. What is the name of this magical village?"

Joseph laughed. "I know it sounds crazy. But it is also a little magical. The village is called Le Chambon-sur-Lignon. I have heard about this village from others in the past year. They are mostly Huguenots who refused to cooperate with the Vichy government and now are refusing to cooperate with the Nazis. Their pastor has made it his mission to hide Jews, who the Huguenots consider the chosen people."

Trudi snorted. "Well, the Nazi government has chosen us, but mostly for deportation."

Joseph ignored his wife and continued, "They also have this network of support in and around their village, so when they hear of an impending visit from the police, they move the Jews to another place. Last year, the Vichy police arrested the pastor, but his wife is continuing his work."

Trudi gasped and exclaimed, "Arrested the pastor? Well, that doesn't sound very safe."

"The pastor has since been released and is in hiding to avoid being re-arrested. But the work continues, and it is our only option."

"But how are we going to get Mama and Papa there? I'm assuming it won't be easy to get there."

Jacob then spoke. "We're not going with you. My health is too fragile these days. We have located a clinic in Lyon where we can stay, and if it gets too risky, there's a farm we can move to not too far out of town."

Trudi was quiet for a minute before saying, "But we've never been separated. How will I know that the two of you are safe?"

Her father gently took her hand and said, "We will be fine. The clinic is well protected. And I will feel better when you are further away from here."

"Since the Nazis put that butcher Claus Barbie in charge of Lyon, life has gotten much worse," said Joseph, "and too many people in the neighborhood know we're Jewish. The sooner we leave here, the better. They'll be ready to move us in a few days. We'll need to decide what to take and we need to talk to Laure."

Lili patted her son-in-law's arm and said, "Laure will be fine."

After Jacob, Lili and Laure had gone to bed, Joseph brought out two glasses of tea and sat down next to Trudi on the couch in the living room. He set the glasses on the coffee table and turned to his wife. "Trudi, I know you're nervous about leaving Villeurbanne and going to this new place. This has been our home for more than three years. But we will be safer somewhere else."

"Joseph, I really do understand that we need to leave, notwithstanding my earlier sarcastic comments. If nothing else, being pregnant has certainly convinced me. It is just hard for me to leave my parents. Especially Papa, who just seems to be getting sicker."

"Chérie, to be separated now when everything is so chaotic will be hard for all of us. It's just that we don't have a choice. But I want you to know I will do everything I can to make sure we return to your parents again, and hopefully soon. I also want you to know how proud of you I am. You have been so brave these last three years, and you have made this house a home for all of us." He had a twinkle in his eye when he added, "And your cooking has really improved."

Trudi giggled, then wiped a tear away. She took Joseph's hand and said, "Who could imagine me cooking for the family and not poisoning everyone? But Joseph, you have been my rock. I could not have done any of it without you. Especially when we lost Ruth." Trudi became quiet and Joseph took her hand and kissed it. He then led his wife up the stairs and to their bedroom.

•   •   •

Two days later, a car pulled up to the small house in Villeurbanne. Each of them carried a single suitcase. Enough clothes to get them through the next few months – or maybe longer. Joseph sat in front with the driver, and the other four sat in the back. Joseph didn't know the driver's name. It was better that way, just in case. The car travelled the ten kilometers to the medical clinic. After hugs and kisses goodbye, the driver took the remaining three to the train station. Joseph bought them tickets to a nearby town, and the three waited until the train arrived. Once they reached that town, they left the station, then returned to the station and bought tickets to another town. The family repeated this ritual three more times that day. Joseph was told that such actions would reduce suspicions among those paying attention, and that appeared to be the case that day. Finally, they reached the station just outside of Le Chambon-sur-Lignon and waited inside the station until their contact arrived.

Trudi took out some cookies for the three. As they were enjoying their snack, a police officer walked up to them. He was not German, and Trudi assumed he was a local officer. He asked Joseph for their papers. Joseph handed the officer their forged identification cards, and the officer scanned each one carefully. He then asked, "What are you doing in our town? Are you lost?"

Joseph and Trudi had been told to say they were visiting relatives, the Bernards, but Trudi spoke first, worried about Joseph's slight accent. "No, Monsieur, we're not lost. We're staying with family for a few weeks. The Bernards. They were supposed to be here, but I guess they're running a little late."

"The Bernards. I don't know them. But I don't know everyone in this region. Of course, it's getting harder to know who's supposed to be here since Jews keep coming here, hoping to find refuge among our good citizens. You wouldn't be one of those kind?"

Trudi answered quickly, "No, sir." But the officer glared at Joseph. Trudi was hoping Laure would not look at the officer, would not say anything. She didn't dare look at her daughter, but she could tell her daughter was simply focused on eating her cookie and not reacting at all. She really had become good at hiding. Trudi was worried the officer didn't believe her, or would wonder why Joseph wasn't speaking, and would soon arrest the three of them. But at that moment, a drunken man walked into the station and began singing loudly. The officer said, "Oh, what now?" and quickly handed Joseph back the papers, saying, "Make sure you leave soon," as he walked toward the drunken man.

Trudi breathed a sigh of relief. She then saw a man signal to them, and the three got up from their bench and walked to the man, who said to Joseph, "Monsieur Reich, follow me." He had a car waiting in front. Joseph got into the passenger seat and Trudi and Laure got into the back. As they were driving off, the man introduced himself. "I am Claude Michel. You will be staying with my wife and me for the foreseeable future. We saw the officer walk up to you and sent in a friend to distract him. I'm glad it worked."

Trudi didn't know why – perhaps it was the relief at not being caught or the ruse of the drunken man – but she started to laugh, and Joseph and Laure soon joined her. Monsieur Michel looked over at the family quizzically and said, "I think we are going to enjoy having you stay with us." And this made the family laugh even harder.

Frankfurt
March 1944
Gertrud sat at the kitchen table, feeding little Heidi. Now two years old, Heidi was a good eater and a good sleeper. Or at least, she had turned into a good sleeper. That first year had been a challenge, and Gertrud was worried that the constant air raid sirens would make her sleep worse. But it actually seemed to help. Whenever they were forced to leave the apartment – even in the middle of the night – little Heidi would just find a corner in the shelter and go right back to sleep. And on the nights when there were no bombings, she would stay asleep in her crib. And she ate everything. Which was a good thing, now that there was very little variety. Mostly potatoes and cabbage these days. But she loved both.

After she finished eating, Heidi went off to play, and Gertrud sat at the table, enjoying the quiet while drinking her ersatz coffee. Her mother was working the very early shift at the bakery and would not be home for another hour. The bakery was now open morning and night, baking brown breads. A few varieties, but to Gertrud, they all tasted the same. No more cakes, no more cookies – the Aryan nation would win the war on brown bread, they were told. Not the white bread that the Allies were eating! Broadcasters on the radio were even claiming that the Jews had created white bread as a way of undermining German health and that the true German only ate dark brown bread. But Gertrud missed her cookies.

She was also enjoying no Karl. Because the German army was running out of soldiers, Karl was drafted last month. And while he ranted on about the greatness of Germany and the German military, he wasn't particularly happy about being drafted. But Gertrud was happy to have him gone. And her mother didn't seem too unhappy about his absence, either. In fact, with Karl gone, Gertrud and her mother were getting along much better.

The apartment was cold, but Heidi didn't seem to mind. She was wearing a warm sweater and a hat, and she was singing a song to one of her dolls. Gertrud was also dressed warmly, including woolen socks. The building's monthly coal rations were nearly gone, and the boiler was run only one or two hours during the night. As she continued to sip her coffee, her mother opened the door to the apartment.

"Anybody home?" she called out.

Heidi rushed to her grandmother. "Oma!"

"There you are," Margarete said, as she gave her granddaughter a big hug. She put her bag down on a chair and reached in to pull out a package. She handed it to Gertrud.

"What is it, Mama?"

"Open it."

Inside the package was a large sausage. Gertrud had not seen a sausage in months.

"Oh, Mama, where did you get this? It's huge!"

"Better not to ask. I had an opportunity, and I took it."

"You didn't break any rules, did you?" Gertrud winked at her mother and smiled.

"You, of all people, should not be asking me that question." Gertrud stopped smiling. *What did her mother mean by that?* But she wasn't going to ask. Instead, she took a sniff at the sausage. It smelled wonderful!

"Mama, I need to go to work soon, but I would love to have a little of this when I come home."

"Don't worry, I won't have any of it until you're back from work. I'll take a nap when Heidi takes her nap, and then we'll go to the store to see if there's anything that we can cook with this sausage. We'll have a party tonight, right, Heidi?"

"Party, Oma," Heidi giggled and twirled around the room.

After she dressed, Gertrud walked to the door and picked up her coat and hat. But she stopped as she was about to open the door, turning back to her mother. "Mama, I want you to promise me that if you hear a siren, you will go immediately to the shelter."

"Of course I will go," her mother said as she tickled her granddaughter.

"But you didn't go last week, and I heard yesterday that it was not a false alarm, that bombs actually fell."

"That was not my fault. I was sleeping, and so was Heidi. We didn't wake up in time."

"Mama, even you can't sleep through the siren. Please, promise me."

"I promise. Now go, before you're late. When I left, there was a long line out the door, so I imagine you will be very busy today."

"Yes, like always. Heidi, say bye-bye to Mama." Her daughter gave her a big hug, and Gertrud left the apartment quickly. If she hurried, she would only be a few minutes late. *It'll be all right*, she thought, since she often stayed a bit later if they were busy, which would certainly be the case today.

Before the war, it would take Gertrud fifteen minutes to walk to work. But because of all the bombings, it now took her more than a half hour. Some streets were now impassible, and some streets required extra care in maneuvering. She had been lucky so far —

many of the inner-city buildings were damaged or destroyed, but much of the destruction had not yet reached her neighborhood.

As she approached the bakery, she could see the long line for bread. *Another busy day*, she thought to herself. She walked to the back of the bakery and entered through the back door. Her boss waved to her, then touched his watch. But he also smiled, so she knew she was fine. She grabbed an apron and asked to help the next person in line. This continued non-stop until six p.m., with just a quick break for lunch. She was exhausted after she helped the last person during her shift. She took her apron off, grabbed her hat and coat, and left by the back door.

Gertrud was happy to be outside and was enjoying the crisp air of the early spring evening. Few lights were on now, a requirement so that the Allied planes would have fewer targets. But it made it more of a challenge to walk. Several times, she nearly fell into a hole and thought that maybe she should bring a flashlight with her. Surely, the government couldn't object to her using a flashlight. Of course, she would have to find one, since they were in short supply. She would also have to find batteries, which she assumed were even harder to find. Maybe she just needed to be a little more careful.

Gertrud could smell the sausage as soon as she entered the building and was excited about a proper meal for the first time in a long time. As she opened the apartment door, she heard Heidi cry out, "Mama!" Her daughter took her hand and walked her to the table and said, "Mama, look!" Before her was a feast – the sausage, plus vegetables and spätzle. Gertrud turned to her daughter and asked, "Did you make all of this?"

Heidi beamed. "Me and Oma."

"Well, this looks wonderful. Let me take off my coat and hat and wash up. Then we can eat this beautiful meal."

Gertrud could not remember having such a wonderful meal. *It must have been the sausage,* she thought to herself. She was so glad that half the sausage was still left for dinner tomorrow. But Gertrud wondered where her mother got the sausage. Gertrud hoped she didn't sell anything. There wasn't much left to sell, but her mother did have a few pieces of jewelry left from her own mother.

After dinner, her mother washed the dishes while Gertrud read to little Heidi. The lights were off in the apartment because of the blackout, so Gertrud took one of the candles into the bedroom. Little Heidi's vocabulary was advanced for a two-year-old, but she didn't have patience for long stories. Mostly, Heidi liked to look at the pictures. But she and her grandmother must have been busy today, because Heidi was already asleep before Gertrud had finished the first story. She kissed her daughter on the forehead and joined her mother in the kitchen. Gertrud dried the dishes while her mother wiped the counters. Then the two went into the living room to read a little of the newspaper. By nine p.m., both were nearly asleep and decided to make it an early evening. Margarete had the early shift, anyway, and said she was happy for the extra sleep.

Gertrud had just fallen asleep when she heard the sirens. Not again, she groaned to herself. She slowly got out of bed and shook Heidi awake. Heidi was so used to being awakened that she just lifted her arms with her eyes still closed so her mother could put on a warm sweater. Margarete was already at the door by the time Gertrud and Heidi left the bedroom. In another minute, they were out of the building and walking up the street to the shelter. As they neared the shelter, they could hear the bombs falling, but unlike other times, the bombs seemed much closer. And as they climbed the stairs of the shelter, they heard a loud noise and the stairs shook violently. Her mother began to fall, and Gertrud grabbed her arm. The three quickly climbed the remaining stairs and found an empty place. They heard another loud noise, and the lights shook and dust from the ceiling fell on them. For the next hour, the bombing and shaking continued. Gertrud worried that a direct hit to the building would cause the shelter to collapse in on them. So, every time she heard a loud noise, she covered up her daughter.

After an hour, they could still hear bombing, but the noise was fainter, and the shelter had stopped shaking. The bombing continued all night.

Gertrud never went to sleep, too worried about her daughter. But little Heidi slept on her mother's lap, and Margarete also fell asleep next to Gertrud. When the bombing had completely stopped and the "all clear" sounded, the shelter door opened and everyone left. As they left the shelter, Gertrud could see the sun rising and realized they had been in the shelter all night. Then she looked around and gasped. Destruction was everywhere! Some building lay in ruins, others were on fire. Gertrud picked up her daughter and gingerly walked down the street. As they approached their block, she and her mother stopped. It took her a few seconds to orient herself, since everything looked different. She finally located her building. Or, at least, where her building was supposed to be. Because it also lay in ruins.

Gertrud turned to her mother. "Mama, you stay here with Heidi. I'm going to try to get a better look." Maybe it was just the angle from where they were standing, that the building was merely damaged. But as she got closer, she could see that her building must have received a direct hit. Their home was gone. They would need to find a place to stay. If there *was* another place available, since they weren't the only ones looking for housing. At that moment, all she could think was, *The rest of the sausage is gone!*

She walked back to her mother and said, "The building is gone." Everything they had, everything they owned, was in the apartment. The only clothes they had were the clothes on their backs. Gertrud didn't know what to do. She had friends, but not close friends. She always kept a distance from everyone, worried they would find out the truth about her. Gertrud was only close to her cousins, and none of them were in Frankfurt. She was thinking about what else they could do when her mother said, "Let's walk to the bakery. We can get some breakfast there, and I'll ask someone if we could stay in their place for a few days." Gertrud was too tired to think of an alternative, so they walked to the bakery. But Gertrud knew her mother was right. They had worked with these people for years, and she trusted them. One of them would certainly put them up for a night, or two, or three. Or maybe more.

Le Chambon-sur-Lignon, France
May 1944

The sun was finally shining after days of rain. Trudi had pulled her auburn hair back into a bun and was retying her scarf, one of the few possessions left from her earlier life. She always loved the colors of her Hermès scarf and was happy to be wearing something pretty – and expensive – on this beautiful day. When Joseph had seen her that morning, he laughed and asked, "Are you going to a fashion show?"

Trudi gave her husband a playful swat on his arm and replied, "Is it a crime to look nice every once in a while?"

Joseph hugged his wife and said, "Well, you do look pretty."

She smiled to herself as she sat looking at the garden, watching Laure and Madam Michel plant the vegetables. Trudi had been helping with the planting earlier, but she began to feel the weight of the pregnancy and finally sat down. She never gardened before the war – they always had a gardener back home – but she and her mother had planted seeds for vegetables in the backyard of their house in Villeurbanne in the early spring, although no seedlings had sprouted by the time they left.

Laure adored Madam Michel and was now helping her plant beans. Carefully paying attention to the rows, Madam Michel made the hole, and Laure placed the bean in the hole. Each time they finished a hole, they would yell in unison, "Voila!"

When it was time for lunch, Trudi happily volunteered to make sandwiches for everyone. As she walked back to the house, she heard Joseph in the barn helping with the cows and the chickens. While Trudi had recently planted seeds, Joseph's only experience with cows was eating them. But he was also enjoying the manual labor. Anything to avoid sitting in the house and worrying about the future.

When Trudi was done making the lunch, she took the food outside to a table and called to everyone. Laure arrived first, yelling, "Oh, Mama, thank goodness. I was about to faint from hunger!"

Madam Michel laughed. "Laure, I don't think you could possibly be hungry with all the strawberries you ate while we planted."

Laure made a face and said, "But I only ate the strawberries that were bruised. No one would eat those strawberries anyway."

Joseph was walking over and heard his daughter's last comment. "And I wonder how the strawberries became bruised." With that last comment, everyone laughed, included Laure.

Madam Michel looked at the spread and said, "Trudi, everything looks so good. You take what I pick, and you make it beautiful."

Joseph laughed and said, "Before the war, my wife never left the house unless her dress, shoes, and purse matched. She had to give that up, but she still knows how to make things look pretty."

Trudi winked at her husband and added, "Madam Michel, I could not have done this without all of these wonderful vegetables."

"Trudi, you've been living here more than a month. I think it's time you called me Marie and my husband Claude."

"I will, Marie. Thank you. Our time here has been just wonderful."

Marie looked over at Joseph and asked, "And where is that lazy husband of mine?"

"One of your neighbors came over and said he needed to speak with Claude. He told me to tell you that we should start eating and not wait for him."

Marie looked toward the barn and said, almost to herself, "One of our neighbors. Hmmm." But then she looked at the Reich family and said, "Okay, let's eat."

About ten minutes later, Claude joined them. The normally easy smile was missing; in its place was a grimace. Marie immediately asked, "Claude, what's wrong?"

"Not in front of the child."

But Trudi said, "Yes, Claude, in front of Laure. She has been through everything with us. She can hear this as well."

"Very well. We've heard that German police will be visiting some of the farms tomorrow. We don't know when and we don't know which farms. But we have to assume it will include our farm. That means the three of you will need to leave before the sun comes up."

Joseph looked at Claude and said, "Okay, Claude. We trust you and your network. Where will we be going?"

"Switzerland."

Without even thinking, Trudi cried out, "Switzerland? How are we going to get into Switzerland? The Swiss have kept the border closed, especially for Jews. And if they catch us, they'll send us back and into the hands to the Gestapo, who will deport us to a camp!"

Claude responded, calmly, "That might have been the case for much of the war, but in the last few months, things have changed. It started when Germany invaded Italy at the end of last year, after Italy surrendered to the Allies. Switzerland began allowing some refugees from Italy to enter. Recently, they have stopped watching many of the border crossings. And when Jews make it across the border, we believe the Swiss have stopped sending them back. Besides, we don't think taking you further into the French countryside will make you any safer."

Joseph looked at his wife. "Trudi, I think he's right. It's not safe here for us. But if we can get into Switzerland and they let us stay, we'll be safe."

Trudi then sighed, perhaps a little too loudly. "For the past four years, we have been in one dangerous situation after another. But nothing like this. Nothing like trying to cross the border. Joseph, remember when my cousin Gustav crossed the border into

Belgium? The Belgium police weren't trying to stop them. The German police were. So even if the Swiss police won't care, the German police will still try to stop us. They won't hesitate to shoot us."

"But remember, they made it across the border!" Joseph said.

Claude added, "Trudi, I won't lie to you. There is always a danger in crossing the border. All I can tell you is that we have found places that the German police don't monitor often. In fact, the most dangerous part of the trip will actually be getting to the border. So, assuming you agree Switzerland is the best place for you, you'll need to do the same thing you did when you came here, taking several short trips on the train. That way, it won't attract the attention of the German police. And you need to give me your forged identification cards. The German police have become better at detecting forgeries, and we have people who can do a better job."

Joseph immediately got up to get the cards. Trudi hadn't even agreed to this approach, and they were acting as if she had. But they were right. They needed to get out of France and she needed to go for another reason, one she hadn't shared with Joseph. She had been spotting. Not a lot, but enough to make her worried. She had seen a doctor before she left Villeurbanne, but there were no doctors she could safely see here. But there would be a doctor – plenty of doctors – in Switzerland. And a hospital, if she needed one. And so, they were going to Switzerland.

•   •   •

That evening, Marie and Claude announced they would prepare a feast for their friends. Claude said, "This is a bon voyage feast, not a farewell feast. When this crazy war has ended, we will see you again. And we can't wait to meet the little one." Trudi insisted on helping Marie with the cooking while Joseph went with Claude to retrieve the identification cards.

When they returned, Claude said he had more news. "The information we heard this morning was confirmed. So, before dawn, I will drive the three of you to the train station in the next town to start your journey."

That night, in bed, Trudi said to Joseph, "We were really lucky finding Marie and Claude. They have taken us in like family and have made sure that we are safe. I know they mean only the best for us, but Joseph, I'm still afraid. We've never tried to cross a border illegally."

"I know, chérie. But we can't stay here, and any place they send us in France will continue to present a risk for us because all of France is occupied by Germany. We won't be safe until we're out of France. But know that I will do everything in my power to keep both you and Laure safe." Trudi wasn't sure what Joseph could actually do to keep them safe, but she liked hearing those words. Maybe she just needed to hear those words because she felt better. She kissed Joseph and held him as she drifted off to sleep.

•　　•　　•

Trudi was up before Joseph and joined Marie in the kitchen to make the food for their journey. Marie had made a pot of ersatz coffee and they both drank the coffee while they chatted. It had been a while since she had made a friend – they were cautious about getting too close to anyone in Villeurbanne – and she was going to miss Marie. Claude came into the kitchen and told them to stop chatting and finish packing, then winked at both of them. They could only take essentials since more than a single rucksack would attract attention. The last thing they did was wake up Laure, who yawned as she said goodbye to Claude and Marie. Trudi and Joseph then both hugged Marie and the Reich family quickly and quietly left the house.

As Claude pulled into the train station, the sun was rising. He told them to quickly leave the car and not to say goodbye since that would draw attention to them. Joseph went up to the ticket counter and bought them tickets to a town three stops away. They waited about thirty minutes for the train to come and then the three boarded the train. They did this three more times that day, making sure no one was watching as they left each station, then returned.

At some point, Laure said quietly, "Mama, we could all be spies." Trudi smiled as she remembered her cousin Gertrud saying the same thing to her when they were younger. When they reached the last station – near the Swiss border – they left the station, as instructed, and walked down the hill to a small café. They went inside and ordered three hot teas. As they waited, a man came up to them and said, "It looks like you are finished with your tea."

Joseph took his daughter's hand and said, "Yes, let's go." They followed the man, who told them to get into the backseat of his car. He said nothing, but started to drive. After thirty minutes, they reached a small hut with a small dirt road beside it. The driver told them to leave the car and walk up the road.

A man was waiting for them at the end of the road. He said, "I will guide you through the woods for the next five kilometers. We need to reach a shallow river in two hours, since that is when the Swiss guards change their shift and there will be no guards at the crossing. Once you have crossed the river, there will be a fence, and you will need to climb the fence. Once you are over the fence, you will be in Switzerland, and you can walk to Geneva. It is another five kilometers. After we start to walk, no one can say a word. If you have any questions, ask them now."

Trudi looked at her husband and said quietly, "I thought there would be no Swiss guards at the border."

The man heard her comment and said, "Don't worry about the guards. Everything will be fine, as long as you do what I say."

Trudi nodded her head slowly, then said, "We trust you and will do everything you tell us to do. But I do have two questions. First, how high is the fence? And I know this is a silly question, but what is the name of the river? I just want to remember its name."

"The fence is about three meters high, but I have a cord and canvas to hold down the barbed wire, and that will protect you. And Le Foron is the name of the river. But I promise you, you will not need to swim across the river. Your shoes may get a little wet, but that's about it. Now, let's go."

Trudi shuddered, hoping the man was right about the guards. He gave no name, and Trudi was fine with that, as long as he guided them safely to Switzerland. It was dark, but the moon was out, and the path was easy to follow. The man kept them moving at a steady pace, and they reached the river in about two hours. The man told them to lie in the grass next to the river while he checked to make sure there were no guards. He returned in a few minutes and told them it was safe to cross the river.

The man was right – the river was little more than a brook, and the rocks in the river facilitated the crossing. Joseph went first, then helped his daughter and his wife. The man threw them the cord and the canvas, wished them luck, and left.

When they turned away from the river, they saw the fence. Three meters somehow seemed higher in person. Joseph climbed to the top of the fence, placed the canvas over the barbed wire, and threw one end of the rope over the fence. He motioned for Trudi to pull down on the other end of the rope. Then he signaled for Laure to climb. She climbed quickly and was soon over the fence. Laure then grabbed the end of the rope to hold down the canvas. Trudi passed the rucksack up to Joseph, who then passed it down to Laure. Trudi then began her climb. She was much slower than her daughter, but Joseph helped her, and she was soon over the fence. Joseph was the last to climb down. Then they were done. They were safe. Trudi could hardly believe the climb went so quickly. She started to cry, and Joseph said, "Chérie, it's okay. We're safe. We didn't even need the new forged documents."

"You don't understand. These are tears of joy. For the first time in four years, I feel like I can breathe." She then stopped crying and her face grew serious. "But I am also sad because our little Ruth is not here with us to enjoy our first taste of freedom." Tears began to flow again.

Joseph hugged his wife, and Laure walked up and hugged both her parents. Joseph said, "Trudi, we will never forget our little Ruth."

After a minute of hugging, Laure said, "Crossing the border was so easy! Maybe *Grand-mère and Grand-père* could join us."

Trudi laughed. "Can you imagine either of them climbing over that fence?" And then all three laughed. Trudi wiped the remaining tears and said, "Okay, family, now we walk to Geneva."

Trudi reached down to pick up the rucksack. She turned around to hand it to Joseph and immediately saw a guard holding a rifle, pointed at her. She stopped, feeling the blood drain from her face, and grabbed Laure's hand. The guard said, "You three are under arrest. Come with me."

Munich
July 1944

Bettina heard her son giggling and yelled to him, "Gregi, I will not be happy if I have to change you a second time!" Gregor only had two nice shirts, and he had already spilled milk this morning on the first shirt. Bettina knew she was being a little cross with him, but they needed to look their best for Colonel Zirngibl. Their lives depended on it.

In early January, one week after Hans left for war, Bettina received a notice that she was to report to Gestapo headquarters and bring her son. She assumed that her time was up and that she and Gregi would be deported. Bettina told Gregor they were going to meet a very nice man, but was nervous the entire ride on the tram.

When she reached the headquarters, she was told by the man at the reception desk to take the stairs to the third floor and go down the hall. When she reached the end of the hall, a Gestapo officer was sitting at a desk. She handed him the notice. The officer looked at the paper, gave her a sinister smirk, then directed her to follow him. He stopped at a closed door, knocked, and walked in without waiting for a response. A blond-haired, middle-aged man was sitting behind a desk. The assistant said, "Colonel Zirngibl, this is Frau Schnitzler, a Jew." He handed the colonel the paper notice and left.

Colonel Zirngibl motioned for Bettina to sit in one of the chairs. He smiled at Gregor and said, "Young man, you can sit next to your mama." He then turned to Bettina and said, "I imagine you may be a little worried about being summoned by the Gestapo, but I can assure you there is nothing to worry about. We only needed to check to make sure that you and your son are all right. And I am assuming you are both all right?"

Bettina immediately nodded her head and said, "Yes, Colonel Zirngibl, we are both doing well." The colonel took out a sheet of paper, asked Bettina a few more questions, then told her to report to his office on the first of every month. And that was it! Bettina nearly cried with relief as she stood to leave.

But then Colonel Zirngibl got up from his desk and walked towards her. He touched her arm and said, "Why the rush, Frau Schnitzler? You're not afraid of me, are you? You needn't be. Everyone will tell you I am very nice to all the Jews who check in with me and I want to compliment you on the way you and your son are dressed today. Very respectful."

Bettina smiled and replied, "Thank you, Colonel." She then quickly turned and left his office, gripping Gregor's hand.

As she passed his assistant, he said to her, "Jew, looks like you get to go home today. Maybe the next time you will not be so fortunate!" Bettina could still hear his laughter as she reached the stairs.

Bettina returned with Gregor the next month, and the colonel was initially as nice as he had been the previous month, even smiling at Gregor. But he soon began asking more personal questions, and as she prepared to leave, he got up from his desk, touched her arm, and complimented her on her dress. She thanked him, but avoided his gaze. When she passed the colonel's assistant, he again suggested that the next check in would be her last.

With each succeeding month, the colonel became a bit more forward. During the last visit, he stroked the sleeve of her dress and said, "I do like the feel of this fabric. Very soft. Just like you."

Today's visit would be their seventh with Colonel Zirngibl. At exactly nine a.m., she and Gregor left the apartment. It generally took them thirty minutes on the tram to get to the building, but she never wanted to be late for her 10:00 a.m. appointment. As she neared the building, she slowed her gait and looked around, mostly to calm herself. Most of the buildings had been destroyed in the recent bombings. The police barracks, where Gestapo headquarters had recently relocated, was one of the few buildings still untouched by the bombings. The large Nazi banners draping the front of the building reminded Bettina of the peril she faced every time she stepped inside. As she entered, Gregor complained she was squeezing his hand, and she loosened her grip, but wouldn't let go.

When she reached Colonel Zirngibl's assistant, he glared at her for a few uncomfortable seconds before directing her to the colonel's office. This was new behavior for this awful man, and she wondered if today was the day she and Gregor would be deported. She took a deep breath and entered his office. Colonel Zirngibl was focused on a document and barely acknowledged Bettina. This worried her.

After a minute, he looked up, sighed, and said, "Frau Schnitzler, we will need to make this visit short. I have something else that requires my immediate attention." He looked at her in a way that made her uncomfortable, then asked, "Has anything changed since your last visit here?" Bettina shook her head, and the colonel then dismissed her and returned to his document.

When she left his office, Bettina exhaled in relief. But as she walked past the assistant's desk, he repeated the same warning he always made to her - the next check in might be her last. She wondered about the document the colonel was reading and worried that it might have something to do with her. She left the building as quickly as possible and headed right home.

An hour later, Bettina knocked on Tante Helga's door, but didn't wait for an answer. She walked in, carrying two large bottles of water, as well as the daily newspaper. Gregor trailed behind her, carrying two smaller bottles. Gregor yelled out, "We're here and we have water and the paper!" Tante Helga came out of the bedroom, and said, "Oh, my heroes!" Then she gave Gregor a big hug.

"I was coming back from my meeting with Colonel Zirngibl when I saw the water truck heading up our street. Gregor and I raced to our apartment, grabbed water bottles, and ran to the truck. Who knows whether they'll come back again today, so I wanted to make sure you had enough water."

"I have plenty now. I filled up some bottles yesterday, just before the bombing started."

"Yes, yesterday was particularly hard. Now they're bombing us day and night. They seem to be targeting just the inner city and the factories outside of town, but who knows where the next bomb will hit. It could be us." Bettina saw Gregor staring at her, so she added, "But I am sure we will remain safe, as long as we always go to the bomb shelter when the siren goes off." Her son smiled and nodded his head.

Tante Helga asked them to sit down, and Bettina and Gregor both sat at the dining room table. Tante Helga went into the kitchen and came back with three cookies.

"Where did you get these cookies? I haven't had a cookie in such a long time!" Gregor stared at the cookie, waiting for his mother to say it was okay to eat it. "Please, Gregi, eat your cookie." Bettina laughed and took a bite. "Wow, this actually tastes like a real cookie, too."

"A friend of mine brought me cookies yesterday. Her husband is a big-shot official with the government. I didn't ask where she got the cookies, but she wouldn't have told me anyway. They are good, aren't they?"

Bettina felt a little guilty eating something prepared for a Nazi bigwig, using ingredients not available to anyone else. But just a little guilty, saying, "Yes, they're absolutely wonderful."

"I'm glad you're enjoying your little treat. It's so nice to have a treat these days." Tante Helga then took Bettina's hand and sighed. "I'm so relieved to see the two of you. I worry each month when you do your check-in with the Gestapo. Each time you go, I worry that this will be the time you won't return. I just wish Gregi could stay with me when you go."

Bettina took Helga's hand and said, "I worry as well. But so far, Colonel Zirngibl has treated me with respect and has not threatened me or Gregi." Bettina never shared with Helga the colonel's behavior towards her and she never told her she had already asked the colonel whether she could leave Gregor home with her aunt and he had refused. She assumed the Gestapo thought she might send Gregi away to hide, like other Jews did earlier in the war. She smiled at Helga and said, "Let's not think about my visit with the Gestapo. Let's just enjoy this treat!"

Helga smiled and said, "I agree. Anything new in the paper?"

"Not much. And now that the paper is only two pages, I was able to read it as I was waiting for the bottles to be filled." Bettina had been in the habit of reading a newspaper since childhood and so continued to buy the paper, even though it was now mostly a propaganda tool. With the paper and ink shortages, the paper had shrunk to the two pages, and with very little actual news. It was only through a conversation she recently overheard at the grocers that she discovered the Allied invasion of Normandy the previous month, which had been reported in the newspaper as a failure, was actually a success for the Allies.

Tante Helga never wanted to discuss the news, instead saying, "I saw you received a postcard yesterday. From one of your cousins?"

"Yes. This postcard was from my cousin Gustav." Bettina was so excited to finally hear from him she thought it was okay to share that Gustav was alive. But she didn't tell her where the postcard was from, or that the postcard was postmarked three months earlier. Gustav said very little in the postcard – only that he was "happy and healthy" and was in a camp in Poland. Nothing in the cousin's code, and those were not the words Gustav ever would use, so she assumed he was restricted in what he could write to her. But at least he was alive! Since Gertrud was still in Frankfurt, she said nothing to Tante Helga about her youngest cousin. Not that she didn't trust her, but she just didn't want to risk her cousin's safety. Nor did she tell Tante Helga about the special code. Bettina was often amazed that none of the letters she had received had ever been censored. *Maybe the code really does work*, she thought to herself.

Tante Helga took a small bite of her cookie, then said, "I am so sorry for you and your cousins, Bettina. I don't like to discuss politics, but I wish things were different for you and for my darling Gregi."

"I wish things were different for all of us, that we had running water, that we had gas for the stove, and that we all had enough to eat."

Tante Helga took Bettina's hand and said, "Yes, I wish that as well."

At that moment, the air raid alarm sounded. Bettina and Tante Helga gathered the things they needed to keep them occupied for the next few hours – knitting for Tante Helga and Bettina and a few toys for Gregor – and left for the shelter. They could hear the bombs falling, but they were so accustomed to the raids that they walked without speeding up. No point in getting there too early, since, on this July day, the shelter would soon heat up. Bettina was glad she had eaten that cookie!

Monowitz
August 1944

It was hard for Gustav to imagine being any hotter than he felt at that moment. The bright sun was overhead, and they had no shade as they painted the side of the factory wall. *But I'm outside and not lifting enormous bags of cement, so I really shouldn't be complaining,* he thought to himself. In addition, his diarrhea was finally gone. He had been in and out of the infirmary since his first admission in February, always leaving at the end of the two-week period. His last admission was in the middle of June, and he thought this might be the last time he could avoid selection for Birkenau. But miraculously, the medicine finally worked, and when he was discharged on July 1st, the diarrhea was gone. And, so far, no relapse. He always said a special prayer for the doctors who devised this way for him (and others) to avoid the two-week rule and certain death in Birkenau.

Gustav continued to paint and must have been daydreaming since Isaac came up to him and said, "The Kapo will beat you if you don't move that paint brush."

Gustav smiled and said, "Thanks, Isaac. I don't know why I stopped. I don't even remember what I was thinking,"

His friend smiled and said, "I know what you were thinking, and you need to stop."

Gustav lowered his voice and said, "I try, my friend. But, sometimes, it just comes. A certain smell, a certain memory. I felt the strong sun and remembered a day that Gretel and I were walking along the Main River, enjoying a warm sunny day. We saw a boat overturn, and the people in the water were laughing and splashing each other. Then Gretel started to laugh. It was at that moment that I realized I was in love with her."

Isaac grunted and said, "Gustav, you should stop thinking about her and about your life in Frankfurt. That will only cause you pain, and that will not help you to survive this place. Right now, things are good for both of us. We have a good work assignment and the Kapo doesn't randomly beat us, like other Kapos. We even get some extra food because of your mending and the drawings you're doing for some of the civilian workers."

"You're right, Isaac. It's almost like a vacation in the Alps."

"Okay, maybe life isn't perfect, but we're alive, and that is always a good thing. Everyone else on the Kommando that lugged the cement bags is now gone."

Gustav nodded his head and said, "I guess it could be worse. Plus, I get to draw. Sometimes, I'm even able to forget I'm here when I draw. And thinking about Gretel helps to keep the despair at bay." Gustav winked at his friend, then grew more serious. "Isaac, is the diarrhea any better? All this time, you managed to avoid it, and now you can't seem to get rid of it. Of course, no one can understand the challenges of diarrhea better than me."

"It's not so bad. Not bad enough to make me go to the infirmary. Especially now. It seems that anyone showing up now with diarrhea is sent to Birkenau. I guess the SS figured out what the doctors had been doing for patients to avoid the two-week rule and put an end to it."

Gustav patted his friend on the shoulder, but was still worried about him. It was never good to be sick at Monowitz.

They continued to paint the wall of the factory, focusing on the work and avoiding the stick of the Kapo. As Gustav was gathering his supplies to move to the adjacent wall, he heard a loud buzzing in the sky. He looked up and saw what looked like tiny bugs. Then he heard the air raid siren. It was the first time the air raid siren had sounded. The Kapo yelled for them to stay where they were. Gustav looked around him, and saw the civilian workers running for safety, and one of the prisoners asked if they could also run to safety. The Kapo said, "No. Everyone must remain here."

Gustav wanted to yell, "That's crazy!" But he knew the Kapo would beat him, so he stayed where he was. As the air raid siren continued, a smoke canister was released, and Gustav could no longer see the sky, or anything else. But he could hear what he knew were bombers and could tell they were getting closer.

He felt a hand in his hand, and Isaac said, "No one can see us now. I'm sure they're going to bomb this factory. If we stay here, we're dead. We need to take shelter." Gustav said nothing, but held onto his friend's hand as they ran from the building wall and found a place under a tree.

It didn't take long for the first bomb to fall. Gustav heard the noise and felt the explosion. He couldn't see where it landed, but he thought it wasn't far from where they were hiding. Gustav grabbed a large piece of metal near them and covered himself and Isaac. He could soon hear things hitting the metal. The bombing continued non-stop for at least another fifteen minutes. And then there was silence.

Gustav's ears were ringing from the bombings. He and Isaac waited where they were lying until he heard his Kapo yelling for help. He and Isaac ran to the Kapo, who was lying on the ground with a large piece of metal sticking out of his leg. They left him and tried to find someone who could help. But as they were looking for help, they turned to the wall they were painting and saw that it had collapsed. Gustav turned to his friend and said, "Thank you."

•　•　•

That night, the men in their barracks gathered in the bunk elder's room and talked about what had happened that day. The painting Kommando's Kapo had died, as had the Kapo for the electrical Kommando. Twenty-five men from their bunk had also been killed in the raid. No one said it, but everyone in that room was happy the Allies had bombed the factories. Gustav had heard from prisoners who had recently arrived that the Allies had landed at Normandy and were retaking France and that the Russians had been doing well in the east, so this bombing gave him and the rest of his barracks hope. The factory making the synthetic fuel had been damaged. And the new factory's walls would have to be rebuilt. Gustav knew of some attempts by prisoners to sabotage the work, to delay the opening of the rubber factory. But this bombing would be a real blow to the Nazis, and everyone was happy. Although they could never say it out loud.

The bunk elder stood and invited everyone to say the Mourner's Kaddish – the prayer for the dead – for those killed in the bombing. They all knew the Hebrew prayer, whether or not they were religious. So, they all began the prayer. Gustav had been educated in an Orthodox synagogue and could recite it in his sleep. And he did one more thing. He thought about his mother. He hadn't admitted it to himself before, but he now knew she was gone. She had been sent to Birkenau and had died in the gas chamber. And so, while he said Kaddish for his fellow prisoners, he also said Kaddish for his mother. *Yit'gadal, v'yit'kadash sh'may ra'ba…*

•   •   •

The following morning was Sunday. The prisoners normally didn't work on Sundays, but they couldn't work anyway since the IG Farben employees were assessing the damage to the complex. As was the case every Sunday, Barracks 20 was preparing for lice inspection. Gustav undressed and waited in the line for the doctor. When he reached the front of the line, the doctor inspected every part of him. After the doctor was finished, Gustav moved to another line to be shaved with the barracks' only razor. After his shave, Gustav waited to be told to dress. Instead, the bunk elder said, "Everyone needs to go outside and stand for roll call. Naked. Out now!" Gustav grunted and walked out of the barracks with his fellow prisoners.

As he walked towards the courtyard, Gustav noticed that the prisoners from the other barracks were also assembling for roll call. Standing for roll call naked was unusual, and anything unusual was a bad omen. Whenever his bunk assembled naked for their weekly lice inspection, Gustav tried to keep his head down to avoid looking at his fellow prisoners. He knew they were slowly starving to death; he could see it in their sallow skin and sunken eyes. But their uniforms hid most of the destruction the Nazis were doing to their bodies. But standing there with his fellow prisoners, Gustav could not help but look at them. He saw sagging, translucent skin and arms that looked like broomsticks. Ribs were visible on many of the men. A few looked like living skeletons. Many had sores, as well as welts and scars from prior beatings. Gustav turned to his friend Isaac and gasped. Isaac saw Gustav's reaction and whispered, "That damned diarrhea."

After everyone was assembled in the yard, SS Hauptstrumfuhrer Heinrich Schwarz, the commandant of the camp, appeared. Tall and clean shaven, with a ruddy complexion and the beginnings of a belly, he took great pleasure in personally beating prisoners to death. Any time Gustav saw the commandant, he kept his gaze down, hoping to avoid his stick. The commandant glared at the assembly with his cold eyes, then nodded at one of his underlings, who began to address the camp. He said, "We suffered a great tragedy yesterday. The Allies tried to stop our great effort to make the world a better place. But they have failed. You will rebuild what has been damaged, and you will make it stronger. And only the strongest among you will accomplish this. Those who cannot do the work will need to leave the camp, replaced by workers who are coming this very day. We have officers who are now walking among you, determining whether you are capable of continuing this important work."

After the speech ended, SS officers began walking through the yard, looking at the backsides of the men. Isaac said to his friend,

"They are looking to see how much fat we have. We have been reduced to cattle."

One officer came to the Barracks 20 group and walked up the line. He looked at Gustav's behind and continued to Isaac. He then stopped and pulled Isaac out of the line, saying, "This one." Isaac tried to object, but two other officers grabbed him.

As he was pulled away, he said to Gustav in Polish, "Say Kaddish for me." Isaac was not religious, but still wanted to be remembered as a Jew. They had talked about this before, about how one would say the prayer for the other if something were to happen. So, Gustav would say Kaddish for his friend tonight.

•   •   •

Just as the lights went out for the night, Gustav heard noise in the barracks. A new shipment of prisoners had arrived. He heard the bunk elder say to one of the prisoners, "You are in this bunk," and Gustav moved to make room for this new prisoner. Now there would be three in the bunk. He thought the prisoner would want him to say something, so he said, "My name is Gustav. Do you understand me?"

The man said nothing, instead looking around. And then he turned to Gustav and responded, "Yes."

"Where are you from?"

"Amsterdam."

"Some Dutch Jews were selected for Monowitz last week."

"That is the name of this place? Monowitz?"

"When I came here in January, it was just called Auschwitz III. But they decided last month to change the name to Monowitz, which is the name of the town. It doesn't matter what they call it, it is still hell."

The man said nothing, and Gustav then said, "But you should be glad you're here. Being selected for Monowitz is better than the alternative."

"Alternative? Maybe I didn't understand what you're saying because of the language. What do you mean by the alternative?"

And Gustav realized that his new bunkmate didn't understand that, as bad as Monowitz might be, he had just escaped certain death. Then again, Gustav had just escaped death. He had been lucky today. And he had been lucky in the past. That seemed to be one of the keys to survival in this horror of a place. Luck. But how long would his luck last? Just before he went to sleep, Gustav said the Mourner's Kaddish silently for his friend Isaac.

CHAPTER 15

Frankfurt
January 1945

Gertrud was struggling to find a comfortable spot on the couch. Every time she moved, she found a new spring. The couch had been old before it became her permanent bed, and the last few months of sleeping on it had only made it worse. But she had to remind herself that she and her mother and daughter had a place to sleep, with a roof over their heads. She knew others who were living in partially destroyed buildings, with the windows boarded up to prevent snow from getting in. The apartment had no heat, but she was dressed warmly and wrapped in several blankets. Little Heidi was on the other side of the couch, sleeping soundly. Heidi loved the fact that she was sleeping with her mama. Every night before they went to bed, Heidi asked, "Mama, are you sleeping with me tonight?"

Gertrud always responded, "Who else would I sleep with?"

She and her mother had known the baker since her mother first began working at the bakery. They didn't know him well – he rarely spoke – but he was the first to offer them a place to live when their apartment was destroyed. The apartment was small, with a tiny kitchen and small bedroom, and a washroom down the hall. Herr Fischer – it occurred to her at some point that she didn't even know his first name – said he would continue to sleep in his bedroom but carried home a mattress the same day they settled in the apartment. Her mother didn't ask where it came from, happy that she had something to sleep on. Gertrud and her mother shared their rations with Herr Fischer, and he was grateful to have someone cook him a meal, which he said every night when he was served dinner. Although the meals tended to be the same because of the severe food shortages – mostly bread, potatoes, and whatever vegetables they could find. Meat could only be found on the black market, and no one had the money. Herr Fischer didn't talk much during dinner and never asked the women any questions about their lives. Gertrud made sure he knew that both she and her mother were married and that both husbands were in the army, but he didn't seem interested in either woman. He only seemed interested in doing the right thing and in surviving.

Gertrud had the morning shift and needed to leave shortly. Herr Fischer had already left for work, but her mother and daughter were still asleep, so Gertrud was quiet as she gathered her things, left the apartment, and walked down the hall to the washroom. Someone else was in the bathroom. Gertrud gently knocked to let the person know she was waiting. Since she moved in with Herr Fischer, more people had moved into the building, displaced from their own homes. The door to the washroom soon opened, and Gertrud smiled at the woman as she went in. *This person is new*, she thought to herself.

Gertrud washed her faced with the soap that still made her gag, and then she brushed her teeth. As she returned to the apartment, she could see her mother taking out plates for breakfast. The same breakfast they had every day – brown break and ersatz jam. Gertrud smiled at her mother and put down her toiletries. She gently nudged little Heidi, who walked with her grandmother to the washroom. When they returned, the three sat down for breakfast.

"Gertrud, you came in late last night. How were things at the bakery?"

"Busy, as usual. And I need to get to the bakery in about thirty minutes. We're short on staff today. I'm surprised you weren't asked to come in too, although they do know we need to take care of Heidi. I would have been home earlier last night, but I stayed a little later since one of the delivery men had some news about the war. Herr Koch, you know him. He said the Soviet army has been having successes in Poland, taking back land we had taken. He believes we will lose the war and soon. He said that, once the Allies landed in Normandy last year and liberated France, it was only a matter of time before Germany was defeated."

"Wasn't he worried about talking that way about the Nazi government?"

"He lost a son at Normandy, and since that time, he's been pretty bitter. He only talks to a few of us, people he has known for years."

"Gertrud, you still need to be careful. You never know who might be listening."

"I'm always careful, Mama. You know that."

"Yes, I do. But you know me. After all these years, I still worry."

Gertrud quickly finished her breakfast and got dressed for work. While the apartment was cold, the bakery was not, with the ovens working non-stop. She put on a light blouse, just in case the bakery got too warm. As she was putting on her coat, the air raid siren went off. Gertrud grunted and called to Heidi to get dressed. Heidi was so used to the sirens that she knew exactly what to do. Gertrud's mother also dressed. Gertrud picked up their shelter bag that included blankets, and the three of them left the apartment and walked to the shelter. Since they had moved to the neighborhood, there had only been a few alarms, but they knew where the shelter was, a large windowless four-story building built earlier in the war.

They entered the shelter and searched until they found a place to sit. The room was cold and dark, and the three wrapped blankets around themselves. Gertrud and her mother began to knit, and little Heidi played with a doll. Another girl about Heidi's age was sitting near them, and the two girls began to play together.

Gertrud was counting the stitches for a sweater she was making when she became aware that someone was standing in front of her. She looked up, and it was her! Frau Müller! That horrible woman who knew her father. Who knew she was half-Jewish. Who knew she wasn't supposed to be in Germany. Who knew she was a liar. The woman looked over at her mother, then at little Heidi. Gertrud looked at her mother and wondered if her mother recognized this woman. She was showing no signs of recognition, but that meant nothing when it came to her mother.

Finally, the woman spoke. "Hello, Margarete. Gertrud, I see your little baby is not a baby anymore. She doesn't look Jewish to me, but then again, Gertrud never looked Jewish, with that blond hair and blue eyes."

Her mother looked at this woman and said, "I don't know who you are, but I would ask you to leave us alone."

"Yes, you would like me to leave you alone, wouldn't you? But that is not going to happen, not this time. I'm going to find a policeman and I'm going to have you both arrested. Jewish filth was supposed to be gone from the city, and I'll make sure that happens with you. With the two of you. Enjoy your time in the shelter, since your time in Frankfurt is about to come to an end." Then she walked away.

Gertrud looked around the room, but no one was looking at them. Her mother then turned to Gertrud and asked quietly, "You know who this woman is? And you've seen her recently?"

"Frau Müller? Actually, I've seen her twice since we moved out of our first apartment. The first time was with Papa. I didn't think it was important and didn't tell you. The second time was after Heidi was born and we had taken a long walk to the zoo. I didn't want to worry you and thought if I stayed away from the zoo, I wouldn't see her again. But she must live in this neighborhood. Do you think she could make trouble for us?"

"I don't know. She used to spit on the ground when your father walked by, always mumbling something under her breath. When I was by myself, she would say I was a traitor to my race. I haven't seen her since your father and I divorced. I can't believe she remembered you or could even recognize you. Although, I have to admit that your face hasn't really changed since you were a child."

"I can't tell if that's a compliment."

"It's a compliment. You were always a beautiful child, and you are a beautiful woman."

"Thanks, Mama. But I'm sorry about this woman recognizing me. I've always been so careful. No one has known anything about me. Even you don't know about some of the things I have done."

"Is that so? Well, I have a question for you." Then she whispered, "How are your cousins?"

Gertrud blanched a little. "What do you mean?"

"I'm not a fool. Do you think I didn't know about your meetings with Gustav or the letters you and your cousins have been exchanging throughout the war?"

"You knew? Why didn't you say something?"

Her mother responded quietly, "I didn't need to. Even though I told you not to go with Gustav to those cafés you liked, you disobeyed me and went anyway and on a regular basis. But I could see you were being careful, and so I let you go. I knew you were writing to your cousins, but I could tell you were also being careful. I found one of the letters, a long time ago, along with that poem, so I knew all about the code, which I did think was especially clever. *Prometheus*? I remember learning that poem when I was in school. I never thought you paid attention to anything in school other than boys. Besides, you would have likely done something more reckless if I had tried to stop you. In that way, you are like your father. I needed to protect you, and letters exchanged with your cousins seemed to make the most sense. If I ever thought you were putting yourself in any danger, I would have stopped it. I knew you needed it, especially after you lost the baby. By the way, I loved the beautiful drawing Gustav made for you when you were in the hospital."

"I can't believe you knew about this all along. And you knew the drawing was from Gustav!"

"So, tell me how they are doing."

"Mama, let's sit in the corner, away from people." They moved to an empty bench a few yards away, and Gertrud began. "I will start with Gustav, since you mentioned him first. Gustav and his family escaped to Belgium at the end of 1941. In September 1942, his mother was arrested, and in September 1943, Gustav was arrested and deported to the Monowitz labor camp in Poland. He has been able to send a few postcards to Bettina. The last time she heard from him was in October, although the postcard was postmarked July. Nothing since." A tear fell down Gertrud's cheek and her mother squeezed her hand.

"Gertrud, I am so sorry to hear that. I know how much you love Gustav. I'm sure he's fine."

"I hope so, but I've heard rumors at the bakery that many of the Jews sent to the east are being murdered by the Nazis."

Her mother looked at Gertrud and said, "I don't want you speaking about that at the bakery. Other people can overhear conversations and get you into trouble."

"Mama, that's not the point. I have been careful. The point is that I worry about Gustav." Gertrud took a deep breath, wiped her eyes, and continued. "I haven't heard from Trudi since last March when she wrote that her family would be leaving their home just outside of Lyon because it was no longer safe. Their daughter Ruth died in 1940, which was really sad for the family. Trudi was pregnant again when she wrote. She was due last October, and I don't know if she had the baby or if something happened to her or the baby. I'm really worried about her. Mail service between France and Germany was poor even before France was liberated, so that might be the problem. When she wrote to me, Onkel Jacob and Tante Lili were being moved to a clinic in Lyon. I hope they're all safe and weren't sent to any of the camps."

"I sometimes had issues with your father's family, but I always liked Jacob and Lili. Now that leaves Bettina. You were closest to Bettina. She really was like a sister to you growing up."

"That's true. She moved to Munich because her husband got a job there. It was hard for me when she moved. She and I have been in constant communication throughout the war, which is how I know about Gustav. Her mother was deported at the end of 1941, and Bettina doesn't know where she is. But, so far, Bettina is safe. They haven't deported her because she is married to a non-Jew. Her son Gregor was born in 1938, just after they moved to Munich, and he has been a great comfort to her. Her husband was drafted last year, but she is close to her husband's aunt, who actually owns the building they're living in. But I do worry about the constant bombing of Munich. It's worse than here, from what I've read. She hasn't left Munich, like many of her neighbors. I think the two of us write so often just to give assurances to the other that we have survived another bombing. Assuming she survives all that bombing, I believe she will be fine. Which is a relief."

Her mother looked over at Heidi, who was playing with her new friend, then looked back at her daughter and asked, "And your father? I had asked you to stop communicating with him after Kristallnacht for your own protection. But I assumed you were still communicating through one of your cousins."

"It was through Gustav. I actually haven't heard from Papa since October 1941, when he wrote he was being deported to Lodz in Poland. Since Gustav left Frankfurt just after I received Papa's letter, he has no way of communicating with me. I am so worried about him."

Margarete took her daughter's hand and gave it a squeeze. "Gertrud, I'm sorry about your Papa. I assumed he was deported after I read all Jews living in Prague had been deported. I'm sorry you thought you couldn't tell me about your Papa and your cousins.

That was wrong of me. But Gertrud, you need to understand why I wanted you to avoid your cousins. Anyone seeing you with them might have suspected that you were not what you claimed to be, a non-Jew. I am sorry that I had to do it."

"They were my family, and being cut off from them was like losing a limb. I didn't understand why you did what you did when I was younger. But, as it turns out, it was the only thing that prevented me from being deported. Who knows where I would be if you hadn't altered my records. I might be living in a concentration camp, or in one of the ghettos. I certainly wouldn't be married to Franz or have little Heidi. And who knows whether I would even be alive."

Margarete looked directly at her daughter and said, "Gertrud, you probably think I wanted to hide the truth about your father because he is Jewish. That's actually not why, although it became necessary after the Nuremburg Laws were passed. I couldn't explain it to you then because you were too young to understand, but I should have explained it to you when you were older. But by that point, you had to deny your father was a Jew. The initial reason, however, was because I worried that your father's political activity would get you into trouble. While he was just a Social Democrat, I didn't worry as much. But after our divorce, he became involved with the Socialist Party, and I was convinced that, one day, he would be arrested. He actually would have been arrested if he hadn't fled to Prague. I didn't want his arrest to affect you. Fortunately, he didn't tell you about any of that activity."

Gertrud chose not to tell her mother the truth about what she knew. What would be the point now? "Mama, you could have told me sooner. I would have understood, and I think it might have made things easier. But maybe not."

The two remained quiet for a minute, then Margarete said, "I'm sure you don't remember what used to be here before they built this ugly shelter, but I remember. It was a synagogue, and it was where Gustav had his bar mitzvah. The building was quite ornate, with lots of stained-glass windows. Your father told me the Rothschild banking family donated the money to build the synagogue. It was destroyed during Kristallnacht. Very sad."

Gertrud nodded, but said nothing in response. She was exhausted from the confrontation with Frau Müller and her mother's explanation of why she had to deny the existence of her father and cousins. Instead, the two women returned to their original bench and their knitting, remaining quiet until the "all clear" sounded. Heidi started to cry when she was told she needed to say goodbye to her friend, but stopped crying when her grandmother said they could walk to the park later. As Gertrud neared the door, she saw Frau Muller waiting, glaring at her and standing next to a police officer. As she got to the door, the woman grabbed Gertrud's arm and said, "Gertrud Heppenheimer, you aren't going anywhere. Officer!"

Margarete pulled the woman's arm away, and Frau Müller fell backwards into the policeman. Margarete grabbed her granddaughter's hand and said, "Come, little Heidi. Let's go home and then to the park." She then turned to Gertrud and whispered, "Don't run. We don't want to draw attention to ourselves." And the three walked quickly into the bright light of the cold January day, joining the crowd leaving the shelter.

Munich
February 1945

Bettina was outside with Gregor, helping to clean the streets from the last bombing. She saw a few neighbors she knew, but most of the people were strangers to her. Had they lived here throughout the war, or had they just moved here because there was no shelter or food outside the city? Bettina concentrated on sweeping and avoiding most of her neighbors. But she saw Frau Becker. Like herself, Frau Becker was a Jew married to a non-Jew. She discovered this only by accident, when Gregor said something to Frau Becker's son, even though he was instructed not to say anything. Bettina worried about what this woman would say, but Frau Becker said, "Don't worry. I am also in a privileged marriage." When they could, they shared any information they had about their privileged status or about the war. Frau Becker's husband had also been drafted, but earlier in the war. She had also lost her forced labor position when her factory had been destroyed.

"Ilse," Bettina said to her friend, "I see you and Rolf are also helping with today's mess."

"Rolf actually likes to clean up, so I'm helping both the community and myself by getting him out of the apartment."

"Gregi doesn't love this, but he sure seems happy to be doing it with Rolf."

"Yes, as long as they stay in the street and away from the craters from yesterday's bombing."

"I think we'll need to watch both of them, Ilse. So, have you heard any news?"

"I actually have." She dropped her voice to a whisper. "A friend heard that the German army has suffered a big defeat in Belgium. This friend thinks this might be the beginning of the end for the German army. The foreign newspapers are calling it 'The Battle of the Bulge.'"

Bettina knew better than to ask Ilse about this "friend." Bettina suspected Ilse might be involved with the resistance, but she certainly never asked. Instead, she said, "Well, we certainly wouldn't have seen any mention of defeat in our newspapers. All they talk about is the greatness of the German military and how victory is just around the corner."

Bettina became distracted by a noise and noticed both boys playing too close to a crater. "Rolf, Gregi, get away from that crater. It's too dangerous." The boys reluctantly walked away and returned to help their mothers.

The day was very cold, and Bettina's fingers were growing numb from the cold, so she decided it was time to leave. She had found some wood and was eager to heat up the stove and get warm.

She said goodbye to Ilse and she and Gregor walked back to their apartment. On the way back, she stopped to see if the market had received any food supplies. The Allies' bombing had destroyed the rail lines, so deliveries had to be made by truck or even a horse-drawn cart. She went into the store and saw that some potatoes and onions had been delivered, and she took out her ration book and purchased some of each. "Looks like we're going to have a potato and onion soup tonight, Gregi." He made a face, and they both laughed.

When they reached their apartment, Bettina told Gregor to ask Tante Helga to come down to their apartment. "I'm sure she is cold in her place and would want to sit close to our stove. We can ask her if she would like to have some of our potato and onion soup."

"And maybe she still has some of those cookies."

Bettina winked at her son and said, "Yes, that would be nice." Gregor ran upstairs, and Bettina walked into the cold apartment. She opened the front of the stove and put several pieces of wood inside. She then took some newspaper, lit it, and added it to the stove. Bettina thought to herself, *This is the only thing this rotten Nazi paper is good for.* As the stove heated up, Gregor and Tante Helga walked in. And sure enough, she had three cookies in her hand.

"I was saving these for a special occasion. Potato and onion soup sounds like a special occasion." The three laughed and Bettina told the two to sit down.

She poured water from one of the bottles into the kettle and said, "How can we have cookies without ersatz coffee?" As Bettina was preparing the coffee, she heard a knock at the door. She wasn't expecting anyone. Then she realized knocks on the door generally meant bad news. Maybe something had happened to Hans. She hurried to the door.

When she opened the door, she saw a man standing there in a Gestapo uniform. Why would the Gestapo be here? Then she started to worry for a different reason. He immediately asked, "Are you Frau Bettina Schnitzler?"

She found her voice and answered, "I am."

"And is that your son, Gregor?"

"He is."

"And who is that?"

"That is my husband's aunt."

"Is she a Jew?"

"No."

He then handed her an envelope and said, "This is for you. Read it carefully and follow the instructions. There will be serious consequences for you and your son if you fail to follow the instructions." He turned around and walked down the stairs.

Bettina immediately opened the envelope, read it, and sank into the closest chair. She sighed loudly and put her head in her hands.

Tante Helga asked, "What is it, Bettina? You can tell me."

Bettina exhaled loudly and said, "From everything I have heard, the war is nearly over. Tante Helga, I know this may come as a surprise, but Germany will lose the war. It may take a month, it may take a year, but Germany will lose. And what do the Nazis care about most? Taking care of the German people? Seeing that no more German soldiers die needlessly? No. What they care about is getting rid of every Jew in Germany."

Tante Helga pulled up a chair, sat down next to Bettina, and asked, "What does the notice say?"

"It informs me that Gregi and I will be deported. Those in privileged marriages are no longer exempt from deportation. They are coming here in two days to take us away. 'For our own protection' the notice says. Gregi and I have survived this long, after my mother was taken, after we have struggled to eat and stay warm, after we have been hit with one bomb after another, after avoiding that Gestapo colonel's advances. And when we are so close to the end of this madness, they are coming to take us away! To who knows where? And who knows what they will do to us?

Why didn't I leave Germany when everyone told me to leave? Why did I believe Hans when he said he would protect us? Liars! They are all liars!"

Bettina had never spoken this way in front of Tante Helga. She had always been careful about sharing how she really felt. But getting rid of German Jews now was pure madness. And evil. She wanted to scream it to Tante Helga. She wanted to scream it to the world. She looked over and saw Gregor. He looked frightened. Then she looked at Tante Helga. She was clearly upset, but Bettina couldn't tell what she was thinking.

Then she regretted that Tante Helga was there. She loved this woman, but she also recognized that Tante Helga was a good German. Plus, her husband was well-connected with Nazi officials. It was not in her nature to break the rules. Especially the big ones. Like deporting Jews. And now Tante Helga knew that Bettina and her son had received a deportation notice.

Before Bettina could say anything else, Tante Helga said, "Bettina, please don't worry. I'm sure it will all work out." Bettina could see Tante Helga wringing her hands.

Tante Helga would be of no help now. Bettina needed cunning; she needed sneakiness. She needed a rules breaker. If one of Bettina's cousins had been there, they could help her figure this out. She remembered Gustav's letter after he made it across the Belgium border, about how his mother had said, "We are not going to be deported," when they first received the notice. She needed a Tante Paula. Instead, she had Tante Helga and Gregor. An old woman and an innocent little boy.

Bettina looked at her son. She knew Gregor had been listening and understood what was happening. He slowly walked up to his mother and asked, "Mama, what are we going to do?"

Bettina knew she needed to be honest with her son. "Liebling, I just don't know."

EPILOGUE

Frankfurt
June 1996

The old woman was looking at the menu when she heard familiar voices. She looked up and saw her cousins walking towards her, waving. She stood up and hugged them both when they reached the table. Through her tears, she said, "I am so happy to see you two." After a few more seconds of embracing, the three sat down.

"Bettina, why are there four menus on the table?"

"Of course you would notice that, Gertrud. I was so caught up in the moment of being in Frankfurt that I forgot there were only three of us today."

"I completely understand. As we were walking into the café, Trudi said that she thought she saw Gustav."

"Gertrud, that's not what I said. I said I was expecting to see Gustav, but of course, we know that won't happen."

The three sadly nodded their heads. They opened their menus quickly, and Bettina signaled to the waiter, who came over to take their orders. As he walked away, Gertrud said, "Bettina, this was a great idea to have lunch here. It's not our café, but it's probably one of the few left from our era."

Bettina nodded, and said, "I was remembering how my mother used to take me here after we went shopping. I was walking around the Zeil earlier – and boy has that street changed – and I remember her taking me to Kaufhaus Wronker. Trudi, do you remember you and your mother coming into Frankfurt to buy your wedding dress there? Gertrud and I met you there to pick out linens. Afterwards, we met your mother for coffee and cake."

Gertrud laughed. "I remember that day. I remember your mother left us to visit family, and we spent the afternoon walking around the store giggling and not actually picking out anything. Your mother was so annoyed and made you and me go back the next day to pick out the linens. The other thing I remember was all the clothes your mother bought you on that trip!"

Bettina winked at her cousin. "I must say I always felt so ordinary whenever I stood next to you in your matching dress, hat, shoes, and purse."

"Bettina, if you notice, I'm only matching my dress and shoes today." All three laughed.

Trudi then took Bettina's hand and said, "I know how hard it is for you to be in Frankfurt. I just want to make sure you're okay."

Bettina sighed and said, "It was a little hard when I first landed in Frankfurt, but I'm okay right now. Maybe walking along the Zeil before I came to the café helped. Or maybe just being with my cousins."

Trudi squeezed Bettina's hand and smiled. "I'm sure that's what it is. Still, I want you to let us know if things change for you." Bettina shook her head, but didn't respond.

Gertrud then spoke. "Bettina, I understand Alfred isn't coming."

Bettina nodded and responded, "I had encouraged him to come, and at first, he said he would think about it. But then he said he would come another time. But I don't think he will. Like me before today, he has not been back to Germany since the end of the war. And I don't think he has any intention of ever returning."

The waiter brought their coffees and salads, and they started to eat their lunch. Bettina then put down her fork and said, "Flying over from America, I was thinking about how all of us were living in Germany or German-occupied lands through the war and how incredible it is that the three of us actually survived, especially since we were Jews. And Gertrud, as far as the Nazis were concerned, you were a Jew. Almost all Jews remaining here during the war did not survive the nightmare, and any one of us could have died at any moment. Each of us faced death more than once during the war, and yet we made it. And with all that he went through, Gustav almost made it as well." Bettina's voice cracked a little, and she took a sip of her coffee. She continued, "It makes me so sad – and angry – to know how close he came to surviving."

Trudi nodded her head and said, "With everything we know now, once he was arrested in Brussels, it would have been nearly impossible for Gustav to survive the war. The three of us always stood the better chance – I was in France, no one knew Gertrud was half-Jewish, and Bettina, you were in a privileged marriage. I remember Gustav writing to me just before he was arrested, regretting that they had registered with the Brussels Jewish Community in the first place. But maybe he still would have been arrested. Who knows? But I agree with you Bettina, it is rather astonishing that all three of us made it, especially the two of you, actually living in Nazi Germany throughout the war and with all those bombings."

Bettina looked at her cousin and said, "Although, Trudi, you scared both Gertrud and me. We didn't know if you were even alive until the middle of 1945. We worried that you and your family had been arrested in France and sent to a concentration camp."

"When the Swiss border guard arrested us just after we climbed over the fence, I was sure they would send us back, and who knows what would have happened to us if that had happened? But the Swiss let us stay and I was able to have my daughter Eiliane in a safe place. I'm sorry I scared the two of you. I tried to write you, but every letter came back. Germany had stopped all mail coming from Switzerland by the time we crossed the border. And I didn't know how terrible it must have been living with almost daily bombings. From everything you both told me, you would have thought it would have been a bomb that almost got either of you. But it wasn't."

Gertrud laughed and said, "That's right. My nemesis was Frau Müller. When I saw her at the door of the shelter, standing near a police officer, I was certain we would be arrested. After all those years of successfully lying and hiding! But after my mother pulled her away from me, Frau Müller fell on the officer and started screaming about her leg. The officer yelled for help, and they were probably too busy trying to calm her down to chase after us. We did avoid spending time outside over the next two months, other than going to and from work, and once I thought I saw her in the street and ran the other way. But Frankfurt was liberated two months later and I no longer had to worry."

"I loved that when you told Franz that your father was Jewish and that he had been deported, the first thing he said was, 'We need to find him.' You were worried about how he would react, and he reacted in just the way you needed him to. He was a good man. And so was Onkel Robert. I'm so sorry that he perished."

"Thank you, Bettina. I still miss my father. Although I had my mother until 1977, and she was a wonderful grandmother to Heidi and great-grandmother to Heidi's children." Gertrud remained quiet for a moment, then said, "But, Bettina, your life in Munich turned out to be even more at risk than mine."

"Gertrud, you mean the fact that Gregi and I were almost deported? When they brought that deportation notice, I was pretty stunned. It was February. The war was practically over, and Germany was about to lose. And they wanted to deport us? But dear Tante Helga really surprised me. She said, 'You two are not going to be deported. You are moving in with me. If anyone asks about you, I will tell them you left town.' So, we moved upstairs. On the day of our deportation, we heard someone come to our apartment, but, of course, we weren't there. No one came again over the next two months, and then the war was over. But in those two months, until the Allies liberated the city, Tante Helga kept saying that no one was taking her Gregi. And she wouldn't let us leave the apartment – she did all the shopping and got all the water. That woman was our hero. I miss her."

Trudi took her cousin's hand and said, "And I really miss your mother. That was one of the hardest things to learn after the war, the way Tante Henny died. Shot a few days after she arrived in the Soviet Union and buried in a field."

Bettina wiped away a tear, took a deep breath, and said, "Both of you know I don't like to talk about the war, except with the two of you. And even then…" Bettina stopped speaking and took a sip of her coffee. She waited a moment, then said, "Still, I often think about my mother. She was a special woman. I'm glad she had time to spend with Gregi and that Gregi has some wonderful memories of her. It's a horror to know how my mother died, but I wish I knew what happened to Gustav. I received two postcards from him at Monowitz; the last was postmarked July 1944. And then nothing."

"Gretel also tracked Gustav to Monowitz, but so many of the records are missing or were destroyed by the Nazis, so she was only able to confirm that he wasn't among those who survived the camp. He might have died there, or he might have died on the death march after the camp was evacuated in 1945."

"Gertrud, I'm so glad you were able to work with Gretel to find out as much as you did. Are you still in touch with her?"

"No, Trudi. We lost touch years ago. I think it was too hard for both of us – every time we saw each other, it was a reminder that Gustav was gone. I know she married and had children, but I wonder if she ever got over the loss of Gustav. On some level, I don't think I ever did."

The other two cousins responded in unison, "Me either."

Trudi took a sip of her coffee and said, "Let's stop talking about the past. Bettina, how is life in America?"

"Life is good. I'm busy with friends and get to spend time with Gregi. And no, Gertrud, I don't miss Germany, in case you're wondering. After everything that happened, I couldn't stay. When

Hans came back from the war, I told him I needed to leave. I didn't expect him to join me, and to be perfectly honest, I wasn't unhappy when he said he wanted to stay. I think he was more upset that I was taking Gregi with me. But he was able to see Gregi a few times before he passed away."

Gertrud nodded and said, "After everything you went through, I would have been surprised if you had stayed. My mother was here, so it made sense for me to stay in Frankfurt. It was mostly sad for me because, when you left Germany, no cousin was left but me. But little Heidi – who is not so little anymore – has blessed me with grandchildren, so I can't complain. Although I do miss Franz."

Trudi sighed and said, "And I miss Joseph. It's hard to be alone. Especially since Eiliane moved to Israel with her family more than ten years ago. I hardly get to see her children, although I like having Laure and her family close by. Who would have thought we would remain in Lyon and not return to Strasbourg? I must admit that I sometimes miss living in Strasbourg, and I will always miss that Matisse painting, which we never recovered!" The three laughed, but then grew quiet.

A moment later, Gertrud cleared her throat and said, "I always thought Gustav would return. Even after the war, and even after we knew he was gone, I expected him to knock on my door and say, 'Hello, spätz.' With that wide grin and that twinkle in his eye. Which is why it has been so hard over these years to remember our last conversation, when he was so upset and so scared, and when I agreed to his request. I can remember every word we said to each other. I even remember when – it was early September 1941, just before Jews were required to wear yellow stars and before we decided it was too dangerous to see each other again."

Bettina reached over and held Gertrud's hand and said, "I've heard the story so many times that it's like I was there. You went to the zoo that morning, excited to share the news that you were pregnant and that the doctor thought things would be fine with this pregnancy. The zoo was busy with families enjoying the sunny

Sunday and you were running a little late, but you didn't worry because Gustav was always late."

Then Trudi picked up the story. "When you arrived at the bench in a remote location of the zoo, you were surprised to see Gustav standing next to the bench, his back turned to you. You whistled a familiar tune so he wouldn't be startled, and when he stood up and turned around, his normal smile was missing, replaced with a grimace."

"Gustav, why the long face? Aren't you glad to see your favorite cousin?"

Gustav walked to his cousin and hugged her tightly. Gertrud waited a few seconds, then pushed back from the embrace. "Gustav, what's wrong?"

Gustav took his cousin's hand and led her back to the bench, but remained standing. He said, almost in a whisper. "Gertrud, I almost didn't come. But I knew you would worry, and so I came. You know about the activity I do when I'm not working?" Gertrud nodded her head, and Gustav continued. "I was to meet my contact this morning to deliver supplies. As I was walking across the street, Gestapo officers raced to my contact and threw him to the ground. I turned and walked the other way. I could hear him yelling and heard the car drive away."

"Oh no. What will happen to him?"

"Nothing good. He will probably be sent to a concentration camp. Or worse. If I had reached him thirty seconds earlier, I would have been arrested as well. I always knew the risks of what I was doing, but somehow, I never thought about the possibility of getting caught. I always said to myself that, as long as I was careful, nothing would happen to me. But bad things can happen to me. And I might die, regardless of how careful I am."

"I have also worried that you might get caught some day. But you aren't doing anything bad. You're just helping sick people."

"Not in the eyes of the Nazis. They don't even see us as people."

Gustav stopped talking and his face took on an even more serious tone. "I don't know if I mentioned to you that over the last year, I have been going to synagogue on the way to work to help make a minyan. In order to pray, there needs to be ten men together, and my mother asked me to help out after my stepfather left for England. They have been meeting in a small building near my apartment since the synagogue was destroyed during Kristallnacht. In the beginning, I was just saying the words. They didn't mean anything to me. But the constant reminders by the Nazis that I am a Jew have made me think about what it actually means to be a Jew. Without my realizing it, the prayers began to take on a meaning. Maybe that's why my mother asked me to do this in the first place. In fact, when I was almost arrested this morning, I never felt more Jewish. Spätz, I have a favor to ask of you. I know you're going to think this is crazy, but if anything were ever to happen to me, I want you and Bettina and Trudi to say the Mourner's Kaddish for me. But I want the three of you to say it together. I know you don't know the words, but you know it's said after someone dies. Bettina and Trudi can help you with the prayer. You three are like sisters to me, and I'll feel better knowing you will all say it together. I will write to Bettina and Trudi and ask them for the same promise."

"You know I would do anything for you, but why is this so important?"

"We had a discussion recently at our makeshift synagogue. The rabbi has escaped already, but the cantor has been leading services, and he spoke about remembering a righteous person after they die. He said that a righteous person may die, but they still live on in the good things they have done. And when the Mourner's Kaddish is said, the good things the person did are remembered by those saying the Kaddish. In addition, for the person you are remembering, the burdens he has carried in his life are released. I don't know if I believe that the prayer would release me from all the things I have done or have been done to me, but it is a nice thought. To have my spirit free. Plus, I like the idea of living on through the three of you."

"And what about Gretel? Should we include her?"

"You know how I feel about Gretel. She is my life. And if anything were to happen to me, I know she would mourn me in her own way. But the three of you are blood. Jewish blood. And I am a Jew. That's why I want just the three of you to do this for me."

"If we can end this depressing conversation by agreeing to this promise, then I promise. And I will make them promise as well."

Gustav's smile returned for the first time, and he had a look of relief. "Thank you."

The three cousins remained quiet for a moment, then Gertrud said, "And here we are, fulfilling that promise. More than fifty years later."

Bettina smiled sadly and said, "I take full responsibility for the fifty-year delay. I never wanted to set foot in Germany again, but it never felt right to say the Kaddish when you two came to visit me in America or when I came to visit you two in France. Or maybe I just didn't want to bring up all those memories. But when we were invited to attend the opening of the Frankfurt Memorial, I knew it was time to return to Frankfurt and for us to say the Kaddish here. I know this might sound crazy, but when I received the invitation, I actually felt like Gustav was encouraging me to attend and to attend with the two of you."

The other two cousins smiled, and Trudi said, "I don't think that is crazy at all. And Bettina, I know how hard this is for you, but it is also very brave."

•   •   •

The Frankfurt Memorial at Börneplatz was a frieze on the outer wall of the Old Jewish Cemetery, with more than 11,000 metal blocks, each containing the name of a Frankfurt victim of the Holocaust. The ceremony dedicating the memorial was to begin at four p.m. Before the ceremony began, the three cousins walked the length of the wall to find three blocks. They were in alphabetical order, making it easy to find the three "Heppenheimer" blocks. The first block they saw was Henny's. It contained her birth date, deportation date, and death date. Bettina touched it first, followed by her cousins. Bettina said, "Mama, I miss you every day." She then wiped a tear.

The next block they saw was Robert's. Gertrud was the first to touch it, and she started to cry. Bettina and Trudi immediately went to their cousin and hugged her tight. Bettina understood. There was something about seeing the block that made her father's death even more real.

Finally, the cousins saw what had brought them back together. Gustav's block. It contained his name, date of birth, but no date of death because no one knew where or when he died. It could have been in the Monowitz infirmary, on his work detail, in the camp yard following a savage beating, in a crematorium, on the brutal death march from Poland to Germany. The cousins stood before the block as the ceremony began.

The Mayor of Frankfurt spoke first, describing the city's large and vibrant Jewish community before World War II, which included a Jewish mayor before the Nazis took power, and noting that, while there were 26,000 Jews living in Frankfurt in 1933, just 100 Jews remained when the Allies liberated the city. He spoke in some detail about the Jews who were deported in the early years of the war and the struggles of others to remain in hiding. Bettina was finding the speech painful to listen to. Any time she spoke about her life during the war, or listened to other speak about that period, she would become depressed, sometimes for days. She would wonder about a world that could allow for the slaughter of six million Jews. One was her mother. And two of those could have been she and Gregor. She expected to have that same feeling of hopelessness after the ceremony was over, but she needed to come for Gustav.

Bettina stopped listening to the speech and thought instead about Gustav. Looking at his block, she started to remember the last time she saw him. They were packing up her mother's apartment for the move to Munich. He was so handsome with his brown wavy hair and blue eyes. As she continued to stare at his block, a fuzzy image appeared. She blinked several times, and the image grew clearer. Then she could see that it was Gustav! Was she going crazy? She shut her eyes and shook her head hard, hoping the image would disappear, but when she opened her eyes again, he was still there. He looked as he did that day in the apartment, young and hopeful. With his whole life before him. He smiled at her and said, "Sorry I'm late. Thank you for bringing everyone together to say Kaddish for me. Just as you promised." She stared at him for a moment, then smiled to herself. She said silently to Gustav, *How could I not come? I promised. And soon your burdens will be lifted.* She closed her eyes, and when she opened them again, Gustav had turned into a blue butterfly. And she remembered – Pandora's box and the butterfly of hope. She had kept the drawing of the butterfly he made for her when they were packing for her move from Frankfurt. It had travelled with her to Munich and then to America, and it was now in her purse. She hugged her purse. The butterfly flew to her, touched her arm gently, then flew away.

After the speeches were finished and as the attendees started to walk away, Bettina passed out the transliterated version of the Mourner's Kaddish - since Gertrud never could read Hebrew and Trudi and Bettina had forgotten how to read it. Bettina had said it at her father's funeral, but didn't say it after she received confirmation that her mother had perished, and had never said it for her. Trudi had said it with her mother Lili when her father Jacob died soon after her return to France from Switzerland in 1945, when her mother passed away in 1956, and when Joseph died in 1975. Gertrud had never said it before. They began, ignoring all the other activity around them, *"Yit'gadal, v'yit'kadash sh'may ra'ba..."*

After they finished saying the Kaddish, each took a pebble and placed it on Gustav's block, to let others know that family had come to remember him. And as a marker that they had fulfilled their promise. Bettina then took her cousins' hands and said, "Gustav, today we fulfilled our promise to you. We remember how well you lived your life and how good you were to others. You were a righteous person, and we love you. May your memory be a blessing." Bettina dropped her cousins' hands and wiped away a few tears.

Bettina soon noticed that she felt a little lighter, a little less burdened and actually a little more hopeful. Then she remembered that, when they were burying her father, Gustav had said to her that the Kaddish was also a prayer for better days, a prayer that expresses hope for the future. She looked at her cousins, and even with tear-stained cheeks, each was smiling. She knew they were both remembering Gustav and that saying the Kaddish also seemed to unburden them a bit. Perhaps it gave them a little more hope.

She then realized this was Gustav's last gift to them. He knew the power of the Kaddish, for himself and for his cousins, and the power of saying it together. That was just like Gustav, Bettina thought to herself. Relieving their burdens and giving the three the gift of hope.

Trudi and Gertrud started to walk away, but Bettina remained in place. Trudi turned back to her cousin and Bettina said, "I would like to spend a little more time with my mother. I will see you both later for dinner." Both Trudi and Gertrud nodded knowingly and continued to walk away. Bettina touched her mother's block and began to recite the Kaddish for the first time.

Author's Note and Acknowledgements

In 2021, after more than three years of research, I published a non-fiction book about my husband Bruce's German Jewish family, *Broken Promises: The Story of a Jewish Family in Germany*. Through this research, I discovered the Heppenheimer family, a remarkable family whose history tells the story of Jews in Germany from the late seventeenth century through the Holocaust. The families of three Heppenheimer brothers – Joseph (my husband's great-grandfather), Lazarus, and Maier – were still in Germany when Hitler came to power. After I finished the non-fiction book, I realized I was not finished telling their stories. I decided to write their stories as novels and to write them as a trilogy. The first novel in the trilogy, *Stumbling Stones*, was published in 2024 and focused on the origins of the Holocaust as seen through the children of Joseph Heppenheimer, especially his remarkable daughter, Alice. *What Remains is Hope* tells the story of the Holocaust through the grandchildren of Lazarus Heppenheimer. The third novel will focus on the children and grandchildren of Maier Heppenheimer.

In the "Author's Note" accompanying *Stumbling Stones*, I wrote of the challenges in telling the story of people I never knew. In *Stumbling Stones*, I was particularly challenged because no one knew anything about the main characters in the story. For this novel, I was fortunate in that I was able to rely on first-hand knowledge from some family members. Trudi's daughter Eiliane's husband Jean Horgan shared with me remembrances about the family's life in France during the war. And Bettina's son Greg (he changed his name from Gregor when he immigrated) provided me with touching accounts of his life in Munich during the war, including when he received the stuffed teddy bear from his Oma Henny (which he still has). These personal recollections allowed me to bring to life the many records I obtained through my research of the family.

As was the case in *Stumbling Stones*, to give context to the various events in the lives of the four cousins, I did extensive research of the period. This was particularly important in answering certain questions I had after reviewing some of the documentation. For example, when I received Gustav's hospital records from the Auschwitz Museum, I was puzzled at his repeated hospitalizations, each of which lasted only two weeks. It was only after I found a chapter in the book *History 1933-1948: What We Chose to Remember* written by Ewa Bacon, a history professor and the daughter of the doctor who established the infirmary at Monowitz, that I learned of the two-week discharge system that the doctors developed that allowed patients to avoid (or at least delay) the gas chamber.

Gustav's brother, Alfred, included in his request for reparations to the German government after the war very brief description of their attempt to escape to France and their successful escape across the German/Belgium border. I looked to more detailed descriptions of the harrowing journeys of others to capture the challenges likely faced by Gustav, Paula, and Alfred during their crossing. And because Gustav's records in Monowitz are limited to his hospital records, I looked to the experiences of others in the camp. Of particular help was Primo Levi's book, *If this is a Man* (also known as *Survival in Auschwitz*), which detailed Levi's experiences in Monowitz.

In researching and writing this account of the four cousins, I thought about what it would take for these four cousins to live through the war, and I concluded that it must have included hope. Hope is a very important concept in the Jewish religion. The late Chief Rabbi of the United Kingdom Jonathan Sachs wrote that "the Greeks gave the world the concept of tragedy. Jews gave it the idea of hope." Gertrud never considered herself Jewish, and of the other three, I imagined only Gustav had a strong connection to religion, at least growing up. However they learned hope, there is little doubt that the three wouldn't have survived the war without it. We will never know how Gustav died – the last record in the Auschwitz files was his release from the hospital in July 1944. In his book *Man's Search for Meaning*, the renowned psychologist and Holocaust survivor Viktor Frankl noted that the death rate in the week between Christmas, 1944 and New Year's Day, 1945 dramatically increased in Auschwitz because the prisoners thought they would be home by Christmas. Frankl wrote, "As the time drew near and there was no encouraging news, the prisoners lost courage and disappointment overcame them." That may have been what happened to Gustav. After years of holding onto to hope, he may have simply, in the words of Frankl, "lost faith in the future."

I don't know whether the four cousins had the kind of relationship I imagined in the book, sharing letters throughout the war using a secret code. But secret codes in letters were used throughout the war to keep families informed. All postcards and letters sent throughout the Nazi-occupied lands were heavily censored, but people found ways of sending coded messages. For example, Hebrew words were camouflaged as family names to alert the recipient of a deportation. Letters from concentration camps were limited to a single contact person, and the prisoners were instructed to inform families they were happy and healthy. But even in these postcards, which were intended to let families know that the sender was alive, coded messages were sometimes included that described the situation in the camps.

As for the three cousins who survived the war, they lived long lives. Bettina passed away in 2006 in Virginia at 94. Trudi passed away in 2007 in Lyon at 92. And Gertrud lived until 2004, having never left Germany. She was 84.

I have a number of people to thank for their support and suggestions as I wrote the book. I must start with my golfing friends Laura Manning Johnson and Julie Isaac, who encouraged me to start this journey of fiction writing. My sister Lisa and brother-in-law Richard Altabe advised me on Judaic content. This is the second book my sister-in-law Rachel Heppen has read and, as always, provided me with incredibly helpful comments. I am grateful for the support provided by my publisher Black Rose Writing and the entire BRW team, particularly my editor Mary Ellen Bramwell, whose suggestions made this a better book. My children Emily and Jonathan (the next generation of Heppenheimers) provided me with continued encouragement as I wrote the book. And I cannot understate the role my husband Bruce played in this book. He read multiple versions of each chapter and provided important suggestions. No writer could have a better editor. He deserves more thanks than is possible.

About the Author

Bonnie Suchman has been a practicing attorney for forty years. Using her legal skills, she researched her husband's 250-year family history in Germany, publishing the award-winning, non-fiction book, *Broken Promises: The Story of a Jewish Family in Germany*, as a result. Those compelling stories became Suchman's Heppenheimer Family Holocaust Saga. The first in the series, *Stumbling Stones*, was a Finalist for the 2024 Hawthorne Prize for Fiction, and recently, her family traveled to Frankfurt, Germany, to install stumbling stones for her husband's Great Aunt Alice and her husband Alfred, the real-life characters in the book. *What Remains is Hope* is the second novel in the saga.

In her free time, Bonnie is a runner and a golfer. She and her husband reside in Potomac, Maryland.

Note from Bonnie Suchman

Word-of-mouth is crucial for any author to succeed. If you enjoyed *What Remains is Hope*, please leave a review online—anywhere you are able. Even if it's just a sentence or two. It would make all the difference and would be very much appreciated.

Thanks!
Bonnie Suchman

We hope you enjoyed reading this title from:

BLACK ROSE
writing™

www.blackrosewriting.com

Subscribe to our mailing list – *The Rosevine* – and receive **FREE** books, daily
deals, and stay current with news about upcoming
releases and our hottest authors.
Scan the QR code below to sign up.

Already a subscriber? Please accept a sincere thank you for being a fan of
Black Rose Writing authors.

View other Black Rose Writing titles at
www.blackrosewriting.com/books and use promo code
PRINT to receive a **20% discount** when purchasing.